The Urbana Free Library

To renew: call 217-367-4057
or go to "*urbanafreelibrary.org*"
and select "Renew/Request Items"

TAINTED
MOUNTAIN

A NORA ABBOTT MYSTERY

TAINTED
MOUNTAIN

SHANNON BAKER

MIDNIGHT INK
WOODBURY, MINNESOTA

FIRST EDITION
First Printing, 2013

Book format by Bob Gaul
Cover design by Adrienne Zimiga
Cover illustration © Robert Rodriguez/Lindgren & Smith, Inc.
Cover images: Mountain sunset © iStockphoto.com/amygdala imagery
            River © Don Paulson Photography/Purestock/SuperStock
Editing by Nicole Nugent

Midnight Ink, an imprint of Llewellyn Worldwide Ltd.

Library of Congress Cataloging-in-Publication Data
Baker, Shannon, 1960–
  Tainted mountain: a Nora Abbott mystery/Shannon Baker.
    p. cm
  ISBN 978-0-7387-3422-4
1. Businesswomen—Fiction. 2. Murder—Investigation—Fiction. 3. Environmentalists—Fiction. 4. Native Americans—Fiction. 5. Ski resorts—Fiction. 6. Arizona—Fiction. I. Title.
  PS3602.A5877T35 2013
  813'.6—dc23
                    2012032917

Midnight Ink
Llewellyn Worldwide Ltd.
2143 Wooddale Drive
Woodbury, MN 55125-2989
www.midnightinkbooks.com

Printed in the United States of America

To Dave: may the adventures keep coming.

AUTHOR'S NOTE

In the interest of accuracy, and to keep people from blowing a gasket, let me lay out a few disclaimers:

Nora's ski resort, Kachina Ski, is a one-lift, one-run, dinky operation on Kachina Peak north of Flagstaff, Arizona. While there is a Flagstaff and a small mountain range north of it, there is no Kachina Peak and, therefore, no Kachina Ski. The beautiful San Francisco range—called *Nuvatukya'ovi* in Hopi and a host of other names by the thirteen tribes that consider them sacred—looks down on Flagstaff.

The Arizona Snowbowl, the ski resort on Humphrey's Peak (tallest of the San Francisco range), is a much bigger, much nicer place than Nora could have hoped for. Founded in 1938, it now boasts 777 skiable acres with 40 runs and 6 lifts. There are 2 lodges on the mountain.

Unlike Kachina Ski, there are no plans to pump water from the aquifer onto Snowbowl's slopes, probably because there is no water source on the Peak. However, approval through the courts was granted and pipes were laid starting in 2011 to pump treated wastewater from Flagstaff for snow making. Several tribes and coalitions have battled this decision and fought the approval for Snowbowl's planned expansion. In multiple cases that teetered on the brink of a Supreme Court appearance, the tribes were defeated again and again.

Just in case you were wondering, the lava tubes are real. How extensive they are and where they lead is a mystery to me; I only went a few feet into one and started imagining Stephen King's *It* and made a hasty retreat before becoming spider fodder.

I took a few liberties in the layout of Flagstaff's downtown and courthouse plaza, though I stopped short of rezoning it. If you haven't visited Flagstaff, I recommend you do. There is a charming downtown surrounding Heritage Square, which is an excellent people-watching venue. Trust me on this, you'll love Flagstaff. I rearranged Flagstaff and moved Heritage Square to the courthouse.

I also made up Benny's village in Hopiland. While I was welcomed at a public dance in Shipolovi on Second Mesa, the Hopi generally don't appreciate strangers wandering around their private villages. Can you blame them? How would you like people peeping in your windows because you live in an historic building? I've endeavored to respect Hopi culture and their privacy and, to that end, deleted certain references and specifics as requested by my Hopi friend. Although I was happy to do this out of respect, I also don't need an angry kachina giving me grief.

ONE

FRIGID AIR RIPPED DOWN her throat, searing both lungs as her heart threatened to burst through her rib cage. Heavy panting announced the pursuer, one step from overtaking her. A final leap put her safely on the ledge.

He blew past her, not seeing the sheer drop-off beyond the ledge. "Abbey!"

Skidding on his butt, two legs dangled over a 300-foot drop to rocky ground. Nails scrabbled on the cold stone.

Fear and adrenaline shot through Nora Abbott's body. She dove toward the edge, her fingers frantic to find purchase. Using all the weight in her lithe frame, Nora flung herself backward to jerk him to safety. Then she closed her eyes.

"Stupid dog," she whispered, as she released his collar and hugged the aging golden retriever. Why couldn't he stay home, snuggled into his warm bed, as Scott had?

Holding Abbey's panting body close in the muted light, Nora turned to the east. She'd nearly missed it. Fearing that failure to be here on time would jinx the day, she'd half ran the entire three-mile uphill hike, something she wasn't really in shape to do. With just minutes to spare, she knelt on the rough volcanic stone, recovering her pulse and breathing.

Wait for it. Wait for it.

Bam!

Sunrays burst over the silhouetted ridge of Kachina Mountain, warm and welcoming, like a mother greeting her child.

Joy filled Nora's mind and heart. This was the mountain's gift to her. "Thank you." Her whispered words drifted over the treetops and the ski lodge below. The sun and the mountain took care of her spirit, and she'd do her best to take care of them.

Maybe the run up the trail hadn't brought her as close to death as she felt at the moment, but her heart and lungs still complained, so she decided to sit a bit longer. Abbey, however, stood and shook, moving away from Nora to sniff and pee.

Nora rolled her eyes. "Sacred moment terminated." But the gratitude lingered, throwing a soft blanket over her anxiety.

She drew in a deep breath and tilted up her face, letting the sun soak in as fortification for today's battle. How could she not triumph? She was right, and right always won.

Didn't it?

Nora blew out a last breath, then stepped back from the ledge and along the precarious footing that would lead her back to the main path. If she slipped, she'd crash six feet onto the trail. Probably not enough to kill her, but with her luck, she'd strike her head. They'd find her broken and in a coma, and her mother and Scott would fight over her brain-dead body for the next twenty years. Or until Scott gave up.

Sheesh, Nora. Over-dramatize much? She steadied herself against a chilly rock.

Woft, woft, woft. Above her head, wings beat the air. Nora looked up and spied an enormous raven sailing over her. Despite the natural glory of her mountain, ravens always seemed sinister. Circling in a wide arc, the black bird came at her like an alpine kamikaze.

Nora started to scramble down to the trail, heart racing once again. Halfway there, her foot slipped and she smashed her tailbone against a rock, sending a shower of knives up her spine, then she slid the rest of the way to the dirt trail, back scraping on a stone.

Nora groaned in pain. Abbey meanwhile barked like a terrier on meth. His outburst added to Nora's jitters, and she started to quiet him. But he wasn't looking at the vanishing raven. Abbey focused on a point farther into the pine trees and closer to ground level. Abbey's hackles rose as he bared teeth.

Nora turned her head from where she lay, her hackle-less neck raising hairs of its own. A man stood in distant flittering light. Even from far away the bright blue that accented the stranger's clothes flared in the forest.

Nora jumped to her feet, ready to bolt down the trail for the safety of home. She blinked. The figure was gone.

Nora squinted and drew in her brows. "How in the … ?" Abbey stopped barking and serenely picked his way down the steep ledge to the trail. He trotted past her, tongue lolling and tail wagging.

Nora shook her head. That wasn't a person. Couldn't be. She glanced around again. Her heart still galloped, even though she told herself her imagination and the spotty light had turned a really big blue jay into a threatening image.

A cloud covered the newly risen sun, blotting out the warmth, just as the stupid raven and huge jay had blotted out the peace in her spirit. Didn't the Navajo believe ravens were a bad omen? Maybe that's why she didn't like the things.

She let out a disgusted breath. Prophecy, bad luck from a broken mirror, and omens existed only in people's imaginations. She really needed to be more practical than that, especially today.

But if she didn't believe in omens, why did she race to within an inch of her life this morning just to greet the sunrise?

TWO

THE JUDGE, IN HIS polyester robe, slammed the gavel onto the podium. "Court dismissed." Wordless prattle erupted in the back half of the room.

Nora's attorney, Raymond, jumped from his chair and slapped her back hard enough to knock her into next week. "Congratulations!" His arm reared back for another celebratory smack, but Nora sidestepped out of his reach.

Not sure she trusted the verdict, she asked, "No more appeals?"

Raymond's guffaw drowned out the excited chatter of the people exiting the room. "Next stop is the Supreme Court, and that's as likely as snow in July." A cheesy grin spread across his face as he looked sideways at her. "No pun intended." He burst into exhilarated laughter.

Snow in July. The future opened before her, ripe with possibilities, rotten with pitfalls. *Focus on the possibilities, Nora.* Snow. Wet, life-giving. Not only to her ski business but to the drought-stricken mountain as well.

"That's a good one," Raymond said. "Now that we won, you *can* have snow in July, if that's what you want." He stepped close again, and his heavy paw landed so hard on her back that her children—if she ever had any—would be born dizzy. "It's okay to whoop a bit. You just won a landmark case, missy."

Raymond had worked tirelessly for almost four years, through appeals and setbacks and the same threats and harassments she'd borne from activists and hell-bent enviros on a mission. This landmark win would skyrocket his career. That made her smile. She raised onto her tiptoes and kissed his cheek. "You're brilliant. Thank you."

Raymond beamed at her. "Coming from a sweet young thing like you, that makes it all worthwhile."

All worthwhile. So why didn't she feel the victory with as much enthusiasm?

Because Scott wasn't here to share it with her. Being too tired to catch the sunrise with her hadn't stopped him from leaving the apartment before she and Abbey returned from the mountaintop.

He said he'd be here. She glanced at her watch. He was late, surely that was all.

Raymond directed her toward the courtroom doors. "The press is gonna set up outside. We gotta get you out there for a sound bite. This will make it all the way to Katie Couric, I guarantee it." He whisked her through a jumble of bodies clustered in the hallway, muttering, "Excuse me, excuse me."

More thumps on the back—thankfully less heartfelt than Raymond's—and congratulatory exclamations followed her. Not watching where he walked, Raymond pulled her directly into the path of a man striding down the hallway.

Her shoulder accordianed into him.

Raymond released her arm and continued toward the media frenzy, not noticing the lost contact.

A tall, athletic man with sandy blond hair and a serious face reached out to steady her. Her eyes rolled down his plaid shirt, fitted jeans, and worn hiking boots. Not normal dress for the courthouse. *Great,* she thought, *an enviro, here to berate me for unnatural acts against the world.* She tensed, ready for a fight. People like him didn't understand that conservation and business didn't have to be mutually exclusive. She'd prove it to them.

"Sorry, ma'am." He hurried past her and down the hall.

Nora grimaced and glanced over her shoulder at his receding back. She didn't believe the contact was an accident.

Still, she'd endured worse than an ignorant shove. Others of his ilk no doubt waited to hurl insults, but hopefully not sharp objects, at her. Tire-slashers, window-smashers, activists who protested each court appearance and sent her death threats lay in wait somewhere outside the courthouse. She scanned the faces in the lobby as she moved to rejoin Raymond. Mostly white, well-dressed. Flagstaff's mayor and business leaders clustered together.

The court decision to allow manmade snow on Kachina Mountain outside of town ensured the success of Nora's skiing business, but it would bolster all of Flagstaff's winter income too. To some, Nora was a hero.

Knots of supporters dotted the courthouse lobby. Raymond waved and shouted comments to several. He leaned close to Nora. "Why don't you slip into the powder room there? The cameras wash you out and you'll want to put on lipstick and spruce up a bit."

Cameras? Sound bites? Slick sweat appeared on her upper lip. She was a business person, not one of FOX's foxes. "Can't you do the talking?"

"I could, but you're much prettier." He nodded and grinned at a rotund man crossing the tiled floor. "Get going. You don't want Big Elk to get all the attention."

She lost her breath as an anvil dropped from the sky and pounded her into a nervous mush. Of course Big Elk, the Al Sharpton of Native Americans, would be around for the decision. He'd be rousing the rabble outside, wooing the media, and working someone into a froth so fiery they might not stop at threats this time.

Raymond gave her a shove. "Off you go."

Nora pushed open the bathroom door and let it bump shut behind her. She peered under the cream painted doors, making sure the space was her own. For added privacy, she stepped into a stall and slid the lock closed.

If I spontaneously combust, I won't have to do any of this. No speaking to news crews. No facing Big Elk. No fighting to come up with money to fund an expensive snow-making operation. And no finding out why Scott didn't show up today.

She braced her arm against the door and dropped her chin to her chest, letting coppery hair curtain her face. The court's decision was a victory. She deserved to relish the achievement, damn it. *Go ahead, Nora. Relish.*

A hand shot under the stall door, driving at her ankle. A glint of metal flashed. Nora leapt back instinctively, slammed her calf into the stool, lost her footing, and fell against the toilet seat. *Good God, was that a knife?*

Rage fueled her scream. "Hey! Stop!" She heard the door thump closed. She fumbled with the stupid metal lock on the stall. This weapon-wielding psychopath was getting away and her fingers felt as useful as water balloons. Finally released, she lunged toward the bathroom door and burst into the lobby panting.

People in the lobby closest to her stared at her abrupt entrance. Raymond boomed midway across the space. "And here she is."

Her eyes darted to dark corners and the busy hallway. The guy couldn't disappear, not in this crowd. Blank expressions met her glance.

A hand rested on her arm. "Miss."

Nora jumped to the ceiling.

"Missus."

Ready to waylay an attacker, she turned to find a withered slip of a Native American gazing up at her with the darkest eyes she'd ever seen. Come to think of it, his soft voice sounded more tentative than deadly. Deep wrinkles lined his face like wadded parchment and skin sagged around his eyes. *He must be a hundred years old.*

This had to be an elder, still embracing the traditional ways. He probably lived in a pueblo with no modern conveniences and spurred younger people to protest snow making. He looked too frail to be the bathroom knife sniper, but he could have encouraged someone else to attack. The threats and insults of the past months had taken their toll, and trust wasn't something in Nora's backpack anymore.

She pulled her arm away.

"Missus. I brought you my kachinas." Though it barely reached her ears, his voice held a strange combination of sadness and strength. He pulled a dusty canvas bag off his shoulder and reached inside.

A kachina salesman? He wore a long, threadbare tunic and what appeared to be ancient leggings and moccasins that reached to his knees. He could easily fade into the desert with his beiges, browns, and deeply tanned skin, except he wore a bright blue sash around his tunic. The old guy must be poor and desperate. Her heart thawed a bit. Nora understood desperate. Her checking account contained fourteen dollars, and Kachina Ski was so far in the hole she'd need carabineers and ropes to get to the surface.

She slid her hand into her side pocket for her last twenty. The one her mother had tucked into personally embossed stationery with the admonition to take herself for a nice cup of coffee after the hearing. Nora had hoped to use it for lunch with Scott, to celebrate their court victory and new beginnings.

She sighed. Bravo for the court victory. Too bad Scott wasn't really on board with the new beginnings part. "I don't want a kachina, but take this."

The little man avoided her money and shoved a small wooden doll into her hand. In an accented voice shaky with age, he said, "Not for sale. For you. For the moun-ain."

She looked down. With its slit eyes and plug nose, the masked face of the doll looked creepy. The doll wore a tunic of the same blue fabric as the old man's sash. He held a hatchet in one hand, feathers in another.

Raymond startled her with a whack on her back. "It's showtime."

Nora looked up to return the kachina doll, but the little man was gone. She searched the crowd for sign of his thick, black hair like a bowl he tied to his head with a weathered red strip of fabric. He'd disappeared. First the apparition in the woods, then the phantom bathroom stabber, and now a harmless kachina salesman? No doubt she was headed for the loony bin.

"Big Elk's got the crowd all fired up. You gotta get out there and have your say or the media will take his side."

Ben-Hur's chariot race couldn't thunder louder than the thoughts in her head. Where the hell was Scott? Kachina Ski was his business, too.

Her slick dress shoes offered no traction to fight Raymond as he propelled her toward certain doom.

Raymond inspected her. "You didn't put on lipstick. And what happened to your ankle?"

Nora followed his gaze and was surprised by the thin line of blood oozing from the slash just above her ankle bone. She felt the sting for the first time.

"Ms. Abbott," a voice spoke with unquestioning authority, drawing her attention. With the confident air of success and an impeccable Western suit and ostrich-skin cowboy boots, Barrett McCreary looked every bit the part he played as an international icon in the energy business.

Raymond clucked like a hen, pulled a handkerchief from his pocket, and bent to dab at the sliver of blood on her ankle.

Already breathless, Nora was now tongue-tied. In business school she'd written a paper on McCreary Energy and its owner. Barrett McCreary was her ideal role model: a tycoon with environmental conscience.

He held out his hand. Raymond elbowed Nora. She transferred the kachina and crumpled twenty to her left hand, wiped her sweaty palm on her dress, and grasped Barrett's hand.

"I'm Barrett McCreary. Congratulations on your victory."

Through the rush of blood in her head, she managed not to stammer or choke. "Thank you."

The sandy-haired man she'd bumped into earlier advanced on Barrett as he moved away from her. She'd read in the paper that Barrett intended to resurrect uranium mining in the area, and she was somewhat grateful for the diversion. Now the enviros would have their pick of causes to attack.

Raymond tugged Nora toward the door as she tried to invoke Barrett's spirit of confidence. She stepped through the courthouse door...

And the confidence evaporated. Nora fought the urge to dive back into the courtroom and slide under a table. The blast of high altitude sunshine didn't blind her to the crowd gathered in the courthouse plaza. Sure, this was Flagstaff, so it didn't take a lot of people to fill the small plaza, but a hundred angry protesters increased the churning in Nora's gut by two hundred percent. She felt sure the tire-slasher, the rock thrower, and probably the ankle-slitter were looming somewhere in the crowd.

A voice issued from a bullhorn with nauseating familiarity. Big Elk. He stood on the steps, his back to her, screeching to the angry mob. "Kachina Ski will pump 1.5 million gallons of water per day during the ski season. That's the blood of our Mother splattered on the ground."

The crowd was mostly young Natives, eager for Big Elk's speech. A few gray heads dotted the bunch. Nora called them the Guilty White People. They followed Big Elk around the country, living off their trust funds and trying to make up for their ancestors' exploitation of the indigenous peoples of the world.

She needed her husband now; she shouldn't have to do this alone. *Where is Scott?* A trickle of sweat rounded the small of her back.

Big Elk's beak-like nose rubbed on the horn as he spewed vitriol. "It's regrettable that the courts place the profitability of a playground over the deeply held religious and cultural convictions of hundreds of thousands of indigenous peoples."

Where was that spontaneous combustion when you needed it?

Since she couldn't achieve incendiary suicide, Nora took a deep breath. It didn't calm her. She squeezed sweaty palms around the crude doll and twenty dollars.

Raymond gave her a gentle shove. "You've done tougher stints than this. Go get 'em, Tiger."

Nora's blood pressure spiked another ten points as she readied to thwart Big Elk.

With his skin looking more sunburned than Native red, Big Elk squawked like an injured chicken. "Why is there global warming? Why 9/11 and the hurricanes, tsunamis, floods, earthquakes? Because we are allowing our sacred mountain to be desecrated. The mountain is home to the kachinas. We must protect their sacred place!" His limp gray ponytail whipped side to side when he raised a fist and started a chant.

Many of the people shouted their agreement.

I can't listen to another plea to keep Mother Earth cloaked in her burqa and hidden from the modern world. Nora loved her mountain as much as any Native, and she would never do anything to harm it. Spraying water meant an end to its suffering from drought and a return to biodiversity. The runoff would eventually filter back into the underground aquifer, so there would be very little net loss to the water table. She'd vowed to fight for her mountain when Kachina Ski became hers. She couldn't back down now.

Like the Leonard Bernstein of activist rallies, Big Elk conducted the crowd to a crescendo. "The courts gave her permission to destroy the home of the kachinas, but there is a higher judge. We must fight for the kachinas of the mountain!"

Raymond nudged her. "You need to make a move here."

Now that Big Elk whetted the crowd's bloodlust, she was supposed to speak reason? Right. Nora couldn't present an argument to Native Americans and enviros who thought today's decision was akin to granting her legal right to blow up the Washington Monument. She'd be lucky if they didn't shoot her full of arrows.

She needed a savior, but Scott riding in on his white stallion to save her seemed about as likely as the sky opening up and ending the drought. Nora took a deep breath. *Be Barrett.*

She marched straight to Big Elk. If her legs trembled, she didn't acknowledge it; if her heart hammered, she ignored that too. No one needed to know her fear loomed so large she barely kept from peeing her pants. With her head erect, she called forth the dignity and poise of her mother, Abigail.

Ignoring Big Elk's murderous glare, she stepped in front of him and noticed for the first time that he stood several inches shorter than her five seven. No wonder he had the vicious bark of a little dog. She shouted, "Thank you, Mr. Big Elk."

She had testified in the courts, given interviews for the media, put her money and life on the line for this. She could certainly overcome fear of public speaking. "I'm Nora Abbott, owner and manager of Kachina Ski."

Boos and hisses.

"How would you like it if I pissed in your church?" someone yelled at her. Nothing new. Tainted water on a holy site. The analogy made sense to them.

People shouted in a jumble of heat and temper. "Go back to your white world and leave us alone!"

Two cops in uniform stood at the back of the crowd. They looked alert and focused on the steps.

More people joined in the insults, and soon distinct words disintegrated into swelling outrage.

Was it her imagination or did the crowd inch up on her?

They'd settle down and act civilized any minute now. Sun penetrated her skin, singeing her insides. Up on her mountain it would be cool with a slight breeze, the pines letting off their summer tang.

Just then Scott rounded the corner of the courthouse plaza, his dark curls as reassuring as a troop flag. Her cavalry of one. Nora nearly collapsed with relief.

A tall Native American with blue-black hair down to his waist stepped forward, his blazing eyes scorching her. "Get the hell out of our sacred places!"

The cops waded through the knot of protesters in slow motion. Others jeered and shouted in a confusion of voices.

Scott wasn't even looking her way now. Nora's courage dissolved like a tiny levy in a big flood. Instead of cutting through the crowd like a knight on his charger, Scott hurried in the wrong direction toward someone else. Barrett McCreary? The older man strode away from the courthouse. Scott bee-lined for him, an uncharacteristic frown marring his mischievous face.

The scene around her deteriorated as her eyes came back to the people in front of her. The livid young man climbed a step, his face angry as the fires of hell. "You can pack up and leave on your own or not, but you will leave."

Others stepped up, and Nora's fear shot from her heart and climbed up her throat. What had she planned to say?

The man climbed again, and a pretty girl followed. His teeth looked like the fangs of a wolf, ready to shred her flesh. "You don't belong on the mountain."

The cries from the crowd grew even louder now. "Save our Peaks!" "Don't desecrate the sacred Mother!" "You don't belong here!" Eyes full of vengeance, mouths opened in escalating rage, they shouted at her.

And Scott was off on his own mission. Cops only halfway to the steps. No help in sight.

The young girl's pretty eyes shone with excitement and she placed her hand on the angry young man's muscled shoulder.

He looked ready to tear out her jugular with his hands.

Nora backed up, panicked and frozen in place.

The guy leapt up the last step and advanced on her. "This mountain was given to us to keep sacred for the whole world."

The girl jumped up on the step, close behind him.

Nora took another step back and bumped into the courthouse wall.

The cops couldn't get to her in time. More people pushed toward her, forming a wall of bodies that blocked her from sight. Scott wouldn't see her now even if he looked.

Malevolence shooting from his eyes, the tall Native American pulled something from his pocket. Impossible against the riotous clatter of the surging crowd, Nora heard the *swisht* of a blade jumping from a handle.

THREE

Barrett McCreary III slid his Serengeti sunglasses over his nose, cutting the glare from the plaza. Too damn bad the glasses couldn't hide the sight of Big Elk and his rant.

"Barrett."

Shit. Another idiot holding him up.

Cole Huntsman. For a smart man, an expert on uranium mining, he sure dressed like an illiterate granola. Cole pushed his shaggy pale hair from his forehead. "I found that study on in situ mining in Canada you asked me about."

"It hasn't been five minutes since we spoke."

Cole held up one of those fancy phones that could contact the moon and download an encyclopedia, if anyone knew how to use an encyclopedia anymore. "I e-mailed it to you."

Even if he looked like a tree-hugger, this guy impressed Barrett. He was smart, efficient, and not one to waste Barrett's time. "Nice work."

A woman's voice sounded from the courthouse steps, startling Barrett with its clarity. Across the courtyard, Nora Abbott stood on the steps, looking remarkably cool for the mess she'd put herself in. Both Barrett and Cole focused on her addressing the hostile crowd. That coppery hair and bright eyes made her cute as a penny, but she had to be smart too, to keep that ski area running through this drought. She should know better than to throw herself in front of that mob.

But that was not his problem. He hurried across the plaza while Cole was distracted. Barrett wanted nothing more than to get home, shed this stupid suit and tie, and get down to business. With the congressional hearings on uranium mining set for next week, there were palms to grease, weight to sling around, and dirt to dig.

He hadn't been quick enough. Around the corner popped Scott Abbott. Just who he didn't want to see. And certainly not in public.

"I need to talk to you," Scott said.

"Not here."

Crowd clatter rose from the platform.

"Tomorrow, then. On the mountain," Scott said.

"Six a.m. There shouldn't be anyone on the trail that early."

Scott squinted toward the noisy courthouse. His eyes widened when he saw his wife and, without another word to Barrett, he elbowed his way into the crowd.

Barrett didn't want to wait around for the finale. Big Elk had succeeded in his typical mischief. The brothers and sisters to the moon and sun were storming the steps. Par for Big Elk's course. He took a last look at the crowd and turned to leave.

Wait.

He spun back toward the steps.

It was her.

How could she be standing there? A train wreck of memory slammed into his gut in an explosion of pain followed by paralysis. His mind spun back forty years. He saw the woman he loved smiling at him, her shining black hair and turquoise necklace catching the sun and tossing it back for everyone's delight.

Ester.

He sucked in air, fighting for reality. Ester, in her velvet skirt, silver earrings, Concho belt…

But this girl on the steps wore jeans. No turquoise and silver glinted.

And Ester would never set foot in this plaza or anywhere else again.

Slowly it started to make sense. The girl amid the mob advancing on Nora Abbott was his Heather. Not Ester. Heather. He didn't know the black-haired delinquent she followed, but he would find out. No Native American jerk-off, angry at the world and looking for a handout, was going to get near his Heather. The boy would disappear from her life.

And that damned Scott Abbott needed to disappear too. All in a day's work for Barrett.

He was a virtual magician when it came to vanishing people.

FOUR

A hand shot out, the blade aimed for Nora's belly.

She lost her balance. One foot slid and she crashed to her knees. She was saved from that thrust, but she had no hope of avoiding the next.

She squeezed her eyes closed, expecting the burn of flesh as the knife sliced between her ribs into her lungs. Instead of the pain of the blade stabbing through her skin, a hand closed around her wrist and jerked her to her feet. She opened her eyes and looked into the face of the enviro who'd knocked against her in the hall and accosted Barrett McCreary. Probably some Earth Firster who would turn her over to Big Elk and his henchmen.

He shoved her behind his back and faced outward. "Back off!" he yelled at the crowd.

The cops finally infiltrated the mob and shouted orders to move back. Nora focused her frightened eyes on the crowd, but the slasher was nowhere in sight. He'd vanished from the courthouse steps as completely as he had from the bathroom. Other hate-filled faces glared at her, still thirsty for blood.

The enviro pulled her through a break in the crowd and down the steps. As they ran across the street, she stumbled on the curb, reaching for his arm.

The kachina doll splashed into the gutter and her twenty dollar bill fluttered away on a breeze. Nora's fingers clutched at the sudden emptiness in her hand. Losing her last twenty stung, but seeing the kachina, its mask broken and floating in the filth of the gutter, punched a hole in her heart. Even if she didn't believe in its supernatural powers, the old man probably carved his heart into the doll, and it felt wrong to abandon it. She tugged away from the enviro, determined to save the kachina.

He closed his hand around hers and dragged her down the sidewalk into a parking lot. He gently pushed her into the shade next to a building and stood in front of her. "Are you okay?"

If *okay* meant terrified, shaken, and mad enough to spit bullets, then yes, she felt okay. She nodded, trying to catch her breath.

He studied her and bent down to wipe the line of blood from her ankle with the cuff of his sleeve. He stood. "I'm Cole Huntsman."

From murder attempt to garden party introductions in a matter of seconds. The day went from weird to bizarre. Still, the impeccable manners she was raised with surfaced. "Nora."

"Hey!" a voice shouted.

Cole swung around, stepping in front of Nora.

Scott strode up to him. "Who are you?"

Of course Scott would be protective against a stranger. Nora hurried to explain. "He helped me get away."

Scott didn't look pleased, but he didn't start swinging. "Well, thanks. But I was on my way."

"Cole, this is my husband, Scott Abbott."

Cole squinted as if assessing. "Scott Abbott." He stood in awkward silence for a moment, then said, "Well, you don't need me hanging around here so … " Cole started to walk away.

Nora jumped forward. "Wait."

A smile, more in his eyes than on his lips, lit Cole's face.

"I just wanted to say thanks."

He put a finger to his forehead as if tipping his hat, a boyish grin spreading across his face. "Good to meet you, Nora." He strode out of the parking lot and around the corner.

Nora switched her attention to Scott, eager to feel the safety of his arms around her. He'd come for her. Late, sure, but he was here now.

"Have you had enough, yet?" Scott's eyes flashed with anger.

She'd expected support, and his reaction smacked her upside the head. Once again, her struggle to please him had backfired. She masked her hurt. "As a matter of fact, I have. Enough of struggling to make Kachina Ski earn a living in a drought. Enough of religious freaks and rabid environmentalists and Crazy Horse wannabees sticking their nose in my business. And I've really had enough of you acting like I'm the devil."

His face didn't soften. "Then walk away from it."

Scott might as well suggest they buy a ranch on Mars. "I didn't even want to run a ski area! But we're in it now. We can't just give up."

He shrugged and looked away from her. "I thought it would be fun."

When she'd been offered Kachina Ski from her late stepfather, she wanted to turn it down. But Scott had practically begged her, promising they'd do it together. But the picture he painted of growing a fruitful business together and raising children free to roam the mountain had faded with the drought. "When we have reliable snow, it *will* be fun," she said.

He frowned. "We have no right to alter the natural environment for profit."

What? Mutiny now they'd just won their victory? He had been on board with the fight for snow making in the beginning. She opened her mouth to remind him of the drought-relief snow making would bring to the mountain. But she simply closed her mouth again. It didn't matter what the issue, he rarely agreed with her anymore. Never laughed with her. She couldn't remember the last time he even kissed her.

The stress of the ski business killed their hope. The drought not only sucked the land dry, but her energy and resources as well. If she could get a good year or two, pay down the debt, ease up the pressure on them both, they'd be okay together, she had felt sure of it. Maybe they'd slow down enough to have a baby. Making snow meant making money, and to Nora, that meant saving their marriage as well.

"Scott, when we started this fight you were all for doing whatever it took to keep Kachina Ski alive. What's changed?"

His eyes darted away from hers. "Things."

Controlling her impatience was like trying to keep a tree upright after the lumberjack had yelled "Timber!" "You said you thought snow making was a good idea."

Scott shook his head. "That was before."

"Before *what*?"

He shifted from one foot to another. "You wouldn't believe me if I told you."

Sudden tears burned. More secrets, when he used to tell her everything. She remembered sitting in a mountain meadow, their packs discarded under a tree. They held hands and Scott told her how he never loved anyone as he loved her. When he laid her down with her back against their mountain and the sun in her eyes, it felt to her that their souls joined in their lovemaking. Now she struggled to get him to talk about his day.

"When have I ever not believed you?" she said.

"Since you stopped believing in anything except cash flows and lines of credit."

A nice one-two to the heart. "Kachina Ski won't run itself, so someone has to think about the business."

He glared at her. "See what I mean?"

Idiot. She always said the wrong thing. "I'm sorry. What changed your mind about snow making?"

"You won't get it."

"I want to get it. Tell me."

He leaned against the building. "Okay. Up on the mountain yesterday when I ran the Ponderosa trail, about four miles into it, near the summit … " He paused as if reluctant to go on.

She and Scott used to run the trails together. Other than this morning, she couldn't recall how long it had been since she'd had time for such outdoor exercise. Now, walking Abbey from the lodge down to Mountain Village constituted a big outing.

Scott started again. "I saw something blue in the trees and I stopped to get a better look."

Nora froze, suddenly alert.

"It was a guy. I mean, he had arms and legs. He was all decked out in some kind of costume and had a mask. He had a blue sash and held feathers and a hatchet."

Like her kachina, the one broken and abandon in the gutter or the guy she didn't see in the forest. A hard pit formed in her stomach. "Maybe you caught a Native American in the middle of a ceremony."

"Yeah, that's what I thought. But I got the feeling he was expecting me."

She ignored the hairs that stood on her neck.

A thin sheen of perspiration formed above his lip. "It was like the whole forest stopped moving and held its breath."

"What happened?"

"I started walking toward him and he raised his hatchet." Scott's eyes lost focus. "He didn't say anything. But it felt like he was warning me."

"Warning you?"

"He was telling me not to make snow."

Her belief lost its suspension and crashed to the ground. "What happened then?"

"I took another step toward him and he ran away. I chased him and he darted behind a tree and then ... he was gone."

"Gone?"

"Yeah. Vanished. Like he was never there. I searched all over but never found a trace of him."

"Let me understand this. Some guy dressed in a kachina outfit met you on the trail and you got the *feeling* he was giving you a message from Native American mythical gods to sabotage your means of livelihood."

His face closed up.

"And you believe this?" She cringed at the incredulous tone of her own voice.

"See? That's why I didn't tell you."

"Why, because I have a firm grip on reality? Because I have some perspective?"

His eyebrows drew together. "Because for you everything is black and white."

"The only reason you can give me for ruining our chance at success is a phantom visit from a mythological spirit. How can you expect me to believe that?"

His ears turned red, a sure sign he was losing his temper. "If you insist on snow making, something bad is going to happen."

"Why are you suddenly so against snow making?"

He bristled. "I told you why." He stared at her a moment. "And... never mind. Forget it."

Her teeth clenched so tight against a retort her jaws hurt. "What?"

"If you don't believe the kachina, why should I bother you with anything else?"

"What else?"

"It's best if you don't know."

He was dismissing her from his life yet again. "Or what? You'll have to kill me?"

He looked worried. "Just don't make snow, okay?"

Nora ached to give Scott everything he wanted and she would, as soon as they started making money. "Scott. This is our only chance at survival." She wasn't talking about the business.

"Then I'm outta here." Scott spun around and took off.

She agreed to take over Kachina Ski because he wanted it, and she fought for four years to make it work. She worked seven days a week, filed lawsuits, sat through court hearings. All for Scott, to somehow make him happy so he wouldn't leave her. Hell, she'd even forgiven him for what he did two years ago. She couldn't let her marriage end in a side alley to a parking lot. "Wait!"

When she burst around the corner onto the sidewalk, Big Elk and his usual knot of devotees stared at her from across the street. Cole stood between her and Big Elk's contingent with his arms crossed. Great. She and Scott were afternoon street entertainment like the noon shoot-out reenactment in Tombstone.

She couldn't worry about that now. "Scott! What did you mean?"

He turned around. "I mean I'm done. Finished. Through with Kachina and through with you."

26

She negotiated and worked deals in business, fought daunting court battles, and created business plans to make Donald Trump weep. A modern businesswoman to be sure. Yet Scott always managed to have the upper hand with her. She wouldn't beg. Couldn't let herself. "Please, Scott." *Damn it, have some pride.* "Don't go."

She could feel the eyes of the crowd on her, sense their interest in her private affairs. Thank goodness her mother, Abigail, was still alive. If not, there would be major grave-rolling-over at this little episode of the *Jerry Springer Road Show*.

Scott's gaze made her feel like a hairy spider crawling across the kitchen floor. "You're strong, Nora. You don't need me." No more shouting and red ears, just a disgusted shake of his head as he turned.

She watched her husband's back moving away down the sidewalk, dragging her heart on the pavement behind him.

FIVE

BARRETT DID NOT LIKE mountain hikes, but he'd learned early on to do whatever it took to keep his family and McCreary Energy safe. If that meant meeting this earth muffin in secret on a mountaintop, then he'd do it.

While they climbed, Barrett let Scott yammer about protecting the environment and people's health. As if the bonehead knew anything about saving people. Life, liberty, and the pursuit of happiness probably came next on Scott's list of talking points.

Barrett was beyond happiness; pursuing it for himself would be a waste of time.

Scott strode along the trail ahead of Barrett. "I want you to know I appreciate you meeting me."

Barrett thought about swatting the back of Scott's head. "You said you wanted to talk about groundwater on the Hopi reservation."

Scott stopped and waited for Barrett. "Did you know this mountain is sacred to fourteen tribes?"

I even know why. Barrett stepped around Scott and kept walking.

Past sixty and overweight, Barrett's main exercise consisted of riding his champion quarter horses on his ranch. His monthly hiking meetings with Scott stretched his patience as well as his stamina.

Scott followed closely on Barrett's heels. "You read the last report, right?"

The trail rounded a curve and Barrett saw what he was looking for, a sheer drop on the side away from the cliff. A boulder field bottomed out on jagged lava rock 100 feet down.

Barrett struggled to get his air. Flagstaff sat 7,000 feet above sea level, so they must be at a good 10,000 feet on this mountain. That left little oxygen. He hated the sweat dripping down his jowls and couldn't wait to get back, to shower and wash the slick film covering his body.

Scott's breath sounded soft as a sigh. "We need to go public with this information right away."

Barrett saved his limited air.

"I know something this big will impact McCreary Energy."

Impact it? You cretin, it would destroy it.

Scott fidgeted in the silence, as if unsure what to do next.

Barrett leaned against the cliff wall.

Scott stared at him, voice incredulous. "You aren't going to do anything about it?"

"Why yes. Your lovely wife is going to make snow on Kachina Mountain."

Scott shook his head. "But—with these results—that's not okay."

Barrett pushed away from the cliff wall and took a step forward. He spoke quietly. "Making snow is good for business. Making snow will eliminate our little problem. Everyone is happy."

Scott looked wounded and stumbled back a step. "I thought … "

Barrett narrowed his eyes. "What evidence do you have about this?"

Scott gazed toward the meadow, hundreds of feet below them. "I submitted the well logs to you. You wouldn't hide this, would you?"

"Did you make copies?"

A spark of panic lit Scott's eyes. "You can't cover this up." As Barrett suspected, Scott was too much of a dolt to keep copies.

Barrett took another step toward Scott. "The problem is being taken care of."

The nervous man glanced down the trail, no doubt searching for escape. Barrett guessed Scott was now regretting trusting Barrett and not making copies. "Pumping water on the peaks is no solution," he said.

Barrett sighed. He hadn't wanted it to come to this, but the moron left him no choice. He might be old and out of shape, but his extra weight wouldn't hinder him now. Without another word, Barrett lurched toward Scott and slammed into the fool, launching him over the edge.

The granola cruncher had been paid well to keep his mouth shut and until now hadn't had any temptation to open his trap and spoil his good deal. The only person who might know about this was his wife, but if she spoke up, the whole snow-making deal would be off. He'd keep an eye on her, but she struck Barrett as too smart to let that happen.

Barrett glanced over the side of the cliff.

Not much blood, but the angle of the neck proved just how dangerous it was to cross Barrett McCreary III.

SIX

Nora stood on the wide lodge porch and gazed across the empty expanse of the ski run. There were so few summer mornings to savor on her mountain, and this one had withered away in worry, meetings, balance sheets, and business plans.

Abbey trotted up the lodge steps, tongue lolling.

Nora scratched his ears. "You don't care if the bank is skeptical about snow making and Scott walked out, do you? As long as there is a rabbit on this mountain and food in your dish, you're content."

He slopped in his tongue, wagged his tail, and sat to survey his mountain.

The restless night alone pounded in fatigue behind Nora's eyes. With her closest neighbors in Mountain Village, nestled three miles down the winding road at the base of the mountain, she felt isolated at the lodge. She'd jumped at every noise, afraid Big Elk or Knife Guy would come back to finish her off. Hoping maybe Scott would return.

The nip of pine wafted in the air and the sun filtered through the branches, creating a camouflage of cheer on the grass. Normally the fiery penstemon, the violet flax, and sunny cinquefoil made her heart light. Today, she forced appreciation for the beauty around her.

She stared at the rocky, red dirt parking lot about two hundred feet down a path from the lodge. She imagined snow piled on the periphery and happy people shrugging into ski togs. She loved those days. Everyone excited and busy, laughter chasing around the mountain. Unfortunately, too many days the parking lot sat empty.

Nora allowed herself memories of early morning skiing with Scott. They often checked the slopes before allowing skiers on the runs. Sharing the thrill of their mountain, the morning runs had felt as intimate as lovemaking.

Nora shook away those memories. Enough emotional torture, business beckoned. The morning's meeting in town with her banker had yielded mixed results. Despite her impressive charts and projections and armed with the court's decision, her banker considered her already sizeable operating loan and the refinanced business loan. Kachina Ski's lifeline showed minimal activity. But making snow would not only speed recovery, it would guarantee robust health far into the future. At least that's what she'd told the banker.

In the end, the banker offered enough to pay for initial construction of the snow-making equipment, providing she came up with investors to furnish the remaining capital.

Set my hair on fire, pull my toenails out with pliers, bury me to my neck in hot sand, but don't make me call my mother for money.

For the thousandth time since dawn, Nora scanned the forest behind the lodge. Scott might traipse back after camping in the forest. It wouldn't be the first time he appeared after a night away and they went along as usual with no mention of the argument.

A ridiculous notion. Failure had been threatening their marriage for months, maybe years. Despite all their efforts, they'd never really recovered from … her mind automatically shifted away.

A flash of bright blue drew her attention deep into the forest. Scott? But then, it might be Knife Guy, back for blood. Isolated out here, he wouldn't have to wait for the cover of darkness. Logic did nothing to stop the electric flash of nerves.

A fat, mean blue jay flew from the forest.

Just a bird, she thought.

A crash behind her sent another zing of fire through her chest. Abbey barked. Nora spun and fell against the railing, arms up, ready to defend herself.

She drew in a breath, probably her last. A figure lurched from the gloomy lodge.

"Oh, God." She slowly exhaled, allowing the panic to dissolve. This heart fibrillation needed to stop or she'd keel over dead.

Charlie—gray-haired hippy, survivor of the summer of love and whatever Jesus freak, earth-loving, peacenik movements surged in the old days—stood in front of the screen door he'd let bang closed. His rusty voice brought his usual good cheer. "Didn't mean to startle you, dear. You are beauty and grace and give me reason to live."

Long live normalcy—at least Charlie's version. "I'm here just for you," she said.

Pabst Blue Ribbon beer can clutched in his hand, Charlie made his way to her, Abbey dancing at his feet. His grizzled face wore a grin and his faded eyes crinkled with affection. "I heard what happened in town yesterday. You ought to keep the back door of the lodge locked."

"I thought it was locked." Her inadvertent vulnerability shocked her.

Though they called the rambling building a lodge, it more resembled an insulated barn with a few dividing walls to separate the small snack bar, rental and locker area, and her office. On snowy days crowds packed the small place, making it hot and stuffy. The rest of the time it echoed and a constant chill filled the air. With a dependable snow supply, they could expand. Why not build a restaurant, get a liquor license? Possibilities—always lurking in Nora's mind—warred against her worry.

"Might think about getting a gun too." Charlie lived in Mountain Village, edged up to the forest, probably born of the pine needles and cinders after the last volcano erupted. He stopped in with his beer to visit Nora a couple of times a week then headed up one trail or another to perpetrate his peculiar brand of peaceful eco-terrorism. The idea of him wielding a gun made Nora smile.

"What's the good news today, Ranger?" Nora asked her usual question.

Charlie gulped his beer and gave his expected response. "Looks like rain."

Nora knew Charlie hung teapots, kettles, coffee cups, and water buckets in a tree in front of his house to encourage rain.

"A gully washer."

He guffawed. "I like an optimist."

With his unflappable attitude and quirky outlook, Charlie often felt like her only ally. Even if he objected to snow making, he never argued with her about it. She felt slightly uncomfortable that he spent his days dragging logs across trails to thwart the wheels of hated motorized vehicles in his forest. But he had given up stringing cable from tree to tree when he nearly decapitated a dirt biker and ended up with a month's jail time.

He reached into a pocket of the oversized army jacket he always wore, probably the one issued to him back in Vietnam, and pulled out another PBR. "Care for a beverage?"

Nora laughed. "That stuff tastes like gasoline."

He popped the top and took a swig. "Coming from anyone else, I'd say that was an elitist comment made by an exclusionary capitalist out to exploit the underclass. A real Barrett McCreary."

"I don't really mind being compared to Barrett McCreary."

Charlie shook his head. "Child, you don't know what you're saying."

Charlie tipped his head back and drained his PBR in one long chug. He crushed the can and slipped it into a pocket. "Got work to do. You be careful and lock that door."

Abbey, tail wagging, joined Charlie and they ambled across the grass, disappearing in the forest. Nora wandered into the dark lodge. She checked the back door. No wonder Charlie walked right in. Scott must have broken the mechanism and forgot to tell her. She needed to rework her revenue projections, but then she'd head back to town to hit the hardware store. No way did she want to spend a night here without sturdy locks.

The sound of a chair scraping over the floor startled her. Her head whipped around, and she searched the vast darkness. "Who's there? Charlie?" Her pulse pounded in her ears, blocking any other sound. Movement next to the white stone fireplace caught her eyes.

"If you're one of those activists, you'd better get off my property." She stepped toward the door. "I'm calling the police." Another step. No replies. Maybe her overloaded mind blew a fuse and nobody was here. She hurried toward the door anyway. In the dim lodge her eyes strayed to a hulking shadow jutting from the wall. Breath caught in her throat.

Knife Guy glared at her from behind the rental counter.

There was no debate between fight and flight; Nora took off for the screen door.

She barely cleared the rental counter when what felt like a brick wall slammed into her back, sending her crashing to the floor in a crush between concrete and two hundred pounds of lean, murderous Indian.

Fingers raked her head and grabbed a handful of hair. He jerked her around and pounded her down, the back of her head cracking on the floor. Fissures of pain blinded her. He straddled her chest, letting only the barest stream of air into her lungs, hatred shooting from his eyes. "You won't destroy our sacred moun-ain." His words came from clenched teeth.

She struggled for breath. "I ... "

His hand smashed into the side of her face, grating her cheek and tongue against her teeth. Agony exploded through her temple, and the taste of blood filled her mouth.

"Shut up!"

His hands wrapped around her throat, squeezing as if her neck were nothing more than a wash rag. Rage turned his dark face into a mask of destruction, eyes glinting with absolute power.

She kicked for her life, fought to buck him off, struggled to shake her head. Yet she barely moved, despite adrenaline pumping through her. Impossible that death could find her so easily. It shouldn't happen this effortlessly. Someone shouldn't simply walk in the door and kill her. No preamble, no preparation. Hardly any struggle. Just dead.

And then she felt a new pain. Real, excruciating, burning her lungs as they dried up, turning in on themselves, begging for air. Her mouth gaped. Blackness seeped into her vision, closing in, shuttering life. Her arms dropped to the floor, her body no longer obeying her dying brain. The twisted face hovering over hers faded into darkness. This was it.

Death brought instant relief. The weight on her chest disappeared. It felt as if air actually raked against her raw throat. But it burned. There shouldn't be pain in death, right? Great gulps triggered coughs that scraped her delicate tissue.

The blackness receded from her eyes and sound returned to her in the form of grunts and pounding flesh. Two men grappled on the floor next to her. Knife Guy, larger and heavier, took a fist to his face. The other man moved with grace and agility, planting another blow and another.

Knife Guy shoved the thinner man off balance and settled himself in an attack stance. And there it was. The knife appeared and the blade emerged with a *schwit*.

Jump, scream, run. Do something! But she just wallowed as though buried in tar. The man, her savior, jumped to his feet. Cole Huntsman. He crouched, his eyes burning into the attacker's, calculating, calling him on.

The heart-stuttering siren of an emergency vehicle sliced through the air.

Knife Guy hesitated only a second, then bounded past Cole and out the screen door.

Before the door even banged closed, Cole knelt beside Nora. "Are you okay?" He put an arm under her shoulders and helped her sit.

She swallowed fire. Her voice sounded raspy and weak. "Yes. No."

"Can you stand?" She nodded and he pulled her to her feet.

Her core shook, radiating out to her arms and legs. She leaned on Cole. "He's gone?"

"The siren saved us. It looked bad when he pulled the knife." He supported her weight and helped her toward a bench.

Sirens. Police? Ambulance? Her brain still felt foggy, and she couldn't think straight. How long since Charlie had left her—minutes, a half hour? He might have been careless, fallen and broken a leg or crushed a foot with a heavy log.

Scott always teased Nora for overreacting. It was probably just a hiker who twisted a knee or something.

Cole lowered Nora to sit. "Where is your husband? You shouldn't be out here alone."

But she wasn't alone, was she? Cole was here. A dangerous environmental activist. Her heart accelerated again. Fear made for a terrific aerobic workout. She glanced at the door, wondering if she could get outside before he caught her. Cole Huntsman couldn't be any more pleased with her making snow than Knife Guy. "What are you doing here?"

He looked startled at her accusing tone. "Well." His Western drawl sounded as if he just stepped in from the range. Even in the dim light she saw a blush creeping into his cheeks. "I couldn't help but notice that things didn't go that great between you and your husband yesterday. I don't mean to butt in, but I just wanted to check to make sure you were all right."

Likely story. He and Big Elk had to be in cahoots and he was taking the "good cop" role. Maybe he came to Flagstaff to stop Barrett's uranium mining—why else would he be hounding Barrett—but he'd obviously joined Big Elk's camp. Still, he saved her life.

Her life. Her throat and neck ached with bruises inside and out and her tremors returned. She'd nearly died. And the man who wanted her dead was still out there somewhere.

Cole's hand rested on her shoulder and rubbed slowly across her back. "Let's get you into the sunshine."

Good guy or bad guy, right now Cole was the only guy around. He'd kept her alive so far. She let him help her stand and stagger to the deck. As soon as possible she ducked from his supporting arm.

The lodge squatted halfway up the mountain. Two short flights of wide metal stairs led from the ground to the deck. Five giant picnic tables spread out on the expansive redwood platform that faced the lift. Nora and Scott's tiny apartment sat on the second story, accessed by a steep outside stairway that climbed the front of the lodge.

A police cruiser pulled into the parking lot, lights swirling, and stopped.

Who called the cops? How did they know about the attack? Odd that they showed up so quickly.

She and Cole watched as the cop walked up the path and clumped up the stairs. Nora recognized him as the same senior officer who had investigated her slashed tires and the broken shed window, the most recent incidents of vandalism on the property. Nora searched her brain for his name. Gary something or other.

Gary glanced at Cole then settled his focus on Nora.

"Hi, Nora," Gary looked down at his shoes then up at her again. "I'm afraid I have some bad news."

It suddenly dawned on her this wasn't about the attack. The ambulance. Charlie.

"We just brought Scott down."

"Scott? What?"

"I'm sorry," he said.

Scott? Brought him down? Down from where? The ambulance. Not in town but on the mountain. Scott.

Her eyes lifted to a hint of red glow through the trees. Scott was there.

Her husband had been hurt on the mountain. He needed her. She sprinted past Cole and hit the stairs two at a time.

Gary called to her, but she dashed on across the parking lot and around the bend in the road. Scott needed her.

The ambulance sat at the trailhead across the road from the parking lot. Its red lights flared off the pines.

"Scott!" Her gravelly screams echoed off the mountain.

No, oh no. He's got to be okay. He's fine.

Then she saw it. The gurney. Two people wheeled it toward the back of the ambulance. There was no face. It couldn't be Scott.

No face.

Because it was covered with a sheet.

SEVEN

BARRETT STOOD AT HIS office window assessing the view. His home commanded the countryside from atop a hill that looked over an expanse of juniper, scrub, and desert. Across the valley the San Francisco Peaks rose in splendor.

The mystery and power of the peaks still had the ability to awe him, despite his years in the sometimes-sordid energy business. God, how Ester had hated the ski resort. He barely remembered his own disgust in those earlier times. Ester wouldn't understand why he'd had to do what he did to Scott. What happened on the sacred mountain this morning would break her heart, if he hadn't destroyed it forty years ago.

But Ester wasn't here to rail against him. Her sacred kachinas hadn't saved her. He lifted the faded photo and stared at the happy young family. Ester, with her black hair falling over one shoulder to her waist, bent toward their two-year-old daughter at her feet, his darling Soowi. Next to them stood the man who used to be Barrett. He was thin and sunburned with a baby resting on his arm: his son, Manangya. In the photo, Barrett's head tilted back, his mouth open in laughter. Try as he might, he couldn't remember what his daughter had said that morning to make them laugh. Just one more thing that haunted him.

The sun slipped below the tallest peak.

Heather skipped down the stairs, the short skirt flipping, a bare strip of brown belly showing. Instead of the usual burst of love and joy at the sight of his daughter, he girded himself for battle. Being a father required more courage, strength, and sacrifice than running a multinational energy corporation.

She ran to him and stretched to kiss his cheek. This affection used to be her normal state. Now it was usually sighs and outbursts, tears and slamming doors. *There should be an Alcatraz for teenaged girls*, Barrett thought. *You send them there at thirteen and pick them up when the hormones settled, whenever that might be. In the meantime, a vast moat would protect them from sniffing and groping men.*

"I'm meeting some friends in town. I won't be late."

A rock sat in his gullet. "You're not going anywhere."

Quicker than a teenaged boy's orgasm, she whipped toward him, her eyes heating with temper. "Why?"

"Because I said so."

"That's not fair."

Bad start, but he was committed. He patiently motioned for her to enter his office and she flounced in front of him. "I saw you at the courthouse yesterday."

She thrust her chin in challenge. "So?"

Screw patience. "You will stay away from Big Elk."

Heather leaned back against his desk and faced him as he dominated the room. She folded her arms, that impenetrable look on her face. She'd never met her, yet Heather's expression matched Ester's. It still took Barrett's breath away. "Do I have your word you

42

won't have anything to do with Big Elk?" He wouldn't bring up Alex Seweingyawma, the boy he'd identified as Heather's *friend* at the courthouse hoopla. Barrett had had no trouble finding the hoodlum's name, or making sure the cops locked him up.

She stared at him, emotionless except the flash of defiance in her eyes. "You have no right to keep me from my people."

Barrett was surprised his clenched jaw didn't pulverize his molars. "Your people are the McCrearys."

"My *adopted* people." Her nearly black eyes glistened with contempt.

He glared back, ignoring the blow. "Nevertheless. McCreary's don't carry signs and stop economic progress. We don't spout fairy tales about sacred mountains."

Though Heather assumed an icy attitude, she hadn't yet established Ester's stamina to hold the calm. She broke and shouted. "You bigot! You think your Christian doctrine, the one that says the world was created for you, is the only viable religion on the planet. It's never occurred to you that you were created to protect the planet. That's what Hopi believe. To you, the whole world is here for you to rape and pillage."

Now Barrett had the upper hand. "I know what the Hopi believe. I spent a fair amount of time on the rez. I've even been inside the kivas during certain ceremonies."

She laughed in disbelief. "When were you ever open-minded enough to learn the true Hopi way?"

"I was young once." It sounded cliché even to him.

She narrowed her eyes as if detecting a lie. "Maybe. But you don't get it."

Déjà vu sent a chilly wind over his skin, raising goose bumps. He remembered when he stood outside a home on Second Mesa, the ancient bricks crumbling beside the newer stone repairs and cinder blocks. Heat radiated from the empty plaza and created a haze across the landscape below the mesa. Sweat drenched his body under his dashiki. His heart was broken, but he made sure Ester didn't see the fracture.

Ester stood in front of him in a colorful peasant dress he'd bought for her in a Flagstaff boutique. It was one of the few gifts she'd let him buy, always insisting she didn't want anything that cost him mere money. If her heart broke too, she did an equally good job of hiding it. She said those same words to him: "You don't get it, do you?"

Barrett's heart had pounded in desperation to make Ester understand. As much as she talked about responsibility to her people, the world, and respecting the Hopi way, she should know he had a responsibility to his family.

But Ester left him sweating on the blazing plaza. Barrett never saw her again. They didn't even tell him when she died.

He couldn't let Heather slip from him like that. Not after all this time.

Barrett cleared his throat. These damn flashbacks had to stop. "The Hopi are wrong," he said. "Their claims of being able to save the human race are nothing but false hope and giant egos. All they amount to is trying to control their youth, ban world progress, and keep the people living in poverty."

"The simple life brings us into balance, lets us focus on what's important."

This from the iPod princess with the plasma TV, driving a new Toyota SUV and charging gas and lattes on his card. "Ask some of your new Hopi clan how they like living in squalor, not having money for food or clothes, and the sorry state of their medical care."

"A spiritual person doesn't need much to be happy."

"A poor person has to be spiritual because that's all he has."

Heather jumped from the desk and started for the door. "If you can't touch it or put a price tag on it you don't believe in it, do you?"

Barrett grabbed her arm and forced her into a chair. "There you are wrong, little girl. Show me where I can touch our heritage and the essence of McCreary. Yet I believe in family above all else. And show me where I can touch the love I feel for you. Because, Heather, *that* is the most important thing in my life."

She ignored his exposed heart. "Hopi have a special bond with the forces of nature. If we don't pay attention, the world will be out of balance." Heather glared at him. "And then it will end."

Barrett's temper threatened to break loose. "Hopi are like children. They don't know how to function in the real world and are afraid of it. We, the McCrearys you think are so evil, have been taking care of them for three generations."

Heather's voice rose to a shriek. "Taking care of them? Is that what you call strip mining their coal and pumping water for a coal slurry? And you paid them a pittance."

Acid ate Barrett's stomach and he wondered if he could mainline Rolaids for the next few years. "You call twenty-five million dollars a pittance? That's what it cost to seal those nine hundred mines. And McCreary Energy reseeded thousands of acres."

Heather swiped at her tears. "Yeah. You hauled off the radioactive tailings and boarded up the bad wells and water holes. But Poppy, before you did that, people died."

His heart went as dry and cold as the mesa in winter. It continued to beat even so. Just as he still breathed and walked around. He couldn't stop the image of the twinkling brown eyes, the soft skin and baby fat thighs, the gurgle of delight from Daddy's embrace. The son that would never swim in the creek, eat a popsicle, or even go to school. He remembered Ester's eyes burning with love and passion the last time they made love.

Barrett drank in the sight of the beautiful girl in front of him, his last chance at redemption. He'd lost everything but her.

"You are forbidden to see Big Elk. You will not go up to the Mesas."

Heather pulled her hand back and swung, smacking Barrett on his cheek with such force it snapped his head back.

They stood toe to toe, breathing hard and staring at each other. Heather's lips peeled back in a snarl. "I hate you."

Even taking into account her teenaged hormones, the words hurt far worse than his stinging cheek. "But I love you. More than you can know."

She walked slowly out of the room, leaving the door ajar.

Barrett sank to his desk chair. He felt her tugging at the blood that bound them together; had felt it for some time now.

Keeping Heather safe in the moment carried urgency, but her long-term security depended on the new uranium mining. Individually, the problems didn't amount to much, but each cog had to work or the whole thing would fall apart.

The congressional committee needed to release the lands they'd temporarily withdrawn. Huntsman had the credentials to give convincing testimony, but he had a troublesome individual streak. Even if he performed for the committee, he might give Barrett problems later on. He was much smarter than Scott, after all, and look how that had turned out.

And there were protesters, specifically that loose cannon Charlie Podanski and the troublemaker Big Elk, constantly in Barrett's way. Barrett would love to smash them, but he had to tread lightly to keep from creating a public relations debacle. Big Elk was a smarmy fake and Barrett could dispatch him easily enough with cash. But Barrett knew Charlie to be relentless and once he got started, he wouldn't quit. Luckily no one really listened to him.

Then there was Nora Abbott. Tough in business but young and easy to manipulate. Now that her husband was gone, she'd need strong guidance. Who better than a wealthy mentor? She shouldn't pose much trouble.

And the Hopi had agreed to recommend mining on their lands, but he couldn't count on them absolutely until their X was on the line.

"Barrett." Cole Huntsman's voice startled him out of his plans.

"Jesus." He had a meeting and he'd completely forgotten about it. *I must be losing my fucking mind.* He never used to forget anything.

Barrett rose from the desk and waved Cole in. "Just finishing an overseas call."

"Thought it might be something like that when no one answered the door. Hope you don't mind that I let myself in." Cole had a country bumpkin face that made him look harmless. It didn't fool Barrett.

"Glad you did," Barrett said. "I've been working on our testimonies for the hearing."

One eyebrow arched on Cole's forehead. "Our testimonies? I figured on speaking for myself."

"Of course. These are just some thoughts to coordinate our message."

"Right." That sincere drawl and perpetually friendly face would play nicely at the hearings.

Barrett picked up a stack of papers from his desk and handed them to Cole. He lowered himself back into his chair. "Sit down and we'll get to work."

Cole took the papers and wandered over to the window, his eyes on Kachina Mountain. He acted as if he had all the time in the world, like he operated on Navajo time. Cowboys and Indians—with their disregard for time, it was a wonder the West was ever settled.

Cole glanced at the pages Barrett prepared for the hearing. "Releasing those claims might be a tough sell to the committee."

Another shovelful of coal was added to his heartburn. God-damned Interior Department withdrawing lands he needed for expansion of uranium mining. "That's why we've got to coordinate our efforts."

Cole nodded. "Be easier if we had a champion."

Barrett could ease Cole's mind by telling him about a guaranteed vote or two, assured by Barrett's behind-the-scenes tactics. But the less Cole—or anyone else—knew about that, the safer for Barrett.

Cole read silently for a moment. "What do you know about a Charlie Podanski?"

Barrett's neck hairs bristled. "He's a kook. Why?"

Cole shrugged. "I hear he's a radical and can disrupt things like hearings. And that he doesn't like you. Is there anything he can use against you in this?"

Despite himself, Barrett laughed. "He's past his prime. Keep tabs on him, but I doubt he'll amount to much."

Cole didn't seem to mind chunks of silence in a meeting. Finally, he said, "I've got a concern about the groundwater."

Barrett's balls sucked into his belly. "Groundwater? How so?"

Cole continued to look at the mountain.

Does he know something? Impossible. Does he suspect?

"I'm not convinced about the stability of the breccia pipe formation. Even with the in situ method, there is risk of crumbling and some of the debris leaking into the groundwater. I'm wondering if anyone on the other side will challenge it."

Barrett leaned back in his chair, the well-oiled springs silent. "This has all been researched. Hell, you did most of it yourself."

The shaggy head nodded. "Might be something I missed someone else caught." Cole moved in slow motion to a leather Morris recliner and sat. He slouched, his long legs stretched in front of him. "When's the last time you logged the water? Wouldn't mind updating our records."

No one needed to find what Abbott's logs revealed. "We've got surveys up the ass, most of which you conducted, that say mining uranium up here is perfectly safe. We had functioning test wells and the green light on everything until this goddamned moratorium. In a few days we're going to give sincere and heartfelt testimony before the congressional committee and get them to release the claims."

"There's no evidence to contradict those surveys?"

Barrett didn't need an employee questioning his decisions. But he did need the esteemed Cole Huntsman on his side. "The surveys are up to date. Let's just get past this hearing. Then you can do more testing. If we see it isn't safe to the groundwater, we'll back off. I'm not interested in polluting the whole Colorado River, for Christ's sake. I've a proven track record with respect to the environment."

No change in expression. "Track records don't mean much against new information. We need to be extra careful."

Cole had joined McCreary energy two years ago. He was a damned good miner and carried a lot of weight in the industry. For some reason, people respected that "aw shucks" personality. He acted humble and down home, but his brilliance in matters of mining and his reputation for environmental ethics were legend. It surprised Barrett that he wanted to work for McCreary since he leaned more toward granola sensibilities than the hard reality of big energy. Barrett figured the cowboy had decided it was time to make some money.

But maybe the cowboy had another agenda. Barrett studied him. "Why all the questions?"

"Can't go into combat without bullets."

The day suddenly piled up on Barrett. He stood, signaling the end of the meeting. "Look over those notes. Be sure to hit the talking points in your testimony."

Cole rose slowly. "Sorry I was late getting here. Had something come up this afternoon."

Barrett walked toward the door, trying to usher Cole out. He wanted nothing more than bourbon and Patsy Cline.

"You know that ski area owner, Nora Abbott?" Cole asked casually.

Barrett's skin pricked. Cole may sound offhanded but if he mentioned the Abbott woman, there would be some thinking going on under that hillbilly mask. Barrett tilted his head to indicate slight interest.

"Her husband fell off a cliff and died this morning. I was out there when they found him. I took Nora to the hospital."

"What a tragedy." What was Cole doing out there?

Cole wasn't making much progress toward the door. "Just before that, some Native American guy attacked her."

This was news. "Attacked her?"

Cole nodded. "Yep. Came right in the lodge and tried to kill her. It was that same guy that pulled a knife on the courthouse steps. Big guy."

"Did she report it?" Alex Seweingyawma. It had to be. He was supposed to be locked up on Barrett's orders.

"Did you know Scott Abbott?"

Shit. Why would Cole even ask? Barrett shrugged and stepped into the hallway, making it plain he expected Cole to follow. "No."

Finally Cole made moves to wrap up the meeting. He offered Barrett his manly Western handshake and walked away, business conducted.

Barrett pivoted, already focused on fixing the Alex Seweingyawma problem. He was halfway to his desk when the thought struck.

Scott Abbott had accosted him at the courthouse. Cole was there too. Did Cole see it? Did he just catch Barrett in the lie?

No, wait. Cole had run off to rescue Nora Abbott on the courthouse steps. He didn't see Barrett's encounter with Scott. Probably. Goddamned loose ends.

EIGHT

RAW, THROBBING, AND ACHING for relief. But it went on and on.

After two hours of standing on the side of the mountain listening to Scott's friends tell stories and give tribute, Nora's pain had reached maximum force. Her agony had little to do with the bruise on her cheek, sore throat, and black-and-blue neck from the attack. The beer, lugged in coolers from the trailhead of Kachina Ski, dwindled to a few bottles and the speeches gave way to anecdotes.

At least Abigail wasn't here to hate this casual funeral, or whatever they were calling it. Nora wanted to honor Scott and give his friends a chance to say goodbye. Now, at the end of her ability to maintain control, she simply wished it would end.

Nora leaned against Charlie, glad for his loyal, if a little beer-bleary, support. Abbey lay at her feet, content to snooze in the dappled shade of the pines.

Charlie put his arm around her shoulder and squeezed. "Mighty fine sendoff. Scott had a boatload of friends, both here and from other places."

People flocked to Scott. He knew how to have fun. It always amazed her that someone so full of life and mischief would hook up with someone serious like her. At first she hadn't trusted it, hadn't trusted him. But he charmed her and won her over so completely that after seven years she didn't know where he started and she ended. So many women wanted to be with Scott, but he'd chosen Nora to be his wife.

One of Scott's buddies finished his story. "Scott pointed his skis down, took that jump, and landed like a giant snowball. He rolled down the mountain. We thought he broke at least twenty bones. But when we got there he was brushing snow off, like, 'Dudes, what took you so long?'" The friend raised his bottle. "You got there first again, man. Guess you couldn't wait."

A few people murmured, most raised their bottles at the simple hat-sized pine box Nora had picked out for Scott's ashes.

After a moment of silence, Nora sucked in a breath. She planned to dump his ashes over the side of the mountain and leave him in a place he loved.

Charlie's watery eyes filled with compassion.

How could she let him go? She could scatter Scott's ashes anytime. It didn't have to be now. Nora stepped from under Charlie's arm and turned to the knot of people. Since trekking up the mountain, Nora had drawn in her body tight so she wouldn't fly apart. She knew his friends had gathered by the sounds of shuffling feet and murmurs. She hadn't been able to turn and see them all.

She inhaled deeply and swallowed. "Thank you for coming. This is the way Scott would have chosen that we celebrate his life." *Celebrate his life. Who comes up with this crap?*

Abbey stood and stretched. He settled his silky head under Nora's dangling fingers.

They stepped forward, hugged her, kissed her, said variations of, "if there's anything I can do." She smiled and accepted that they loved Scott and cared for her. But she wanted to be alone.

Charlie and Nora stood by the box as everyone else wandered away. God, when would this end? A mass of blonde drew Nora's attention to the edge of the clearing, where people were starting to make their way down the trail.

A big-ass ugly mule kicked Nora's belly, followed by instant nausea. That face always caused the same reaction.

Charlie followed Nora's line of vision. "You got something against that girl?"

The blonde threw her arms around one of Scott's cycling buddies. She sobbed into his chest, and he patted her back.

Already tender, Nora's emotions shredded into piles of gore. "I can't believe her nerve."

Charlie took a step down the trail. "If you don't want her here, I'll send her on her way."

Nora didn't want to remember that face. Two years ago, the night she'd driven to town for a beer. Alone because Scott was supposedly competing in a bike race in Utah, she stepped into the bar. She expected happy greetings from friends, but their faces froze. It took about two seconds to see Scott cozied up to that athletic blonde at a back table.

Just seeing that bleached head of spun shit brought back the pain, humiliation, and betrayal. Nora wanted to honor Scott today, not relive that pain.

Charlie put a hand on Nora's arm. "Looks like she's ready to leave."

Nora stomped to the rock and picked up Scott's box. "She's got no breeding." *And doesn't that sound just like Abigail. Gaa!*

The tethers of her control snapped. She sprinted toward the blonde, weighted down by the heavy pine box.

Abbey let out a bark and raced with her.

"Hey. Honey, wait," Charlie called.

Outrunning Charlie wasn't hard. Nora's vision narrowed to a red laser focused on the tacky blonde. The bimbo turned just as Nora slammed into her side, driving her into a tree like a croquet ball.

The girl regained her balance. "What the hell?"

Abbey bowed his front legs and barked, tail wagging.

The two guys with the bimbo stood back—just the cowardly sort of friends she deserved.

"How dare you show up here today." Nora fought the urge to slam Scott's box into the girl's nose.

Silence fell for a moment while the woman stared at Nora.

Charlie caught up to them. He waved his arm at the blonde as if she were a wasp. "Go on. You're not wanted."

Nora's words spit at her. "Don't you have any pride? I'm his wife." *Was his wife.*

The girl narrowed her eyes and glared at Nora. "How long do you think he stayed away from me?" When Nora didn't answer, she said, "Try two weeks."

Blood rushed through Nora's ears. This wasn't true. It couldn't be. They'd been trying to put their marriage back on track for almost two years.

The bimbo nodded. "That's right. There is a lot about him you don't know."

Breathe. Stand up. Do not fall apart. Pride was all that kept her alive.

"He used to call you Mom. You squeezed the life out of him. That's why he came to me."

Despite Herculean effort, Nora slumped against Charlie.

Charlie held out his palm. "You stop talking now."

Bimbo stuck the dull knife in farther. "He planned on leaving. He almost had enough saved for us to leave together. But you found out and you killed him!"

Money? "Liar." She pulled away from Charlie. "There was no money."

The smug look on Bimbo's face infuriated Nora. "Maybe Scott felt sorry for you and didn't want to hurt you. But I won't protect you."

Charlie shooed her away. "You're out of line."

Bimbo shouted at Nora. "You didn't know anything about him. He had a job, his ticket to freedom. That's what he said. And he was finally going to leave." Suddenly she broke down in heaving sobs. "And now he's gone."

Nora couldn't feel her own body.

Tears streaked Bimbo's makeup. With her red eyes and dripping nose, she looked more like the grieving widow than did Nora. Bimbo shrieked and ran at Nora. "And I know you did it. You killed him. I know it!"

Bimbo drew her arm back and swung toward Nora's face. Just before her palm slapped Nora's cheek, a hand shot out from behind Nora and caught Bimbo on the wrist.

Abbey set up a string of agitated barking.

Cole Huntsman lowered the woman's arm, giving her a fierce look. "Leave her alone."

No one moved for a full three seconds. Then the two guys, Bimbo's cowardly friends, shrouded her and spirited her down the trail.

Nora's knees trembled. She bent over and heaved, the acid of bile burning her sore throat.

Charlie appeared at her side, grabbing a handful of her hair and patting her back.

Strength trickled back. It didn't matter how many deaths Scott died to her, she would have to keep breathing. She stood and stared into the forest, gathering her forces.

The branches, logs, flowers, and shrubs shifted from fog to focus and she realized she was staring, not at a Ponderosa as she'd expected, but at a man. Or at least he seemed like it. He wore a mask, the scary kind with the slit eyes and plug mouth. His clothes and body paint jumbled in a tangle of blue and red. This living vision of the kachina doll the little man had forced on her sent chills racing over her skin. He only had to spring forward and raise his hatchet to hack her to pieces.

Nora cried out.

Charlie patted her back. "Let it out."

She glanced down, backing away. When she swung back to avoid his attack, the man was gone. She pointed. "Where did he go?"

Cole whirled around and studied the forest. "Who?"

"That guy. That Native American." Even to her it sounded crazy. But there were plenty of people who would like to harm Nora. Seeing strange men in the forest—and then not seeing them—freaked her out.

Cole pushed his hair from his forehead. "I'll check it out." He started away.

The whole thing stank. "What are you doing here?"

Charlie swayed slightly. "Cole was keeping that girl from clocking you."

Wait a minute. How did Charlie know Cole's name? "You know him?"

He shifted and mumbled. "Why wouldn't I? Working for the enemy, out to cause mischief."

Not unusual for Charlie to head off on a tangent that made no sense. Did Cole's face turn red? Probably a sign he was hiding something. Why did he always show up to save her? Was he keeping her safe so the masked guy or Knife Guy could get her later on?

The red deepened on his face. "I was … wanting to pay respects to your husband."

She scowled at him. "You didn't know him."

He stammered. "But I sort of know you and it seemed like something I should do." He looked at the ground as if he were an embarrassed kid. No wonder Big Elk sent him. He played up a boyish charm. It might fool some people, but Nora had dealt with threats and harassment for a long time. She was no sucker.

"I'll go see if I can find the person you saw," he said.

"You do that." She watched him walk away.

She marched down the hill ahead of Charlie. *And now I will put my life back together. I will run Kachina Ski and do all the things I need to do.*

Scott and Bimbo. Together. Molten lava exploded inside. Nora heaved the pine box. It sailed up and crashed to the forest floor. The top landed three feet away and the plastic bag of ashes flopped out.

She sank to the ground. Every cell in her body weary, Nora said to Charlie, "What am I going to do without him?"

Charlie gathered the bag of ashes and placed it back in the box. He slammed the lid on. "You'll do what you've been doing all along. You'll take care of everything and everyone around you."

Nora shook her head. "Scott gave me courage. Knowing that he'd picked me, I felt… And now I'm all alone."

"That boy didn't give you anything."

God, she was tired. Nora pulled herself up and trudged down the trail.

Charlie followed her, carrying the pine box.

They walked in silence. The ache in Nora's heart pounded in her brain. She'd never feel good again. The last curve rounded into a long straight decline to Kachina Ski's parking lot.

All Nora wanted to do was climb the stairs to her apartment and fall into bed.

She looked down the trail and froze. The worst day of her life just cranked up another full turn.

Bimbo and her friends were gone, but something far worse waited for her down there.

NINE

LIKE STRATEGIZING THE NEXT chess move, Barrett chose the exact words to reassure the congressional committee members. He maintained relaxed body language and a sincere expression, leaning slightly forward in his chair and looking each vote-hungry vulture in the eye.

Since the meteoric rise in uranium prices recently, McCreary Energy, among others, had filed hundreds of mining claims in the vicinity of the Grand Canyon. Environmental alarmists scurried to block them and repeal the 1872 mining laws that made mineral rights king over every other public lands use. Climate change, clean fuel, faltering economy—all of it stood squarely in Barrett's way as he readied McCreary Energy to go after the uranium windfall. Now this hastily convened congressional committee thought they had the power to pull Barrett's plug.

They wouldn't stop him.

Wheelan Deavonshire, Senate representative for northern Arizona, hosted this on-site hearing. Barrett owned Deavonshire, which meant this asinine mining moratorium would go away. Or else.

Christ, he hated squeezing his feet into the fancy ostrich-skin boots and confining himself to a suit and tie. Didn't matter if it happened to be the finest fabric, tailored to fit his growing bulk. He might despise this and other actions, but it was a small enough sacrifice for family. For Heather.

Barrett studied the congressional panel while keeping a keen ear out for the media and other participants filling the conference hall behind him. He spoke with authority. "Withdrawal of these lands from mining is unnecessary and if enacted will degrade the environment of the Grand Canyon, reduce public visitation to the area, increase America's dependence on foreign energy, and negatively impact the economy of both the region and the country."

He paused to let that digest. "With China and India pushing for nuclear reactors, it's our patriotic duty to develop uranium here and reduce our dependence on foreign oil. If you withdraw this land from uranium development, a valuable resource capable of producing clean electricity for millions of people will be sacrificed to appease the emotions of a few special interest groups."

Barrett sounded reasonable. "This union of special interests is attempting to justify withdrawing lands by attacking the mining industry. They grossly exaggerate environmental damage of an operation closed for more than forty years. They assume we'll use the same outmoded techniques today we used in the 1970s. I can assure the American people that McCreary Energy has cleaned any contamination that remained from earlier operations and that today's techniques are far safer.

"If this attack is successful, you will send a clear message to the American people that the federal government doesn't care about the price of fuel, domestic jobs, or the environment."

Barrett thanked the committee, and the chairman declared a break.

Before Deavonshire could escape, Barrett gave him a hearty slap on the back and directed him toward the senator's office.

Once inside Barrett settled into the comfortable client's chair and waited for Deavonshire to close the door and seat himself behind the glossy desk. Even in a district as cash-strapped as northern Arizona, the senator managed to surround himself with tasteful and expensive trappings. All on McCreary's dime.

"The opposition's lined up an impressive roster for testimony today," Barrett said, eyeing the glad-handing, ingratiating slime.

The senator nodded his head with annoying enthusiasm. "Thank goodness there aren't more people like that Charlie character badgering the committee."

At least Charlie had kept his heckling outside the courtroom and behaved himself in the hearings. In their youth, Charlie carried more threat. His bark, as well as his bite, had certainly weakened with age. "Charlie's made a career of being a pest."

Deavonshire matched Barrett's insincere smile. His tanned face, wavy hair, and toothpaste-ad radiance didn't quite hide his discomfort. "Uranium mining close to the Grand Canyon is a hot button issue. At the end of the day, people are concerned with preserving the beauty of one of the Eight Natural Wonders of the World."

Seven, you idiot. "The committee was receptive to Huntsman's testimony about the safety of modern mining techniques. With your support, Senator, they'll have no problem giving us the go-ahead."

When Deavonshire's only response was an uncomfortable silence, Barrett hardened his voice. "You understand McCreary Energy is responsible for putting you where you are now." The grin slipped from the senator's face. Good.

"You know I'm grateful for your support."

"Bring home the votes. We're set to start drilling immediately."

Was Deavonshire's smile the tiniest bit shaky? "It's a tough issue, Barrett. I'll do what I can."

Barrett rose. "Deliver."

The senator held out his paw for the firm politician's hand job. "Big Elk sure isn't helping our cause. The Hopi council was ready to recommend the mining, but they cancelled their testimony for this afternoon. Rumor has it Big Elk convinced them to change their position."

Fire blasted through Barrett at this unexpected setback. "I'll take care of Big Elk."

"I'm sure the committee is going to call for another environmental impact study."

Goddamn it. "You'll convince them it's not necessary and a waste of taxpayer dollars. Last year's EIS is sufficient."

There was that patronizing attitude, as if Barrett didn't know how the system worked. "This is a small issue and might be something we can concede to appear cooperative."

"Another EIS is non-negotiable. No new studies, no delays. Get the vote."

"Absolutely." Could teeth get any bigger or whiter?

Barrett wasn't convinced of Deavonshire's sincerity. "How rude of me. I haven't asked about your wife and adorable daughter. Angela, isn't it?"

The senator grinned. "She's a corker."

"The world can be a dangerous place for a three-year-old, don't you think?"

Deavonshire's face froze. He might be stupid but, apparently, not retarded. The color drained from his face.

Barrett showed his teeth, only slightly resembling a smile. He patted the senator on his shoulder. "I'm looking forward to the committee releasing those claims." He sauntered down the hall, spying Cole chatting with, of all people, Charlie goddamn Podanski.

Cole spotted Barrett and ambled over. A young reported scurried to them, her notebook and pen poised. "Mr. McCreary, what do you say to those who are worried uranium mining could destroy the landscape and pollute the water? That, ideally, mining should be forever banned in this region?"

Barrett barely kept himself from growling at the ditz. Obviously, he shouldn't talk to the press now. "Let me introduce Cole Huntsman. He's McCreary's expert on uranium mining." Barrett stepped back and let the ever-charming Cole disarm the reporter.

"Mining techniques have changed dramatically since uranium was mined around here in the seventies," Cole said. "The typical footprint of the mine is smaller than a Walmart parking lot. Each mine would only last about five years and as it closed, a new one would open. So we're not talking about hundreds of mines operating at the same time."

The co-ed scribbled and nodded. With the reporter occupied and the hearing room emptying, Barrett moved on to his next problem. He needed Nora Abbott under his thumb. Not necessarily out of the picture like her meddling husband—though if it came to that, he wouldn't hesitate.

Cole continued with his smooth press voice. "Uranium is deep underground, so mines won't be exposed to wind and water. The water table is way below mine level. There will be no blasting, no unsightly pits, and no lasting contamination."

Problems roiled in Barrett's gut and he swallowed acid. Was this how his father felt before he'd keeled over from a heart attack?

"The Arizona Strip, a land area of 1.7 million acres, contains one of the richest uranium resources in the world." Cole was wrapping up the soft sell. Touting the benefits of nuclear energy wasn't difficult. Barrett himself was a true believer.

Barrett slipped away. He pushed open the smoked-glass courthouse doors, stepping into the blinding sunshine of the courtyard.

How could he expedite snow making? Left to her own devices Nora Abbott might not get around to it this year, what with mourning the loss of her dumbass husband.

He tossed Nora to the back of his brain and shuffled the next issue to the top. Big Elk. Didn't that asshole ever quit? Like an annoying gnat under Barrett's nose, he meddled with the Hopi Tribal Council and stirred up do-gooders who didn't have lives of their own. Barrett could neutralize him; it would only cost money. Lots of it.

Deep in his plots, Barrett paid little attention to crossing the street and arriving at his shiny black Escalade. He pushed the unlock button on a key he didn't remember pulling from his pocket. Damn, age whittled his awareness. Used to be he could manage McCreary Energy's five-year plan, train a quarter horse to pace, and enjoy Heather's preschool antics all at the same time.

Focus, you old fool. Barrett drew in a breath and glanced across the park at the edge of the courthouse parking lot.

A gunshot through his temple wouldn't have been a bigger jolt.

Cuddled under a tree, Heather leaned forward and shared a sloppy kiss with that fucking Indian.

Goddamn it. He'd paid good money to send that thug to jail.

Barrett wanted to kill the boy, just tear him apart and watch wolves fight over his flesh. He wanted Heather safe at home in a ten-year time out. Red hot rage coursed through his blood. He couldn't get to Heather fast enough. His hands ached to close around the boy's throat and see the life drain from him.

Heather's eyes widened when she saw Barrett charging toward her and Alex. She recovered and jumped to her feet, hardening her face in challenge.

Suddenly it was Ester in front of him with that same expression: "I have made my choice, Barrett."

Barrett froze.

Heather stepped in front of him, chin raised. "Hi, Poppy."

Not Ester. Heather. Years ago he'd wrap his arms around her and take her into his lap, her little ponytails bouncing. But like Ester, his sweet little cherub didn't exist anymore. The teenager in front of him burned with enough anger to heat a Siberian village for a week.

Barrett took Heather's hand. "It's time to go."

His touch hit her like acid and she pulled away. "I belong with Alex. With my people. Honoring Mother Earth and the kachinas of the sacred mountain."

The stinking pile of shit dared to speak. "She is finally with her people. Don't try to corrupt her with shiny toys."

This scum didn't understand the thin ice he skated on. "Shut up."

Alex tossed his veil of black hair with an aggressive thrust of his shoulders. "You can't talk to me like that. I got friends. More powerful than you."

Barrett barely held on to his rage. "What friends?"

"Big Elk. Don't fuck with him, dude."

Nice nail to your coffin, asshole. Barrett pulled Heather's hand again. "Let's go."

The young man's shifty eyes focused across the park and he took a step back.

Heather resisted. "I've tried to talk to you about this and all you talk about is cost of living and making money. You don't listen."

Heather's brave boyfriend took another step back and hurried away. She watched him with a puzzled frown.

A man's voice sounded behind Barrett's shoulder. "Mr. McCreary?"

He turned to the gray-haired uniformed cop and flipped through his mental Rolodex. "Mike Tomlinson, isn't it?"

The cop returned his smile, probably impressed Barrett could come up with his name. "That's right."

Heather inched away. Before she could take another step, Barrett put his arm over her shoulders and drew her to his side. "Have you met my daughter, Heather?"

Tomlinson lost his smile and hesitated a moment.

Ice floes threatened Barrett's heart. There was a reason Alex disappeared, a reason the good officer approached—and he understood it all had to do with Heather.

Tomlinson looked Barrett in the eye. "Actually, Mr. McCreary, we have a situation involving your daughter."

Heather stiffened next to him but kept an implacable expression.

"There was an incident here a couple of days ago at the courthouse that involved your daughter."

"What sort of incident, Mike?"

Tomlinson shook his head. "That activist, Big Elk, stirred up a bunch of people and things got out of hand. The owner of Kachina Ski, Nora Abbott, was threatened."

"That's terrible."

"Afraid so. Anyway, several witnesses identified your daughter as one of the assailants."

If he'd had any doubts before, this sealed Alex's death warrant. "How is Ms. Abbott?"

"She wasn't injured. Unfortunately, the next day the main assailant, Alex Seweingyawma, attacked Ms. Abbott at her home and nearly killed her."

Heather drew in a sharp breath. At least this news surprised her.

"Attempted murder? And this criminal is at large?" No need to tell Tomlinson that Alex had been here. Barrett was more efficient and lethal than the legal system.

"We've got leads but, frankly, when these people retreat to the rez, it's hard to get our hands on them."

"I understand, Mike. This is a disturbing situation and I promise we'll take care of it."

Tomlinson nodded. "Seweingyawma is a dangerous man. Your daughter needs to keep her distance."

"Of course. Thank you." Barrett started to walk away.

"There are consequences, you know," Tomlinson said.

Barrett clenched his teeth. "Consequences?"

"To your daughter's involvement. Heather will have to appear before a judge. In cases as serious as this, juvie lockup isn't out of the question. But sometimes, if the family can come up with suitable restitution and the youth shows appropriate remorse, probation is a possibility."

Heather didn't balk when Barrett led her to the Escalade.

A black wave of panic gathered at the back of Barrett's brain. He forced calm to take over. He'd made a fortune turning problems into opportunities. He needed to think like Barrett McCreary III, not some addled peon.

How could he stop Heather from this teenaged rebellion stage and get her back on track? When Heather threatened Nora Abbott, she also threatened her own future. Fear of her next self-destructive act terrified him. At the very least, she'd made his next move trickier.

If Nora held resentment for Heather's part in the attack, Barrett would have a hard time manipulating her. And he needed Nora Abbott on board. Barrett cleared his mind and waited. He put his trust in the wheels and cogs that operated on the other side of his consciousness.

It happened again, as it always did. A solution sprang into his head, fully formed like Athena bursting from Zeus's temple. Barrett hadn't lost his touch, after all.

By this time tomorrow, Nora Abbott and Heather would both be under his control.

TEN

CHARLIE BUMPED INTO NORA on the trail, Scott's pine box stabbing her in the back. "Oh man, it's the Heat."

She thought the death of her husband, revelation of his betrayal, and looming financial ruin might be more than she could take in one day. And yet, the black cloud just got darker.

Maybe she could walk back up the trail like the Von Trapp family at the end of *The Sound of Music.* Just run away. She'd trudge onward until she found sanctuary.

"You go," she said to Charlie. "I'm heading up the mountain to find a place to sit until I petrify."

Charlie frowned down the trail. A crowd milled in the lot, but Charlie's sole focus was Gary something or other in his uniform.

Cole Huntsman stood next to the cop, probably spilling his guts about Bimbo accusing Nora of murder. And Big Elk stood in the middle of a circle of protesters like a ringmaster. With the righteous following, this circus wasn't short on clowns. A dozen or so Native Americans and the Guilty White People chanted "Make love, not snow." As bad as all that seemed, what froze Nora's blood and made her want to swallow a cyanide pill was what had just stepped out of a taxi.

Abigail.

Charlie sucked in a breath of awe. "I am in love."

Cold sweat slicked Nora's forehead. "Forget it, Charlie. Abigail is like carbon monoxide. You don't realize how deadly she is."

"Abigail. The name sings as if spoken by the hosts of heaven."

Right on schedule the news van pulled up and a camera woman jumped out. Big Elk had to be disappointed the crew was local. Still, a network affiliate left hope for national exposure.

Charlie all but floated down the path. "Who is this vision?"

Reluctantly Nora followed. "My mother. Abigail the Perfect."

Abbey trotted down the trail like a one-tail welcoming committee.

From their location on the trail, Nora could hear Big Elk's booming voice. He held his hand out to quiet the chanters. "This is our sacred mountain, home to the kachinas since the beginning of the Fourth World. When our Hopi brothers and sisters received responsibility to balance the world, they agreed to protect the Mother and this sacred home."

The minivan that served as Flagstaff's taxi sat in the parking lot. As if spotlighted by the sun, Abigail stood in her beige silk suit and gold sandals, her arms crossed, scowling at the demonstration.

The sanctuary of the lodge sat across the minefield of the parking lot.

Run back up the trail while you still can. But Nora knew she couldn't hide on the mountain forever; they'd already hauled off the beer.

The taxi driver reached into the back of the van and brought out an enormous tapestry-covered suitcase. He hefted it onto his shoulder, picked up a smaller bag, and started up the path to the lodge. Nora saw that two large suitcases and a couple of smaller bags already sat on the deck.

Charlie's joy was unmistakable. "It appears she's here for a long spell."

"Hard to say how long she plans on staying. Being fabulous requires supplies." A tiny Abigail troll appeared at the base of Nora's neck and turned a control knob from 0 to 1, sparking a headache in her temples.

Big Elk raised his arms like a televangelist. "The fire-bearer of the mountain is demanding we listen to him. If we don't stop the desecration, he will bring fire to the mountain."

Charlie didn't take his eyes off Abigail. "I only want to bask in her presence."

"You don't know what you're in for." Nora now set a determined pace for the lodge and Charlie fell in beside her. Together they walked across the parking lot. Involved in his performance, Big Elk didn't notice Nora. Too bad. She'd rather face Big Elk and his evangelistic army than greet Abigail.

Nora took a deep breath and braced herself. "Hello, Abigail."

Abigail spun around. A reactionary frown flitted across her face. She quickly rearranged her face in a show of sorrow, probably practiced in front of a mirror. Abigail opened her arms. "Baby! Oh, baby. Mother's here."

Nora had stopped just outside her mother's reach. She wondered how much rehearsal Abigail had done to get her words and facial expressions just right. The parking lot full of protesters might have thrown a less experienced performer for a loop, but Abigail excelled at improvisation.

Nora rubbed her temples. "What are you doing here?"

"Excuse me." The authoritative voice behind her could only belong to a cop. Gary Something or Other approached Nora.

Abigail looked confused that Nora hadn't run into her arms. "Where else would I be when my baby needs me so?"

Hawaii? Italy? Outer Mongolia? "I thought you were on an Alaskan cruise."

Officer Gary stepped closer. "May I have a word with you?"

Abbey pushed his head under Abigail's hand. Her upper lip curled slightly and she pulled her hand away. "I caught a plane at the first dock as soon as I heard. I knew you'd need my help planning the services."

Welcome to the Abigail Show, Nora thought.

"I'm sorry to disturb you today." Gary's persistent and official formality grated on her nerves.

Cole inserted himself between the cop and Nora. "Then why are you? I asked you to come back tomorrow."

Enough of Cole's rescuing. Even though she didn't want to talk to Gary, she said, "What's going on with Alex Sewe-something? The guy that attacked me."

He hesitated. "Alex Seweingyawma. We're sure he's hiding on the Hopi reservation." Obviously, this wasn't the topic the cop had come to discuss.

"He's still missing?"

"We don't consider him a threat to you at this time."

Charlie nudged Nora with the pine box and gushed at Abigail. "How kind of you to fly to your daughter's side."

Traitor.

Abigail's Mary Kay smile froze on her lips.

The cop attempted to bring the focus back to business. "This is an urgent matter."

"And a murderer running loose isn't?" Nora asked.

" . . . fire on the mountain." Big Elk's bleating ceased making sense to Nora's addled brain.

"That about does it, Mrs. Stoddard." The taxi driver returned to Abigail as if approaching a sacred altar, having deposited the last of the matching baggage on the deck.

Abigail pulled a bill out of a small bag dangling from her shoulder on a long gold chain. With both hands she pressed it into the taxi driver's palm. "You must call me Abigail, Ted. Thank you so much for all your help. I would have been lost without you."

Shoot me now. The troll at the base of Nora's head clicked the knob to 3 and her headache traded in amateur for professional status.

Cole lowered his chin, a big horned sheep readying for battle with Officer Gary. "Why not make yourself helpful and get rid of that asshole?" He pointed to Big Elk.

Gary glared at Cole but shifted his focus to Big Elk. "He *is* an asshole." He marched to the protesters and raised his voice above Big Elk's, ordering them to disperse, but Big Elk wouldn't take that lying down.

"The whole world will shake and turn red and fight against those hindering the Hopi."

The picketers took up their stupid "Make love not snow" refrain while Big Elk and Gary had words. Bless Cole's heart for calling off Big Elk and Gary with one remark. Now, if he could just make Abigail disappear Nora might forgive his environmental activism and even promise him her firstborn. Not that she'd ever have a firstborn with her husband gone. Her heart squeezed yet again.

Abigail flashed Cole a dazzling smile. "Could you be a dear and take my bags from the deck up to the apartment? That dog of Nora's is likely to get underfoot and those stairs are so treacherous. I'm afraid I'll fall and break my neck."

"No! This man is not your servant."

Charlie looked ready to jump. "I'll haul your bags to heaven if that's your wish."

Cole smiled at Nora. "It's okay."

Nora looked straight ahead, her neck stiff. "It's not okay."

Abigail's tone set Nora's teeth on edge. "Really, Nora. There's no need to be so prickly. Here is this young, strapping man willing to help us out."

"I'm perfectly capable of dealing with your bags. It doesn't make me more of a woman to act helpless and stupid."

Abigail drew in a breath of offense. "Same Nora, always cutting off your nose to spite your face."

The scene in the parking lot was getting to be too much. All Nora wanted was to curl up in a ball and ignore the betrayal she felt at Scott's lies.

Balancing the pine box with one arm, Charlie pulled a Pabst Blue Ribbon from a jacket pocket. He held it out to Abigail. "Can I offer you a beverage?"

Abigail stood as if she'd turned to a pillar of salt.

Cole meanwhile strode ahead. Lean and tall, he looked like he spent more time outside than in, probably camping and living off the land. A younger and less crusty version of Charlie. Nora imagined that, like Charlie in his radical days, Cole wouldn't hesitate to protect nature with violence if he thought it necessary. He kept turning up at all the right times and acting helpful, but she figured his agenda dealt more with finding her vulnerabilities. But if his issue was uranium mining and his nemesis Barrett McCreary, why would he be stalking her? Nora couldn't begin to sort that out.

Undaunted by Abigail's rejection, Charlie pulled the tab on the proffered beer and took a gulp. He smiled and delivered his normal opening line. "Looks like rain."

Abigail jerked her head to the cloudless sky and shot Charlie an offended look.

Nora smiled and felt a slight decrease in the pounding in her temples. "A toad strangler."

"I like an optimist."

Abigail walked next to Nora and put a hand on her arm. She kept her voice low and barely moved her lips. "Who is this person?"

"This is my friend Charlie."

It didn't take Queen Abigail long to assert her authority. She eyed Charlie. "I'm Nora's mother and this isn't a good time for a visit. She's suffering stress and needs to rest."

If what Jim Bowie went through at the Alamo was called stress, maybe you could say Nora's day was stressful. "Charlie is my friend and he's always welcome." *Even if he is struck with momentary insanity and thinks you're a goddess.*

Officer Gary had temporarily won the battle with Big Elk. Either that or the news crew shot their footage and sound bite and Big Elk had no more incentive to hang around. The chanting had subsided and the protesters now climbed into their vehicles, slammed doors, and started engines.

Nora trudged up the stairs to the deck. Abigail tapped up behind her, probably struggling to keep her sandal heels from getting stuck in the metal grating. Charlie followed them.

Cole waited next to the luggage. "Where do you want these?"

"Timbuktu." Nora headed for the apartment stairs. The world could turn or stop for all she cared. She wanted to climb into bed. "Abbey, come."

Abigail folded her arms. "I wish you hadn't named your dog that way."

"He's named ... "

Abigail's annoyed voice finished, "I know, after Edward Abbey. An *anarchist*."

Charlie perked up. "Ed Abbey was a god."

"A great environmentalist, Mother."

"*Now* she calls me Mother."

As opposed to Queen of Darkness? Nora's inner voice snarked.

Abigail tried to enlist Cole to her side. "I think she calls him Abbey to annoy me. I don't know why she couldn't call him Rover or Spot."

With a straight face and slow, serious drawl Cole said, "He doesn't really have any spots."

For the first time in days, Nora almost laughed.

Abigail reestablished her calm and smiled at Cole. "You can take those upstairs to the apartment. I need to get settled in so we can discuss the funeral."

Oh lord. "We had the ceremony today."

Abigail's eyes widened. "Today? What church?"

Nora squared her shoulders. "No church. We did it up on the mountain. We just got back."

"What?"

Nora didn't reply, sort of enjoying the strangling sound coming out of Abigail.

"Did you say you just came back?" Abigail sputtered.

Nora nodded "Yep."

She couldn't have sounded more shocked if she heard Nora really had murdered Scott. "And you wore ... jeans?"

"It's hard to wear heels on the trail, Mother."

Abigail waved in Charlie's direction, indicating the box. "And that ... ?"

"Is Scott's ashes." Nora stomped over and took the box.

Though Scott's unusual ceremony must have thrown Abigail's world off kilter, she recovered quickly. She tossed her head, sending her bob fluttering. "You look tired."

My husband is dead. I just found out he was cheating on me. Again. My business is drying up and I'm not sure I care. I'm being stalked by an abnormally large and angry Native American who would like to see me dead. A rabid activist calls me names on the news. Some strange masked man appears and disappears in the forest. A confusing and probably dangerous environmentalist keeps hanging around being weirdly nice. And now the woman who tortured me all my life, the one who makes me throw up and have diarrhea at the same time, the diva of demons, just dropped in for a visit.

"I haven't been sleeping," Nora said.

Abigail hurried to her bags. While Charlie and Abbey watched, Abigail bent to one of the smaller bags and rummaged inside. She held up a small bottle. "This is absolutely the best concealer on the market." She handed it to Nora. "We'll have you looking decent in no time."

The troll gave the knob a good crank to 6.

Cole picked up a suitcase. "I think Nora looks great." An obvious lie, but greatly appreciated.

Abigail smiled at Cole. "It's a woman thing."

Cole started up the stairs. Nora shouldn't allow him up to her apartment in case he wanted to plant a bomb or something. But it seemed that being blown up might actually be better than lugging her mother's bags up the steep flight. Exhaustion didn't begin to cover what she felt. Nora moved aside to let Cole pass.

Thudding on the metal stairs alerted her to Officer Gary. He stepped onto the deck and walked to Nora.

Cole stopped. "Didn't we decide you'd come back tomorrow?"

Gary spared him a stern look and turned to Nora. "I know this is a bad time but I need to ask you to not leave town for a few days."

"Sure. I'll cancel my Mexican vacation." It was stupid to be belligerent with cops, but Nora was beyond reason.

Charlie held his fist in the air, some hippy symbol of power to the people. "Unless you have a warrant, you're harassing my friend."

Abigail put her hands on her hips and stared down Charlie. "You stay out of this." She flashed Gary a smile. "I'm sorry, Officer. It has been a trying day, what with a funeral and those people in the parking lot and I don't even know why they were here. Nora's nerves are shot."

Okay, maybe Abigail had her usefulness. She spoke with a tone of warm tea. "Nora doesn't intend on traveling, of course. Can you tell me what this is all about?"

Gary studied Abigail and let out a deep breath. He addressed Nora. "There is evidence of foul play in the death of Scott Abbott. As his wife, you are an official person of interest."

The deck tipped and swayed. Scott's box hit the deck and for the second time that afternoon, let loose the bag of his ashes.

"Scott was . . . ?" She couldn't say it.

"Murdered," Gary finished.

A suitcase hit the stairs behind her and tumbled after Scott's ashes just before Cole's arms closed around her and kept her from doing the same.

ELEVEN

ONE WAS NOT REQUIRED to bang the frying pan on the stove, slam the cupboard door, and clang the lid to make eggs. Yet Abigail never had mastered the art of making breakfast with the volume turned down. Nora wanted nothing more than to sleep again.

She rolled over and squinted her eyes. The vast empty bed bored a hole into her chest.

If what Bimbo said was true, Scott had posted the vacant sign over Nora's bed long ago. She'd been one argument away from sending him packing herself. It didn't stop the pain welling in her chest, nearly stopping her heart.

Murder. Her eyes flew open with the thud in her chest. It made no sense. Suspecting Nora as the murderer would be logical, though. No one else was ever angry with him. If Cole had told Gary about Bimbo's accusations, not even suitcase carrying could clear him of suspicions in Nora's mind.

Had someone really killed Scott? It had to be that Alex guy. After all, he'd attempted to murder Nora two, maybe three times already.

Scott had died as collateral damage, an exchange for Nora. Which only made her feel guilty on top of battered.

The door swung open and Nora held her breath. Maybe Abigail would see her sleeping, take pity, and leave her alone.

No such luck.

"It's eight o'clock. You can't stay in bed forever."

Nora rolled away. "Yes I can."

The blinds zipped up, the window slid back, and the cawing of a crow exploded into the room. "I know it hurts, baby. But you have to put your life back together and the sooner you start the better."

"Why do you hate me? I tried to be a good daughter."

Abigail tsked. "None of that self-pity."

Even if she wanted to, Nora couldn't rise. Her body morphed into something made of a substance more dense than lead.

"It's a new day. You can't hide away."

"I'm not hiding, Mother. I'm mourning."

Abigail sat on the side of the bed and patted Nora's shoulder. "I'm sorry about Scott's passing, of course. But he wasn't the quality person you deserve."

Nausea welled in the pit of Nora's stomach. "I expected too much from him."

"I tried to keep it to myself, but I never thought you should have married him."

Nora sat up, toppling Abigail from the bed. "Keep it to yourself? You've never missed an opportunity to trash Scott," Nora said.

Abigail managed to keep from splatting on the floor and smoothed her shirt. "You should have married someone like Cole Huntsman."

Age slowed Abigail not one bit. She still held the Flabbergaster Master world title. "What?"

Abigail stooped and whisked Nora's jeans from the floor. "He stopped by this morning to check on you. Now that's considerate."

Nora swung her legs out of bed and snatched the jeans from Abigail. She stared at her mother and dropped them back on the floor. "You're sticking up for an environmentalist?"

Abigail let out a superior chuckle. "He's not an environmentalist. He's from Wyoming. Besides, I embrace the green movement. I recycle."

"Do you eat local too? Ride your bike instead of drive? Or do you just throw your empty water bottles into the correct bin?"

Abigail put a hand on her hip. "Again with plastic bottles in landfills! I'm not a fanatic like you, if that's what you mean."

"For the love of Pete." *Gaa!* She had just used one of her mother's favorite clichés. "Would you go away?" She needed Scott. He provided Abigail Protection, one of Nora's favorite things about being with him. His deficiencies deflected Abigail from Nora's failures.

Scott. She saw his dark eyes twinkling with humor and heard his deep laughter. A slap of pain hit her like a physical blow. She sank back to the bed.

Abigail grabbed her arm. "No, you don't."

How was it possible her cheeks were wet with tears? Scott didn't deserve her tears. But he hadn't deserved to be murdered, either. "I can't do this alone, without him."

Abigail put her arm around Nora. "Of course you can. You've always been able to do anything you set your mind to. You've got decisions to make."

"Like what?"

"For one thing, you'll need an attorney."

Oh. That.

Abigail picked up the jeans and folded them. "Sooner rather than later. That podunk Officer Gary said you haven't been accused of anything yet but we need to be in control."

"When they have that Alex guy in custody, it won't take them long to prove he pushed Scott and then came after me."

Abigail tilted her head. "Of course. But in the meantime, you need counsel. I've watched enough *Law & Order* to know that without a lawyer you could be in trouble."

Nora tugged against her mother. "I just want to sleep."

"I know you do. What you're going to do, however, is brush your teeth. Then you'll come out to the kitchen and eat the omelet I'll make for you."

Nora wouldn't admit it to Abigail, but she did feel better once she showered and dressed. She took the omelet to the deck and only worked through a fourth of the conglomeration before it fell to her stomach's floor. Leaning her head against the wood siding of the lodge, she closed her eyes to the sun and rested her hand on Abbey's head.

Bubbles of worry fought the murkiness of her brain. They needed to begin construction on the pipeline immediately if they— she—was going to make snow on the main run by Christmas. And what about money to pay the attorney?

Jail and/or bankruptcy loomed unless she drummed up the courage to ask Abigail for a loan. It was impossible to calculate the years of verbal sniping ahead of her for failing badly enough to beg Abigail for money.

The screen door of the apartment opened and the keeper of Kachina Ski's financial future, the heel that would grind Nora to emotional dust, descended delicately to the deck. "I was thinking we should get spiffed up and go shopping. New clothes will cheer you up."

"My clothes are fine."

Abigail didn't vanish, despite Nora's fervent prayers to any and all spirits of the mountain. "I don't want to be indelicate, but you must face the reality of your situation. You're no longer an attached woman. If you don't make yourself attractive, you may spend the rest of your life alone."

"I'm not in the market for a new husband."

"You say that now but loneliness sets in surprisingly fast and it's not fun. I miss Howard terribly."

Nora stopped herself before saying, *Good thing he left you with yet another fortune to help you heal.* Nora was wicked and no doubt heading for the fires of hell.

Abigail's eyes filled with tears and, as if she controlled it, one single drop spilled from her eye. Not enough to ruin her makeup, just enough to make her appear vulnerable and strong at the same time. "It has been an extremely difficult year. I've fought every day to remain true to the Stoddard dignity."

"You've been strong."

Nora's husband died just four days ago and yet, all sympathy and attention needed to focus on Abigail's loss. Situation: Normal.

While things were bad, Nora girded herself to ask Abigail for money.

"Good morning, lovely ladies!" The shout came from across the ski run.

Saved by the hippie. She blessed the kachinas for their mercy in sending Charlie.

Abigail's hiss reeked of disapproval. "Honestly, Nora. I don't think you should allow that man around here."

"I like Charlie."

"But, dear, he's not really ... "

Nora waited while Abigail trailed off, then finished for her. "Our kind?"

Charlie stepped on the deck.

Abigail let out a deep sigh. "You know what I mean."

Charlie walked over to Nora. "You are the sun and moon and bring meaning to my life." He bowed to Abigail. "Your glittering visage takes my breath away."

Abigail clasped her hands behind her back. "Oh posh."

A black SUV crunched the cinders in the parking lot.

Great. Visitors.

TWELVE

BARRETT SHUT THE DOOR of the Escalade and waited.

After a moment he reopened the door and put his head inside. "Staying in the car won't make me change my mind."

Heather glared at him from the passenger side. "I don't see why I have to do this."

"Be on your best behavior or Nora Abbott can make your life difficult."

Heather didn't move.

Barrett shrugged. "Fine. You don't have to go with me to ask Nora Abbott's forgiveness and offer your services."

She smiled and sat upright. "Thank you, Poppy. I'll be good, I promise."

"You can wait for the judge to send you to juvenile detention."
Boom.

Out came that lower lip. "The judge might come up with something besides jail."

Barrett raised his eyebrows. "We are McCrearys. We don't wait for others to decide our future. We take control."

She crossed her arms. "What makes you so sure this Nora woman will hire me?"

"I've got ways."

"You mean you've got money."

"Something like that."

Heather grabbed the latch and shoulder checked the door open. "Someday you're going to come up against a situation where money won't buy you out."

She didn't know he couldn't buy the one thing he ever truly wanted.

Heather came around the Escalade and together they walked across the cinder parking lot and up the path to the lodge.

The girl stopped at the top of the stairs and Barrett gently pushed to move her forward. An attractive blonde about Barrett's age stood next to Nora and a few feet in front of the woman a decomposing mountain man gulped from a beer can.

God. Charlie. That dried-up piece of idealist turned up everywhere.

Barrett reached for Nora's hand. "How are you, Ms. Abbott?"

He'd read her profile. Graduated at the top of her class, smart, ambitious, not a bad looker. But she'd certainly struck bad luck with the drought. He'd seen her around town. She carried herself well, her red hair usually shiny, bouncing around a cheerful face with intelligent eyes. The last few days had been hard on her, making her pale and adding a shadow of grief to her eyes.

Barrett couldn't afford to feel guilty for causing her pain. Heather's well-being and protection came first. It was Scott's own fault he got in the way.

Nora gave Heather a stony expression but her face softened when she shifted to Barrett. "I'm fine, thank you."

Charlie sipped his beer and narrowed his eyes at Barrett. He sank to a bench beside an older dog. "She's a woman of uncommon strength and breeding."

Barrett looked away from Charlie without comment. It was just like Charlie to use that phrase, the old joke the three of them had shared about Ester.

The classy looking blonde smiled at Barrett. Now here was a woman worth looking at. He held out his hand, enjoying the rush of pleasure when she placed her delicate fingers in his. "I'm Barrett McCreary," he said.

Her lips were full, inviting. "Nice to meet you, Mr. McCreary. I'm Abigail Stoddard, Nora's mother."

"Barrett, please." His blood pumped to places he'd ignored for too long.

"Barrett," she repeated, looking into his eyes.

THIRTEEN

THE LEGEND. BARRETT MCCREARY here at Kachina Ski. What was he doing with that Native American girl? She was the one at the courthouse with Alex the Knife Guy. Should Nora run from her or slap her? Either way, she wanted the girl off her property.

Barrett put a hand on the girl's back and brought her forward. "I'd like to introduce my daughter, Heather."

Daughter? She was more the age of a granddaughter and clearly not of his European background.

Barrett shot a pointed look at the girl and she glared back. The standoff felt as familiar to Nora as an old movie. Although Barrett and this girl didn't look at all like Nora and Abigail, the body language was their same tango from fifteen years ago.

Finally the girl turned her attention to Nora. "I'm here to apologize for my part at the courthouse. I'm sorry."

Maybe the girl lost the silent battle with her father, but she didn't shirk her duty. She impressively held Nora's gaze and her voice sounded strong.

What do I do with that? she wondered. Maybe Heather hadn't actually harmed Nora, but she'd been with a very dangerous man. Her friend had pulled knives, strangled Nora, probably killed Scott. "You're hanging out with bad people," Nora said.

Barrett nodded in satisfaction, apparently approving Nora's firm stand.

"Nora!" Abigail sounded as though Nora scalped the poor girl. "Heather came to your home and humbled herself. She deserves your gracious forgiveness."

Abigail didn't need facts; she made them up for herself.

Barrett shook his head. "Nora's right. An apology isn't sufficient."

Heather inhaled. "I know there's nothing I can do to change what happened. But I would like to make restitution by working for you the rest of the summer."

No way. "That won't be necessary."

"Actually, it is," Barrett said. "If you'll agree to Heather working here it will probably save her from time in juvenile detention."

Maybe locking her up would teach her a lesson.

"While she might deserve that treatment," Barrett said, as though he could hear her thoughts. "I believe in rehabilitation."

And I get to have the murderer's apprentice on my property? Hell no.

Barrett continued his sales pitch. "She's a good worker."

Heather obviously fought to keep her dignity in the face of what amounted to a slave auction. Abigail in all her evil glory couldn't have been any worse.

Abigail focused her feminine attention on Barrett. "What a caring father you are. Raising children isn't easy." She probably didn't know Barrett McCreary steered the course of one of the largest energy companies in the country, but Abigail certainly had the ability to smell money, even in the fresh mountain air. It was a valuable skill, her version of Nora's MBA.

Charlie crushed his can, put it in a pocket, and stood. Surprising bitterness crisped his voice. "You'd have to look far and wide to find a more caring father than Barrett McCreary."

If Nora could harness the frosty look her mother shot Charlie she wouldn't need snow-making equipment.

Barrett chose to address Abigail. "I think Nora is an inspiration to young women."

Abigail beamed. "Well, growing up she gave me some challenges, but she turned out well."

Just like that Nora felt like the prize pig at a stock show. In the newly revised History According to Abigail, the only reason she'd achieved anything was due to Abigail's steady parenting. What credit would her mother accept for the financial ruin of Kachina Ski? Nora couldn't help feeling a connection with the sullen teenager. While Barrett and Abigail focused on each other, Heather and Nora made eye contact.

Charlie simply produced another beer from a jacket pocket and popped the top.

Abigail took a step closer to Barrett. "Now, dear," she said to Nora. "Didn't I teach you about giving back?"

What you taught me was to smile, keep my nails painted, and if I acted really pleasant, I could marry rich. Well, it had worked for Abigail—three times. Her mother lived a life of leisure with no worries.

"I believe your mentoring would be a turning point for my Heather," Barrett said.

The poor girl was doomed. With this bull of a father it's no wonder she raced down the wrong path. Nora looked at her with a smidgeon of compassion. "I really hope you don't have to spend time in jail. But I can't help you out."

"Nora!" Abigail said.

Nora shook her head. "To gear up for snow making, I'll be devoting all my time to raising financing. I can't take on mentoring."

Barrett's smile reminded her of Dracula. "If it's a matter of money, we should be able to work this out."

Incredible. She'd spent years straining for ever more creative ways to keep Kachina solvent and suddenly money was as easy as turning on the faucet. Even more incredible, Nora felt a real aversion to the obvious salvation Barrett offered. "Actually, I'd prefer to keep this a family business."

Abigail's eyes looked wide in her pale face. "Nora, honey. Can we talk?"

And leave our guests unattended? This must be serious. "I'm sorry you came all the way out here for nothing," Nora said to Barrett. She nodded to Heather. "Good luck."

Abigail placed her hand on Barrett's arm. "Would you mind waiting while I talk to Nora?"

She couldn't tell if Barrett was pleased with Abigail's attention or angry with Nora. "Of course."

Abigail took hold of Nora's arm and pulled her into the lodge.

"What's this about?" Nora said.

A bead of sweat appeared on Abigail's upper lip. "You have to take this offer."

Confused by her own reaction, Nora could only say, "Something about it doesn't feel right."

"What other options do you have?"

This wasn't how Nora hoped to broach the subject. *Here goes.* "I thought you might want to loan me the money for a few seasons."

Abigail's voice squeaked. "You have to talk to Barrett right now, before he changes his mind."

"Mother, you aren't listening to me. I don't want to work with Barrett."

Abigail paced across the room and back to Nora. "You can't get any money from me."

Ouch. Abigail had no faith in Nora. She scrambled for other options.

"You have to keep Kachina. I'll help you run it," Abigail said.

"What?"

"I'll be living with you anyway so I might as well earn my keep."

"You are not living with me."

"I have to. I sold my house in Denver. I sold the condo in Boca."

Nora's stomach started to churn. "What are you saying?"

Abigail stared out the window.

"Are you out of money?" Nora hated asking such a ridiculous question.

"I met a man at church. He had this idea of a great investment and it was making money hand over fist. Even in this crazy market."

Nausea pushed at the edges of Nora's belly.

"Remember the Madoff news story?" Abigail said.

"Madoff? Ponzi-scheme Madoff?"

Abigail nodded and looked sick. "It was something like that."

Nora sank onto the bench. "You're broke?"

"We're family. We need to take care of each other. And right now we need Barrett McCreary."

FOURTEEN

For the third time in less than two weeks, Nora wore her business suit and played the professional entrepreneur. This time the uniform felt more like a collar and leash, complete with muzzle. Four years ago she sold her soul to Kachina Ski for Scott. Today she mortgaged her future to Barrett for Abigail.

Barrett shook the attorney's hand while everyone gathered papers and pushed back from the conference table. It seemed that power and money created efficiencies Nora had only dreamed about. In an hour they'd seen two top attorneys, who Barrett had flown in from his law firm in Los Angeles. One was a corporate tax expert who'd magically drawn up partnership agreements ready for Nora's blood signature. The other was a criminal attorney prepared to shield Nora from any inconvenience associated with being a person of interest in the murder—*murder*—of her husband.

In a few short days she went from destitute and alone to secure under the wing of Barrett McCreary's millions.

She felt like her life was careening downhill like a sled on an icy luge run.

Abigail, perfectly coiffed and looking every bit equal to Barrett's bank account, smoothed her skirt and lifted the chain of her slim bag over her arm. "We should have lunch to celebrate this happy arrangement."

Happy. Yep. All Nora's heavy money problems were over. She should be floating like a helium balloon, not sinking like a bowling ball. "You and Barrett go ahead," she said. "I've got to call the snow sprayer contractor."

Barrett gave a final back pat to the tax attorney. "Don't worry about that. I contacted a firm in Colorado and they've expedited the equipment. Should be on its way."

"You ordered it? Without talking to me? When?" Heat rose from her belly to her face.

"Work crews are due by the end of the week. We'll have snow by Christmas."

Abigail already had a soft hand on Barrett's arm. "I was thinking Thai."

Barrett walked toward the door. "I'll take care of the snow making and leave the rest to you. You've got enough to do with operations."

Nora pressed her foot to the brakes but it looked like Barrett had cut the lines. "You said you'd be a silent partner and let me run things. I know what kind of eco-friendly equipment I want up there."

Barrett barely slowed his exit. "We have a limited window to get the equipment functioning. I've got contacts and, dare I say, some weight to throw around." He winked at Abigail and patted his belly.

"For once, just let someone help you, dear," Abigail said.

Help or take over? she thought. "We can't put just any equipment up there. It has to be energy efficient and work with the environment."

Abigail scowled at her. "Don't be so controlling. Barrett hasn't gotten this far by making poor decisions."

Frustration twined through Nora. Abigail was right. Barrett had created an empire, while Nora succeeded in nearly destroying one small business. She could use a mentor, not to mention a bank-roller. She waved them off, keeping her temper in check. "Go ahead. Enjoy the Thai. I'll see you later."

Abigail took Barrett's arm. "If you're sure … "

Nora waited a few minutes before leaving the conference room and stepping into the hall. Her high heels sank into the plush carpet of McCreary Energy's corporate office. After years of struggle and worry, snow making was a reality. The sunrise of opportunity shone just below the horizon. Too bad it felt more like an alien spaceship aiming a laser at her.

God, what happened to me? Nora used to be happy and hopeful. Challenges sparked her blood and the possibility of winning thrilled her. Somewhere in the seven years since meeting Scott, obstacles had become mountains that required exhausting effort to scale. Gone were the hurdles she sailed over on her sprint to the finish line.

The hallway led to the finely appointed reception area, escape only a few feet away. She'd head up to the mountain, get Abbey, and hike away this dread.

Abigail stood with arms crossed by the front door, her face impatient. Nora followed her gaze to a conference room where Barrett's muffled voice sneaked out. The door to the room stood ajar a few inches. Now would be a good time to tell Barrett to cancel the equipment he ordered. She needed to stop his intrusive management before it went any further. Since the receptionist no longer manned the desk, Nora veered around the corner, heading for the conference room.

She stopped outside the door to gather courage. A deep chill hardened Barrett's words. "How trustworthy is this information?"

Nora froze at the ice in Barrett's tone. Through the slit of the open door, she saw Cole Huntsman's lean form.

"Pretty reliable," Cole said.

Something crashed like a chair thrown into a table. Barrett sounded as if his temper barely held. "Fucking Deavonshire. He said he'd get the votes."

Cole's drawl contrasted with Barrett's heat. "Doesn't look likely. We'll need to switch gears. Do you have something up your sleeve?"

"Like what?"

Cole paused. "Favors to call in, maybe? Cash to spread around? Congressmen aren't angels."

Cole worked for Barrett and advocated bribes to Congress? So much for her theory that Cole was a righteous enviro out to get Barrett. If he was working with Barrett, he was far more dangerous than she'd thought.

Barrett's voice became clearer as he headed toward the door. "I'll get that greaseball Deavonshire to pony up the votes."

"How are you going to do that?" Cole hung back.

Nora hurried away from the door, slipping into the restroom across the hall.

She leaned against the door.

There was no hint of Barrett's anger as he obviously rejoined Abigail in reception. "How about that lunch? I'm hungry enough to eat a bear."

Abigail laughed, her impatience vanishing along with Barrett's terrifying threats. "Bear curry with Thai spice. Sounds yummy."

Nora waited inside the restroom door until Abigail and Barrett had time to leave the building. Then she moved as quickly and silently as possible from the restroom to the front door. The receptionist was back at her desk and issued a pleasant goodbye as Nora exited.

She hurried past the courthouse, her Jeep in sight. Barrett and Cole had to have been talking about the uranium hearing and the vote to withdraw lands from mining. Cole must be some sort of double agent working for both Big Elk and Barrett. He advocated bribing congressmen. She should tell someone. But who?

What a power-hungry maniac. Barrett tampered with Congress, ran a multi-billion dollar company, raised a teenage delinquent, and still had time to mess up Kachina Ski. The man was like a chainsaw juggler.

"Nora."

Cole's voice slashed across her thoughts. He must have followed her out of Barrett's offices. She pretended not to hear him. Only two blocks down the sun-drenched sidewalk to the parking lot and ten miles north to the serenity of her mountain.

"Nora, wait!" Cole trotted to her.

This guy was a ruthless criminal who could very well hurt her if he suspected she knew about his duplicity. She froze and waited for him.

His face lit in a boyish smile. "Good to see you." That flush started up his neck again. "Have you had lunch? Would you like to?"

What was his game? "I'm on my way home."

"Oh." He looked disappointed. "So, what were you doing at McCreary?"

"What were you doing there?"

"Business."

"Same here."

He studied her face. "What's your business with Barrett?"

"He's my partner."

He scowled at her. "You and Barrett are partners? I don't like this."

"You don't like it? I'm sorry to hear that." She took a step away.

"That didn't come out right." His face flared as if he really were embarrassed. "Obviously you can do what you want. But getting involved with Barrett isn't a good thing."

A few minutes ago she'd been thinking the same thing, but she wasn't about to let one more person tell her what to do. "I see. It's okay for you to work with Barrett on whatever you do, but not okay for me to work with him and make snow."

He didn't seem the least upset that she'd discovered he worked for Barrett. "It's not about snow making."

"Of course not. Suddenly you're all for desecrating the sacred peaks and ripping uranium out of the Grand Canyon."

"I don't necessarily think we should mine uranium at the Grand Canyon. There are places that should be left alone. I'm not sure we should risk this important watershed." He stopped when he noticed Nora staring at him, probably with her mouth open.

"If you were any kind of environmentalist, you'd be screaming about uranium mining up there. But you're not cheering for Barrett, either. What team do you play for?"

He stared at her as if she'd gone bonkers. Finally he shook his head. "We're talking about you and the fact you shouldn't be involved with Barrett."

She was as involved with Barrett as a person could get. Not only was he financing and making decisions on her business, he might be courting her mother, as well as placing his daughter in virtual daycare under Nora's watch. Having Cole confront her on it only made it worse.

Cole frowned and leaned forward. "You're in all kinds of danger. You've got Barrett with a hidden agenda, Alex Seweingyawma has already tried to kill you, and Big Elk is out to get you. Who is he, anyway?"

"Big Elk is exactly what he seems: a fake chief, beating his drum and creating attention for himself. Other people, on the other hand," she glared at him, "are not at all what they seem."

Cole didn't respond to her accusation. He was one smooth player. "But where did Big Elk come from?"

"He's Sioux. From Nebraska, I think."

Cole shook his head. "That's just it. I have a Hopi friend who's pretty tight with several people up in Nebraska, near Rosebud. They don't know where Big Elk came from. He never spent time up there. He just came on the Native American activist scene working for other tribes, saying he was Sioux."

"You know what? I don't care," she said. "I just want to run my business and be left alone."

He shook his head, his eyes full of concern. "That's not going to happen. You're in the middle of this mess and I'm worried about you."

This was too much. "Worried about me? Maybe you should quit lying to me. Why not tell me what you really want?"

Dumbfounded. He stood mute for several beats. "You saw the meeting with Barrett just now, didn't you?"

Good one, Nora. Now he knows and he'll have to kill you. "The one where you and Barrett plotted to bribe Congress?"

He grabbed her arm. "Forget about what you heard."

"You'd like that, wouldn't you?"

"You don't need to put yourself in any more danger. These people don't mess around."

"Sure. I should forget about it to protect myself. Right."

He let go of her arm and ran a hand through his hair, agitation coming from him in waves. "Hell, Nora, someone killed your husband. Do you know why? Who? How can you ignore the danger you're in?"

Her knees buckled. *Scott. Murdered.*

Cole put a hand on her elbow to steady her. "I'm sorry."

She tried to pull on her armor. "Leave me alone."

Cole led her to a bench and they sat. The heat of the sun-warmed concrete soaked through her suit.

He looked her square in the eyes. "The woman at the funeral said Scott was working for someone. Do you know who it was? Maybe that has something to do with his murder."

What was wrong with her? Cole might be all nice and warm and kind on the outside, but he'd already proved he had a dark side. It might be blacker than she thought. She jerked away. "I've got to go."

Cole jumped up. "I didn't mean..."

Her panic pounded in her heels clicking on the sidewalk. Just before jerking the door open on her Jeep she saw Heather in the park, leaning against a tree, scanning the area as if waiting for someone.

Nora glanced behind her and didn't see Cole. She headed toward Heather. "Aren't you supposed to be shoveling dirt from around the lift house?"

Unruffled, Heather waited for Nora to get to her. "Abigail said since everyone else was going to town, I could have the afternoon off."

Two days on the job and already Nora had lost control. "Abigail's not your boss."

"Your mom's cool."

"Yeah. I thought that once, for about two seconds." *Now who's being a bratty teenager?*

"You don't even appreciate what you have." Bitterness tinged Heather's words.

As if Abigail couldn't irritate her enough, now her mother had her very own groupie. "I suppose you think your father's cool too?"

Heather's eyes narrowed. "My *adopted* father."

Uh oh. The mention of adopted fathers brought Nora's thoughts to her own adopted father figure. The pressure overwhelmed Nora. It had nothing to do with Heather; the levy simply gave way. No more banter, no more holding it together. Nora fought one last moment and then tears overtook her. "What am I doing here? I never wanted any of this."

Heather's eyes opened in alarm "Whoa. I can go back to work if it means that much to you."

"I mean the whole thing. I never wanted the ski area or Flagstaff or snow."

Heather relaxed a little. "Then why are you here?"

Nora sank to the grass, getting control of her sobs. "It was for Scott. And for Abigail. And for Berle."

Heather sat across from her. "Who's Berle?"

"Berle was my mother's second husband. I loved Berle. He was good to my mother. I think maybe she really loved him."

Heather's confused gaze encouraged her to talk.

"Not long after Scott and I married, Berle got stomach cancer. I was finishing business school and had some nice offers. I was going to live in a plush high-rise condo in Chicago or L.A. and vacation on sunny beaches."

Heather sat quietly, waiting for her to continue.

"But Berle went from alright to almost dead in less than two weeks. One of the last days, he begged me to promise I'd always take care of my mother. He had a fortune and it would all go to her but he worried. He said he owned this ski area in Flagstaff. Kachina Ski. He'd give it to me, free and clear, with the one caveat that if my mother ever needed financial help, Kachina would be her safety net."

Heather's eyebrows drew together as she worked it out. "This must have been before the drought. I can see where that would be a good move."

"I told him of course I would take care of my mother, but I didn't want a ski resort. I assumed I'd have a great career in finance."

"But you ended up here."

"When I told Scott about it, he latched on to the idea and couldn't see anything else. He was full of dreams of us running the place together and spending our days on the mountain. He wanted it so much, I couldn't say no."

"But it didn't work out as you'd planned."

She shrugged. "I was naïve to think Scott would enjoy the business side."

"Your mother says he played and you worked."

"It was more than that. I couldn't have done any of it if he hadn't been with me. Scott made me feel … " she searched for the right words. Being Scott's wife made her feel special. If he loved her, she must have worth. Sheesh, it sounded so Abigail. But since Bimbo's appearance in their lives, she'd lost even that measure of confidence.

She shouldn't be talking like this to a teenager. Heather might seem mature and, well, like a friend, but this kind of sharing with a sixteen-year-old was inappropriate. Nora wiped her eyes. "Enough of this. Tell me something about you."

Heather shrugged. "What do you want to know?"

"Why don't you tell me about what interests you?"

"Hopi."

"Okay. Tell me about Hopi."

Heather eyed her and began slowly, as if testing her. "On either end of Earth's axis, twin brothers sit and hold down the head of the serpent. They are the balance of the world. If they let go, Earth will tilt and there will be chaos. Hopi are responsible for keeping the brothers there."

Nora nodded.

"Every Hopi belongs to a clan, sort of like families, and each clan performs ceremonies that together maintain balance of the natural forces. See, each of us has a good side and a bad side. Like an elder told me, 'black and white threads wind together in our ceremonies.' So we have to balance our two selves to protect the world."

"Hopi are in charge of the whole world?"

Heather's shiny black hair bounced to her nod. "We're the smallest tribe, but we have the biggest job."

"Balance in life is important," Nora said, wondering what it would feel like to be balanced. "Really, the *whole* world?"

"We do the ceremonies and that's what keeps the balance."

Why not? "So tell me about kachinas."

"Kachinas are spirits. They aren't saints like Christians have or like the Greek gods. It's kind of weird. They can help people or cause problems or just sort of be there."

Nora thought of the doll the old man had given her. What spirit did he contain?

Heather held Nora's eye. "Thanks for not laughing at this. Poppy won't listen. But your mom, she's great."

"You're talking about Abigail? You told her this?"

"Yeah. She's really interested in it. I just picked up a bunch of library books to take to her."

Could it be her mother's mind had expanded a notch or two since Nora was young?

Heather stiffened and her eyes hardened to flint at something behind Nora. "Douche bag."

An oily voice floated over her shoulder. "If it isn't Ms. Abbott. Taking a break from destroying Mother Earth?"

Big Elk.

Nora ought to climb into her Jeep and just drive away, but her dander was running high. She rose to her feet and took a step toward

Big Elk and his usual entourage of Guilty White People. "Face it: you lost, I won. Go pick another fight somewhere else."

"The courts granted you permission to gut the Mother. But they aren't the ultimate law." The followers murmured assent. He raised his voice in excitement. "The kachinas promised fire on the mountain if you continue your destructive path."

Heather shifted her hips and crossed her arms. "Knock it off, Big Elk."

Venom filled his eyes as they moved to Heather.

Nora jumped in to distract him from the girl. "Go ahead and send someone else to kill me. But snow making will happen. Kachina Ski has a partner now, McCreary Energy."

Dismay washed across Big Elk's band, but his arrogance never wavered. "I haven't sent anyone to kill you, Ms. Abbott."

"Don't bother lying to me."

"Lying is the way of the white man. Native Americans don't hide behind falsehoods."

Rage erupted in a fiery furnace. "Is that so? You haven't been behind all the vandalism and protests? You didn't send that Alex guy to murder me?"

Heather blew a disbelieving breath from behind her. "He wasn't going to kill you."

Big Elk remained irritatingly calm. "You're the one spreading untruths, Ms. Abbott. Alex, our brother of the Hopi, went out to the sacred mountain to pray and offer gifts to the kachinas. When you attacked him, he had no choice but to defend himself."

"Defend himself with his hands around my neck!"

"The Hopi value peace and he wouldn't react unless threatened."

Unchecked words shot from her. "You and your bullshit! What do you know about any of this anyway? You're not even Native American."

"My ancestors…"

"Your ancestors were probably European farmers. You aren't any more Native American than I am. Where are your records, huh? You're not Sioux."

He may or may not be indigenous, but Big Elk's face turned a violent red. "My people were with Dull Knife at Fort Robinson. I…"

She stepped forward and pointed. "Yeah? No one up there knows you or your family. You're a fake."

She'd gone too far.

She thought she felt hatred from him before, but that was mild displeasure compared to the noxious wave that came at her now. He looked at her with Charles Manson eyes. "You'll regret uttering those words. The kachinas protect their own."

He turned slowly, his murderous eyes lingering on her.

FIFTEEN

BROODING AGAIN. BARRETT LEANED back in his custom-made leather desk chair and gazed at Kachina Mountain.

McCreary Energy was one very profitable privately owned company. Thanks to Barrett the Third. But he wouldn't have had the opportunity if his grandfather hadn't planted the family in Northern Arizona and if Barrett's father hadn't seen the benefits of mining.

It's what McCreary's do. Grandfather started it. Father almost lost it but if he hadn't died young, he probably would have turned it around. I staunched the hemorrhage and turned it into a powerhouse. But I have to strengthen the family chain even more. Heather needs a company with wealth and a diversified position. McCreary Energy has to move into the future.

Uranium.

Northern Arizona is the Saudi Arabia of uranium and that's Heather's future and my legacy. If I let this opportunity slide by, McCreary Energy will become a third-rate has-been and Heather will have nothing.

A lesser man might fold under the forces against him: Enviros hated the idea of mining close to the Grand Canyon. Those radical long-hairs wouldn't go away quietly. Native Americans feared uranium mining on their lands, and he didn't blame them; they'd suffered from the industry's earlier ignorance. But none suffered more than Barrett.

He grabbed the Rolaids from his desk drawer. Beneath the bottle, Ester and their children smiled at him from the Kodachrome memory. He slammed the drawer closed.

No, mining techniques had improved. That disaster would never happen again. He had to move forward. He owed it to Heather. *Forget the past, old man. Look ahead.*

Like a cool breeze on the desert, the image of Abigail wafted before his eyes. She had class and intelligence and a fine ass for a middle-aged gal. Maybe when this was all over they could get together.

Romance could wait. Right now, Abigail was good cover so he could keep an eye on Kachina Ski.

He'd like to get rid of Nora. Her balkiness over snow making irritated him. But it would look suspicious if Nora disappeared and for now, he had her under control. Her life expectancy would change, though, if she ever found out Scott was working for him.

Barrett sank back in his chair. Abigail was a fount of disturbing information at their lunch. For instance, Barrett learned about Scott's affair. Who knows what he told his floozy on the side. Another loose thread to take care of.

Dust on the road signaled an approaching car. He glanced at the clock. Right on time. That alone proved Big Elk was no real Indian, just a damned mercenary.

Big Elk's black Escalade, now dusted with dirt, braked in front of Barrett's house. He turned off the ignition and sat behind the wheel talking on the phone.

The irksome imposter drove the same vehicle as Barrett. Before he rose to answer the doorbell, Barrett sent a quick e-mail to his assistant at the office in Phoenix telling him to trade the Escalade for one of those Mercedes SUVs.

"Nice place," Big Elk said when Barrett opened the door.

Barrett led him to the great room. "It's home. Drink?"

"Whiskey, straight up."

Barrett poured two fingers and handed it to him.

Big Elk settled himself on the leather sofa. "What's on your mind?"

Barrett wanted business with this varmint concluded quickly. He stood by the window. "Stop influencing the Hopi council against uranium mining."

Big Elk sighed. "The Hopi are a simple people. I'm merely a voice for them to the outside world."

Barrett figured he knew more about the Hopi and cared more for them than Big Elk ever would. He knew what served their best interest. "Convince them of the benefits of mining."

"I see no benefit to raping and mauling their pristine lands to satisfy your avaricious desire."

It was a good thing for Big Elk that Barrett's gun rested in his desk drawer across the room. Too bad for Barrett the Rolaids sat in the same place. "The benefits of mining royalties to the Hopi are something I'm sure you can imagine. What's more important for *this* discussion is the benefit to Big Elk."

Big Elk sat back with satisfaction. "Go on."

"What's your price?"

Big Elk feigned shock, coming closer than he knew to a fist in his face. "This is about an ancient people's land and their right to sovereignty."

Barrett waited.

"I can't say you're much fun to do business with."

"I don't like you."

Big Elk's eyebrows shot up. "Ouch."

Again Barrett waited.

Big Elk stood. He reached in his back pocket for his wallet. "Two million. Deposited equally to these accounts." He pulled out a handwritten note.

Barrett didn't move. "One."

"With uranium selling at an all-time high and you panting after one of the world's largest deposits, you won't miss two million, my friend."

"I'm not your friend." Barrett let the clock tick. "One point five."

Big Elk took a moment, as if weighing the decision. "And a warehouse in Flagstaff."

"A warehouse? I won't be involved in drugs."

Big Elk laughed. "Nor would I. I'll spare you the details but saving Mother Earth isn't the only game in town for this Indian."

Barrett snatched the paper containing the bank accounts from Big Elk's hand.

Big Elk smiled. "I'll let myself out."

"One other thing," Barrett said. "Keep Alex Seweingyawma away from my daughter."

An oily smile slid onto Big Elk's face. "I can't control the boy."

"If I find out he's been anywhere near Heather, the deal is off and you're going to jail."

Big Elk shrugged. "I'll do what I can to protect your innocent daughter. But understand this, Barrett: I have as much on you as you have on me."

Barrett glared at Big Elk until the small man snorted with arrogance and sauntered toward the hall. Barrett craved a disinfectant shower. It sickened him the way Big Elk had no principles, no loyalties. He might do some shady things himself, but at least everything he did was for family.

Big Elk tossed off words over his shoulder. "You don't have any attachment to Nora Abbott, do you?"

Barrett waited in silence while Big Elk faced him.

"I've heard she's accident prone," Big Elk said.

An accident, such as a fall from a cliff? Maybe a malfunctioning Jeep engine? The lodge apartment ran on propane and those pesky fuel bottles could blow under heat or pressure. It would be nice to have the Nora Abbott problem eliminated . . .

Barrett bent to pick up the empty whiskey glass so Big Elk wouldn't see his smile. Good. Just let Big Elk take care of her.

The front door opened and closed as Big Elk left.

Barrett headed to the kitchen and realized he hadn't heard Big Elk drive off. One glance out the window made his veins fill with ice.

Heather stood next to Big Elk's Escalade. Damn it. She said she'd be gone all day riding her horse and here she stood, talking to Big Elk. Heather seemed to have a talent for finding trouble these days. Maybe Barrett should install a tracking chip under her skin.

Heather's eyebrows drew together the way they did when she made a serious point.

Barrett stomped onto the front porch. "Heather."

She jumped and turned toward the house, not finishing her sentence.

"Come inside now." Barrett glared at Big Elk while Heather stomped up the stairs and into the house.

If Big Elk didn't stay away from Heather, he might make Barrett truly angry.

SIXTEEN

WATCHING THE TRUCK LOADED with pipeline inching up the slope should fill Nora with triumph. Three months ago, she feared she'd end up selling the ski lift on eBay and peddling used rental skis on the street corner.

Back then, Scott was still alive and planning to leave her. The 9th District court was weighing its decision on snow making. Abigail was shopping in New York and though Nora fretted about losing Kachina Ski, she hadn't yet learned real fear.

A ski area in Arizona sounded crazy. But Kachina Ski opened in 1935 and was one of the oldest ski slopes in the country. Sure, the drive to a desert took only an hour, but this mountain rose to nearly 13,000 feet. The runs didn't rival Colorado or Utah resorts, but Kachina Ski held its own and even managed to be profitable. That is, until Nora took over, which happened to coincide with a five-year-long—and counting—drought.

But this pipeline proved she could conquer the drought, and with Barrett's help, she'd have Abigail shopping for shoes in another time zone in no time. By Christmastime this mountain would be covered in snow, whether Mother Nature felt up to the task or not.

Why did it make her stomach ache to think of it?

The sun glared overhead, heating the pines and releasing their pungent perfume over a mountainside covered in June's wildflowers. Enormous black ravens cawed and glided from treetops and over the wide swathe of grass-covered ski run. The day sparkled brilliantly on her mountain, but it might as well have been sleeting.

Nora plodded up the slope, following the truck with its load of pipe rolled like giant spools of fire hose. Its tires tore the ground like the Jolly Green Giant's golf divots.

A quiet voice filtered through the truck's struggle. "Miss."

The slip of a man, the kachina salesmen from the courthouse, stood behind her. His approached must have been masked by the roar of the truck. He stood without moving, his black eyes focused on her face.

If he breathed, Nora couldn't see the movement. Though nothing about him was threatening, Nora's pulse quickened. Maybe he'd brought Alex with him. "You. What do you want?"

His eyes shifted slowly to the truck, which stopped at a level place to unload the hose. The sorrow on his face was clear and heart wrenching.

The rolls of hose stacked on the flatbed would be unrolled and laid on the ground alongside the run. The pump would shoot water and air through the hose to the sprayers. Snow, directly from the abundant aquifer. God, it was good to be an American.

It should have been a triumphant day on her mountain—well, her sliver of it, anyway. *I will not feel guilty, damn it.* This guy needed to go away.

He brought his gaze back to her. "Will you...?" He spoke in clipped words, as if English wasn't natural for him. He pointed to the hose.

He didn't look like the placard-bearing, rally-calling, hysterical religious fanatics that fought her for years. That didn't mean he wouldn't turn on her any minute. "It's for snow making, yes."

He nodded so slowly he barely moved. Those eyes carried deep sadness.

Nope. I am not feeling bad for bringing water to the mountain. Nora turned away from him and hiked to the truck. Maybe if she ignored him, he'd disappear like he did at the courthouse. She waved to the driver when he climbed from the cab. "We want to stack the rolls right here."

He pulled a clipboard from the cab. "I gotta do the paperwork."

Nora walked next to the rumbling truck, ignoring the diesel fumes. She put a hand on the sun-heated hose, the veins that would pump the blood to keep Kachina Ski alive.

"Miss."

Nora jumped. That gentle voice raised the hairs on her neck. She hated it, but it almost felt like he belonged here more than she did.

He pulled a ratty bag from his back. "I brought you my kachinas."

The crude doll with the blue mask broken and floating in the gutter flashed in her mind. "No thanks. I lost the last one."

While his hand rummaged in the bag, he stared into her face.

The two top rolls shifted. Nora skittered away from the truck.

They settled. The driver must be ready to unload. "Excuse me," Nora said to the little man. She strode away to talk to the driver.

Holding his bag in front of him, the man stared up at the hose.

Something moved on top of the truck.

The top two rolls of hose shifted again and the straps holding the stack upright slipped to the ground. Lightning flashed inside Nora as she realized the hose was no longer strapped to the truck. If the little man didn't move now, the hose could fall and flatten him.

The unstable roll slipped from the top.

Why didn't the little man react?

The whole pile started to topple. Still the Native American man stood motionless.

The top of the load rolled, followed by the others. Nora's body took over, legs pumping up the slope, perhaps her voice shouting, hands in front of her.

The man stayed rooted to the mountain.

Nora smashed into him like a defensive tackle, pushing both of them out of the way of the crashing hose. She landed on top of his small frame. The ground vibrated with the impact of the nearby falling freight.

Still pulsing with adrenaline, Nora dug her feet into the dirt and tried to scoot them farther away.

Too late. A heavy weight crushed her ankle, sending hot waves of pain shooting up her leg and spine. Several more hits felt like someone with a sledgehammer pounding her shin.

And then silence. Not even a raven cawed.

Nora opened her eyes and pulled her face from the ground. She still lay on top of the little man and tried to move but the hose pinned her calves. She managed to shift enough for him to wiggle out. Throbbing pain made everything below her waist ignite in flames.

Behind her, the truck bed sat empty except for two rolls of hose. The remainder of the load spread across the slope, with one roll on her legs.

"Nora!" Cole appeared next to her head. He reached for her hand, his eyes searching her face. "Are you okay?"

Her throat tightened and she fought panic. He always showed up just as something awful happened, and that couldn't be a coincidence. Somehow Cole caused this accident in an effort to shut her up about the bribery. She struggled with the desire to get away from him.

Cole shouted at the driver. "Help me get this off her!"

The overweight driver scurried around Nora's head and grunted. The weight on her legs lightened and Nora held her breath against the throbbing. It hurt like hell but she could move her legs. Celebrate life's little victories.

Cole knelt beside her. "Can you stand up?"

She struggled for strength but her voice sounded weak. "What are you doing here?"

"What are you thinking jumping under the hose?"

"That man ... " *Yee-ow!* No way could Nora stand. "Ankle," she said between clenched teeth.

Cole bent over to examine the foot she raised. His lean fingers tested the purpling flesh.

The raw agony nearly made Nora pee. "Stop!"

"Sorry."

She gently rotated the ankle in question slowly, the pain galloping all the way up her leg.

"It's sprained. I can wrap it," Cole said.

"Just leave me alone!"

"Hey, buddy." The driver stood next to the hose. "What do you want me to do?"

Cole shrugged. "Finish unloading the truck and stack it."

The driver shot Nora an annoyed look. "I was told there would be help."

Maybe the kachina man could use a few bucks. "What about that guy?"

Both men gave her a puzzled look.

She scanned the slope, suddenly worried he'd been injured. "Where did he go?"

Cole followed her gaze. "Who?"

"That Native American guy I was talking to."

"Before the hose fell? I didn't see anyone," Cole said.

Nora looked at the driver. "You saw him. I tried to shove him out of the way of the falling hose."

The driver shrugged. "I was doing the paperwork."

The aching in her ankle overrode everything else. "Load it, leave it. I don't care."

No doubt drawn by the roar of tumbling hoses, Abigail appeared out of nowhere, just as she used to whenever Nora was in some kind of mischief. "What is going on? Oh! My baby!"

Cole put Nora's arm around his shoulder. "Stack it. You've got a dolly on your truck."

Nora shrugged, trying to back away from Cole. But she couldn't stand on her own.

"I gotta get back on the road, man," the driver said.

The little guy had been right here. Where could he have gone? Was he working for Cole and Barrett too?

The expression Abigail turned on the trucker would make a werewolf whimper. "If you looked before you unstrapped the load, you would have seen my daughter and not released the strap. I'm sure your supervisor won't like that report."

The driver jutted his head. "Hey lady, I didn't unstrap the hose. I was in the cab."

Abigail pulled a cell phone from her pocket and looked at the phone number of the company advertised on the side of the truck. "And why do you suppose the hose suddenly let loose?"

Pain was making Nora sweat now. The sun beat on her head as well, giving her maybe two minutes before her hair burst into flames. "It doesn't matter whose fault it is. Let's just move."

Controlled anger tightened Abigail's voice. "You might have been killed." She glared at the driver. "Your negligence caused bodily harm, so be helpful or you could be in worse trouble."

Nora felt sorry for the driver. He probably had nothing to do with the accident. Cole, the man who held her upright, was Nora's main suspect.

The driver puffed up his shoulders. "I ain't in any trouble, lady. I checked out at the yard. You don't have nothin' on me."

Nora's head and ankle throbbed in rhythm. She wanted off the slope. "Buddy, *lawsuit* is her middle name."

The driver's shoulders dropped slightly. "Whatever."

Cole helped Nora take a step and spoke to the driver over his shoulder. "I'll come back and help."

In the presence of witnesses, Cole might as well help her to the lodge. He couldn't do anything to her now, could he?

The slope opened wide before them with the lodge looking like it sat in another country. Each step they took wiggled her injured ankle and sent waves of hot lava shooting through her. *Another day in paradise.*

They hadn't gone far when the driver called out, his tone smug. "Hey, lady. Take a look at this."

The driver held one piece of strap and tugged the end from under a roll of hose. He held up both pieces.

Abigail marched to him and snatched one away. After inspecting, she dropped it and stomped toward Nora and Cole.

"I need to call the police." She marched closer. "This will convince Officer Gary that your life is in danger and you didn't kill Scott for the life insurance."

Ankle, head, now her nerves were on fire. "What do you mean convince him I didn't kill Scott?"

Abigail waved her hand at the annoyance of it all. "Gary called on your cell and I answered. He wanted to know about Scott's life insurance so I found it. Your files are a mess."

What about Barrett's expensive lawyer? Nora was pretty sure he wouldn't want Abigail handing over anything to the cops. Nora gritted her teeth at the pain in her ankle. "I don't know who killed Scott, but I've got a good idea who's behind this accident." She glared at Cole.

The man acted as if he didn't know what she meant. "Use that cell phone in your pocket," he said to Abigail.

"Battery's dead. It's this high altitude. Nothing holds a charge for long."

Cole laughed. "Good thing Mr. Truck Driver didn't know that."

Nora planted her good foot. "What is going on?"

Abigail squinted in rage. "Someone sliced the straps."

"Cole sliced the straps, Mother."

He froze under the arm that was held over his shoulders for support.

Abigail laughed. "Don't be ridiculous." She marched ahead then turned around. "Let's go. Nora can't stand out here in the sunshine on that bad ankle."

SEVENTEEN

HOURS LATER NORA LEANED her head against the warm siding of the lodge and closed her eyes to the sun. Resting on an old lawn chair Abigail had scrounged up, her examined and bandaged leg elevated on a stool, she reached down and patted Abbey's head.

The peaceful setting warred with her emotions. Being relegated to sitting on the deck felt as bad as imprisonment. She needed action to calm the growing panic.

"There you are." Abigail came from the lodge.

"Right where you left me."

"What a beautiful day. I've made mint iced tea and we can sit here all afternoon and talk."

Was it possible the falling hose actually killed Nora? Because she had to be in hell. She closed her eyes again. "When are you going to find a new home?"

Glasses clinked on the bench next to Nora. "I couldn't think of leaving you now."

"Abbey and I can get along fine on our own."

"Don't be silly. Your dog can't fix you tea and provide conversation."

"No. But I like him better." Why did she say things like that? Abigail didn't cause these problems. Her mother needed help and a place to stay, not hurtful comments just because things were going badly for Nora.

Charlie's voice boomed from the base of the deck stairs. "Greetings mountain nymphs."

Abigail froze momentarily. She then sprang to her feet and leapt to the apartment stairs.

Pretty spry for her age, Nora thought.

But she was too late. Charlie bounded onto the deck in his own spry move, not like a graying, hippie alcoholic, but more like a teenager in love. Abigail was caught.

Despite Nora's earlier resolve to be a kinder, gentler daughter, she cracked up.

"Look who I found on the trail," Charlie said.

Cole appeared behind Charlie. His sandy-colored hair fell across his forehead. "How are you feeling?"

Cole pretended to be charming and Abigail obviously bought into it. He'd acted all shocked and hurt when Nora accused him of slicing the straps, but maybe he was an excellent performer. She should go to Officer Gary with her suspicions, and tell him—what? That she overheard a conversation between Cole and Barrett about illegal things? That would hardly prove Cole tried to smash her, and it would only make her sound like a hysterical peabrain.

But he was always around to "save" her.

Exactly. Why was he always around when things went south?

Gee, Nora, maybe because everything *is going bad lately?* If he was going to be around at all, he'd be witness to bad things.

"How thoughtful of you, Cole," Abigail said.

123

Nora waved a hand at her foot propped on the chair. "I hate to disappoint you, but the falling hose only gave me a sore ankle. Not even sprained."

"Nora!" Abigail acted predictably aghast.

"Come on, Mother. Why was he here when the hose fell?"

Cole looked embarrassed. "I wasn't stalking you. I was at Scott's murder site looking for some clue to who killed him."

Charlie nodded. "That's right. We've been over that place again and again. Cole says you don't know who Scott worked for. D'you 'spose he left some papers or something around so we can figure out who offed him?"

Charlie and Cole were working together? Charlie always protected Nora. Abigail trusted Cole. Cole gave off honest and kind vibes. Trust him or not?

"If you believe the cops, I did it," Nora said.

Cole sighed. "I don't believe the cops and that means you're in danger until we figure out who did it and why. Case in point," he said, gesturing to her raised foot.

"And you care, why?"

"Of course he cares," Abigail said.

Abigail was in full match-making mode.

Cole stared at her ankle. "Someone has to take care of you. You won't do it for yourself."

Nora closed her eyes and leaned her head against the lodge. "Are you taking care of me or planning to kill me?"

Charlie and Abigail both laughed.

No one took her seriously.

"You could talk to the police," Abigail said to Cole. "That Gary man said they'd look into it, but he's incompetent at best. And I'm sure he's out to get Nora."

Nora aimed daggers at Abigail with her eyes. Now Cole knew the cops had no leads. "Charlie, didn't you tell me columbine's blooming behind the lodge? I'm sure Abigail would love to see that."

Charlie had Abigail's hand tucked into his arm before she could break and run. "It is beauty to rival mortals, though it doesn't come close to your heavenly dazzle."

Abigail's eyes pleaded with Nora for rescue as Charlie led her away, extolling her beauty with each step.

Nora smirked at the iced tea Abigail had brought out and then up at Cole. "My mother just made tea. Please have some."

He sat next to her on the bench and took a glass.

Nora watched him raise it to his lips, weighing whether setting him up like this was cruel and unusual punishment for him nearly killing her.

He took several gulps, his Adam's apple bobbing. When he lowered the glass his eyes grew wide, his mouth contorted. "Your mother made this?"

Nora gave him her sweetest smile and nodded.

"And you think *I'm* trying to kill *you*?" He picked up her glass and hot-footed it to the railing, dumping both glasses over. "You don't need to thank me."

Nora fought giggles.

Cole set the empty glasses next to Nora, then sat down and leaned forward, eyes intense. "Who do you think cut the straps?"

"You."

His eyes crinkled with laughter. "Seriously."

"I am serious."

He stood up and paced the deck, long legs striding. He stopped in front of her. "I'm trying to keep you alive, but you're not help-ing. Get out of this deal with Barrett. Quit snow making. You know it's not good for the mountain, and hooking up with Barrett might get you killed."

These words echoed her own doubts, which only made Nora angrier. "You're in Barrett's back pocket! Suddenly you're all environmental and down on McCreary?"

"You don't know what's going on."

"Enlighten me."

He stared at her, an obvious battle waging in his mind. Finally he puffed out air. "Please. Just trust me. In the meantime, you and Abigail should move to town."

"We're not going anywhere. All your scare tactics won't work to stop snow making." *Forget about stopping it—with Barrett at the controls, I can't even slow it down.*

"I don't care about the snow making. I mean, I don't think it's a good idea, but that's not the point. Barrett is dangerous."

She batted her eyes at him. "I get it. You don't want Barrett to be my partner because you're concerned for my *safety*."

"Yes."

And he looked earnest. How could he confuse her so much?

The putter of a car floated to the deck.

A soft tinkle of Abigail's laugh preceded her arrival from the back of the deck. When she caught sight of Nora, she sobered. "I don't appreciate you sending me off with that Gonzo."

Charlie appeared with the satisfied grin of someone awarded a blue ribbon. He winked at Nora.

Abigail hurried to the rail. "I wonder who this could be?"

If the current trend held, it wouldn't be good news.

Abbey let out a mild woof as they all stared down the stairs and waited.

In a moment a young, heavy-set woman with too much eye makeup trudge up the stairs. She sidestepped a curious Abbey. "Are you Nora Abbott?" She carried a cardboard box that looked heavy.

Nora nodded.

The girl plopped the box on the bench, knocking over one of the iced tea glasses. "Sorry." She didn't look sorry. Despite the heavy black outlining her eyes, they were red and puffy and her whole face looked swollen. Her thick lips turned down at the edges.

Abigail hurried over and picked up the glass. "We haven't met. I'm Nora's mother, Mrs. Stoddard." She held out her hand as if meeting a dowager at a garden party. "This is Cole Huntsman." The warmth in her voice plummeted to subfreezing. "And this is Charlie."

The girl looked confused. "I'm Teresa. Maureen's roommate."

A garrote sliced through Nora's neck.

Abigail smiled warmly. "Maureen? I'm sorry, I don't … "

Nora held up her hand and interrupted. "Never mind, Mother." She looked at Teresa and made her voice as unwelcoming as possible. "What do you and *Maureen* want?"

A little hiccup of distress slipped from Abigail.

With surprising speed, Teresa's eyes filled with tears that then gushed down her face. "Maureen would want to be alive."

Silence. The confusing sentence started to make dreadful sense. Nora would rather sprint to the other side of the mountain on her painful ankle than ask. "What do you mean?"

Teresa wiped a pudgy arm under her nose. "She's dead. I don't know what to do with this stuff and since it belonged to your husband anyway, I thought you might want it, but if you don't I'll take it away." Teresa dissolved into great heaving sobs.

Always ready, Abigail pulled a tissue from her trouser pocket. Of course, it was unused. "You poor dear."

It seemed hard to recall that Abigail was Satan's handmaid. She didn't know Teresa or Maureen, had to be repulsed by Teresa's physical appearance, and yet here she was, all comfort and grace.

Unlike Nora, who hadn't the slightest idea how to react. What do you say when your husband's mistress (now that's an old-fashioned term) dies? Maureen wasn't high on her list of favorites, but she didn't wish her dead. "I'm sorry."

Charlie and Cole couldn't even drum up that much.

Teresa lifted her head from Abigail's shoulder. The black smear on Abigail's dry-clean-only shell proved that waterproof makeup wasn't perfect. "It's just not fair, you know? Not long ago she was so happy. She was planning on getting married ... "

To my husband. Nora's stomach lurched.

Another sob. "You can't imagine how hard it was for her when he died."

Can't I?

Abigail patted Teresa's back. "I'm sure it was awful."

Teresa nodded. "At least she's not in any more pain."

What a stupid thing to say. Nora would learn to live without Scott, and she was sure Maureen could have gotten over him too. But Maureen would never have the opportunity to love again. She wouldn't feel the sunshine on her face or eat a bite of dark chocolate or even be annoyed by a deranged mother.

Nora's throat closed and an artesian flow rushed through her head, forcing tears. "I'm sorry," she said again.

Cole sat next to Nora and put a hand on her back. Surprisingly, Nora didn't want to brush it off.

Teresa gave Nora an appraising look. "You don't seem like such a bad person. I mean, you don't know what goes on in someone else's life, but you don't seem as cold as he said."

Nora's stomach lurched again.

Cole stood up. "Do you need anything else?"

"Well, there's that box of stuff and ... I guess that's all."

Cole held Teresa's arm and walked her away.

Abigail took over from Cole and ushered Teresa down the stairs. "Thank you for bringing his things," Abigail said. "I'm sure you understand. Losing a husband is one of the most difficult situations to endure. I myself have buried two husbands ... " Their voices thankfully faded.

Nora struggled to remember something she'd thought earlier. Yes. Sunshine on her face, dark chocolate, annoying mothers. Small things. She lifted her face to the sun and reached down to pat Abbey's head.

Light footsteps tapped across the deck and stopped in front of her. "You need to develop dignity," Abigail said. "You can't fall apart at every revelation of Scott's secret life. You are above that tacky display. Now pull yourself together because Barrett is on his way up the trail."

"Barrett McCreary?" Nora leveled her head and looked at Abigail.

"How many Barretts do you know?" Like a general dismissing his troops, Abigail nodded at Charlie and Cole. "We have issues to discuss regarding Kachina Ski. Thank you for stopping by."

With her arms outstretched, she herded them toward the back of the lodge. She returned to stand in front of Nora. "You really ought to go inside and put on some makeup, but I suppose you'll do."

Nora took the offered tissue. Did Abigail have a never-ending supply in her pockets? And yet, her slacks had no telltale bulges. Too bad she didn't use her magic for good. "Thanks for the compliment."

Abigail patted her own hair and applied lipstick from some other hidden pocket. "He's important to us."

"Us?"

Abigail faced the stairs, flexing her shoulders like an athlete stretching for competition. "Don't forget it's his funding that's keeping this place alive."

Right. Nora studied her leg propped up on the bench. Kachina Ski might survive, but would she and her mother?

Abbey's tail thumped the deck and Charlie trudged around the corner from the back. "Hidy ho, ladies."

Abigail rolled her eyes. "You couldn't just go?"

He sidled over and sat next to Nora in a puff of beer and forest scent. "I've got interests to protect." Nora welcomed Charlie's warm hand over hers.

Abigail just turned her back and flounced to the rail.

EIGHTEEN

BARRETT SLAMMED THE DOOR of the new Mercedes SUV. Damn Big Elk. Barrett had really liked the Escalade. Maybe it wasn't the new car that had him irritated so much as it was the meeting he'd just had with Heather's school counselor.

Heather clicked her door closed. "Grades are just white man's way to control and catalogue people."

"You have to at least pass to make it into community college."

She shrugged. "Even if I wanted to go to college—which I don't—all you'd have to do is fund a science building and I'm in."

His jaw clenched. The women he loved most in the world could always ignite his temper. But not Abigail. He may not feel the same passion for her as he did Ester, but passion was overrated. Just the thought of her feminine and pleasing ways soothed him. "Bring your grades up next year or we'll be looking at military schools."

Abigail waved from the deck. Her soft blond hair glimmered in the sun and her trim body was draped in well-fitted slacks. So unlike Ester, but he found her immensely appealing. He allowed the five-second fantasy full run. By the time he and Heather climbed the stairs, he'd had his imaginary climax and stubbed out his imaginary cigarette.

Abigail took Heather's hand. "How was the meeting with the counselor?" Abigail was a good influence on Heather and measured up as a suitable companion for him.

While Heather complained about the unfair American educational system, he turned his attention on Nora. She sat on a bench with her foot elevated. Ignoring Charlie next to her, he said, "Feeling any better?"

Abigail pulled herself away from Heather. "She's in some pain, of course. But she's managing with over-the-counter painkillers. She was lucky."

"The company agreed to give us the hose at half price." Barrett had argued a half hour to convince them the discount trumped a lawsuit for negligence. "Of course, it's not worth the pain you're going through."

She didn't seem as pleased as he expected. "It wasn't their fault. They should get the full cost."

"The hose didn't jump off the truck on its own. There has to be recourse for poor safety procedures," he said.

Abigail's pleasant smile slipped from her face. "No, Barrett. It wasn't an accident. Someone cut the straps."

Heather's small gasp said it all. Alex was at it again. Still, it wouldn't hurt Barrett's feelings if Alex eliminated Nora.

"Did you talk to the police?" Barrett asked.

Even Abigail's folded arms appeared feminine. "Of course. But that Gary is more interested in Scott's life insurance, which was paltry by the way, and some alleged threat Nora made to Scott's mistress at the funeral."

His deepest protection instinct kicked in, as well as his male pride. Abigail needed the shelter he could provide. "I'll hire a detective and get to the bottom of this."

Nora gave a weary sigh. "Great. What I'm really concerned about is the snow making. The pipe is fine. But the sprayers you ordered are all wrong. I stopped the order this morning."

Abigail drew in a breath. "Won't that slow the process?"

Nora nodded, keeping her focus on Barrett. "I doubt we'll get delivery until early spring."

Temper swirled below the surface of his control. "That's ridiculous. Do you realize how much that delay will cost us?"

Nora bristled. "I've been running this place for a few years; I think I know the costs. But the sprayers I ordered are more fuel efficient, less noisy, and generally more environmentally friendly."

"Don't give me the fuel efficiency line. And the noise issue is moot since they run at night when no one is here. You're afraid to move forward." It was hard to stay calm when he'd rather smack her.

"Nora, we do not cave to eco-terrorists," Abigail said.

At least Abigail stood on his side. "You've had threats for years."

Nora struggled to her feet. "I won't deny I'm scared and worried about protecting Abigail. But this mountain needs care too. I'll do what's right for it."

Charlie raised his fist. "Right on."

"For just once listen to someone else, Poppy," Heather said.

Barrett sent Heather a scathing glare. "You're in enough trouble right now." He looked at Nora and tried to sound soothing. "You're obviously distraught. Let's give this a day or so and we'll discuss it again. If you still want to delay snow making by changing the equipment, of course I'll abide by your decision."

Big Elk's little buddy better hurry up or I might have to take care of Nora myself. Barrett noticed Charlie narrow his eyes and stare at him. *What a waste of skin that guy is.*

Abigail brushed her hands together at the job well done. "Letting it sit for a while sounds reasonable. I've got a pitcher of iced tea. Let's enjoy the beautiful sunshine."

To make Nora feel less attacked, Barrett backed off a few steps. He glanced down into a large cardboard box. He had a meeting with Big Elk tomorrow and would encourage the Alex situation—

His mind registered what his eyes had been reading for the last seconds. Logging records. Water composition. Well numbers. Signed by Scott Fucking Abbott.

Proof. Goddamned evidence that Scott worked for Barrett and of exactly what he discovered. Barrett struggled to hide all emotion. He had to get that box, destroy it. Right now.

"Iced tea sounds nice, but Heather has already missed several hours of work. She needs to earn her keep." He gestured toward the box, concentrating on not letting his hand shake. "This looks like a box of old records that needs burning."

Nora collapsed to the bench, all fight sucked out of her. "Yes. Burning."

He reached down and picked up the box. *Slowly, no rush. Don't act desperate.* "I'll help Heather take it around back."

Nora looked like a whipped dog. "Good idea."

Abigail nodded approval.

Barrett hefted the box. "Let's go, Heather."

"Wait." Nora looked up.

No! Burn it now. Do it.

Nora stood and hobbled across the deck. "Leave the box."

Abigail rushed to throw Nora's arm over her shoulder for support. "You need to let it go."

Nora's face was little more than enormous, tortured eyes. "Leave it."

Barrett inhaled slowly. "Of course. Where would you like me to put it?" Goddamn it!

Abigail frowned, arguing wordlessly with Nora. Just as mute, Nora held firm.

Barrett wanted to close his hands around Nora's scrawny neck and wring the life from her.

Abigail finally relented and sighed. "Let's put it upstairs for now, shall we? In the back of a closet perhaps."

Way to the back, where Nora wouldn't want to retrieve it and where he could snatch it before she ever got the courage to look at the incriminating reports.

NINETEEN

NORA ROLLED OVER FOR the billionth time, her wrapped ankle wadding up the sheet. Across the hall, Abigail slept like a baby. Except babies don't snore like lumberjacks. Maybe she exaggerated. Abigail's snoring sounded more like a soft purr.

Nora couldn't sleep anyway. Like worms chewing into her guts, apprehension gnawed at her. She felt a growing resistance to making snow and the only reason she could name was that it felt wrong. Which was pretty much what Scott had been telling her before he died.

Of course having Barrett on her side was a good thing. He knew how to make money. She should be grateful for his help. But he wasn't helping; he was running things. And the closer they got to pumping water onto the mountain, the more uneasy Nora felt. At least she got the right sprayers. One small victory.

Abbey woofed on the deck below the apartment. His claws scratched the wood as he scrambled to his feet.

Nora tossed off the covers and stumbled to her bedroom window. Her ankle still throbbed but felt stronger all the time. She slid the window open farther and leaned out to see Abbey. He barked again, focused on the woods.

Resting her hands on the ledge, she stared into the dark forest. It was as if electricity didn't exist and the stars jumped from the sky like footlights on a stage.

How many summer nights had she and Scott cuddled in a sleeping bag on the slope and stared at those amazing stars? They'd talked and laughed and made love, caught up in the magic and the newness of owning Kachina Ski and living in such a beautiful place.

Just as the chasm in her heart started to crack and bleed, she hardened it. How often had he done the same thing with Maureen? The stars were just cosmic facts, not divine sparks, and Scott proved to be nothing more than a common cheater. Nora lowered her eyes to the forest and that's when she saw the distinct flicker of fire.

Abbey barked for real now. He ran down the stairs, high-tailing it for the forest.

Nora's skin froze. Maybe the pinpoint of light deep in the trees was Alex's dying fire and right now he snuck through the forest, planning to slit their throats.

"Abbey!" Like the well-trained and obedient dog he was, Abbey kept on barking and running across the slope.

Abigail snored on. Should she wake her and head for town? But they would have to get to the parking lot—Alex could jump them on the way. Should she call the cops? And tell them what? That someone was camping in the woods, on public lands, for which they have every legal right.

She strained to see the flame but lost sight of its glow. In the old days—just two weeks ago—when she'd taken the time to look at the mountain, the sky, or the forest, she saw nature's beauty. Now it seemed she was constantly squinting into the shadows looking for danger.

Abbey stopped at the edge of the trees and kept barking.

The campfire either flickered its way out or was deliberately doused. The only lights now came from the stars and they refused to help Nora.

Without warning a fireball ignited at the edge of the slope.

Nora gasped. The flames leapt higher than a man. But there was nothing except green grass where it burned, no fuel to feed a fire. It looked like an independent monster, living on its own.

Abbey dove into the shadows. A moment later, his bark turned to a yelp of pain.

"Abbey!" Nora spun from the window, her heart pounding like an unbalanced washing machine. She pulled on her jeans and awkwardly shoved her feet into shoes, gasping at the discomfort in her ankle. She grabbed the flashlight by the door and took the stairs two at a time, keeping more of her weight on her good leg. She paused at the deck railing and stared into the trees. Abbey made no sound.

The fireball slipped up the slope for several yards and then turned into the forest. It moved with the jerky gait of a runner, but it was quicker than any sprinter Nora had ever seen.

Was it Alex? For all she knew, it could be Cole out there running up and down with some high-tech eco-terrorist lantern. Except it didn't look like a real person running. It moved too quickly, with random fits and starts. But where was Abbey?

Nora raced across the open ski run as best she could, dew quickly wetting her shoes. Despite the chilly mountain air, a film of sweat covered her body and her heart rampaged against her ribs. After several yards, she didn't even feel the pain in her ankle.

Nora searched the forest ahead but didn't see Abbey, a flare, a dying campfire, or anything except thick darkness. Picturing the fireball, she slowed her paced and tried to figure where it would have gone. She entered the trees, her breath sounding like a freight engine.

The moon gave scant light. She was no stranger to nighttime on the mountain, but this was no jaunty moonlit hike.

Nora gripped the flashlight, expecting Alex to jump from behind every tree, his knife poised for her throat.

"Abbey!" To her left the night lit up. Abbey barked. Fire. It blazed too far away to make out any details, but the ball of flame appeared to be about the size of a laundry basket and it hovered six feet off the ground. It was definitely not a campfire because it moved, winking in and out behind trees. The flame slipped through the forest about 50 yards uphill and Nora took off after it, following Abbey's excited bark.

Nora chased the fire through the pines, stumbling over fallen logs and piles of brush, wondering what the hell she'd do if she caught up to it, not even sure what "it" was. Did she expect to beat it to embers with her flashlight? Was it Alex with some Native American flame carrier?

She followed the light uphill until her thighs burned and ankle protested despite the adrenaline, then turned back toward the ski run and downhill, executing a circle. Abbey barked occasionally but now it sounded more like play. The closer she came to where she entered the forest, the more nervous Nora grew. Just before the flame stepped—if *stepped* was even the right word—out of the trees, the light disappeared.

Nora stopped and Abbey trotted out of the trees toward her, nose to the ground. He whined and sniffed at the edge of the clearing.

Nora knelt and ran her hands over Abbey. He licked her face once but had more interest in smelling the forest. He seemed just fine.

"*Pas pay um waaynuma.*" The quiet voice made Nora gasp and spin around.

The little kachina salesman stepped out from behind a tree, the top of his head nearly two feet lower than the fireball had been.

Nora tried to keep from bolting. "Who are you?"

"You must protect dis moun-ain."

Abbey shoved his muzzle in the man's hand. The little man greeted Abbey as if they were friends, speaking to him in a quiet, guttural speech.

Nora gripped the flashlight, doubting she'd need to defend herself physically from this gentle man. But he was just plain scary in the forest in the middle of the night. Strangely, she felt like she needed to justify herself. "I'm not out to ruin Kachina Peak."

He spoke in soft, halting accent. "You can do much good. Or you can do much harm. You choose."

The fear and anger that propelled her on this foolhardy journey clung to her. "What is that fire? Why are you here?"

"You love dis moun-ain. You mus' care for it." His words fell to the forest floor with no inflection.

She turned away from him and searched the trees for Alex.

"Bad men are here." A speck of sadness shone in his eyes in the moonlight. "Do not understand the Hopi way."

"If slicing me with knives, strangling me, and crashing freight on me is the Hopi way, I think they understand it just fine."

"Hopi is balance," he said.

The fireball was gone, she didn't see Alex anywhere, and cold seeped under her skin. She wanted to go home. "Are you here to tell me not to make snow?"

His eyes showed an intensity not evident in his voice. "You are protector of our moun-ain."

"I'm not Hopi."

He shrugged. "You love our sacred peak."

Was she really having a conversation with a shriveled Native American in the forest in the middle of the night?

"Watch for spirits of the moun-ain," he said. "Beware men speaking for Hopi. They do not speak our true way."

"You want me to watch for kachinas?"

If doing the kachinas' bidding made her end up living like this little guy did, she'd say no thanks. It was impossible to tell when he'd showered last, if ever. Come to think of it, he had no smell. Dust covered his black hair down to his thick moccasins. He looked like nothing more than skin and bones and bad teeth, a walking lifetime of malnutrition.

He inclined his head and words formed in slow succession. "Watch for giver of fire, spirit of death, owner of upper world. No hair, no eyelashes. Skin marked with scars of many burns."

"Sounds like an attractive guy."

The little man didn't acknowledge her sarcasm. "He should not be living on our moun-ain dis time of year. But there is loss of balance."

"Is he the one running around here with the fire?"

"Do not meet him face to face. No man can look upon his face."

With no eyebrows and scars, who would want to?

"Nora!" The sound of Cole's voice boomed in the still night. He jogged down the trail from deeper in the forest.

Nora sucked in a breath to quiet her startled heart. "What are you doing here?"

He stopped in front of her. "You shouldn't be out here alone."

"Why? Are you here to hurt me?"

Cole clenched his teeth. "I'm out here trying to keep you safe—apparently, from your own stupidity."

She needed to get out of here, back to the safety of home and to check on her mother. "I don't need your protection. I've got this guy here keeping watch over the forest."

"What guy?"

She knew before she turned that the little man had vanished. "Never mind. I may not understand what this fireball thing is or how you're doing it, but I want you to stop."

Cole pushed his hair off his forehead. He stared at her a few seconds and let out a breath. Good. He was going to confess. "I saw it too. What do you think it is? I followed it but couldn't catch up to it."

"Right."

His head shot up as if she'd slapped him. "I'm not your enemy, Nora. I've been camping out here for days keeping watch. You don't seem to understand the danger you're in."

Damn right. She needed more protection than a flashlight if she continued to stand in the forest with a virtual stranger who just admitted to spying on her.

"Big Elk is messing around up here on the mountain. I think it has something to do with the lava tubes," he said.

She stared at him.

"You know about them, right?"

"I know about the opening next to that old plane crash site. There are more?"

He nodded. "The tubes crisscross the mountain and have openings all over. It's like a tunnel system. My Hopi friend told me about them. I'm not sure what Big Elk is doing with them, though."

"What could he be doing with them?"

"Most people think there are one or two isolated tubes. Like you know about the one at the crash site. Benny told me it's more like a subway system with connecting routes. It's another secret of the tribes and they can use them to move around the mountain."

"If they're lava tubes, though, aren't they sharp and dangerous, like the lava fields?" She tried not to think about the razor edges of the lava rock where Scott fell.

"Actually, the stone is smooth in the tubes."

"So you think Big Elk has his Native American gang running through the tubes to jump out and scare people?"

"It's got to be something bigger than that."

She backed away and started for the lodge. "I'm calling the cops."

"Good. Tell them someone is using the springs for a camp. I think it might be Alex."

Her heart leapt to her throat. "What makes you think that?"

"I saw Heather leave some food and supplies there a couple of days ago."

Knife Guy had been in the woods for days, watching, waiting.

"Come on, Abbey." Nora backed away, ready to sprint for the lodge despite her now-throbbing ankle.

Cole's hand shot out and grabbed her arm. With Hulk-like strength, he jerked her back toward him.

Nora pulled away, but he didn't give.

A loud *shshshsh* hit her ears. She followed the sound to the lift house halfway down the mountain. Cole stared in the same direction.

She didn't have time to focus her eyes before the world erupted around her. Light exploded and her eardrums boxed with pressure. A blast of heat added confusion to the fire at the lift house. The jet engine roar of the explosion echoed across the mountain.

Nora fell fully against Cole or he might have pulled her to him. He shrouded her, blocking the heat of the explosion with the cocoon of his body. Yellow flames danced in the distance.

TWENTY

NORA STARED AT THE gnarled metal that used to be the lift house, now drenched in water from the firefighters' hose. The grass and top-soil around the lift base washed away, leaving a red and muddy sludge of rocks and cinder. The cables weighted down with bent and twisted chairs eventually rose to the next pole, heading up the mountain into the gray dawn. The lift house sat as a bent shell, blackened with soot.

Abigail shoved a steaming cup of coffee under Nora's nose. Nora couldn't think what to do with it.

Abigail picked up Nora's hand and wrapped it around the cup. "Drink this, dear. It will help."

Help what? It wouldn't rebuild the lift or save them from Big Elk and his gang. She longed to feel Scott's arms around her, let his warmth reassure her. The last bit of blood drained from her heart, knowing even if he were still alive, Scott probably wouldn't be here with her.

Abigail stepped back. She might have jumped to Tibet for all Nora knew or cared; she couldn't pull her eyes from the wreckage and her vision narrowed to block everything else.

The police had scrambled over the area, taking notes, asking her questions, and stringing yellow crime scene tape.

Cole had answered the police's questions but asked a lot more. He finally tromped into the forest, grumbling about incompetent police investigations. The cops left awhile ago. Now the mountain rested in early morning silence.

"Those sons of bitches." Nora suddenly shouted, feeling some life at the echo of her words on the mountain.

"Nora, language." Armageddon could strike and Abigail would demand good manners and linen napkins on her luncheon table.

Nora at last turned to look at Abigail and was shocked out of her stupor. Abigail stood next to Charlie, wrapped in his army jacket. It enveloped her so she looked like a camo version of SpongeBob SquarePants. Her hair and makeup, of course, were perfect.

Charlie appeared scruffier than usual, probably because he'd hurried over when he heard the explosion and hadn't had time to supply his jacket with beer. "This is not cool," he said.

"We can't stand around here all day staring at this mess." Abigail took her all-business tone. "I'll fix some breakfast while you shower and dress. You'll feel better."

"No, Mother. I don't think putting on a happy face is going to fix this."

"For heaven's sake, of course not. But action is better than moping around."

Charlie rubbed his hands together. "Breakfast with you two lovely ladies would be the highlight of my life."

Abigail huffed in disgust.

"You go ahead. I'll be right up," Nora said.

"You're just saying that to make me go away." Nothing escaped Abigail. She sighed in an injured way. "Stay out here staring at the ruin all day then. I am going to behave in a civilized fashion." She stomped toward the lodge.

Charlie put a hand on Nora's shoulder. "Do you want to be alone with your thoughts?"

The old rascal couldn't wait to go after Abigail. "Go get some breakfast."

"I could stay with you."

"Better take advantage of this opportunity. Breakfast is her best meal."

Charlie bowed as he backed away. "It's not just the food, you know. I'd eat sand if she prepared it for me."

"She's so mean to you. Why do you adore her?"

Charlie's eyes got a soft, faraway look. "You think she's all sharp angles and cold surfaces. But I see the light in her eyes that opens the way to a loving heart."

Nora blew air out her mouth. "Come on." She changed the subject to what really nagged. "Don't you think it's suspicious that Cole is always around when something bad happens?"

Charlie's eyes lost their floating quality and sharpened. "You noticed he's hanging around?"

"Here's the thing: You and Abigail act like he's this great Wyoming guy. But he works for Barrett. He's against snow making but for uranium mining. Sort of, I guess. And I swear I heard him and Barrett planning to bribe congressmen."

"Bribery, huh?"

"He's full of contradictions. I don't think we can trust him."

For a moment Charlie looked like a general planning strategy. Then he glanced at Nora and a lopsided grin crept onto his face. "You coming to breakfast, darlin'?"

Nora shook her head then watched his lurching gate as he hurried across the grass to the lodge. Even Charlie, her one constant, seemed off his norm.

The rumble of an engine brought Nora back to the mountain. Barrett's black Mercedes slid on the cinders. The slamming door rebounded around the empty forest. With powerful strides, Barrett hurried up the trail and across the slope.

Maybe he'd been her idol for years when she thought he was the compassionate entrepreneur; now she knew him for a controlling jerk.

"What the hell happened here?" Barrett bellowed.

"When the spaceship landed, it crushed the lift." *Ask a stupid question …*

He glared at her. "Is that supposed to be funny?"

Irritation blasted into her brain. "Someone blew up my lift to stop snow making. My mother and I could be the next target. That's not a real knee-slapper."

An angry storm clouded Barrett's face as he focused on the smoking debris. "This is the work of cowards. Surely you aren't in any physical danger."

"Thanks for the words of comfort."

Footsteps crunched in the cinders behind Nora. "Good morning, Barrett. Isn't this awful?" Abigail said.

Like an eraser on a schoolroom chalkboard, Barrett wiped anger from his face and replaced it with sorrow. "Despicable. I'm just glad you and Nora weren't injured."

Abigail pshted as if it were a silly idea. "Oh I'm sure we aren't in any danger. Cowards did this and they wouldn't dare mess with me and Nora physically."

Déjà vu or simply hell?

Charlie sauntered up behind Abigail and she looked surprised, as if he hadn't been at her side all morning. She shrugged out of his jacket and shoved it at him.

"How was breakfast?" Nora asked Charlie.

His adoring gaze never drifted from Abigail. "I made sure to turn the burner off after she rushed out."

"You need to abandon ship, Charlie. Throwing men overboard is what she does best."

Charlie's mischievous grin lit his faded eyes. "I'm tied to the mast, sweetie. Don't worry about me."

An Escalade, as ostentatious as Barrett's Mercedes, cruised into the parking lot, followed by a ratty pickup and a compact car.

If only the parking lot were this busy during ski season.

All the doors of the Escalade swung open and people spilled out. Big Elk climbed out of the passenger side and the whole troupe headed up the slope.

Dorothy Black, the incredibly young reporter from the *Daily Tribune* popped from the little car and quickly passed a few Guilty White People, catching up to Big Elk, notebook and pen leading the way.

Satisfaction and self-importance swarmed around Big Elk like flies on a corpse.

"Do you think he did it?" Abigail asked, not taking her eyes off the growing crowd.

"Of course he did it," Nora said. Or maybe it was Alex. Or whoever sent the death threats. Or maybe the little kachina salesman. Or whoever carried the fireball. Or maybe Cole. Who knows?

Abigail's eyes flashed with that mother bear intensity. She glared at Big Elk as he approached, but her words were for Nora. "Pull your shoulders back, lift your chin, and put a confident smile on your face. Why didn't you listen to me when I suggested you clean up for the day?"

Charlie stepped next to Abigail and faced Big Elk and his entourage.

Over the shoulders of the invading hordes, Nora caught sight of a police cruiser easing into the parking lot. They must be tired of traipsing out here for fires, riots, murders. It would be fine with Nora if police-worthy events stopped happening to her.

Big Elk gazed at Nora. "Are you okay?"

You'd think Mr. Soundbite would come up with something more original. Maybe, "Ha-ha" or "Take that."

Abigail raised a regal chin. "Turn right around and march down this mountain. You are not welcome here."

He ignored Abigail and addressed Nora. "I didn't mean for this to happen, but I warned you."

Barrett's low voice carried threat. "If you don't want a restraining order, I suggest you leave."

"And I suggest you keep on my good side, Mr. McCreary."

Barrett narrowed his eyes in a look that foretold epic destruction, torture, and mayhem.

Enough of this. Nora didn't need others to protect her. She eased in front of Charlie and Abigail and opened her mouth.

Dorothy Black, who had interviewed Nora on several occasions, slid from behind Big Elk and into Nora's personal space. Perhaps sensing she held center stage, Dorothy spoke with volume and drama. "Ms. Abbott, what is your response to this morning's *Tribune* article?"

As if Nora had time to peruse today's paper. It didn't matter what Dorothy asked, Nora had a few things to say that she'd kept bottled up for too long. "In Arizona and New Mexico, at least forty to fifty mountains are sacred to tribes. There are over forty thousand shrines, gathering areas, pilgrimage routes, and prehistoric sites in the Southwest, all of which someone claims are sacred. We want to spray water on one-fourth of one percent of this one mountain."

Dorothy brushed that aside. "In light of this destruction, can you respond to today's article in which Big Elk calls for the Hopi and other pueblo tribes to rise up in rebellion against you?"

"He called for what? Against me?"

Big Elk raised his voice. "I was speaking metaphorically."

Dorothy scribbled away, eyes jumping from her small notebook to Nora's face. "You're familiar with the Pueblo Indian Rebellion of the 1600s? He compared snow making to the missionaries quelling the culture and enslaving the Puebloans."

Charlie put his arm around Nora's shoulder and turned her away. "The press, man—use them, don't let them use you."

The reporter took another step toward her, speaking to her back. "The Hopi, known for being a peaceful tribe, actually rebelled against the Spanish priests and flung them off the mesas to their deaths. Big Elk said the Hopi should do something similar to stop snow making."

Big Elk sounded desperate. "I did not call for violence against Kachina Ski. I merely said we need to recapture that spirit."

"Bullshit!" Nora spun around and let her anger shout back at Big Elk.

Abigail spoke quickly, maybe to save Nora from poor press. "If you think your terrorist shenanigans will stop us, Mr. Big Elk, you have greatly underestimated our fortitude. We won't run away like frightened field mice."

Good one, Abigail. Your ability to throw an excellent cocktail party will surely protect us from murderers.

Gary and another uniformed officer finally arrived and pushed past the reporter. Gary's freckles nearly disappeared in his flushed cheeks. "All right, everyone calm down."

Charlie whispered to Nora, "You can't trust the Heat."

Nora's stomach tightened and sweat slimed her underarms. The last two times Gary showed up, he brought news of Scott's death and accused her of murder. Maybe now he'd haul her off to jail for blowing up her own lift.

The small knot of followers behind Big Elk started to chant. "Make love, not snow, make love, not snow!"

Gary spoke to Big Elk, his voice barely discernible above the activists. "What are you doing back here?"

With a glance at Dorothy, who moved closer and stood ready to scribble a quote, he said, "We came to assure Ms. Abbott that violence is not what we stand for. We want to demonstrate our solidarity to peaceful means, even as we vehemently disagree with Ms. Abbott's determination to disrupt Mother Earth's balance by making snow and sending us on the path to certain destruction."

Blah, blah, blah in capitals and quotation marks.

Gary's face remained expressionless, despite the red slashes high on his cheeks. "I see." He unhooked handcuffs from his belt. "You're under arrest for destruction of property."

Whoa! He wasn't going to haul Nora away? Maybe her luck was turning. Well, aside from the blown-up lift, the death threats, and financial puppetry.

Big Elk held his hand up. "I had nothing to do with this, even if I'm not sorry to see it."

Gary interrupted. "You've got your press coverage. Let's go."

"You have no proof." Spittle flew from Big Elk's lips as he shouted.

Gary shrugged. "Anonymous tip from a reliable source. I consider you a flight risk, so I'm not taking chances."

"What about my rights?"

"You'll get the spiel on the way to the car," Gary said.

"You're behind this." Big Elk's finger pointed at Nora. Death. Violent, painful, endless. That's what Big Elk's eyes told her plainly. Eyes able to command from prison. Her knees wobbled.

"You won't get away with this." Though he said it under his breath, the words shouted through her veins.

Gary pulled Big Elk's hands behind him and clamped on the handcuffs. The other officer took Big Elk by the arm and directed him across the slope. "You have the right to remain silent..."

"False accusations," Big Elk launched into one of his famous rants. He twisted his head to shout at Nora. "Your prejudice against Native Americans is well documented and now you're tainting Flagstaff's finest with your lies. My people will carry on this battle in my name for our Great Mother."

Gary looked as if a headache of biblical proportions banged behind his eyes. "Knock off the histrionics."

Evidently deciding Big Elk was the more dramatic story, Dorothy scurried to his side.

Abigail stepped close to Barrett and put a delicate hand on his arm, looking into his face. "Can't you do something about him?"

Though his features seemed calm, there was something about Barrett's face that brought to mind scorched fields of ash and death. "He won't bother Kachina Ski again."

Somehow, that didn't make Nora feel safer.

Gary exhaled as if exhausted. "Nora. I need to talk to you."

Scott was dead and she'd been accused of his murder. Not to mention Gary's suspicions about insurance fraud. What other disaster could he bring?

"Do you know a Maureen Poole?"

The name stabbed her heart and she couldn't begin to pull apart all the connected emotions. Betrayal, sadness, tragedy. Anger or compassion. She nodded.

"She was recently killed in a one-car accident. We discovered a connection between your late husband and Ms. Poole."

Nora tried to swallow but her mouth was too dry. She barely squeaked out, "They were having an affair."

Gary studied her face. "We suspect her death wasn't an accident."

Knife to the lungs, air gone. Murder again. Gary was saying someone killed Maureen. Probably her. Unthinkable, though maybe she should have expected this. Things like this didn't happen in real life. Nora needed to get Abigail out of here, to someplace safe. People were being killed, and Abigail or Nora could be next.

"As a person of interest in the murder of your husband, this obviously makes you"—he hesitated—"more interesting."

Like a fish jerked toward the pole by the painful hook in its mouth, Nora felt herself reeling toward disaster.

TWENTY-ONE

Barrett's boots thudded on the yellowed industrial linoleum. He'd orchestrated Big Elk's arrest to illustrate that he was CEO of more than McCreary Energy. The noble Officer Gary had no idea who gave his chief the reliable tip. Now Barrett and Big Elk would have their Come to Jesus meeting and Big Elk would deliver the vote of the Hopi Tribal Council.

Three small barred cells left room for a walkway in the cinder-block structure. Dull yellow paint covered the walls.

Big Elk had the only cot in the cell farthest from the door. A bleary-eyed drunk hung his head in the next cell. Other than that, they had the place to themselves.

Barrett's steady footsteps down the linoleum corridor didn't disturb the prone figure of Big Elk. He lay on his back, arms under his head, staring at the ceiling.

Barrett stopped outside the cell. "Enjoying your stay?"

Only his lips moved. "Not five-star quality, but what can you expect for the sticks?"

"As a Native of the land, one funded with the hard-earned donations of a faithful following, isn't five stars out of your league?"

Big Elk chuckled and sat up. "Mr. Barrett McCreary. How good of you to call. And how generous to arrange my release."

Despite the difficult things he'd been forced to do in his life, Barrett didn't like violence. Still, he thought he might enjoy ripping this guy's throat out. "At least you understand the chain of command here."

The smirk on Big Elk's face stretched Barrett's control. "So you got the local yokels to toss me behind bars. Good for you. Now get me out."

"Not until you guarantee prompt delivery of what I paid for."

Big Elk rose from his cot. He stretched his arms overhead, took a deep breath, exhaled, and bent over in downward dog. When he stood, he ambled to the bars and faced Barrett. "I'll get the Hopi Tribal Council's endorsement for uranium mining, but not because you think you have power over me."

"I do have the power. This incarceration is a warning. If I decide to let you out, understand that any delay in the Hopi agreement will result in something much more costly than repairs to the ski lift—which you'll reimburse me for, by the way."

Big Elk's arms went overhead and he bent to his left, inhaled up and bent to the right, eyes full of malicious humor. When he straightened he said, "People of the Earth feel strongly about white men desecrating their sacred lands. But I won't be giving you a dime, Barrett. In fact, I want another mil deposited in that account."

Ripping out his throat might be letting him off too easy. "Do you have a death wish?"

"Like Scott Abbott?"

This prick didn't know the first thing about Scott Abbott. He was fishing.

When Barrett didn't react, Big Elk narrowed his eyes and considered. "I don't know how or why, but I'll bet my best horse you have something to do with that."

"Get the job done and get the fuck out of my playground or rot here in jail."

"You don't want to threaten me, Mr. McCreary."

"That's not a threat."

Big Elk appeared as casual as if he was relaxing at a picnic. "Your daughter might not be happy to see me abused like this."

It took all of his control not to fly at the bars and smash Big Elk's skull. Through a jaw locked as tight as Attica, Barrett said, "Leave her alone."

Big Elk shrugged. "Okay. You ought to know, though, that I'm the only thing standing between her and considerable jail time."

Barrett's lungs hardened to stone.

Big Elk chuckled again. "The authorities you think you hold in your pocket might be interested to know the name of the brave eco-terrorist who blew up that ski lift."

Barrett was riveted to the floor and his ears rang at the words he didn't want to hear:

"Heather set that explosion, and her prints are all over the evidence."

TWENTY-TWO

NORA'S ANKLE THROBBED AS she stepped on the clutch of her old Jeep and downshifted. Maybe running all over the mountain, standing in front of her burned-out lift, and driving to town for supplies wasn't the best recovery plan. Abbey rode shotgun on the return drive home, head sticking out from the passenger window and tongue hanging out. The Jeep swung from the highway into Mountain Village.

During the court battles, she'd thought about the financial benefits of snow making, not only to Kachina Ski but to the whole town. She had sincerely believed in the advantages of making snow. But now those doubts wouldn't leave her alone. Was it right to create a playground, rip out more trees, and scour the mountainside so more skiers could spend their weekends and their cash tearing up the wilderness? Would unnatural snow benefit the mountain as she'd thought? After years of battling, the victory had come at her too fast. She addressed Abbey. "Scott was right. We should get out while we're alive."

Abbey pulled in his tongue, glanced at her, swallowed, and hung his tongue out again.

Wish I could find something to bring me as much pleasure as riding in the Jeep gives him. Pleasure, my ass—I'd settle for a little less pain and fear.

She coasted into the parking lot of Kachina. Barrett's black Mercedes reflected the late morning sunshine. The metal cordon defining the edge of the lot lay on the ground and a set of deep wheel ruts ran over it.

At the far side of the slope, next to the gnarled remains of the lift, several pickups parked and a dozen men in hard hats milled around. Barrett stood with a man who had to be a crew foreman.

"That son of a bitch." Nora hurried across the slope. About half-way there Barrett noticed her and he walked away from the men to meet her. She held his gaze as she slowed and stomped toward him. The ache lingering in her ankle fueled her determination.

"What is this?"

"The contractors to start trenching for the sprayers."

"The sprayers won't be here until spring. We'll trench then."

Barrett put a hand on Nora's shoulder. "I reordered my sprayers. They'll be here next week. It's been a tough day for you. Go on back to the lodge and get some rest."

She felt like smacking him. "You can't do this."

Condescension oozed from Barrett. "I understand jitters. This is a big step. It's the beginning of taking Kachina Ski from a one-run mom-and-pop operation to a resort rivaling Lake Tahoe. It's scary and you're understandably nervous. But you're up to the task and I'll be with you every step of the way."

"I don't have the jitters. I will not allow this."

His steady gaze held a hint of danger. "Bigger and more powerful people than you have tried to stand in my way, and they were crushed. One thing you should know about McCrearys, we get what we want."

"Really?" Volcanoes of molten rage made her face burn. "One thing you should know about me, I won't be railroaded."

"Glad to hear it. That kind of determination will transform this mountain into a destination resort. There is no limit to the winter Disneyland we can create."

"I don't think you understand. I mean I won't kneel before you, the Crown Prince of Assholes."

"You're overreacting." He spoke as if quieting an unreasonable child.

Nora raced away, heading to the foreman. He looked startled. She ran behind the men and herded them toward the pickups. "Get out of here. Now. Go!"

Confused, they stared at her. She probably seemed deranged to them. She didn't care. Eventually, the foreman must have decided she was crazy enough that he didn't want to argue. He motioned for the men to leave.

As soon as the men began loading up, she stomped across the slope and up the stairs to the deck. Voices came from inside the lodge. She slinked outside the screen door and looked in.

Abigail, Heather, and Charlie gathered around the large front window. Charlie stood on a chair and hammered something above the corner of the window. Heather carried a waterfall of bright yellow fabric with tiny blue flowers. Abigail stood with arms folded supervising.

Heather rambled on her favorite topic. "When the first people climbed from the Third World to the Fourth World, the leaders gathered and each choose an ear of corn. Other tribes quickly grabbed the largest ears, leaving only the smallest for Hopi. According to their choice, each tribe went on their way to settle in their lands. Because the Hopi chose the smallest ear, we were told our lives will be difficult and we'll always be a small tribe. But we'll survive the longest."

Abigail handed something to Charlie. "But why here? Why didn't they settle where survival is easier?"

"The Hopi clans migrated for a very long time. We left behind maps and histories in the rock paintings that are all over. One day the Bear Clan made it to the Mesa and they met a powerful spirit. They wanted him to be their leader and stay with them. He refused but said they could stay as long as they lived his way. As time went by, other clans settled on the mesas and were accepted into Hopi."

Abigail nodded to Heather. She stepped toward Charlie. "If you raise that bracket a smidge you'll have better luck getting that nail in."

Nora opened the screen and stepped inside. "What's going on?"

Heather looked over her shoulder, the expression on her face like a child at a birthday party.

Abigail didn't turn. "We're sprucing up the place. Don't you think these curtains add cheer?"

Maybe her head would just explode. "No. What I think is that they'll turn into a giant Kleenex for skiers with runny noses."

Abigail clucked. "Heather and I spent the morning sewing these. You could at least say thank you."

Nora was speechless. Which was good, because anything she said would be bad.

Abigail gasped. "Not like that. Charlie, you must measure so they'll be even."

Charlie smiled at her, sweat dripping from his face. "Aw, Ab. No one will ever be able to tell."

Heather laughed. "They'll be too busy blowing their noses."

Abigail gave her a playful swat. "You dickens."

Just one happy party until Nora, the Big Green Ogre, entered. *What's the matter with her, anyway?* Nora wondered.

Barrett walked into the lodge. Nora turned on her heel to confront Barrett, put a hand on his massive chest, and gave it a shove. "Get the hell out of here."

"Nora!" Abigail scolded.

Barrett held up his palm. "I can see you're upset."

"Upset?" She sounded shrill. "Why should I be upset?!"

Abigail came to Nora. "I don't know what this is about, but hysterics will get you nowhere."

"Be quiet, Mother."

Abigail stomped her foot and clapped her hands. "That's enough! You will not speak to me that way."

Heather's eyes widened as she stared at the scene.

Charlie climbed down from the chair. "This sounds like the kind of discussion best undertaken with beverages. Might I suggest a trip to the Mountain Tavern?"

Nora stared at Barrett. "I don't care what agenda you plan. This is my business, and I'll run it my way."

"If you'll recall," Barrett spoke with infuriating calm. "The deal was that I'd give you money to make snow. An ethical business person doesn't renege on a deal."

"Using responsible methods is not reneging."

"Will you sit and talk about this?"

Abigail drew in her chin and straightened her shoulders. "Of course she'll discuss this in a rational manner."

Nora took another step toward him. "Why are you pushing this? It's not as if you need money."

"Nora, really. Barrett is our benefactor."

Barrett's voice dripped with false kindness. "You have the brains and savvy to steer Kachina to the success it can achieve. But you're overwhelmed with the burdens thrust on your narrow shoulders. I'm only here to help."

Her brain felt dry as a desert, all the neuro-pathways like sandy washes. Let him handle the details, why not? She and Abigail could move into town for a while. Nora would recover from Scott's death and betrayal, though she didn't see how. The business would thrive and she'd pick up her life again. Alex would eventually make a stupid move and end up in jail. A smooth transition orchestrated by the great Barrett McCreary himself.

Her term paper research told her he cleaned up uranium contamination, built clinics and schools, all while increasing profits and moving McCreary Energy into the forefront of the industry. He'd achieved success more complicated than running a tiny ski resort. So why did everything in her body rebel against letting him make decisions for Kachina Ski?

Abigail put her arm around Nora, her hands cool and soft. "There now, you see? Barrett is trying to help."

Nora looked up, exhausted. "Fire that contractor. Cancel the sprayers."

Barrett shook his head. "It's not good to make rash decisions right now."

"This is not a rash decision."

Abigail patted Nora's shoulder. "You won't have to do it alone. Barrett is going to help you, aren't you, dear?"

Dear? Abigail took to rich men like foie gras to champagne.

Barrett looked pleased with himself. "People will be here tomorrow to begin the lift repairs."

"What?"

"Leave it to me. I'll take care of everything."

Blood pumped back into her brain, flash-flooding the synapses. "No. I'll make the decisions about snow and the lift."

The *p-shew* of a beer can opening broke the silence. Charlie slurped then said, "Perhaps Miss Abigail and I can wander down to the Tavern and reserve a table. You guys could join us later."

Abigail let out a deep sigh. "No, Charlie. Barrett and I are on our way out."

Charlie didn't sound daunted. "Okay, then. Might I interest you in an evening stroll?"

Nora and Barrett still faced each other. Nora breathed fast and shallow.

"I'm sorry," Abigail said, sounding anything but. "I'm not interested in strolling with you, having supper at the Tavern with you, sharing a six pack with you, or doing much of anything with you except wishing you a nice day."

Charlie chuckled. "I like a woman with some vinegar to her."

Barrett's smile looked benign enough, but something nasty lurked around its edge. "You're still general manager here, Nora. In fact, I'd planned on giving you an actual salary and benefits, like a real corporation."

Nora put her hands on her hips. "Unlike Abigail, I'm not interested in being your kept woman."

"Hear me roar," Charlie said.

Abigail glared at Nora, color high in her cheeks. "That was uncalled for and cruel."

She's right. "I'm sorry, Mother. I didn't mean that." Guilt felt like tar in Nora's throat.

Abigail's gold lamé sandals clicked across the floor to grab her bag by the front door. "Are you ready for lunch, Barrett? I'm half starved."

Barrett hesitated a split second and started after Abigail. "There's a quaint bistro in the old mining town of Jerome."

Nora spoke to Barrett's back. "Cancel your equipment."

Just before he walked out of the lodge, Barrett said. "Don't try to stop me, Nora."

She followed them onto the deck, seething. They strolled down the path to the parking lot. Charlie and Heather stood behind her not making a sound, as if in thrall at the climax of an adventure movie.

Barrett opened the Mercedes's door for Abigail and helped her to settle inside.

Without much thought Nora raced down the steps to the parking lot. Two pickups full of trenchers idled in the lot and she ignored them. Nora jumped into her Jeep, cranked the key, and slammed it into gear. The Jeep lurched backward, spraying cinders as she popped the gear shift from reverse into second and aimed for Barrett's Mercedes, which was poised to turn onto the road. She braced herself on the steering wheel and stomped on the gas. The Jeep shot forward and crashed into the bumper of Barrett's gas-guzzling black monster.

She grabbed the gear shift and shoved it into reverse, backed up a few feet, then slammed it to second again, giving it gas. The next impact created a satisfying explosion of taillights.

The car's driver side door opened and Barrett jumped out, motivating his bulk with impressive speed. While he approached she backed up again, put it in neutral and revved the motor.

Barrett put a hand on her door, as if that could stop her. "What the hell are you doing?"

She faced the rage in his eyes. "I don't know, but it feels good."

Ram into gear, stomp the gas, slam into the bumper a third time.

"You're crazy!"

"That's right."

Abigail appeared next to Barrett. She put an elegant hand on his massive arm and turned him toward the Mercedes.

The fire inside Nora died as Abigail saw Barrett into his seat, gave him an endearing smile, and turned to walk like a queen to her side of the vehicle. She opened the door and, just before stepping in, looked at Nora.

Instead of anger and disappointment, Nora saw pain and confusion. Barrett and Abigail drove away.

The trenchers idled in their pickups.

TWENTY-THREE

AND WHAT DID THAT little stunt prove? Only her incredibly unstable nature.

Heather and Charlie gave her a standing ovation from the deck.

First one pickup then the other inched toward the road. No doubt the trenchers would be called as witnesses at the murder trials of Scott and Maureen. They'd testify to Nora's deranged actions. Maybe insanity would be a good defense.

Charlie walked over to her window and reached in, tilting her chin to look at him. "You are a magnificent woman."

At that, a sob escaped her. "So magnificent that I poured years into a doomed business that led to the death of my husband. A husband, by the way, so impressed with my magnificence that he was boinking some other woman. And I just went berserk and smashed my Jeep for nothing!"

Charlie shrugged. "Sure. But you're not passive. You've got life and passion, and that's a great thing."

Heather stood at the trail to the lodge. "That was some crazy shit."

Nora climbed from the Jeep and plodded past Heather. "I'm sure that's not the example your father wants you to emulate."

Heather turned and followed her. "No one ever treats Poppy like that. Whatever he says goes."

Charlie followed them up the path, popping a beer and slurping. Abbey trotted along behind.

"If you really believed he's invincible, you wouldn't be getting in trouble and doing time with me," Nora said.

Heather shrugged. "Okay, so I'm fighting uranium mining and snow making. It won't make any difference. Poppy always gets his way."

"Not this time."

A light sparkled in Heather's eyes. "Maybe not this time. Too many forces are against him."

"Thanks for the vote of confidence. I'm only a small force but I've got controlling interest in Kachina Ski."

"It's not only you."

"If you think Big Elk is such a douche bag, why are you helping him?"

Heather's face turned as blank as a pack mule's. "I don't work for him. We just happen to support some of the same causes."

"I support Ponderosa pine and Mexican spotted owls, and no motorized vehicles in my forest," Charlie said.

I support staying alive, thought Nora. "Okay. Let's see if we can salvage anything of this day."

Heather sounded eager. "Charlie and I could finish hanging the curtains and surprise Abigail."

"To see her smile I'd hang a curtain to China," Charlie slurred.

"Much as I'd love to please my mother," sarcasm injected Nora's voice, "I think we should finish inventory of the rental stock. Besides, Charlie shouldn't be climbing chairs."

Heather walked next to Nora. "How come you don't like your mother? Abigail is so cool."

"Abigail the Horrible? Abigail the Intrusive, Controlling, Disapproving, Demanding Mother From Hell?"

Heather's eyes took on a hard glint. "She's really proud of you. You should hear her talk about all the great things you've done."

"You're kidding." Nora stopped and looked at Heather. "Abigail went to bed for a week because I wouldn't attend my undergrad graduation. She was so busy planning a month-long cruise after my stepfather's death that she never noticed I took over Kachina Ski. By the way, between graduation and Kachina, she barely spoke to me in protest of me marrying Scott."

"You have to admit she was right about that."

Now Abigail was recruiting troops? "I suppose she spent the morning gossiping about my marriage and how she tried to save me."

"She cares about you," Heather said.

"Cares about me." Noxious memories of Abigail's "care" swirled in Nora's brain. What about the preppy outfits Abigail bought, purely out of concern for Nora? It had nothing to do with Abigail's friends' disapproval of Nora's hiking boots and flannel shirts. Abigail's concern overflowed when Nora struggled the last semester of her senior year of high school. She said Nora simply *had* to be valedictorian because Abigail had already invited so many people to the reception. The list of Abigail's "loving concern" was endless.

Nora inhaled to begin her litany of abuse, but Heather's sad face halted her momentum.

"I'd give anything to have a mother."

Nothing like a tire iron to the temple. *I am self-centered, insensitive, and callous*, Nora thought. She put her arm around Heather. "I'm sorry. From now on, I'll share her with you. Maybe you'll get a little of that doting mothering you've missed and I can get a break."

This felt kind of good to Nora. She'd never had a little sister and she liked talking with Heather. Maybe this whole mentor thing would work out for both of them. "Look. I know I've been hard on you. I don't mean to be. I just don't want you to get hurt."

Heather's eyes misted. "That's nice. But I can take care of myself."

Nora gave Heather's shoulders a squeeze and felt her tense. The girl stared at the corner of the lodge.

Nora followed her gaze.

Alex leaned against the lodge, arms folded, a smug smile on his lips.

Nora dropped her arm from Heather's shoulders and fought to keep from screaming. "What's he doing here?"

"I don't know."

Nora spun and sprinted for the apartment and her phone.

"Wait!" Heather called. "He's not going to hurt you."

There wasn't a waiting kind of bone left in Nora's body. She hit the stairs and took them two at a time. While her heart threatened to explode, she told the 911 dispatcher that Alex was loitering on her property.

Heather spoke to him right below the apartment window.

Somewhere Charlie had found a shovel and stood a few feet from the couple, the shovel poised to attack.

Whatever Heather and Alex discussed, it wasn't roses and sunshine. Their body language telegraphed anger. Alex grabbed Heather's arm and pulled her a step toward the forest.

Nora didn't hesitate. As quickly as she'd flown to the apartment, she doubled her speed to get back. By the time she arrived, Charlie had moved closer and held the shovel like a javelin.

Heather raised her hands in a calming motion. "It's okay, Charlie. He's not going to hurt me."

"You'd best clear out of here, young man."

Nora stepped next to Charlie. "Why not stick around a few more minutes. The cops will be here by then."

Heather turned on her. "You called the cops? You bitch!"

Alex laughed. "Go ahead and call the army for all I care. They can't save you." He waved at Charlie, dismissing him. "This old man won't help. If I wanted to kill your lily-white ass, you'd be dead by now."

In another couple of minutes her heart would burst from fear and save Alex the trouble of killing her. "Come on, Heather. Let's go back to the lodge and wait for the cops."

Alex flipped his hair back. "You gonna let that white bitch tell you what to do?"

Heather narrowed her eyes at Nora. "I can't believe you called the cops. I told you I'd take care of it."

"He's a murderer, Heather."

She shook her head. "He's never killed anyone."

"Yet." Alex grinned at Nora.

Nora grabbed the shovel from Charlie. "Damn it, Heather. Get away from him!"

Heather shook her head, tears accumulating in the corner of her eyes. "He's the only one who loves me." She took Alex's hand and together they ran into the forest.

TWENTY-FOUR

WHEN OFFICER GARY SUSPECTED Nora of murder, he drove to the mountain, but a threat on her life only warranted a visit from a junior Mouseketeer. He took notes but never even scouted around the property. Finding Alex on the mountain probably presented an impossible mission. The officer flipped his notebook closed and headed toward his cruiser.

Heather hid somewhere alone out there with Alex. With all the confidence of youth, she thought this badass loved her and wouldn't hurt her. What a mess.

Evening pushed around the corners of the afternoon. Nora wanted Abigail home and safely locked inside before darkness covered them all. Abbey and Charlie provided some comfort, but not any real protection. Both of them dozed by the lodge in the last strength of the sun.

A middle-aged couple with daypacks strapped on their backs appeared near the top of the run and tramped across the slope, disappearing into the forest. At the peak of hiking season, today couldn't be any more perfect. The forest might seem empty, but Nora counted four or five hiking couples that afternoon; they appeared for only a few minutes, then disappeared into the woods, present but unseen.

Cole swung into the lot on his mountain bike. He braked by the cop and climbed off the bike.

Great. Nora turned from the railing. "I've got to do something about Barrett."

"Hmm." Charlie picked up a beer from the bench beside him. Nora noted that it was the same can that had been sitting by him for two hours. Maybe he didn't drink as much as she had thought. Could be he carried around an open can out of habit. "I hate to see you leave this mountain, sugar. But she needs a rest from the skiers."

Nora stared at the grassy slope. Instead of enjoying a mountain lawn, as she used to, she cringed at a bald swath once covered by pines. To add salt to the wound, the tire tracks from the trenchers had left muddy scars. "I thought making snow would fix all my problems. We'd have money, Scott would be happy. I'd be the success my mother always wanted."

"Hold on there." Charlie sounded almost energetic. "Your mother is proud of who you are, not what you've done." Super. Now Charlie *and* Heather tag-teamed for Abigail.

"Anyway," Nora said. "Nothing has changed about making snow. Kachina Ski won't survive without it and with it, I'll be rich in a matter of a few years."

Charlie's voice settled back into half consciousness. "True."

Her mouth almost couldn't form the next sentence. "But it's wrong."

"Now you're talking."

"The arguments are still valid: Kachina Ski only uses less than one fourth of a percent of the mountain; more moisture would be good for biodiversity and vegetation; more commerce would help the local economy. It's all there. That hasn't changed."

"Yep."

"So why have I changed?"

"You're seeing the light."

She wouldn't admit the little kachina salesman held any sway over her, but his words about her protecting the mountain sank deep into her heart. "It's Barrett. He's desperate for snow making and I don't know why. It's like he's sprinkled evil powder over it all, and now it feels bad."

"Mac has that effect on life."

Mac? That sounded too familiar. Nora left the rail and sat next to Charlie. "There's something between you guys, isn't there?"

Charlie stared at the beer can. "Not anymore."

"What happened?"

"It was a long time ago, honey. All I can say now is don't trust him."

Nora waited while he gulped his beer. "Come on, Charlie."

He considered a moment. "We were all young and out to save the world."

"Who's 'we'?"

His eyes gazed decades into the past. "Me and Barrett and Ester."

"Ester?"

"A woman of uncommon strength and breeding. The only woman on this green Earth that could rival your queenly mother for beauty, grace, and intelligence."

Nora rolled her eyes.

He patted her knee. "Pain is best left to the past."

They sat together for a few moments letting the last of the day's sun soak the rawness from their hearts.

Cole climbed up the stairs to the deck. "Hey, Nora. Charlie."

Charlie stirred and stood, crushing his can and dropping it in a pocket. "Got some recon to attend to."

Nora jumped up, now nervous. "Wait. Don't go."

Charlie glanced from Nora to Cole. "Aw, honey, he's okay."

Cole raised his eyebrows at Charlie as if asking a silent question. Charlie answered with a slight shrug and walked down the steps.

It surprised Nora that evening had advanced so far she needed to squint to see Cole. "What's up with you and Charlie?" Abbey trotted over to Cole with a wagging tail. Too bad Nora couldn't trust the dog's character instincts. On the other hand, Abbey had never been all that fond of Scott, and he had turned out to be a bad investment.

"We have a pact to keep an eye on you."

"Charlie I trust. You, not so much."

He gazed off toward the mountain. "Lots of people out here this evening."

She shrugged. "It's a good time of year for hikes and camping."

He considered her for a minute, a slight lift to his lips. "That stubborn streak of yours is hard to get around sometimes."

"I'm not stubborn."

He laughed. "Right. What do you call fighting an uphill battle for years just to get the right to do something you don't really believe in?"

He was treading on dangerous emotional turf. "How do you know I don't think snow making is exactly the right thing to do?"

His shrug said her defensiveness sounded too silly for him to argue with. "And for a long time you stuck by a guy who didn't deserve your loyalty."

"You don't know what you're talking about."

"I know enough. He worked for someone else, lied about the money, and cheated on you."

Thankfully dusk was far enough along he couldn't see her face flame with embarrassment and anger. "You never met Scott. Maybe he had reasons."

"A man can't justify betrayal."

"I guess bribing congressmen doesn't qualify as betrayal in your book."

Cole let out a sigh. "Now you don't know what you're talking about."

She stood up and turned her back to him, crossing her arms against the chill of the night. "Maybe not, but you're lying to someone about something."

He'd moved beside her without a sound and his warmth radiated to her back. His voice rumbled low. "I'm not lying about wanting to keep you safe."

His protectiveness rankled her pride. "I can take care of myself."

"Really? How prepared are you to face Big Elk?"

She waved him off. "Big Elk's in jail."

"*Was* in jail. He's out and the cops lost track of him already."

Nora quit breathing. Big Elk out and at large? She wanted to jump in the Jeep and roar away. She gripped the rail. Hang on. Big Elk wouldn't attack her. He might send someone else after her, but he wouldn't expose himself that way. She faced no more danger now than she had when he was in jail.

Probably.

Cole took hold of her arm and turned her to face him. "Benny said—"

"Benny?"

"My friend on Second Mesa."

"Second Mesa as in Hopi?"

"Yes. He said the kachinas are supposed to be off the mountain and on the mesas this time of year. But they're still here."

"You believe they're real?"

Cole pushed his hair from his forehead. "Hell, I don't know what's real. I know Benny believes, and that's good enough for me."

Nora had felt the same way when Heather spoke about Hopi. "You think if someone else believes it that makes it true?"

"What I think is the Hopi have traveled throughout the Southwest way before our ancestors knew a continent existed here. They built shrines and worshipped and developed a relationship to the land or Mother Earth or whatever you want to call it. The Hopi communicate with the world in ways others can't."

"You may be better looking than Big Elk, but you speak the same language."

"Fine, believe what you want, but I'm saying that everything is off kilter. People are upset. That translates into you and your mother being in danger. You should stay in town until this is over."

Nora swallowed the lump of fear rising in her throat. Dangerous liar with a clever delivery or nice guy who cared about her?

"Okay?" He insisted.

She nodded. "Yeah. Soon as she gets back, we'll pack up."

Cole stood for another moment looking as though he might add something more. Instead he plodded down the stairs.

Cole's friend said Big Elk had planned something. Hadn't there been an unusual number of hikers today? And hadn't most of them been gray-haired, like many of Big Elk's groupies? In Charlie's words, something was going down on the mountain.

And Heather was out there somewhere, alone with Alex and his knife.

TWENTY-FIVE

NORA HAD TO FIND Heather. Okay, she didn't *have* to. Heather was now doing everything she could to push Nora away, and she excelled at it. But the girl needed help, and Nora felt responsible. Cole had said he suspected Alex camped at the springs that nestled at the base of a rock pile a fifteen-minute hike from the lodge. Nora hollered for Abbey.

True night settled in. Like fireflies, lights flickered here and there. These weren't awesome fireballs like the night of the lift explosion, but ordinary flashlights. Maybe the activity was nothing more than teenagers out for a party. Heather might just be drinking with a bunch of friends. Which was dangerous in its own way but not in the same league as Big Elk's campaign.

Heather tugged at Nora's heart in an unexpected way. She didn't owe the girl anything and yet she felt connected. It was probably some stupid transference of affection for the little sister she never had and always wanted. Or the baby she thought she'd have with Scott. Whatever. She'd confront all that wishy-washy malarkey later and figure out a more appropriate relationship with her employee. For now Nora just wanted to make sure Heather was safe.

Nora sucked in a deep breath and hurried deeper into the forest. Not far ahead, three people scurried along, their voices close to a whisper. Nora reached down and grasped Abbey's collar to keep him from joining the group.

The distant *boom, boom, boom* of drumming thumped in Nora's head.

"They've started. We're going to be late," an older man in the group ahead of her said. Definitely not an underage-drinking party.

A thin woman with stringy gray hair breathed hard but managed to whine. "It wasn't my fault. The fuse wouldn't stay connected."

The third person, a woman, jogged a few paces to keep up. "I think there are other sites, so even if it doesn't work it'll still be spectacular."

What were Big Elk's Guilty White People so worked up about? Something with a fuse. The ski lift wasn't enough, they planned to blow up something else?

Nora followed as the three veered onto an uphill trail. A short but strenuous hike brought them to a clearing. The drumming beat loud enough now that Nora didn't worry about being heard. They were gathering at the site where a plane crashed into the mountain in the early 1970s. Some of its wreckage still rested in this spot next to an opening to the lava tubes. An easily identifiable landmark, it was a popular place to gather.

And gathering they were. A bonfire flared next to the bit of fuselage and Big Elk stood on a flat rock, facing a growing crowd of Natives and Guilty White People. With Abbey's collar firmly in her grasp, Nora crouched in the shadow of trees.

Big Elk raised his hands and brought the drumming to a halt. "People of the mountain. Holy people. It is time for us to gather in strength and do what the spirits of the mountain demand of us. The Hopi have a responsibility to care for the world, and that starts with this mountain. We are joining with our brothers and sisters to take a stand for our Mother when she can't defend herself."

The drums pounded several times and people shouted.

"A powerful kachina came to me last night. He stood outside my shelter with his fire and told me to gather the people on the mountain. He wants to show us his displeasure with what is happening and make us understand that we need to stop the white rapists from destroying our Mother."

Nothing but a summer repeat. Nora needed to find Heather and get the heck off the mountain.

Big Elk raised his arms. "Show us, great kachina. What would you have us do?"

Nora took a few steps into the forest. Vibration in the ground shocked her feet before her ears caught the roar. An astonished gasp rose from the forty or so people around Big Elk.

A ball of flames burst from the lava tube, making Big Elk's bonfire looked like a candle flame. The Wizard of Oz couldn't have created a better illusion.

"He is with us!" Big Elk shouted. "He's giving us a message."

Another explosion erupted from the forest below. Flames leapt above the trees and escaped into the air. The flash had barely extinguished when another flare and rumble surged from several hundred yards to the left. Another exploded toward the top of the peak. The crowd gasped and applauded at each successive fire burst.

Big Elk had cleverly staged his mystical pyrotechnic theater from the lava tubes. Maybe he'd rigged fuses through the tubes to connect with each other or maybe he used timers. That must be what the folks walking in front of her were talking about. The balls of flame would ignite the night, but since they originated in the rock openings, the risk of forest fires would be slight. The show exhibited drama and flare—literally. But who really believed mountain gods created fire to demonstrate their wrath?

"Are you going to allow Nora Abbott to desecrate the kachina's home?" Big Elk might be a thin, short man, but next to the fire, with the momentum of the supernatural display, he resembled a roaring lion. The shouts and enthusiasm of his followers left no question: they hungered for blood. Or at least, more destruction of property.

"She ignored our pleas. She plunged the needle into our Mother's veins and will pump her blood to stain the scars she cut into our Mother's flesh. Brothers and Sisters of the Earth, I beg you. The spirit commands you—don't let this happen."

She had to get out of here before the riled up crowd discovered their enemy was nearby and alone save for an aging canine companion. Nora raced down the path with Abbey in thankfully silent tow, hoping she could make it to the springs to get Heather; that is, if Heather was even at the springs. She crashed along the trail, stumbling over rocks and roots. Each step ignited more fear.

Finally she made out a weak light shining from the springs. Alex and Heather stood in a clearing, surrounded by the forest on three sides. A huge boulder pile created the fourth boundary. A flat granite rock looked almost like an altar at the base of the boulders and to the side of this, green ferns and yellow flowers ringed a small spring about the size of a child's backyard wading pool.

"I don't trust Big Elk," Nora heard Heather say as she drew nearer. "Just don't do what he says without talking to the elders."

Alex picked up a wad of bright turquoise-colored cloth. A dead animal lay next to a half empty bottle of Wild Turkey. She'd caught them in the middle of a ritual animal sacrifice.

Wait. The dead animal turned out to be some sort of costume with leather and feathers. It didn't take a genius to figure out where Scott's mystical kachina had really come from.

"Babe, the kachinas want us to act now."

Heather put a hand on his arm. "I'm just asking you to wait and talk to the elders. Do it for me."

He kissed her and smiled. "Only for you."

Nora burst into the clearing with Abbey on her heels. Like a squirrel chased by a dog, Alex spun and fled without stopping to see who attacked. He dove for the rock pile ... and disappeared.

Heather turned to the forest and scowled. You'd think a sixteen-year old would be skittish in that situation, but she acted more put-out than nervous.

"Heather, we need to get out of here!" Nora grabbed Heather's arm.

Heather pulled back and glared at her. Wherever Alex had gone, he might reappear with some of Big Elk's explosives or that knife of his. Nora didn't want to wait around for that.

Abbey climbed around the boulders and whined. The lantern only cast enough light to create shadows that danced with menace. Nora didn't want to go near there.

"Let's go."

"You shouldn't be here. This is a sacred place, with the lava tubes," Heather said.

Duh, Nora, the rock pile is an opening to the tubes. Stupid! She grabbed Heather's arm and tried to jerk her away, now afraid of fire in addition to Alex's knife. "Please, you have to come with me."

"Leave me alone!"

"The tubes. Big Elk. We've got ... "

A click and whoosh came from the direction of the rocks. Whatever high-tech device Big Elk commissioned must be engaging. It was going to blow.

Nora dove for the dirt just as Armageddon broke loose in the clearing. Flames engulfed the space then rose before igniting her skin. She felt as if her eardrums were bursting. Incredible light and heat flashed, and Nora knew she would soon be nothing but a sooty skeleton scattered on the forest floor.

Then it ended.

She couldn't hear anything. Acrid fumes burned her nostrils and her face felt scalded. Heather had been closer to the opening. Was she okay? In the blindness from the flash and smoke, Nora rose to her knees and searched for the girl.

Oh God, where was Heather? She should be close by, but there wasn't anyone there except Abbey, who, probably having heard the coming explosion before Nora, had sprinted to safety before the fire erupted.

Movement next to the springs drew Nora's eye. Through smoke, Nora watched Alex heft a motionless Heather to his shoulder and disappear into the trees.

TWENTY-SIX

Nora ran across the slope, slipping on the wet grass and coughing up the smoky taste of fire. Abbey galloped behind her. Heather had looked like a Raggedy Ann doll draped on Alex's shoulder. *Please let her be okay.* But even if Heather survived the explosion at such close range, Alex might be the bigger danger.

Behind her, the mountain erupted with random bursts of flame. Far off, drums pounded and people cheered.

Nora raced by the lodge, noting the lack of lights. Abigail still hadn't made it home. Nora didn't like Abigail being with Barrett, but it beat getting caught in the middle of an incendiary riot. Whatever. Nora couldn't take care of Abigail tonight.

"Nora!" Cole's shout stopped her before she made it to her Jeep. "Thank God you're okay." He sat in his pickup, the engine running. "I saw flames and was afraid…"

She jumped into the pickup and Abbey scrambled in after her. Nora scooted over to share the bucket seat. "Go! Alex has Heather. We need to save her."

He backed out of the parking lot. "He has Heather where?"

"The rez I'll bet. I don't know. Somewhere. The lava tube blew and he took Heather."

Cole drove down the mountain. "You aren't making sense. Start from where I left you at the lodge."

Nora told him about Big Elk and the explosions and the kachina costume. She explained everything.

He braked as he pulled into town. "We're going to go to the police station and tell them what you just told me."

Nora shook her head. "No. We should go to the rez. I'm sure that's where he'll take Heather."

"Which rez?"

"Hopi!"

"Do you know which mesa?"

Nora hadn't been to the tiny reservation completely surrounded by the Navajo Nation. She didn't know all the details, but the Hopi had been in this area for centuries before the Navajo made their way here. The Navajo tribe grew and little by little moved onto traditional Hopi lands. When the United States government, showing their usual even-handed, understanding ways, divided up the area for reservations, they reduced the amount of land the Hopi considered theirs and placed the reservation smack in the middle of the immense Navajo Nation.

Thus the Hopi lived on in a remote part of the desert on three mesas north of Winslow. About a two-hour drive from Flagstaff.

Cole pulled into a parking space in front of the police station. "If we don't get any help here, I'll get Benny to help us."

Benny? Oh, Cole's Hopi friend. Okay. She'd give the cops a chance but if they didn't do something immediately, she and Cole would rush to the rez.

But after entering the station, it was clear they wouldn't get the action Nora was hoping for. Every spare hand was up patrolling the mountain to create order after the amazing fireworks show. Worse, the cops dragged their feet before even talking to them.

After what felt like an hour, they took Cole one way and escorted her the other way, to a room where they told her they'd take her statement as soon as someone was available. More hours passed. Twice Nora tried to leave, telling them her dog was outside, but uniformed officers led her back to the room. As a person of interest in two murders, the cops didn't feel magnanimous toward her.

Finally Gary showed up, took brief notes, told her not to worry, and let her go.

Not worry that Heather could be injured and in the clutches of a murderer? Fat chance.

A grumpy cop in the lobby relented and let her use the office phone to call Abigail. The apartment phone rang uselessly. Nora slammed the receiver down. Her mother wasn't home, and her cell didn't get reception in most places around here.

Either Abigail held a grudge against Nora for her demolition derby or she'd experienced a romantic encounter with Barrett that stretched all night. Staying at a low-rate hotel just to indulge a snit seemed far-fetched for Abigail. But Nora couldn't calculate the cost of therapy to cope with the image of Abigail in Barrett's bed. She blocked the thought.

So where else could she be? What about Heather? Nora stepped out of the police station into the inky predawn quiet, not sure what to do next.

Cole popped out of his pickup, followed by Abbey. "I'm sorry. I had no idea they'd keep you like that."

She glared at him, patted Abbey, then marched toward his pickup. "Did you find Heather?"

He shook his shaggy head. "I checked the hospital and she's not there. I talked to Benny. There's a public dance out there today at Second Mesa. Alex is supposed to dance, so there's a good chance she'll be there."

Nora opened the passenger door and let Abbey in. What if Heather was seriously hurt in the explosion? Would Alex be selfless enough to take her to a "white man's" doctor? "Let's go to the rez."

"You can't just go out there. There are certain rules."

"Like what?"

"It's sort of like a church service, and you're supposed to dress nice."

"You're taking me to church?"

He opened the door and settled in. "No, I'm taking you home. Benny will help Heather."

She jumped into the passenger's seat. "We've got to go out there now. Heather probably needs us."

He started the pickup and maneuvered through the silent town. "Benny has a better chance of getting her home than you or I."

Nora argued and reasoned during the ride and still Cole held firm. He might be right. Nora wasn't exactly Heather's best friend and she'd fight coming home with her.

But somehow, it didn't matter. The stubborn girl needed someone to help her. The cops certainly didn't care, and if Barrett found out, he would crush Heather's spirit. She might not want the responsibility of Heather, but Nora couldn't turn away.

They pulled into Kachina's parking lot. Cole said, "There is something else."

She hated those words and the serious way Cole dropped them.

"I found out the cops were about to extradite Big Elk to South Dakota when he disappeared."

"Only to reappear on my mountain. What did he do in South Dakota?"

"Well, his real name is Ernie Finklestein. He's wanted for a scam that stole the investments of a bunch of retirement home residents. They lost his trail several years ago. Turns out Ernie got a sunburn and changed his name and now he's into something here."

"Aside from destroying my property and threatening my life?"

Cole nodded. "Looks like he's importing cheap crap from China to sell as authentic Navajo crafts."

"A real hero." She stared out the window. "Maybe he knows the cops are on to him and after last night's Bonfire of the Kachinas, he'll go underground."

"He doesn't strike me as the underground type." Cole pulled up in Kachina's parking lot.

"Don't worry about us." Abbey scrambled from the cab and Nora followed. She was a few paces up the path when the truck's other door slammed. She whirled around. "I can handle it from here."

"I'm not leaving you out here alone."

Punching him might feel good. Not that he'd blown up the mountain or caused Heather to run away, but because of him, she'd lost precious time. Had he not been here, she would have been out at the rez hours ago. "Just leave me alone."

He paused. "Have you found out anything new about Scott?"

Why would he ask that? Was there something he thought she was close to finding, something that implicated him? Except he'd have no possible reason to kill Scott. Unless he felt far more strongly about no snow making than he let on. Despite all his claims to want to help her, Nora couldn't trust her judgment after being so wrong about Scott. Her suspicion must have scrolled across her face.

His face hardened. "I'm only trying to help. The key to everything lies with figuring out who killed Scott. Once I know that, this nightmare will be over for you."

Which nightmare did he mean? Alex's hands crushing her larynx? Big Elk blowing up her property? Barrett ruining the mountain? Abigail taking up residence in her home? She stomped up the path while Abbey went off to conduct his own business.

After a few moments she heard his pickup door open and close more gently. But he didn't start the engine.

Nora slid her hand into her pocket for her key but when she held the knob to insert it, she realized the door was unlocked. She'd locked it last night. She knew it.

Indecision froze her. What to do? Something caught her eye. The screen on the window next to the front door was bent. It looked as though someone peeled it back. The sliding window was open just a crack—someone had broken into her house. She should run.

And wouldn't you know, Cole sat in the lot waiting to "rescue" her once more.

A slight shuffling sounded behind the drawn blinds. Someone was inside.

Damn it. No more being a victim. She would fight back this time. Casting about wildly for a weapon, Nora grabbed an old ski pole she used to shoo raccoons that occasionally climbed the stairs.

Nora held the pole like a bayonet and reached for the knob. One, two, three...

With a mighty leap she opened the door, lunged inside, and stabbed into the kitchen where she heard the shuffling.

"For heaven's sake, Nora! What are you doing?"

Nora stopped mid-attack, confused. "Mother?"

"Whom did you expect at this hour?"

Abbey trotted inside, his tail wagging.

A silent figure stepped from the hallway. Nora raised the ski pole again, sure this was the intruder who used Abigail as a hostage.

"Hey, Nora," Charlie said. He walked from the bathroom.

Nora lowered the ski pole.

Abigail tied an apron behind her waist then opened the refrigerator.

What the...?

Charlie fumbled for a chair at the table and her mother banged a fry pan onto the stove.

Abigail glanced up. "If you're going to join us for breakfast, at least comb your hair."

Nora turned questioning eyes toward Charlie but his head rested on his hands, gazing adoringly at Abigail.

"What is going on?" Nora managed to ask.

Abigail didn't look up from beating the hell out of the eggs. "I refuse to talk to you until you make yourself presentable."

"Oh for the love of Pete." Perplexed and without a target for her adrenaline, Nora went off to change clothes and brush her teeth.

Bacon sizzled and coffee dripped when she returned, which seemed fairly normal. What made Nora wonder if one of the Hopi warriors had let go of a serpent head and thrown the world off its axis was the way Abigail sat at the table across from Charlie and spoke in a soft voice.

Keeping an eye on them, Nora snagged a cup of coffee.

Abigail turned to her. "Please pick up your feet. Shuffling is low class."

The mug warmed Nora's hands. "Where have you been? Why did you break into my house? What are you doing with Charlie?"

Abigail raised her eyebrows. "The tables are turned and she's giving me twenty questions."

Charlie looked up at Nora and grinned. "I've been taking good care of her."

Nora ran a hand through her hair. "Excuse me, Charlie, but you can barely take care of yourself. Why would you overwhelm yourself with Queen Abigail?"

Her mother giggled. "See?" she said to Charlie. "That's why I like to be around her. She's always so witty."

"Not witty, Mother. Tired. Worried. Confused. And pretty freaked out."

Abigail and Charlie exchanged a look that said "isn't she cute?" Abigail patted Charlie's hand and got up to fiddle with the bacon and start the eggs.

Nora sipped her coffee, trying to clear her head. "I thought maybe you were staying in a motel or something."

"Now why would I do that?" Abigail poked a strip of bacon with a fork and transferred it to a paper towel–lined plate.

Her mother was practicing her typical form of punishment. She'd force Nora to detail the offense, then she'd demand an apology.

Frustrated, Nora took a breath and recalled their last conversation, before the fire on the mountain. "I'm sorry I called you a kept woman. I didn't mean it."

Abigail nodded and continued with the sputtering and popping bacon.

"I'm sorry I ran into Barrett's bumper and probably ruined your lunch date."

Abigail grabbed the eggs and whisk and let them have it again. "You didn't ruin our date. We had a lovely time."

Nora couldn't fathom what a lovely time with Barrett looked like. Her imagination balked at anything romantic with that man, and thinking of her mother that way was just plain wrong.

"You're not mad at me?"

Abigail poured the eggs into the warm pan. "I'm not pleased with your performance, no. But you are grieving. Perhaps you should see a therapist."

Nora looked at Charlie, hoping for some help.

He dozed, head resting on his hand.

Nora fortified herself with coffee. "Where were you last night, and how did you end up with Charlie?"

Abigail folded the omelet in a move that impressed Nora. "I was understandably upset when I got back to Mountain Village. Honestly, Nora, you wear me out sometimes."

"So what about Charlie?"

"When Barrett dropped me off, I went for a stroll instead of going directly home. I ran into Charlie and he took me for a cocktail at the Tavern."

Nora choked on coffee. "You went to the Tavern. With Charlie."

Abigail shot her a withering look. "Really, Nora. I'm not an ice queen."

Nora tried to keep from laughing.

"We had a few drinks and he bought me supper—"

"At the Tavern? You know they only serve fried food there."

"I had a fairly nice salad."

"Okay, salad. How did you get from drinks and salad to spending the night with Charlie?"

Abigail's eyes blazed and she shot a look at the still-dozing man at the table. "*I did not spend the night with Charlie.*"

Nora grinned. "You're right. You're home before dawn."

Abigail pulled the skillet from the stove. "Sometimes you're so crude."

"So what happened?"

"You know I'm not much of a drinker…"

Nora laughed, "You have a cocktail or two every day."

Abigail gave her a warning look. "While we were walking home I felt queasy and Charlie gallantly took me to his cabin. He gave me seltzer and aspirin, and I'm afraid I fell asleep."

"You passed out at Charlie's house." This was getting better and better.

Abigail slid the omelet onto a plate and picked up a knife. "Would you please try to act like an adult?"

Nora lifted her mug to hide her amusement. "Sorry. Go on."

"That's all. There's nothing more. I woke up, Charlie walked me home, and I promised him breakfast."

Nora followed Abigail as she carried the plates to the table and set one down in front of Charlie.

He opened his eyes and smiled at Abigail. "This looks perfect."

Abigail sat. "You need some companionship, Nora. Charlie and I think you should start seeing Cole Huntsman."

Nora nearly spit her coffee. "Good idea. It will make it easier for him to kill me."

Abigail laughed.

"You agreed with this?" Nora asked Charlie.

Charlie smacked his lips, loving the omelet. "He's a fine man."

"Well, if you love him so much, why not take him a cup of coffee—make stalking me more comfortable?"

"What do you mean?" Abigail said.

"He's sitting in the parking lot right now making sure I don't get away."

Abigail smiled. "That's so sweet."

Nora wanted to go to bed forever. She glared at Charlie. "You approve of what he does for a living?"

Charlie sat back and patted his belly. "Nuclear energy is cleaner and more efficient than coal, though I don't think they need to gut the

Grand Canyon for uranium. But Cole's a good man and he's working on other things. "

"What else? Murder?"

Abigail set down her coffee cup. "Really, Nora. You should get more rest. You sound confused."

Charlie stuffed a giant bite in his mouth and closed his eyes in ecstasy. Or was he hiding something about Cole?

When he swallowed and opened his eyes, he saw her staring at him. "You ought to get that front window fixed," Charlie said.

"I'll get to it later." She sipped her coffee. "Did you rip the screen or just bend it?"

Abigail sighed and got up for more coffee.

"And why didn't you use your key?" Nora asked.

Abigail filled Charlie's cup and gave her a puzzled look. "I did."

Nora reached for a piece of bacon from Abigail's plate and received a slap for her effort. "If it was so easy for you guys to break in maybe I ought to put bars on it."

Abigail's head snapped up. "Are you listening? We didn't break in, Nora. I told you, I used my key."

TWENTY-SEVEN

SHE LEFT CHARLIE TO the window repair and as soon as Cole drove away and Abigail turned her head, she jumped in the Jeep and started for the rez. Maybe Cole could sit around and wait for his friend to intercede, but Nora needed action. She had to help Heather and do something to stop Alex before he broke into their home again. The next time, Abigail might be home and ripe for murder.

Nora traveled as fast as she dared the nearly seventy miles to Winslow. She turned off the interstate onto a two-lane paved road and pushed the accelerator even more, the bumps and swells of the poorly maintained surface creating a sway like a sailboat. The sign to Second Mesa told her she had to travel another sixty miles on a road that ran straight to the horizon.

She headed toward the three Hopi mesas, each with some villages. Nora had heard that Old Oraibi, on Third Mesa, was the oldest constantly inhabited village in North America. Cole had said today's dance would take place on Second Mesa.

Poor farms and ranches of the Navajo Nation dotted the roadsides miles apart, each compound with a hogan, the traditional home structure of the Navajo people.

After what seemed like five hundred miles, the road ended at a T. On the right, a mesa rose and Nora barely detected the symmetrical lines of structures on the flat surface above her. The buildings blended with the yellow dirt of the desert, effectively camouflaging the town. A sign pointed left to Second Mesa. She passed a large, new school and turned right on a road leading up the side of Second Mesa. Around a switchback the road tilted sharply upward. It continued to get steeper with two more switchbacks. Shanties and worn buildings with signs identifying them as tribal and U.S. government and health facilities squatted alongside the road.

The third switchback, about halfway up the mesa, brought her to a stretch of road occupied with cars, people, and several card tables set up under bright awnings. The tables displayed food and crafts.

Whatever Nora expected of the ancient village, the truth disappointed her. The settlement looked like a Third World country. Dirt dominated everything. Yellow dust covered the paved strip of road, which broke off in uneven edges and dropped to windblown dirt shoulders. Houses made of cinder block, rock, and cobbled-together materials clung to the bare dirt hillside.

Nora stepped out of the Jeep. A candy wrapper fluttered under her feet. Feeling uncomfortable and unsure, she headed for the sound of drums.

Several groups of Native Americans meandered up a route etched into the side of a nearly vertical mesa. Nora crossed the road and started onto a rocky trail that switchbacked up the steep mesa. The path was ground to fine yellow powder by centuries of feet trudging through the village.

From time to time bunches of weeds survived, covered in yellow dust. A few food wrappers and other trash flitted across the ground on the dry, hot breeze. The sun beat on her; with no sunscreen or hat, she'd be crispy in a matter of minutes.

Nora topped out on the mesa and the savory smell of roasting meat struck her. The muffled sounds of men singing joined the constant beating drum. The people on the roof of a two-story building looked down the other side at whatever activity caused the singing and drumming.

She assumed the building held two stories because it rose that high above the mesa, but no windows showed on this side to indicate its structure. Built of natural rock, it became a part of the mesa as if it had been uncovered by shifting desert dirt. Cars and pickups ranging from shiny and new to rusting heaps, all under a coating of dust, crowded the narrow alley behind the building. Smatterings of Native Americans moved in and out of the confusion. Like any other outdoor celebration, they carried camp chairs, water, and bags full of necessities.

Nora approached a friendly looking older woman. "Is this the way to the dance?" A few heads turned toward her, but Nora didn't feel hostility or even much curiosity.

The older woman eyed Nora's jeans and though she didn't change expression, Nora felt chastised. "This your first time?"

How could she tell? Nora nodded. "I'm not sure what I'm supposed to do."

"Follow me," the woman said. She led Nora to the corner of the solid structure, where another building stood at a right angle leaving a narrow passage. People crowded into the opening all facing toward the drumming and singing. A young woman with a little girl about ten years old shuffled aside and made room for Nora. She nodded her head at the older woman.

The two buildings comprised half of the parameters of a village square, with an identical set of buildings making up the other half. Nora stood transfixed by the scene in front of her.

The plaza was about as wide as a basketball court and twice as long. Color, drums, and singing whirled around her as she tried to sort out the images. A circle of bare-chested men lined the length of the plaza—all wore masks, their long black hair falling down their backs. In a symphony of feathers, paint, leather, bells, plants, and animal skins, the men danced in their vibrant costumes, each one different from the others. Or maybe some looked similar to one another; the alien mix made it impossible for Nora to capture all the details.

The fifty or so men chanted and stomped their feet. Some held rattles they shook in rhythm to the drumming. It sounded like unintelligible syllables to Nora, but apparently they were singing words and verses because suddenly they all stepped back and turned in a line dance more synchronized and impressive than one in any cowboy bar.

"Wow." She couldn't muster more intelligent words.

The older woman didn't take her eyes from the dancing.

The dancers continued to sing and move in unison. The drums pounded, rattles kept time, spectators sat quietly and watched. Time and place vanished from her normal life of businesswoman in the middle of American society. Through the space between the buildings across the plaza, the desert stretched from the mesa into eternity. The sky offered bunches of clouds in the expanse above.

"What is this about?"

The woman whispered. "Those are the kachinas. They come from the sacred peaks every spring. They perform dances, most of them secret in the kivas. This is a summer dance. Just a celebration."

"What exactly *is* a kachina?"

The old woman considered before answering. "The kachinas represent things that are important to Hopi. There are more than three hundred of them. They act as a kind of go-between for Hopi and the supernatural world. Mostly they are spirits, like animals or ancestors or plants, clouds, stuff like that." She shut her mouth as if the conversation officially ended.

The celebration resembled a Fourth of July picnic. Smells of cooking wafted around the plaza. Women in aprons moved in and out of the houses, taking a moment to sit and watch the dance, then going back to attend to whatever emitted the wonderful aromas. Unlike the American holiday where children ran and shot off fireworks amid a buzz of activity, for the most part the crowd focused on the dancers. It seemed like a mix between church and a barbecue.

With a final hard pound of the drum the dancers stopped chanting and stamping their feet. The bells and rattles ceased, and the kachinas took up a moaning sound. Perhaps it was in lieu of applause. Their chorus sounded strange; like the deep cooing of doves or the low whine of dogs, but not really either of those. Maybe a combination. Maybe it was a Hopi amen.

A man in the middle of the circle shouted as the cooing accented whatever he said. Sometimes the drums beat or the rattles sounded. Several men moved from the circle to the crowd to distribute parcels of food. Nora couldn't unravel the mystery of why certain women received these. They offered no exchange of smiles and thank yous, as she'd expect. The women simply accepted the food and passed it back to other women, who disappeared through the doors with it. It looked like an arbitrary mixture, store-bought white bread, home-made cakes and pies, fresh vegetables, cooked ears of corn, melons, bags of chips—all gathered in various containers such as cardboard soda flats, plastic storage containers, baskets, and bowls.

The food distribution and oration went on for a while. Nora tucked herself next to a building, taking advantage of a sliver of shade. Time became irrelevant. How long did she stand watching the dancing and gift giving?

The kachinas eventually formed a line and exited the intersection of the buildings opposite Nora.

Whatever the ceremony meant, the Hopi had performed it in almost the exact same way for centuries. The masks and costumes might have gained a few modern touches over the years; the jingle bells on the dancers' legs wouldn't have been available until after Europeans brought trade goods, and there were probably other bits and pieces constructed of synthetic fabrics, though none were obvious to Nora. How was it possible that these customs—older than the castles in Europe—had survived intact?

The heat and yellow dirt yielded the answer. The mesa didn't welcome stray visitors. Outsiders who did venture up here didn't want to stay. Even early settlers coveted rich farmland and easy water sources. The harsh environment here kept the Hopi isolated and able to focus on the old ways.

Nora's gaze wandered back to the crowd and she realized how off-track she'd gotten. She couldn't waste time on a cultural mission. She needed to find Heather. With a thudding heart, she scanned the plaza. She finally spotted Heather on a rooftop across the plaza. At least she appeared uninjured from the lava tube blast.

Heather stood with folded arms, her body rigid. She had no interest in the plaza. Behind her, a decorated figure moved into sight. He towered above Heather. His hand shot out and grabbed her shoulder.

Alex.

Nora gasped and ran several steps across the plaza, but a glimpse of a familiar beaked nose and sunburned red skin stopped her in her tracks.

Big Elk.

TWENTY-EIGHT

IT WAS A REGULAR convict convention, with no law enforcement around to protect them. A costumed Alex now stood within a few feet of Heather, and they were alone on the rooftop. Nora could tell by his body language that he was very upset. Who knew what he could do to Heather up there?

And Big Elk. He hated Nora enough that her white hide would be worthless as soon as he saw her here on the rez.

Alex reached out and Heather let him touch her arm. Nora had to get up there without being seen. Even without horses available, being drawn and quartered seemed possible if Big Elk spied her.

Big Elk held several young women in thrall. He could look over here any time. He'd sic his minions on her and she'd disappear into the desert wind without a trace.

Sweat dribbled down Nora's spine and she dared not move from her shady safe spot. Big Elk now spoke to a middle-aged woman. She considered his words then shook her head and walked away.

Big Elk scowled after the woman. He glanced in the other direction and hurried from the plaza. Today's faithful following was noticeably devoid of Guilty White People. He must have thought they'd bring down his cred out here and asked them to stay away from the rez.

Alex pulled away from Heather and she reached to stop him. He shrugged her off and disappeared off the back of the rooftop.

Here was her chance. Nora lit out after Heather.

A hand on her arm made her squeal.

A man decked out in yellow mud with facial features painted in black frowned at her. He looked like a clown. "You can't go back there, miss. That's for the kachinas."

Heather disappeared down the back side of the building, following Alex.

"But a bunch of other people went that way."

He stared at her. "Only Hopi are allowed. The next dance will start pretty soon. You can go down and look at the art or try the piki bread."

"Sure. Thanks."

She felt the man's painted black eyes on her as she sauntered toward the displays. She had to grab Heather before the girl got into trouble, get her to come back to town with her, and keep away from knife-wielding Alex. But Nora couldn't just traipse off anywhere she wanted. Obviously, a white woman wandering by herself over the mesa spelled trouble.

The mud-caked man watched her. Many of the spectators had disappeared, and those left in the plaza visited with each other. Nora acted as if she intended to wait for the next dance.

She glanced behind her. The alley was empty. Wherever the audience went, they weren't loitering there. She looked back to the center of the plaza, her muddy guardian now nowhere in sight.

What to do? The rez was foreign territory—a misstep could get her into trouble and not help Heather.

But Big Elk shouldn't be here. Whatever he had planned might involve more explosions. Nora stepped out of the shade into the alley.

A hand clasped her arm, squeezing her heart into her throat. Expecting Alex or another of Big Elk's foot soldiers to drag her off and dismember her, Nora threw herself out of the grasp.

"Come on," someone hissed into her ear, "we've got to stop Big Elk."

Heather! Nora sucked in a breath. "Are you okay? Where's Alex?"

Heather pulled in a breath and straightened. She arranged her face into a calm mask. "I'm fine. You didn't need to come rescue me, but since you're here you can help. "

"How did you know I was here?"

Heather gave her an "oh, please" look. "You don't stand out at all."

Nice. "Let's get out of here before someone decides to kill me."

"We can't go. We have to save the dance."

Teenagers and their distorted sense of priorities. Big Elk plotting murder constituted a crisis, and Alex attacking Heather reeked of disaster; one ruined dance performance didn't really matter. "It's just a dance."

Heather glared at her. "You don't get it. Nothing is 'just' anything up here. Follow me."

"There will be other dances," Nora said, keeping close to Heather's back as they walked.

"Maybe there won't be any more. Maybe this is the last test and we fail."

"What makes you think this is a failure?"

"Big Elk. The guys need to be in their kivas doing whatever they do, and he's got them listening to his stupid shit instead."

"Kivas? What do they do?"

They wove between a rusty Ford pickup and a newer compact car. Heather said, "Every clan has a kiva they get into by a ladder through the roof. It represents the way people climbed from the Third Word to this one. I don't know what they do in the kivas. Each clan does their own secret ceremonies. And now they aren't doing it because of stupid Big Elk."

A young woman walked by with a baby on her hip. She nodded to Heather.

They rounded a corner and Nora saw the backs of three or four young men, Alex among them. Big Elk spoke, his face red.

Big Elk was nothing but a poseur out trying to stir up trouble to make himself important. As much as she'd like to charge into the center of the circle and wring his neck, her coward's heart balked. Nora pulled back, trying to slow Heather. "What do you want me to do?"

"I don't know. I saw you ram Poppy's car to prove a point. I thought you'd come up with something."

Nora felt her face flush in embarrassment. "That wasn't one of my best moments."

"We've got to do something. You think Alex can hurt me, but Big Elk can hurt *everyone*." Heather took Nora's hand and dragged her forward.

Bad idea, bad idea, her brain screamed. "Let's just … "

"Hey!" Heather yelled.

Clever plan, Heather.

Big Elk barely glanced up. His eyes flitted over Heather and lowered to the men, his mouth never ceasing the sales pitch. "The way to power is wealth. White people with money crave the spirituality and connection of the Hopi. They'll buy a kachina doll or pottery in hopes some of your wisdom will rub off. I'm telling you we can give them what they want and help the tribe at the same time."

But a few lines later, his gaze found Nora and his lips stopped moving. He straightened. The men in his circle turned to see what distracted him. Alex stiffened like a dog with raised hackles.

"Well, well." Big Elk swaggered past his posse to stand in front of Nora. "It's not enough you desecrate the sacred peak, you have to bring your vileness to the mesas?"

Heather shook her hair back. "I brought her here so she can understand the Hopi way. You're the one destroying the ceremony."

Big Elk raised his eyebrows. "Miss McCreary, Uranium Princess. Maybe you look Hopi, but we all know you're your daddy's little pawn. You want to rape this land and disrupt the balance."

The exchange drew a group of women. Except for the four young men with Big Elk, the other dancers must have gone in their kivas. These young men looked like a pack of hungry wolves waiting for their Alpha to turn them loose.

"I belong here," Heather said with a touch of defensiveness.

Big Elk turned to Alex. "What do you think? How dedicated is she to our cause?"

Alex's face looked as hard as his fingers around Nora's neck, his voice as sharp as the knife that sliced her ankle. "I'll take her back to Flagstaff."

"You want me to leave?" Heather's eyes couldn't hide the betrayal she felt.

Alex looked at Big Elk, waiting instruction.

Heather scowled at Big Elk. "The Hopi way is not one of inhospitality."

"How would you know the Hopi way?" Big Elk spat out. He jutted his chin toward Nora. "You're smoking the peace pipe with the enemy, babe."

"Nora is not the enemy," Heather said.

Big Elk shifted his malevolent force on Nora. "You killed your husband on sacred ground and the kachinas are punishing you. She's here to bring discord to the peaceful dance of the Hopi," Big Elk said, revving the angry men around him like race cars at the starting line.

Nora hoped her words wouldn't stick in the dry desert of her throat. "Big Elk has been desecrating the sacred peak himself."

"Enough talk," Big Elk said.

The young men crowded behind him.

Nora heard a quiver in her voice. "The kachinas weren't up there last night 'bringing fire to the mountain.' Big Elk manufactured the whole thing with some explosives and a couple of old white people."

Confidence oozed from Big Elk like blood from a tick. "You don't know what you're talking about."

"You made a good living by pretending. Why not tell them your real name, Ernie."

Big Elk stepped closer to Alex. "Don't listen to her. She's a deceitful *pahana*."

Her hands shook and her stomach churned, but Nora forged on. "Big Elk doesn't know about Hopi or respect for your land. Before he became Big Elk, champion of indigenous people, he was Ernie Finklestein, robber of the helpless."

Heather made a fist. "I knew it!"

Big Elk turned on Heather. "Go back to your white mansion. You have no business here."

Alex's face roiled with anger like a thunderstorm about to break loose.

Nora pointed at Big Elk. "He's importing fake Native American art that he plans to sell to line his pockets and ruin your people's reputation. Talk about angering the kachinas."

"I gave you a chance to walk away. Now it's too late." Destruction flashed in Big Elk's eyes.

The mud-caked clown who had accosted her in the plaza pushed his way from behind Alex. "What are you even doing here?"

"She's disrupting the dance! Spreading lies and discontent!" Big Elk said.

Heather sounded like a volatile teenager. "He's the bad one! The kachinas won't like what he's doing."

Big Elk directed Alex. "Get her out of here or I will."

Heather folded her arms. "I'm staying."

"Do it," Big Elk said.

"All right." The clown held up his hands in a calming gesture. "Let's settle down." He pointed to Heather. "She's from a powerful clan and has a right to be here." His gaze swung to Alex and the other young men. "I see some of you are Hopi. Go to your kivas." He addressed the others, including Big Elk. "The rest of you are from other tribes. You're welcome to observe the dance. But please stay in the plaza. This area is reserved for Hopi only."

He turned to Heather. "Sikyatsi, I'm glad to see you." His gaze held affection, then he shifted gears to business. "You're welcome here, but bringing her"—he nodded in Nora's direction—"wasn't a good idea. She should go now."

Gladly. With relief, Nora took a step backward.

Heather didn't move. "She's not leaving until he does." She pointed at Big Elk. "He shouldn't be here."

The clown sighed. "He's helping us to save our sacred mountain."

"He's ruining the dance and messing up the balance." She might as well have been stomping her feet and crying.

Since Heather wouldn't allow them to get away while they could, Nora added, "And he's using Hopi beliefs to manipulate you."

Big Elk's face turned redder than his usual sunburn. He looked over the clown's head to the young men behind. "We can't let this evil *pahana* destroy Hopi. Where will the kachinas live when the mountain is clear cut for skiing and water is pulled from the veins of the Mother and She is trampled on by white men's skis?"

When had the crowd multiplied? Where there had been four young men and some curious spectators, now what seemed like a large group of Native Americans glared at her.

"Everyone calm down," the clown said again, but his voice disappeared in Big Elk's bellow.

"Our ancestors didn't allow the *pahana* priests to destroy our way of life. In this time, when the Fourth World hangs in the balance, we need to have the courage of our grandfathers."

The clown held his hand up to silence Big Elk. "Hopi people value a humble life, self-respect, respect for others, compassion, integrity, self-control." He inhaled. "We are not activists in the white man's way. We protect the world by carrying out our clan responsibilities."

Nora took hold of Heather's arm. "Let's get out of here."

Heather pulled loose. "I'm not going." She raised her voice. "I belong here, and I won't let Big Elk ruin it."

Big Elk's shout rose above the mesa. "Lies from the rich white girl! This was foretold in prophecy—it's our duty to stop you."

"Now, Heather!" Nora said.

Any attempt at calm was drowned in Big Elk's ranting. Of course the people listened to Big Elk. In their eyes, the money-chasing whites—that would be Nora and Heather—had set out to destroy their sacred lands. They had lived and worshipped here for over a thousand years. The courts wouldn't listen, the governments wouldn't listen. Now frustration built to the breaking point.

Add a dance that was deeply rooted in religious significance, being on their own ground with their own people, and a talented instigator, and this combination could lead people to forget their normal sensibilities, embrace the mob mentality and ...

Big Elk continued to stir the pot. "We need to take extraordinary steps, like our grandfathers did when the white priests tried to ruin Hopi with their baptism. If we don't, it will be like the time of Lololama, when they took our children to their white schools and tried to wipe us out. But we won't let them this time."

Nora grabbed Heather's arm and tried to run.

Heather fought her. "We're responsible for the balance of the world. I can't let this bastard ruin it all!"

Alex lurched forward and grabbed Heather around the waist. He jerked her backward, pulling her into himself and off her feet.

Heather's arm was wrenched from Nora's grasp. "Heather!"

Alex backed into the growing crowd. They closed ranks and Heather disappeared. Two of the young men moved with purpose toward Nora.

TWENTY-NINE

"You shit!" Though Nora couldn't see Heather, there was no mistaking the fury in her voice.

Nora lunged after Heather only to face a wall of thugs. No way could she get through them. Rescuing Heather became impossible. Rescuing herself was up for grabs as well.

"You disrupted our sacred ceremony and brought evil to the mesa." Big Elk's words diced the air like a razor through flesh.

One young man pulled back like a ball in a pinball machine, ready to fly forward, grab Nora by the neck, and draw her into the pack to be torn limb from limb.

She spun away before he could spring.

Nora wove through the cars and bumped startled women, certain she outpaced the younger, stronger men by only a few steps.

She raced to the path, dodging rocks and pits, praying she didn't slide off the side of the steep slope. Her legs stretched and she felt the impact of each footfall up her back. Her blood pounded: *faster, faster.*

Shouts melted into a roar. Even though she ran past the vendors and crafts booths, no one tried to stop her. Nora dashed forward, not knowing where she headed.

Pot holes and ragged concrete made the road treacherous, and she concentrated on each step to keep from crashing into the dirt. She dared not slow enough to look behind her, but she heard feet pounding and heavy breathing. Any moment a hand would slam on her shoulder, grab her shirt, drag her to the ground.

Then what? They'd take her to the mesa ledge and toss her over to dash on the rocks below. Maybe Hopi believed in peace and hospitality, but some of Big Elk's guys belonged to less friendly tribes. Her shattered death would bookend Scott's.

Nora turned off the main road onto a path that narrowed into an alley between two stone houses. This part of the village looked as if it had grown from the desert of its own volition. Ancient, crumbling; ashes to ashes, dust to dust. No one here would help her. Nora's last moments on this Earth would be spent running for her life.

The dirt path of the alley T-boned and Nora ran to the right. The houses crumbled away until there was only a low wall on either side. The last turn proved to be a fatal mistake.

The walls ended. Nothingness lay beyond them. Nothing except the edge of the mesa ... and death. She faced the same fate as those priests four hundred years ago. Broken and bleeding under a culture they didn't understand.

She ran on parallel to the edge, hoping to see a path down the side of the mesa. The sheer cliff wall dropped impossibly far to rocks below. Like a cornered dog, she turned to face her enemy. Panting and frantic, Nora could do nothing but watch them approach.

Two young men stopped about fifteen feet away. The taller one squinted at her. "Now where're you gonna go?"

The other one, sweat dripping through the dust on his chest, said, "She's goin' down."

"You insulted our Mother."

They walked toward her. "You shouldn't have messed with our peak."

They blocked all paths of retreat. The mesa formed a point and she stood at its apex, nowhere to go but the rocks below. "This isn't the sixteen hundreds. You guys will ruin your lives if you kill me."

The tall one shrugged. "If we let you make snow, our kachinas will turn their backs on us. Then the lives of all the people will be ruined."

The sweaty one took two quick steps, his arms up, ready to push her.

Nora swung to the side and he missed, losing his balance. He didn't go down, but humiliation burned in his face. He let out a growl and lunged for her again.

Nora sidestepped, but he wasn't fooled again. The man crouched like a football linebacker and moved with her. His hands connected with her shoulders.

She couldn't scream. Could only understand that her life was over. Her body anticipated free fall. The painful crush of pointed rocks. Blood, broken, death.

But she didn't fall backward. Strong, small hands on her back held her upright.

The man in front of her staggered backward himself, as if she had shoved him instead of the other way around.

The little kachina salesman stepped from around her. He glared at the two younger men and spoke in a quiet voice. His Hopi words carried an obvious message of shame.

They paled. Stepped back. Lowered their eyes.

The little man barely moved his head but he made eye contact with Nora and, in a gesture so slight she wasn't sure he did anything, he indicated she needed to follow him.

Dizzy at the prospect of escape, Nora struggled to keep up with the man's sure-footed gait, especially since she kept turning around to see if the men chased them.

This little man must be a revered elder to have such an impact on the thugs. Maybe he could make Alex let Heather go.

The kachina man trotted around the last corner and pointed to Heather's RAV4. Alex must have driven Heather out here using her car after the lava tube explosion near the ski resort.

Heather paced in front, looking the opposite direction. Like warm honey, relief spread through Nora.

He nodded in dismissal.

Nora bowed her head, not sure how to express gratitude to him. "Thank you."

He nodded again.

"What did you say to them?" she asked.

He spoke slowly, his words halting. "I said this is not the Hopi way, to harm people. We are a people of peace."

"That did it?"

"They are not Hopi. Navajo."

"And they obeyed you anyway?"

He shrugged. "Our mother villages have mysterious powers to protect. If someone defies the power, we all suffer. Maybe all humankind."

This guy should be president. He should be mediating in the Middle East. Such simple words and she felt compelled to spread peace and harmony throughout the world. She believed it could actually make a difference.

"Nora!" Heather ran toward her. "Where were you? What happened?"

Heather launched herself into Nora's arms and exploded in a monsoon of tears.

With equal relief at Heather's safety, Nora hugged back. "I'm fine. Are you okay?"

But Nora couldn't make sense of the sobs. Something about Heather's embrace and tears tapped Nora's heart like a tiny jeweler's hammer. This girl with the courage of a lion owned the vulnerable heart of a child.

Nora let loose with her own storm of tears, holding Heather close. When was the last time someone had touched her with this much raw love? She'd suffered her mother's dutiful hugs, the well wishes of Scott's friends. She'd appreciated Charlie's affectionate pats. But this girl cracked open the shell of her heart and it gushed with pain and loss—but also with hope and healing.

THIRTY

Barrett's Hopi contact leaned against the black Mercedes with his arms crossed. The shade of the juniper concealed the meeting from the interstate but didn't do much to buffer the roar of semis running down I-40.

Barrett had faced any manner of business problems in the past and overcome personal tragedies that would leave a lesser man a puddle of slush. But the last few years he had relaxed into complacency. He relied on the easy pickings of the energy boom and the domestic tranquility of a daughter who adored him.

All that had changed in the last six months. His emotional and intellectual softness needed to harden into granite again. He needed to be the Barrett McCreary III he used to be.

He gave the councilman a steady stare. "You said the Tribal Council was on board. They've got to know uranium mining will make the Hopi a rich people."

The man shrugged. "Rich don't always matter to Hopi. The elders don't want nothing to do with mining after the sickness last time. But the younger ones, some of them want the electricity and water lines brought to the mesas."

"Big Elk said he was making progress with the elders." Scalding blood pumped into Barrett's brain. Just the opposite of his cool-headed image.

The cadence of the councilman's voice sounded as if a drum beat in his head. "It's Benny. He's against uranium and lots of guys listen to what he says. Big Elk ain't convincing no one to go for uranium. He's just gettin' the younger ones mad."

"Doesn't matter now that Big Elk isn't around anymore."

"I don't know who told you that. He's out at the rez right now. He's got them so's nobody's even thinkin' about uranium."

Barrett had sprung Big Elk from jail in hopes he'd hold up his end of the Hopi deal. He should have known Big Elk wouldn't act with any honor. "What's it going to take to change a couple of votes? Another clinic? A school? Untraceable cash? What does Benny want?" There was always a price, and this one wouldn't be cheap.

The Hopi man's face showed little emotion. Indians hardly ever did. "I can ask, but I don't know how far I'll get. The people are gettin' pretty worked up now, with the government okaying the snow making and the woman laying pipe and all."

"Get me the votes and you'll be a rich man."

Barrett slid behind the wheel of his Mercedes, leaving the Hopi man to his dilapidated pickup. He drove over the hill and out of the juniper.

The peaks commanded the landscape along the highway. His peaks. Barrett ticked through the issues needing his attention as he waited for a break in the sparse line of cars so he could merge onto the highway.

Deavonshire assured him the congressional committee was leaning toward allowing existing claims to go ahead. Barrett could start work on the current mines, but that wouldn't make major expansion possible. He needed the Hopi endorsement. Barrett shuffled the uranium mining issue to the bottom of his agenda.

Big Elk had become too much of a liability. He punched in a number on his phone and when a low voice answered, Barrett gave the details.

Now, the next problem: water had to be pumped onto the mountain immediately. More importantly, he needed to find and destroy Scott Abbott's papers before someone figured out why Barrett wanted the water pumped.

He turned the Mercedes onto the highway and headed for the mountain.

Next, he had to check on Heather. Without looking, he took his phone from his shirt pocket, flipped it open, and pushed speed dial for the house. No answer.

Goddamn it. When she'd called last night and said she was staying with her ditzy friend Sheryl, she promised to be home early to clean horse stalls. This rebellion phase of hers had to stop.

Barrett simmered in a stew of problems, making phone calls to lobbyists and staffers the whole drive to Kachina Peak.

Sun sifted through the pines and dappled the hood of Barrett's Mercedes as he pulled into Kachina Ski's parking lot. Good, the decaying wreck of a Jeep was gone, so he assumed the raving redhead wasn't home.

He stepped out of his SUV and started toward the lodge, pasting on a pleasant face and formulating a plan of attack. He'd put off getting rid of Scott's papers too long. He didn't usually let loose ends dangle like this.

Maybe after the pumps were up and running here and he'd made a start on the uranium mines, he'd take Heather on an extended vacation. Get her away from everything Hopi. His chest loosened slightly. Good plan.

He clumped up the deck stairs and into the lodge. "Hello." He waited for his eyes to adjust to the gloom. No one answered him. He tried again. Silence.

Barrett knew a gift when he received it. He retreated, heading for the deck. Seemed strange Nora would keep Scott's things. If it were him, he'd have sifted through the leavings looking for anything of value and destroyed anything else. But women thought differently. Nora would probably cry over that stupid box for years.

Barrett planned to grab the box from the bedroom closet and reduce it into ashes within an hour. He reached for the screen door but it opened, startling him.

Abigail looked up and yelped. She sucked in a breath and let it out, a welcome smile spreading across her face. "Oh. Barrett. You scared me."

Barrett met her smile, feeling that goofy balloon in his chest. What an exquisite woman. Her face glowed smooth as porcelain. Her eyes lit up with an enchanting sparkle. He felt foolish and delighted in a way he hadn't felt in years—no, decades.

Right now, though, he needed to find Scott's papers and get rid of them. "Abigail. It's wonderful to see you."

She gave him that inviting smile he longed to see in his bed. "It's always nice to see you. What are you doing all the way out here?"

"I wanted to see if the sprayers had been delivered. We've got a tight schedule if we want to have snow for Christmas."

"You could have just called. No sprayers, it's been quiet out here."

She usually offered him something to eat or drink by now. What was the holdup? "Could I trouble you for a glass of water? I am really dry."

"Of course. Come up."

He followed her up the stairs, enjoying the gentle sway of her hips. His blood rushed to pleasant places. Yes, he'd have to find a way to keep Abigail.

Not an item seemed out of place in the little apartment. Abigail hurried to the kitchen. "I'm afraid we don't have bottled water. Nora insists it's environmentally abusive. But I made mint tea this morning."

"That would be wonderful." At least he didn't sound as frantic as he felt.

She handed him the tea, and he took a sip. "That's great."

She seemed pleased. "I picked the mint behind the lodge so I suppose it would pass Nora's test for natural."

"You aren't having any?"

"I hate to fill up on too much tea. I'll have to excuse myself all afternoon if I do." The way she said it made him think she was trying to tell him something.

He noticed her handbag and a notebook sitting on the table. "I'm sorry. I should have asked sooner, are you on your way out?"

She smiled in that enticing way again. "It is my club afternoon. I'm secretary, which is funny, really, since I'm the newcomer. But I wanted to get involved in the community and this club does such good work."

"Oh, I'll get out of your hair." Where was Nora?

She gestured toward the sofa. "Don't be silly. Please sit and enjoy your tea. I've got a couple of minutes."

She pushed him to sit and perched on the sofa arm, swinging her foot.

He started to get up. "I'm keeping you."

She put a hand on his shoulder. "You just sit. Finish your tea. But I do have to run downstairs and get something. I'll be right back."

Barrett couldn't have scripted this any better. "Thank you, Abigail. You're amazing."

"Oh, you." She giggled like someone thirty years younger and hurried out the door. Oh yes, he wanted her. No reason he couldn't have her.

The door clicked shut and Barrett moved as quickly as his bulk allowed. He dumped the disgusting tea down the drain and returned his glass to the coffee table, only losing twenty seconds. Another couple ticked away as he hurried into the bedroom.

They lived like mice in a box. Abigail would love his spacious home with its open floor plan and towering windows, plenty of closets and cabinets to store all the pretty things he'd buy her.

Barrett opened the closet and plunged into the back where he and Heather had placed that stupid box the other day.

Gone. She'd moved it.

He spun, frantically searching the room. A filing cabinet shoved into a corner. What was stored inside? Did Scott keep copies? He ought to blow up the whole place to make sure there were no loose ends. This slum would be no big loss.

A memory blindsided him. He'd lived in more cramped quarters than this. It had been the happiest time of his life. Their bed was nothing but a mattress on the floor, the crib crammed next to the threadbare sofa. Flyers for the next rally sat on a Formica table. He stretched out on the rumpled sheets with his daughter sitting on his flat belly chattering about sister stars. Ester clattered the dented coffeepot and lit a match to the rusting stove. He loved to watch her naked body move with such fluid motion. His son made sucking noises from the crib.

Ester insisted they rise and greet the sun on the mesa so she could offer corn dust and prayers. In those moments he had everything he ever needed.

"Barrett?" Abigail's voice jerked him from the mesa memories.

Damn it. He'd lost time and opportunity. Was he losing his mind, as well?

"What are you doing?" she asked, her eyes sweeping the bedroom for clues.

He cleared his throat. "I'm sorry. I know this is rude. I have to confess I didn't come up here because I was thirsty."

"Oh?" Her eyes narrowed in suspicion.

Barrett tried not to look at the closet door; instead he walked to the window. "I wanted to see the view. I think this lodge could use an overhaul. Maybe even a scrape off and start over."

Her eyes lit up.

If spending money made her glow like this, he'd make sure she never had another bad day. "That's a good idea."

At least he hit upon a decent excuse and maybe not such a bad idea after all. "If we incorporate a living quarters in a new lodge what should it look like?"

She joined him at the window. "It should be much larger. And more secure. I feel completely exposed up here."

Her soft scent tickled his nose.

"I hate to chase you out, Barrett, but I do need to get going if I'm going to be on time."

He nodded. "What about storage? This apartment doesn't seem to have much closet space."

Her laughter tinkled. "Closets are a myth here."

"It must have been cramped with Nora and Scott here. There can't be much space for your things."

She blushed, probably thinking he made an overture about moving her out. "We manage."

"Are all of Scott's belongings still here?"

She led him from the room and sighed. "I've urged Nora to clean it out. I've been through this before and the sooner you bring yourself to discard the belongings, the sooner you move on."

"How is she doing?"

"She's made little progress, I'm afraid." Abigail picked up her handbag from the table and reached for a peg by the door. "Oh, poo."

Poo?

"I forgot Nora's gone with the Jeep. You wouldn't mind taking me to town, would you?"

He held the door for her. "Of course." It felt right having this attractive, charming woman in his life. She might provide the missing piece to settle Heather and give her a true sense of home. With Abigail they would be the family Heather longed for.

Abigail descended the apartment stairs and didn't hesitate before stepping across the deck. He followed her to the parking lot, the idea sounding better with each step.

The iron seemed hot enough for him to strike now. "Abigail, there's something I want to say."

The slightest impatience darted into her eyes, and he decided that would be the color of the aquamarine ring he'd buy for her.

He reached out and took her delicate hand, youthful passion tingling in his veins. "I've grown more than fond of you."

A rosy blush appeared on her cheeks. "Barrett, I ... "

He squeezed her hand. "Let me finish. Since I've met you, I can think of little else. I hope I'm not out of line when I say I think you feel the same way."

For the first time he saw her control slip. That he could catch her off guard and send her heart racing made him bolder.

"We're not youngsters, and I'd like to spend whatever years we have left together. Will you marry me?"

The roses vanished from her cheeks, leaving a floury shock. Her lips lost the lift of her perpetual smile, revealing crevices in her cheeks and wrinkles around her mouth.

He'd made a terrible miscalculation.

Her hand jerked as if she'd like to pull it away. "Barrett. That's sweet … "

He wiped the sappy look from his face. "I caught you by surprise." He laughed. "To tell the truth, I surprised myself. I got carried away by the moment. Please excuse my impulsiveness."

"I don't know what to say."

"Let's just forget the whole thing."

"This is unexpected. And I'm flattered, of course. I am terribly fond of you."

A police cruiser turned into the parking lot. That put an end to that conversation. The officer climbed from the car and approached them. He nodded to Barrett and addressed Abigail. "Ms. Stoddard. Is Ms. Abbott around?"

"Good afternoon, Gary," she said, always the perfect hostess. "Nora isn't home."

"Do you know where she is?"

"She left early this morning to bring Heather home from the reservation."

Heather's on the rez? A sledgehammer crashed into Barrett's brain.

Thoughts might be processing in Gary's head as he stood looking up at the lodge. "I have a warrant to search the lodge and apartment."

Abigail gasped. "You will do no such thing. What possible reason would you have for this outrage?"

"As a person of interest in two homicides, searching Nora's home is routine."

Searching this place, with Scott's papers somewhere inside, could not happen. Barrett contemplated how to step in.

Abigail lifted her chin. "I won't allow it."

Gary let out another exhale. He seemed to have a lot of air in him. "I need to ask you a few questions too," he said to Abigail. "Can you come down to the station?"

"Now?"

Gary nodded. "Now would be good. You can ride with me."

"I'm sorry. I have a previous engagement."

Gary held up his hand as if directing traffic toward his cruiser. "I'll bring you back when we're through."

Barrett's jaw ached where he clenched his teeth. *What the hell was Heather doing on the rez?* But more urgently, he had to make sure the cops didn't find Scott's fucking papers.

Barrett stepped close to Abigail and put an arm around her. "I'll call my attorney and have him meet you there."

Now came the grateful eyes. He felt tides shifting inside Abigail as it became clear to her what Barrett could do for her. She was a bright woman. "Thank you, dear."

He nodded in his most protective way.

She leaned into him. "Could you please follow us to the station? I don't want to be there alone." Before she slid into the cruiser beside Gary, she sought Barrett's eyes. "The answer to your question is yes."

He watched them drive away, his mind shifting into overdrive. Even if he didn't have to go hold Abigail's hand, he wouldn't have time to search the apartment thoroughly, and there was no telling what he'd leave behind for the cops to find.

Scott's papers. Heather on the rez. Big Elk fucking up his plans. Alex getting dangerous too.

Barrett certainly had business to attend to.

THIRTY-ONE

THE HORIZON STRETCHED ACROSS sparse grassland. Rain clouds threatened a patch of desert miles away. The speedometer of Heather's SUV wavered around ninety. Nora wanted to put miles between them and the mesas as fast as possible. She hated leaving her Jeep on the rez, but Heather was in no shape to drive herself.

Heather's head rested on the center console, and Nora laid her arm over the girl's shoulder. They'd barely made it to the highway before Heather fell asleep.

Nora stroked Heather's black hair, soothing the child as she slept. What a fiercely courageous girl with a committed heart. But so blind.

At sixteen Nora had also been full of insecurity and angst. Abigail circulated in a world of Junior League fundraisers and cocktail parties. She introduced Nora to preppy boys in Izod shirts who were "going places."

And Nora snuck out the back door during formal dinner parties to hike in the foothills. She wore Birkenstocks and jeans with holes in the knees. Maybe to the world she looked committed to saving the Earth as she passed petitions for Green Peace and protested the Rocky Flats Nuclear Facility outside of Denver. She listened while friends ranted about the evils of capitalism, took hits off the passed joint, and nodded her head when they complained about how grades were just society's way to control the creativity of youth.

Then she went home and did her homework, studied college catalogues, and dreamed of a corner office on the eighteenth floor. Being valedictorian pleased her mother, disgusted her friends, and left her feeling like she usually did: without a place.

Nora couldn't offer any advice or answers to Heather. She was still a misfit—a nature lover trying to make a living off exploiting the land.

But making snow responsibly wouldn't ruin the mountain. Would it?

Heather stirred and sat up. "Where are we?"

"About ten miles from the interstate. Fifty miles and counting from the rez."

Heather nodded and stared out the window. "He said I was from a powerful clan."

"Who said?"

"Benny. The clown. He knows who I am. He knows my mother. Children take on their mother's clan."

"Is Cole's friend the same Benny as the clown? How would he know about you?"

Heather smiled with satisfaction. "I'm going to find out who I am."

They rode in silence for a while.

"Alex said he loves me." Heather's voice sounded as weak as a melted ice cube.

Nora thought about not answering but couldn't keep her mouth shut. "Kidnapping you isn't a good way to show love."

Heather swallowed hard. "I would have gone with him even if I hadn't been out of it."

"He didn't seem to have any trouble stealing your car. You sure he didn't hurt you?" Nora asked for the hundredth time.

Heather shook her head and studied the passing landscape. "Not this time."

That stabbed at Nora's gut. "What do you mean?"

"He's scary. We had a fight about Big Elk earlier and he told me he'd do whatever Big Elk told him to do, that it's time for Hopi to quit being passive and take charge."

"Was that on the roof today?"

Heather nodded. "I tried to break up with him, but he wouldn't let me." She sounded like she almost couldn't believe it had happened.

Nora shifted her glance from the road to see Heather's frightened eyes.

"I don't know what he'll do, but he scared me."

"You have to stay away from him."

"He's changed."

"Maybe you're getting to know him better."

Heather's voice hardened like cooled lava. "It's Big Elk."

"Alex was probably a creep before Big Elk, but Big Elk knows how to bring out the asshole in people."

"I think we were warned about Big Elk. The prophecies say a *pahana,* a white guy, will try to destroy Hopi and we have to be strong and not follow."

"What prophecies?"

"We have all these amazing prophecies from over a thousand years ago, and they've all come true."

"Such as?"

Heather counted off on her fingers. "Roads in the sky. Those are jets' contrails. They say there would be moving houses of iron, and those are trains. Horseless carriages are cars. They said we'd be able to speak through cobwebs. Pretty descriptive of phone wires, don't you think?"

"How do you know these were given a thousand years ago?"

"They've been passed down in the stories. Here's a scary one. They said that an upside-down gourd of ashes would explode in the sky and cause rivers to boil and bring disease that medicine can't cure. That's the atomic bomb."

"Okay, so back to the *pahana* one."

"I always thought it meant Poppy. It says the *pahana* will gather us under his wings and feed us and care for us because he sees something underneath that he wants. And soon we'll be dependent on him and act like his servants and give away the Mother."

"I can see Barrett in that."

Heather shook her head. "But it could be Big Elk, turning the young men away from the true way. Even if he's not the evil one in the prophecies, we need to stop him."

Except he slithered away from restraints like a snake. He stole pensions and stirred normal people to criminal acts, and still he sashayed out of prison like a prom queen at her coronation.

"Yes, he needs to be stopped. But not by you," Nora said.

"Then who?" This girl may be adopted, but her determination and the look in her eyes made Nora think of Barrett.

"What about the man dressed as a clown? He tried to talk reason to them," Nora said.

"Benny? Look how much good he did."

"But weren't the other elders in the kivas? There's got to be enough of them to calm the young ones down."

"The thing is, Big Elk has a point. We need to protect the peak for the kachinas. A lot of people are getting frustrated. They might see this as the time to act."

"What about the whole Hopi concept of peace?"

Heather's voice rose in frustration. "What has that gotten us? Sure, Hopi believe in peace, but we also need to keep balance and take care of the land."

"I thought you were against Big Elk?"

Heather slammed her palm onto the seat. "That's just it. I know Big Elk is wrong. But everything is out of control and something has to happen. We need guidance."

"Don't you have a Tribal Council?"

"The council can't agree on anything."

"What about a chief?"

"A *kikmongwi*? Each village has its own. In Hopi every person gets to make their own decisions. The government doesn't make laws. People use persuasion and discussion to get agreement."

"What about that old man who helped me?"

"What old man?"

Nora felt a growing irritation, as if Heather wasn't trying to find a solution. "That old guy who walked me off the mesa. He's the same one who keeps trying to sell me kachina dolls."

"I didn't see anyone with you."

"He's little and wrinkled and old. He wears knee-length moccasins and a long tunic shirt."

Heather raised her eyebrows at the urgency in Nora's voice. "I haven't seen him."

How could she be oblivious? The man had been right there. "He wore his hair in a bowl cut and it looked sort of ragged. He looked so odd. I can't believe you didn't notice him."

Heather shrugged. "Sounds like a real traditional guy." She hoisted herself to her knees and reached into the backseat. "Anyway. I got these for Abigail." She turned around with a library book, plopped it on her knees, and started turning pages.

Oh the resilience of youth, thought Nora. A minute ago Heather was ready to blow up, now she flipped pages like she was perusing a fashion magazine.

A whole array of black-and-white photos passed under Heather's fingers. She stopped at a picture of a little man standing in front of a dusty stone house. "Here is how they used to dress."

Nora glanced at the photo. "That's him. That's the guy."

Heather rolled her eyes. "They all look alike to you, huh?"

This kid could be so annoying. "No. They don't all look alike. This is the guy. He's got that unique look in his eyes."

Heather stared at the book. "Can't be."

"Why not?"

"This is Nakwaiyamtewa. He's one of the greatest *kikmongwis* the Hopi have ever known."

"That's what I mean. You need him to straighten out the Hopi."

"Nora, he died like a hundred years ago."

Karate chop to the gut. Nora pressed the brakes and pulled the RAV4 to the side of the empty road.

"What?" Heather's eyes opened wide in alarm.

"Let me see that." The book lay on Heather's lap and Nora pulled it close, studying the little man. No doubt. This was the same man, except in the picture, he didn't wear the blue sash.

That proved it. She was crazy. She dropped the book back into Heather's lap and stared into the sandy desert.

Heather touched her arm. "What's the matter?"

Nora didn't understand it and didn't want to tell anyone in case they locked her up. "I swear that is the guy."

Heather looked at the picture, then back at Nora, considering. "The spirits of ancestors can become kachinas."

Great. Now she was being haunted by an old chief. No, not chief. Heather called him a *kikmongwi*. Much better than an ordinary chief.

"I'm sure there's an explanation. Like maybe Scott's kachina was Alex. And he didn't really disappear, he went into the lava tubes."

"What do you mean?"

"Before he died, Scott said he saw a kachina in the forest who warned him not to make snow."

Heather stared at Nora. "It wasn't Alex. He just made that costume yesterday." Some tinny rap song blared from a bag in the backseat. Heather jumped and reached for her bag. "It's probably Poppy. What time is it?"

Nora glanced at the clock in the dash. "Three ten."

Phone in hand, Heather plopped back in the seat. Worry creased her forehead. "It's not his number."

Damn it. Nora knew that expression. "Where does he think you are?"

The phone continued to blare and Heather gave her a mischievous grin. "Spending the night with a friend. It's okay—I told him I'd be home early and I'm only a little late now. No biggie."

No biggie, you just lied to your sure-to-be-irate father who I suspect already doesn't like me much. Nora put the car into gear and pulled back onto the road.

Heather thumbed a button on the phone and held it to her ear. "Hello. Hi!" she settled back. "You won't believe what happened. This guy on the rez called me by a Hopi name. *Sikyatsi.* I think it means little bird or something like that. Anyway, he knows who I am. When I asked him about it, he wouldn't tell me any more but I'm going to find out. Maybe from Charlie." She listened a moment. "Because Charlie said he knows a lot of Hopi. Said he spent lots of time there when he was young. He's got to know my real parents."

233

While Heather chatted in her animated way, Nora resorted to her constant state of worry. First, there was Big Elk and his followers. Should she go to the cops? They had no jurisdiction on the rez and had already proved they couldn't keep hold of him. Then there was Nakwa-What's His Name, the ancient *kikmongwi*. And that was too bizarre to figure out. Now she'd probably have to face a livid Barrett for bringing Heather home late and from somewhere other than where she was supposed to be: not her favorite thing.

Heather tapped Nora's arm with the phone. "It's for you."

"What?"

"Your mother."

The cherry on the top of a disaster sundae. Nora took the phone. "You have Heather's number?"

"Of course. I also have her e-mail and have friended her on Facebook. She's my *friend*. You remember about having friends, don't you?"

The little Abigail inside Nora's head banged a sledgehammer against the backside of her forehead.

"It's a good thing Heather had her phone. Yours is in the apartment," Abigail said.

One hand on the wheel and her eyes straight ahead, Nora said, "What do you want, Mother?"

"Oh. Well. I just wondered when you'd be home."

The sledgehammer thudded inside her head. Dick Cheney and his gang had nothing on her mother. They could have conserved buckets of water if they'd used Abigail instead of waterboarding.

"Cole called this afternoon. He's such a nice man and so concerned about you. Really, Nora, he's quite a catch."

"Mother." The word packed so much warning Heather raised questioning eyebrows.

"All right."

"If you only called me to matchmake with Cole, thanks but no thanks. I'll be home later."

Abigail drew in a breath and let it out. "I have something I want to discuss with you."

"I thought you had your club meeting today."

Abigail let out a sigh. "I did. But your officer friend, Gary, decided to search your apartment."

"What?"

Abigail lowered her voice. "Don't worry. I put him off and he ended up taking me to town for questioning."

Thud, thud, thud. The tiny Abigail fiend worked on Nora's brain.

"Barrett sent his attorney to help me and when the man showed up, I excused myself to go to the powder room."

"That's good, Mother."

"I didn't have to use the facilities, Nora."

"Okay."

She paused. "I snuck out and ran to the club meeting and had Marilyn drive me home."

Nora snapped to attention. "You left a police interrogation?"

"Just like Emma Peale. Now I'm home. What do I need to hide before the cops get here?"

"You think I've got something to hide? You think I murdered Scott and his girlfriend?" Even calling Maureen Scott's girlfriend made her heart feel like a bruised pear.

"Don't be ridiculous, darling. Of course you didn't murder anyone. But everyone has something to hide. Like maybe," she whispered, "a vibrator."

"Mother!"

"Oh please. We're both grown-ups. I don't know where you keep yours, but I thought you might want me to get rid of it."

The Abigail in Nora's skull found another sledgehammer and delightedly slammed them both into Nora's head.

"Wait." Abigail said.

Nora waited.

"Someone is outside," Abigail whispered.

"Mother."

"Shhh."

"Mother!"

"I'm going to hang up now." Nora strained to hear Abigail's words. "Hurry home."

"Call the cops," Nora said.

"I can't do that. They think I'm in interrogation."

"I'm on my way home."

"One more thing," Abigail still whispered. "Don't tell Heather, I'm sure her father wants to be the one. But congratulations are in order."

Nora's stomach now throbbed too.

"Barrett asked me to marry him and I've accepted!"

THIRTY-TWO

MAYBE ABIGAIL THOUGHT SHE was playing some *Cagney & Lacey* game, but life didn't mimic TV where everything always worked out. Scott's and Maureen's murders proved that. An hour ago Abigail told Nora someone lurked at the lodge. Abigail's phone had put all messages to voicemail since then, and Nora had raced back to Flagstaff with growing concern.

Now she and Heather sped up the mountain road toward home.

A hint of anxiety crept into Heather's voice. "Poppy's going to be mad."

"Because you ran off with your boyfriend and ended up in the middle of a lynch mob?"

"Ex-boyfriend." Heather rolled her eyes.

"Parents can be so unreasonable." Was Abigail alright?

Nora whipped into the Kachina Ski parking lot and jumped out of Heather's car. "For the record, I don't blame him."

Heather followed. "Now you're going to go all adult on me."

Her heart hammered while she rushed up the path. "Being irresponsible is not cool."

"That sounded just like your mother."

The mother she hoped would be waiting with musty mint tea and tales of outwitting the cops.

Heather hurried beside Nora. "I really like your mom, but this whole dating thing with Poppy is creepy."

Even if it meant Abigail moving out, taking all her perfectly hung clothes on newly purchased hangers, packing the potions lining the bathroom counter, and eliminating processed foods from her refrigerator, the idea of Abigail with Barrett gnawed at Nora too. "Why do you say that?"

"He's my father and I love him and all that, but . . . " A raven cawed while she hesitated. "He's like a king. People always do what he says, even if they don't want to. I'm afraid he'll change Abigail. She'll turn into a robot, like everyone else around him."

"Are you afraid that's what will happen to you?"

Heather laugh. "Poppy won't ruin me. I'm so much like him I'm worried I'll ruin other people."

Heather and Nora climbed the deck stairs.

Charlie and Cole stood by the lodge door so immersed in their conversation that they didn't hear Heather and Nora approach. They looked up, startled.

"What's going on?" Nora asked.

Cole pushed his hair from his forehead. "Benny said you caused all kinds of trouble at the rez."

Nora shrugged. "I brought Heather home in one piece." Barely.

"Damn it, Nora. Why didn't you tell me you were going to Hopi-land?"

"Like you and Charlie tell me everything?"

"Now, honey," Charlie started.

She interrupted him. "Where's Abigail?"

Charlie looked sad. "She's at her club meeting. You didn't notice the muted colors of the mountain?"

It would break Charlie's heart when he found out Abigail was engaged to Barrett.

"She didn't go to the meeting," Heather said.

Nora looked up at the apartment and a jolt of fear hit her. "Didn't you fix that window?" she asked Charlie.

He followed her gaze to see the edge of the screen peeled back.

Cole's head whipped toward the window.

A crowbar lay in the shadow of the deck railing, as if dropped from the window. Why hadn't she seen that before? Nora sniffed the air. "Propane."

Charlie cocked his grizzled head. "You smell gas?"

"Where's the tank?" Cole was already moving to the back of the lodge where Nora pointed.

Heather sniffed. "Now I smell it."

Charlie inhaled deeply. "Nose ain't been the same since the Radio Fire in ninety-nine."

Nora leapt for the apartment stairs. "Mom!"

Charlie pushed Nora back with surprising force for a degenerating alcoholic. He cleared two stairs with his first leap, Nora on his heels. "Abigail!"

"Mom!"

Charlie reached the landing while Nora was only halfway up the stairs. It felt as if cement filled her shoes. She imaged Abigail collapsed on the living room floor, her face contorted in agony, gassed and left for dead.

Charlie pulled the door. Locked! Someone had snuck in the window and locked the door on the way out. They probably hid inside before Abigail got home. And Abigail, pumped from her jailhouse escape, wouldn't notice a crowbar or wrecked window.

"Abigail!" Charlie's voice sounded like Nora's heart, splitting with fear. He lunged for the window, wrenching the screen. Nora grabbed a corner, her hand ripping on the sharp metal. She braced herself and pulled it back. Charlie dove inside.

"Mom!" Propane wafted around Nora.

"I've got her," Charlie yelled. "Stay back." He coughed. "There's too much blood."

Blood? "No!" Nora fought the screen. *What blood?*

Charlie coughed again.

"I'm coming," she yelled.

"Don't … "

Ka-whump!

The world erupted in fire and sound.

Blinding light seared Nora's eyes for a second time in two days. Shattered glass and other airborne objects crashed into her, stinging and bruising. The stairs disintegrated and suddenly there was nothing under her feet. The sickening drop of her heart and stomach ended when she crashed onto the deck amid shards of glass, splinters, and burning debris. Pain exploded along her spine and she couldn't breathe. It seemed like forever before her mind caught up to her body and she sucked air into her lungs.

Flames leapt from the window and stretched out the apartment doorway, with the door itself now tilted off its hinges. Smoke scorched the blue sky and blistering heat seared Nora's face and legs. She jumped to her feet and screamed before she was aware she'd opened her mouth.

"Mom!"

She charged for the ragged remains of the stair railing and tried to climb the wobbly structure to the apartment. "Mom! Charlie!"

Rough arms pulled her back.

Through the roar of the flames Heather yelled. "You can't go in there!"

"Mom!" She fought against the arms but they dragged away.

Heather stepped in front of Nora. "Charlie will get her out."

The arms around her felt like iron, but Nora fought to escape. She had to get to Abigail.

Nora succeeded in twisting away long enough to see that Cole held her. She didn't get more than half a step away before he latched onto her, pinning her arms to her sides and lifting her off the ground.

She kicked and jerked. "Abigail needs me!" Nora had to pull her mother and Charlie out of the apartment before they burned. God, why wasn't her mother on a cruise somewhere? And Charlie, he didn't deserve to be hurt.

"Call the fire department," she screamed at Heather.

Panic ringed Heather like a sulfuric aura. "They won't get here in time."

It didn't matter how hard Nora fought, the arms around her didn't weaken. "Help them! Don't let this happen."

Her mother was vital and beautiful. Abigail couldn't burn up. She had too much to do. She had to stick around and straighten Nora out. She had to keep breaking men's hearts and spending too much money. *Oh please God, let her be okay.*

"If you quit fighting I'll go get them," Cole said, his mouth close to her ear.

Nora remembered a self-defense class she'd taken and with the one move she'd actually practiced, she lifted both arms.

Not prepared, Cole lost his grip.

Nora lunged for the railing, determined to save Abigail.

Heather shouted something, probably trying to get Nora to stop.

Nora launched her flight, aiming for a spot several feet up the railing where a small portion of a step remained, hoping momentum would carry her to the entryway of the apartment and the wall of flames.

She flew by Heather before she registered that Heather had the crowbar in her hand. There was only a split-second before it smacked into the back of her head.

White pain exploded and the world disappeared.

THIRTY-THREE

NORA SURFACED TO THE sway of Heather's RAV4 and the *thrump-thrump* of wheels flying across seams on the highway. Where was the cannonball that struck her head? Her skull throbbed.

Abigail.

Nora tried to sit but her arms wouldn't push her off the backseat. "What the hell?" Pain shot across her back and every muscle felt like a giant pulsing welt. Her arms and face stung with an army of cuts. At this rate Nora felt sure she wouldn't survive another day.

Heather glanced over her shoulder then back to the road. "Good. You're awake."

"I'm tied up. What's wrong with you? Let me go." The pounding in her head made her want to throw up, and she'd gladly aim for the back of Heather's neck if she could sit up.

"If you didn't wake up, like in the next five minutes, I was going to take you to the hospital in Winslow. And I didn't want to do that."

"Where's Abigail?" Nora tugged at the loose knots trussing her wrists to her ankles.

Heather didn't respond.

"What happened? Is she alive? What about Charlie?" The knots loosened more.

"I don't know. Cole pulled them out of the apartment and then we got you to the car. After that he went back and I tied you up and took off. The ambulance was there before we got off the mountain. I'm sure she's okay."

Nora slipped her wrists out of the rope. Where did the rope come from? "You're not sure of anything. Take me to the hospital."

Heather shook her head. "Cole is there. He'll take care of them."

Nora sat up and reached over the seat. She wanted to grab the wheel and stomp on the gas but they were speeding down the interstate. "Did it ever occur to you Cole might have set the explosion? Where the hell are we?"

"Twin Arrows. Cole is on your side, Nora."

Halfway between Flagstaff and Winslow. "Turn around."

"Cole said to take you to the rez."

"No."

Heather's phone jangled with that rap bullshit. She pushed it to her ear and mumbled. She shoved the phone at Nora. "It's Cole."

Nora grabbed it. "How's my mother?"

At the sound of Cole's Wyoming drawl she wanted to reach through the line and pull the words from him. "She's in the emergency room now. I don't have any information. She's burned, but I can't tell much. She was unconscious and has a big gash on her forehead. They don't know if there's any internal damage from the explosion."

"What does that mean?"

He let out a breath. "We just don't know."

She shouted above the rush of blood in her ears, fighting to stay focused. "Charlie?"

"He's at least got a concussion and bad burns on one of his hands. They're working on him too."

Nora slammed the back of the seat with her palm. "I need to be there."

Cole's reasonable tone tethered her. "Listen, Nora. You have to stay away. The cops—"

"I don't care about the cops."

"Okay, how about this: someone tried to kill you. It might be Big Elk, might be someone else. Whoever it is, they aren't going to give up. The rez is the safest place for you right now."

"The same rez where they tried to shove me off the cliff this morning?"

"Nora, trust me. I wouldn't put you in danger."

"I can't just hide out there when my mother's in the hospital."

"Just until tomorrow. I'm close to figuring this out."

"I won't stay there."

"Heather can make sure you do."

"Right. She can't tie a knot to save her skin."

Exasperation crept into his voice. "Don't force it, Nora. Heather knows enough people at the rez that keeping you won't be a problem. And if you'd like another knock to the head, my guess is that it can be arranged."

"Kidnapping."

"If that's what it takes to keep you safe."

"Did you try to kill my mother?"

"Damn it! Quit being stupid!"

She breathed fire into the phone, imagining it branding the side of his face.

"Nora?"

"What?"

"I … we care about you. I'll take care of Abigail and Charlie."

She didn't answer.

"See you tomorrow." He hung up.

Nora slumped in the back of the Toyota. She spent the remaining hour-and-half ride churning. They drove to a different mesa than where they'd gone to the dance that morning and turned onto a dusty road. Heather pulled in behind a dilapidated shed and cut the engine.

"We'll hide the car here and walk the rest of the way. There's a village at the top of this mesa. We'll stay there tonight."

Nora folded her arms. "I'm not moving from this car. Take me back."

Heather pulled the keys from the ignition and shrugged. "Whatever." She climbed from the car, slung her leather bag over her shoulder, and slammed the door.

Nora wasn't going anywhere without the keys. Maybe she could steal them. That being her only plan, she needed to stay with the keys and wait for an opportunity when Heather was distracted. Nora climbed from the vehicle and tromped up the trail after Heather in silence.

The sun hovered over the western horizon, casting ominous shadows. She didn't see anyone lying in wait for her, but that didn't mean they weren't there.

She followed Heather up a worn yellow dirt trail, switchbacking along the side of the nearly vertical wall. A narrow paved road wound its way up the mesa some distance from the trail. Too bad Heather hadn't felt it safe enough to drive up; it might have saved Nora from marching in rhythm to the pounding pain in her head, the ache in her back, and the dull returning throb of her ankle. She named the lump on the back of her head Mount Heather.

Once the trail intersected the road, where at some point in the last two centuries some hopeful Native American had built a structure, long since abandoned. "Why didn't you park behind this place?

Your car would have been hidden and we wouldn't have to walk so far."

Heather grinned. "I could have. If I'd remembered it was here. Sorry about that."

"You're sorry. Right."

They topped the mesa not far from a tall structure with a flat roof similar to those in the village they'd been in earlier. They walked around the edge of the building to the plaza. Buildings like aboriginal pueblos constructed of desert sand created the enclosure.

Heather looked over her shoulder and knocked on one of the doors. Without waiting for an answer, she opened it and directed Nora inside.

A ruin of a couch covered with a pale yellow sheet furnished the cramped room with cracked linoleum floors. One single bulb hung from the low ceiling, casting shadows on the round kitchen table and three chairs. Two folding lawn chairs, a stack of boxes, and general clutter clustered in one side of the room. A small refrigerator and stove several decades old were shoved into a corner of the room next to a long table that served as a kitchen counter. Everything looked shabby and second—maybe even third—hand.

"How's your head?" Heather asked.

Nora wanted to pummel the girl. She kept silent.

Heather plopped her bag on the table and rummaged in it. After bringing out a bottle of pain relievers, she poured water from a pitcher into a plastic cup and brought it to Nora. "I only hit you to protect you"

"You didn't enjoy it even a little bit?"

Heather scowled at her. "I didn't hit you hard."

Nora's neck felt like cement and the dim space closed in on her. "Take me back to Flagstaff."

"I can't. It's for your own good."

Nora struggled not to choke on the pills sliding down her throat. "I've got to see her."

"See? I knew you loved Abigail." Heather's eyes filled with tears.

"She's the most annoying and strongest woman I know. She's made my life hell. Of course I love her."

"You don't show it."

Nora couldn't deny her guilt, so she changed the subject. "Who lives here?"

"Benny." Heather looked around and headed for a closed door. "I've got to pee."

The leather bag didn't quite cover the car keys. As soon as the bathroom door clicked shut, Nora snatched them and sped out of the house, sprinting for the RAV4.

It would take a couple of hours to return to Flagstaff. She'd go straight to the hospital and make sure Abigail was okay. But of course Abigail would be fine. Nora couldn't allow herself to think her mother might be seriously injured.

Nora rounded the corner of the building and raced for the trail. She needed to get a head start on Heather. Crashing down the path, she rounded a switchback to the ruins that intersected the road. She spotted a sparkle of metal behind the pile of stone and stopped to listen.

Someone else was out here on the mesa. Alex? Big Elk? Some other Native American who would love to see her disappear? She slowed her breathing, hoping to be invisible and tiptoed closer.

A black Mercedes. Barrett. Maybe not her favorite person, but at least he'd take her back to town. He was probably out here looking for Heather. Maybe Nora would rat Heather out and Barrett would lock her up. Might not be a bad way to keep the foolish girl out of danger.

Voices floated to her at the same time the top of another black vehicle came into view. It didn't really matter who Barrett spoke with, at least he could take her back to Flagstaff. Nora started forward, opening her mouth to call out to him.

Something slammed into her face and wrapped around her mouth. A hand. An arm pulled her against a hard body and dragged her back into the shadows of the crumbling rock wall.

Alex! He'd found her and would slit her throat. Nora bucked against the immovable captor, who seemed not much taller than herself.

Suddenly Heather stood in front of her with sweat running down the side of her face. Her eyes wide, she pointed toward the vehicle and shook her head in frantic insistence. "Big Elk," she mouthed.

Nora stopped struggling.

The man's hand still clamped Nora's head in a vise with her lips pressed into her teeth. Her head was smashed into his chest, pressing painfully on the lump from Heather's batting practice.

"And Poppy," Heather whispered. She nodded to the man holding Nora.

The pressure lessened as if testing Nora; when she didn't scream, the arm fell away. She spun around to see the man dressed in the clown costume, still covered in yellow mud and black face paint. Benny. He stared at her with no expression.

Fight, run, scream. Or stay here and hide. Nora had to choose: Benny or Big Elk? Big Elk definitely wanted her dead. Benny seemed less dangerous.

Heather dropped down and crept to the edge of the ruins. Nora followed. They peered around the rubble. The sun sucked daylight from the mesa, taking it beyond the horizon, leaving Nora and Heather in deep shadow. Barrett and Big Elk stood between Barrett's black Mercedes and Big Elk's black Escalade, a convoy of death.

THIRTY-FOUR

"BOTTOM LINE IS THAT you didn't deliver." Barrett had found it surprisingly easy to contact Big Elk to meet him here. Where the possibility of extortion existed, Big Elk would be first to the party.

Big Elk faced Barrett with the insolence of a terrier unaware he's about to be ripped to shreds in the jaws of a Rottweiler. "I'm waiting for the balance to go up in that bank account. When that happens, you'll get your vote."

Barrett was going through the motions. He only had to keep Big Elk talking for a couple of minutes. "Too late."

"You might change your mind when I tell you I've figured out you killed Scott Abbott and his girlfriend."

Bluff and bluster. Barrett remained expressionless.

Big Elk grinned. "You covered your tracks pretty well."

The back driver's side door of Barrett's Mercedes whispered open, and two black cowboy boots stepped into the dust. The rest of the rough-looking dark man seemed to float out of the vehicle like an oil slick on the ocean. He moved like a shadow, silent, out of Big Elk's periphery.

Barrett kept his eyes riveted on Big Elk's while the dark man slipped behind Big Elk. Barrett would enjoy seeing that smug look fade from his face.

"Okay, you got me." Big Elk laughed. "I don't have proof. I don't even know why you did it. But I can get the cops sniffing around. You don't want that, do you, Mac?"

Barrett didn't move. *Enjoy your last seconds, little prick.*

As if the shadow man worked magic, Big Elk seemed unaware he existed. "Don't play games with me, McCreary. Either that money hits my account pronto or I expose Heather as an eco-terrorist. Sure, she's a minor, but she'll do time somewhere, I guarantee. Blowing up a ski lift is serious business."

Barrett's self-control strained to the breaking point. He should have saved his money and killed Big Elk himself. On the other hand, it was almost comic how Big Elk didn't even sense the black menace behind him.

"That's where you made your big mistake, Mr. Elk." Barrett heard the sneer in his voice. "I could tolerate your low-class ways. I would even pad your accounts. But you should know to never, ever threaten my family."

Barrett dipped his chin slightly like Caesar giving a thumbs down. The dark spirit behind Big Elk raised his hand and drew it in a fluid movement across Big Elk's throat.

Big Elk made a sound like a gag, then slid to the yellow dust.

It looked so easy and clean, aside from the gallons of blood gushing into the dust. No struggle. No last words. One second alive, the next ... dead. Expensive, but you got what you paid for.

Barrett pulled a thick envelope from his pocket and handed it to the phantom. "Tempting as it is to keep the Escalade, get rid of it as completely as you do the body. You'll get the rest when I read the next obit." What a waste of a great vehicle. He stepped briskly to the Mercedes and climbed in.

Scott Abbott: check. Big Elk: check. Abigail: check. Alex: soon to be a check. Now to get the congressional committee in line, get snow making up and running, and find Heather and get her under control.

Cole was still a wild card though. And Nora needed to go.

THIRTY-FIVE

BACK AT BENNY'S, THEY closed the door and all three took their first deep breath since the man in black had severed Big Elk's jugular in front of them.

Heather finally spoke. "Poppy and Big Elk were working together?"

With his yellow body paint streaked with sweat, Benny nodded. "Charlie and I suspected it. Big Elk was secretly buying up the council to vote for uranium mining."

"That was worth his life?" Nora asked.

Benny shook his head. "Don't think that's what Barrett said."

What Barrett said was that Heather blew up the lift. Nora stared at Heather. "Did you really do it?"

Heather froze. "Well, sort of. Yes. I helped."

"Why?"

Heather looked lost. "I don't know. I got all caught up in saving the mountain and doing the right thing, and Charlie kept talking about all the cool stuff he'd done. And your mom said you'd been such an activist when you were young. It was a mistake."

Mistake didn't begin to cover it, but Nora couldn't confront Heather today. Not with the smell of Big Elk's blood swirling in her nostrils. "We'll talk about this some other time. Right now, we have to figure out what to do about Barrett."

Heather sank to the couch, tears falling without care. "He's a monster."

Nora nodded. "And Abigail just agreed to marry him." The words tasted sour.

Heather's head shot up. "Poppy and Abigail are getting married?"

"Over my dead body," Nora said, knowing that phrase might be all too true.

"I gotta clean up," Benny said and disappeared into the other room, clicking the door closed.

Heather curled up on the couch and in seconds she fell asleep for the second time that day. A psychologist would probably say sleep was her coping mechanism. At least Heather could find a moment's relief. Nora wanted to pace but the small, windowless room wouldn't allow much movement.

Benny emerged in ten minutes looking like a normal person. The yellow mud and clownish makeup gone, his hair damp and combed, he wore jeans and plaid Western shirt. Though dressed in normal clothes and larger all around, he reminded Nora of the little kachina man. Maybe it was his dark eyes that didn't seem to miss much.

Nora's insides twisted so tight she could barely breathe. "I need to know how my mother is."

Benny nodded. It seemed to take him forever to answer. Did he rehearse everything he said before it came out of his mouth? "It's best if you stay here tonight."

She couldn't twiddle her thumbs out here when Abigail was in the hospital. "At least call and find out how she is."

"Can't call." If he spoke any slower she'd need someone to translate. "No cell service and we don't have land lines here."

Frantic now, Nora wanted to punch something. "How can you live like this?"

He watched her with annoying calm. "I have everything I need."

"Sure. If you're an Aborigine in the outback. You live in isolation with no phone, no television. You use kerosene for light and haul water. Maybe you're surviving, but what kind of quality of life is this?"

Pause, pause, irritating pause. "Tomorrow I will greet the sun and the Creator with prayers and thanks. My family and neighbors will be happy to see me. I have enough corn to last until harvest. I have the work of farming to keep me busy. The simple life avoids waste and misuse. There is no over-production. I live in harmony and balance."

This philosophy wasn't new to her. She'd grown up in Boulder, Colorado, after all. Communal, back-to-nature living and all that New Age spiritual stuff drifted off the foothills with the pine pollen. But she noticed that when even the more dedicated hippies reached middle age, most had real jobs, mortgages, and health insurance like everyone else.

Benny's words beat in cadence to a rhythm in his head. "We live like this to develop a strong spiritual life so we can care for the land and protect it. Our spirit people looked after the human people and taught us many things. They gave us language and our ceremonies and many sacred and secret things. But with this knowledge came great responsibility. When we live as instructed, we are happy and the world stays in balance."

Benny inhaled deliberately and let it out slowly. "Taking water from our sacred aquifer and spraying it on the sacred moun-ain is disrupting the balance. You shouldn't do that."

Sacred everything, Nora thought. *I'm so sick of hearing that.* "There have been scientific studies that show making snow will not harm the mountain." Even as she spoke, it sounded flat and unconvincing.

Benny shook his head as if sad at her ignorance. "Western science compartmentalizes; we know everything is connected. To say taking water from the ground and spraying it on the surface won't change anything is denying the relationship. It's like saying your thumbs are not connected to your toes."

"You know the court ruled that Native American religious rights are not harmed by making snow as long as there are other places on the mountain where you can perform your ceremonies."

If she'd been trying to goad him to temper, she'd failed. He considered what she said. "Everything depends on the proper balance being maintained. The water underground acts like a magnet attracting rain from the clouds. The rain also acts as a magnet raising the water table under the roots of our crops. Drawing water from the aquifer throws everything off. Our elders tell us if this happens, everything but Hopi will disintegrate. They warn us that time is short."

Heather didn't stir. Suddenly exhausted, Nora sank to the couch. What she wouldn't give for a bath and to change from the sooty, dirty, sweat-soaked clothes. She realized she hadn't showered since yesterday morning.

"It would be great if the Indians could live the way you did two hundred years ago and have all your sacred places and follow the buffalo and smoke peyote and all that. But this is the real world, and you can't halt progress. Indians need to stop living in the past and acclimate to the modern world."

"We need to live our way. It is what we are made to do."

Nora kneaded her forehead. "And destroy or kill anyone who gets in your way?"

256

"That is not the Hopi way." He didn't move, simply watched her with his unreadable dark eyes.

Nora couldn't argue with his logic. If he wanted to live in poverty and believed it saved the world, she had no right to tell him any differently. Heather's soft snoring filled the room. "Sleep will do her good," Nora said.

Benny pulled a folded blanket from the back of the couch and laid it over Heather. He walked to the door with his steady pace. "You can stay in my cousin's house tonight. She works in Winslow as a night clerk at the Holiday Inn."

Nora didn't follow him. "I want to see my mother."

He continued as though he hadn't heard her. "Her house is just across the plaza."

"Can't you take me back to Flagstaff?"

He held the door open for her. "Do you really want to go back tonight?"

"Of course I do."

His deadpan expression didn't change. "Someone, maybe Barrett, killed your husband and tried to kill you. The cops think maybe you're a murderer and suspect you're trying to swindle the insurance companies, so going to them won't help you."

Someone wanted her dead. Even if that someone was Big Elk and he couldn't get her any more, his faithful followers might not want to call it quits. If Barrett killed Scott, maybe he'd kill Nora too. She couldn't go home. Couldn't check on her mother. Like Fay Wray in King Kong's grip, she felt trapped. "How do you know so much about this?"

Benny waited by the door, letting cool night air into the cluttered room. "Cole told me."

"What does he have to do with me?"

One of Benny's eyebrows lifted slightly, what for him was probably a hissy fit of some kind. "He cares about you."

Not sure what that meant and too tired to figure it out, Nora gave in. She'd go to Flagstaff at first light. She plodded across the plaza. The pitch-black night closed about her and she stayed on Benny's heels. Even if she didn't believe in spirits and ghosts—which she reminded herself she definitely did not—she could imagine the place teemed with malevolent forces that knew she intended to desecrate their home.

Benny walked her out a small arched entry to a dark door. He pushed it open and pulled the little chain to the light hanging from the ceiling. The place looked similar to his.

"I hope you don't mind staying alone. My house doesn't have another bed." He slipped behind an old door, the kind that easily broke if someone fell against it. This one looked like someone had accidently kicked it. He emerged with a blanket.

She took the blanket. "This is fine, thanks." Nora wasn't sure if Benny had kidnapped or saved her but, as Abigail taught her, it never hurt to be polite.

At the thought of her mother, Nora's throat tightened and tears pricked her eyes. Burns were painful. And what about disfigurement? Was her face ravaged by flames?

"Are you going to be okay?" Benny asked.

She swallowed. "Yeah. I'll be fine."

He nodded and left.

The quiet of the village, along with all the creepiness of the night and the native-ness of the whole place, pushed against her. She hugged the blanket and sank to the couch. The light would stay on tonight.

THIRTY-SIX

SOMETIME LATER THE CHILL forced her to move her stiff muscles and wrap the blanket around her. And later still she must have dozed.

Panic blasted through her sleep and vibrated in the blackness. She gasped and sat up. Darkness covered the room so deeply she barely made out shapes of furniture. The bare bulb she'd left burning no longer glowed.

There it was again. A terrible crashing on the roof must be what woke her. It sounded like a boulder dropped overhead with a shower of smaller rocks and pebbles following.

Nora huddled into the blanket, imagining Alex outside. Of course he knew she hid on the rez and came to terrorize her. It was only a matter of time before he burst through the front door with a knife. Or maybe only his bare hands to shut off her windpipe. How stupid to think she was safe here. Maybe Barrett lurked outside. Probably not; his style called for a silent assassin or a quick shove. He had no interest in toying with his victims.

The noise stopped. Nora waited. And waited. Apparently Alex only wanted to scare her because no one stormed through the front door.

How she could have dozed despite the anxiety over her mother, the threat of death, the very real attack by Alex with his rocks and boulders mystified Nora. But she jerked awake to more of the rocks crashing on the roof and windows.

It happened two more times before the first hint of dawn penciled the horizon. Each time Nora clutched the blanket to her and stared at the front door, expecting someone to break it down and find her alone and unarmed. But the attacks broke off abruptly each time and, eventually, exhaustion overtook her again.

Come dawn Nora turned the doorknob with a shaking hand and creaked open the door. Her fear conjured the image of Alex on the other side, ready to wring the life from her. But no one was in sight.

She crept from the house, sure there would be a pile of loose debris and rocks. But the dirt surface in front of the house sat empty. She climbed a low stone wall and worked her way up another ancient building until she surveyed the roof of her nighttime shelter. No rocks. No pebbles. Just a flat roof.

The sun slept just below the horizon, casting enough light to convince her the morning would arrive soon. The snatches of sleep she'd gotten in between rocky crashes hadn't done a thing to soothe her nerves. She had to get out of this place before Alex or someone like him killed her and tossed her somewhere in the wilderness never to be found. Maybe that wouldn't be such a bad thing; at least if Nora were gone, her mother would be safe. That was assuming Abigail recovered from the blast.

But if Nora never made it back to Flagstaff, would Heather warn Abigail about Barrett's true colors? Her empty gut clenched at the image of Big Elk's surprised eyes, his last gurgle, all that blood.

Nora ached with worry for Abigail and Charlie. Maybe it wouldn't make a difference if she were at the hospital for them, but she needed to be there all the same. As soon as she saw her mother was okay, she'd report Big Elk's murder and get Barrett locked up.

Nora barely discerned a footfall, a tiny scratch of sand on rock. Her heart leapt up her throat and she swallowed it, fearing she'd look down and see an enemy.

But that's not what made the noise.

Standing below her was the little kachina man. What had Heather called him? Nakwaiyamtewa—Nora had sounded out the word in her head several times since Heather showed her the photographs in the book.

He looked up and his calm, deep eyes searched hers. Without a word, he walked away. He made no sound, and Nora suspected he purposely made the earlier noise to get her attention.

Like a kitten in a tree, Nora found climbing down the building much tougher than climbing up. She searched for each foothold and eventually got low enough to drop the rest of the way. Her landing in the quiet dawn sounded like a buffalo stampede.

She hurried after the little man. As if he'd been waiting for her to catch up, she caught sight of him as he rounded the corner in what appeared to be an alley. Although she'd seen newer buildings in the first village yesterday—some made of cinder block, some framed and covered with cheap government siding—this village consisted of stone structures snugged closely together. It felt ancient and primitive.

The little man continued toward the edge of the mesa at his calm pace, limping a bit on his left foot. She shouldn't go out there. Maybe it was a trap; the area was completely exposed. But then, the little man had saved her before. He never made her feel threatened; a little freaked out maybe, but not in danger.

She wondered if she was acting like the stupid waifs in the black-and-white horror movies, stepping up to the attic in the dead of night while Count Dracula waited hungrily. But she felt compelled to follow the old man.

The sun inched toward the horizon, taking the chill off the frightening night as the little man stopped at the edge of the mesa. He reached into a small leather pouch hanging around his neck and brought out his thumb and forefinger pinched together. In a quiet voice he made strange noises.

Sure, he would probably say he sang, and it did have a certain rhythm, but Native American songs never really sounded like music to Nora. His voice wavered with age and he dipped his head to the east. Just then, the sun burst out with surprising warmth and fire over the horizon. He held out his hand and let whatever he held in his fingers loose into the calm air. It looked like a fine dust.

Tears sprang to Nora's eyes. She might not understand what he said or all the implications, but she knew he prayed with thankfulness for the new day. It didn't matter to whom he addressed the prayers. The gratitude and beauty of the dawn seeped into Nora's heart.

He motioned her forward without turning. Nora obeyed, not even worrying about how close to the edge she stood.

He held out the pouch and nodded to her, indicating she take whatever it contained.

She reached inside, felt a rough powder, and pulled out what looked like a pinch of crushed corn. The little man did the same. He sang again in a quiet voice and tossed his pinch toward the sun. His eyes urged her to her own prayer.

His eloquence, though she didn't know his words, made her feel like a galumphing elephant. Stiff with embarrassment at her inability to say a simple prayer of thanks, she felt her face grow red.

The little man began his song again. The quiet bleating of his old voice sounded like a lullaby.

Nora's tears flowed, melting her reserve. She longed to sing, to offer thanks for another day. But she didn't know who to thank.

What was she so damned thankful for, anyway? Another sunrise and a chance for whoever wanted her dead to succeed? A day of painful recovery, at best, for her mother? The first day of the rest of her life fighting battles alone?

"What are you doing here?" Benny's voice made her jump. She spun around to see him frowning at her.

Her mind felt muddled and she realized the old man's song ended. "I came out here with him."

"Who?"

Of course the little kachina man didn't stand next to her. Obviously, Benny hadn't seen or heard him singing.

Remember when the most horrendous thing you could imagine was Scott having an affair? Now her life revolved around murder, terrorists, mothers in hospitals, and some ancient Indian *kikmongwi* only she could see.

"What are *you* doing here?" she said instead, to turn the challenge around.

He stepped beside her. "Offering my morning prayers."

She stood next to him as he took a pinch of corn from a pouch he carried. He ignored her and sang his song, bowing and tossing his offering over the mesa. He sang faster and louder and without the holy feel of the older man, but it felt like church, all the same.

Benny finished and stood straight.

Nora bowed her head slightly and let go of the corn she'd taken from the little kachina man's pouch.

Benny eyed her curiously.

She lifted her chin. "Nakwaiyamtewa gave it to me." She waited for his reaction.

He nodded, not looking the least surprised. "That's good."

Dirty and sore, Nora faced the warmth of the sun. "Someone waged a war of terror on me last night."

Benny laughed. "How is that?"

Maybe it sounded funny to him, but he hadn't sat through hours expecting to be murdered any minute. "Probably Alex trying to scare me. He succeeded."

A glint of humor showed in Benny's eyes. "What exactly did Alex do?"

"He threw rocks at the windows and roof."

"Rocks?"

Anger and embarrassment heated her face like the sun. "Big rocks. Boulders from the sound of them."

Benny raised his eyebrows. "I didn't see any boulders when I walked by the house."

You infuriating, rational man. "I don't know what happened. He must have cleaned them up."

It sounded lame to her, but what other explanation was there? He'd attacked her four times with the noise—that wasn't something a wild imagination conjured up.

Finally Benny seemed to take her seriously. "I wondered if they would come visit you."

"Who?"

"The kachinas."

"Funny."

"I'm serious. This house is on one of the energy lines. The highways of the spirits. You aren't the only one to hear them."

She gave him a skeptical look.

"Just because you don't believe it doesn't mean it don't exist. There are certain lines of spiritual power that run across the world. One happens to pass through where that house sits. Lots of people hear the spirits when they pass. Even a few white ones."

"You had me stay there on purpose."

"I wondered if they'd pass by. Yeah."

She didn't believe him, of course. The idea of kachinas or any other spirits knocking on the house was ludicrous. There had to be another explanation. But who could have done it and where did the boulders go?

Benny turned and meandered down the path.

Day or night, the village, with its crumbling and ancient buildings felt creepy. She trotted to catch up. "Where are you going?"

He didn't look at her. "Breakfast."

In normal life she wouldn't be the least bit curious about his prayer or what it might mean. But normal life ended with Scott's death and had spiraled into Bizarro Land since then. Her mother lay in a hospital nearly two hundred miles away, murder was now commonplace, and last night spirits from some other world had played Bowling for Sanity on the roof.

"What did you say over there? To the Creator or whatever?" Okay, that was the epitome of rude. Heart-stopping fear caused her to lose the manners Abigail had tortured into her.

"I thanked the Creator for another day and gave him some corn meal. I said, 'It is your way to live the simple life, which is everlasting and we will follow. I ask that you speak through me with prayers for all the people. We shall reclaim the land for you.'"

"Yay for the simple life of hoping the generator holds out."

A smile touched Benny's lips. "If the rest of the world faced disaster and there was no electricity or running water, they would perish. Here we would go on as usual."

"You've got all this talk about keeping the old ways and ceremonies and poverty that, for some reason, balances the world. It's as illogical as one man's death accounting for the sin of mankind. Where is the proof that would make any of what you're doing reasonable?"

They crossed the plaza, less menacing in the morning light and more Third World. Benny held the door of his house open for her. "You want proof as obvious to your senses as this door is to touch. I think maybe you need to expand your perceptions and develop new senses."

She couldn't come up with a polite response, and blowing air through her lips while rolling her eyes would be wrong.

The blanket sat folded on the back of the couch. "Where's Heather?"

Benny's face showed no emotion. "She left."

A tide of salty anxiety surged into Nora. Without Heather, she was a prisoner on the rez. "How will I get to Flagstaff?"

"I can give you a ride." Benny opened a cupboard and pulled out two granola bars. He handed one to Nora. At least breakfast wouldn't be a painfully slow-cooked meal.

"Let's go." She hurried out the door, hoping to get Benny moving.

He drifted into the daylight of the plaza and stopped, his face to the sun. "You've heard of the Anasazi?"

Who blew up my apartment? Barrett? One of Big Elk's followers? What did Alex have to do with any of it? Was Cole a good guy or Barrett's henchman?

Benny waited for an answer.

She backtracked to his question. "The Anasazi are the cliff dwellers. The people at Mesa Verde and Walnut Canyon. They disappeared and no one knows what happened to them, right?"

He stretched as if urgency didn't thunder in Nora's blood. "It isn't a mystery to us. We are the ancient ones. They didn't just happen to disappear in 1100 A.D. like the archeologists say. Each of our clans was instructed to migrate and we did. For centuries we wandered over this country, up to the glaciers, down to South America. We left our history etched in stones along the way. We left our broken pottery and homes made of stones and mud. When we reached the mesas, clan by clan, we settled in the place chosen for us."

She took several steps and waited for him to meander in her direction. "If you're a chosen people, why would you get this hard country where you can barely survive?"

"This is the center of the world. All life depends on what happens here."

By the time he plodded to his vehicle and drove at an idle down the mesa, Nora was sure she would need a walker and adult diapers and her mother would be dust.

"Many of our young people are not keeping to the Hopi way. They want all the material things of the white man, and it's causing disturbances."

Nora nodded and hoped she looked thoughtful. She'd get a ride out of here sooner if she didn't irritate Benny.

"Now Mother Earth is in pain. McCreary is taking her guts for money. Coal is her liver and uranium is her heart." They walked out of the plaza to the alley. Benny's molasses pace made her want to scream.

"You're against mining on the rez?"

He nodded. "Don't matter what McCreary says or how clean it is or how many jobs and royalties it will bring. Would you cut out your mother's guts for money?"

Barrett seemed to be involved in everything. Snow making and uranium mining. Other than both being damaging to the religious sentiments of the Native Americans, what did she even have in common with him, her former idol?

Benny's old Ford pickup used to be white. Now it was tied-dyed with waves of rust and dirt. Bright Indian blankets covered the bench seat that sloped hard toward the door. A large crack split the dash, showing yellowed foam rubber filler. Enough dirt was accumulated on the floor that he could probably plant a garden.

As Nora's head whirled in five different directions, they eventually made it down the mesa and a few miles south on the highway. Benny turned onto a trail hidden by tall summer grasses.

Worry twanged through Nora like an out of tune ukulele. A Hopi shortcut didn't seem like something that would get her to Flagstaff quicker. "Where are we going?"

Benny didn't look at her but maneuvered the truck down the bumpy trail. "I have to see to my corn."

"I have to get to the hospital."

Benny shrugged.

"What about my mother?" She had to protect Abigail from Barrett.

Benny braked the pickup and got out. He headed to the side of the road beyond the tall weeds and started singing in Hopi. His low guttural consonants made a beautiful ringing on the desert floor.

Nora jumped out and ran to him. "Please. I've got to get to my mother."

He stopped singing and turned to her. "All your worry and impatience won't make your mother well. Let go of your stress and listen to Mother Earth." He continued on his way.

Arguing didn't turn Benny back to the pickup. And his stubbornness didn't halt her arguing. She followed, topped the ridge still making her case and then stopped, amazed. In the dry desert, surrounded by hills of sand and scruffy weeds, Benny's cornfield grew lush and green.

He turned to her. "Do you know why I sing to the corn?"

She shook her head.

"The corn is like children. I sing to the seeds when I plant them. I sing when I tend them, bringing water or thinning the weak plants. That way, they learn my voice. They will grow toward it, wanting to please me the way a child would."

Nora wondered if she finally suffered the effects of too much stress. Benny's mystical gumbo sounded logical. "How do you get the corn to grow with no water?"

He smiled proudly at the bushy plants, so different from the endless fields of corn encompassing all of Nebraska and Iowa. "The cloud people have been good to me this year. They have given enough rain but not too much to flood the young plants."

"Why do you plant them spread out like this and not in straight rows?"

He reached down and pulled a weed growing close to one of the leafy stalks. "I don't use a tractor so there is no need to make straight rows. And spacing the corn like this confuses the cloud people. When you plant in rows all close together, the cloud people know where the corn is and they rain and leave quickly. But when you plant like this, the cloud people must look around and they stay over the field longer, giving more rain."

Cloud people—really? But he spoke as if he believed it, and he didn't seem like a stupid man.

He focused on her. "We've been growing corn here for a thousand years. The cloud people live on the sacred peaks. If you destroy their home, there will be no rain for my corn."

"You don't really believe this, do you?"

He walked between the plants, touching their leaves in a loving caress. "Hopi have a respect for life and trust in the Creator. We were told that white men would come and try to take away our lands. But if we cling to the ancient ways, we will prevail."

"Seems like you could grow more corn if you used a tractor or irrigation sprinkler. Why would your spirits want you to do everything the hard way?"

Benny straightened and brushed his hands together. "Making things hard prepares us for what may happen. Like a runner practices every day, building strength and endurance so he can run the marathon, we Hopi live a meager and hard life so we're ready to survive when the time comes."

He handed her a stick about a foot long and as thick as a broom handle. He reached into his pocket and brought out a small plastic bag of corn seeds. "You stay here and plant these seeds over there." He pointed to a sandy spot next to the outer corn plants.

Nora's frustration boiled over. "I can't plant seeds when my mother is lying in a hospital and I don't know how she is."

He nodded. "I have to tend to another field, then I'll take you to Flagstaff. You plant the seeds and if you can, sing to them."

"I don't have time to plant corn, Benny."

He shook his head. "I won't tell you what to do—that isn't the Hopi way. But I urge you to plant these seeds. Do something good for Mother Earth and it will go well for your mother."

"Like a prayer?"

He nodded. "Yes. Like a prayer."

She dropped the stick. "I don't believe in prayer."

Benny started walking toward a low hill, presumably to another cornfield. "Since you've got nothing to do until I'm done, you might as well plant the corn. No one is around to hear you, so go ahead and sing to the seeds. It will help them grow."

She followed him. "Please, I need to go."

He topped the hill. "I'll be back soon."

She waited a minute before moving. Then she trudged back and picked up the planting stick. Might as well, as Benny had said.

Planting corn was a stupid idea, and she didn't want to do it. Just because Benny told her to plant was good enough reason not to plant his stinking corn. She ought to sit down in the dirt and wait for him to come back. If he came back.

But action might help ease her frustration. She squatted down and thrust the stick into the ground. It surprised her the dirt held moisture a couple of inches below the surface.

Planting corn while my mother is in a hospital. As if that will help anything.

She dropped in a few seeds and packed the earth around them. She took four steps away, the distance she estimated Benny's other plants were spaced, and squatted down again.

What if Barrett comes after Abigail or Charlie?

The seeds dribbled from her hand into the hole she dug and she covered them with dirt. She thought of Abbey, patting him on the head and seeing the devotion in his eyes.

Oh, God. Abbey. Had he been caught in the fire?

Hands shaking, she poked the next hole, carefully selected the three largest seeds. Scott. Abigail. Abbey. She dropped the seeds into the hole and patted the loose soil on top. She saw Scott's sweat-drenched face as she climbed from the SAG wagon at an Adventure Race last year. He grinned at her as she handed him his Gatorade and a fresh inner tube for the flat he just suffered. She'd taken care of him for years, holding back the real world by finagling the finances and keeping Kachina Ski running, making sure he had time for the hiking, biking, and outdoor play that seemed to keep him alive.

She'd wanted to care for him with all the love in the world. Love he sucked up without thought. Barbed wire wrapped around her heart and squeezed with every memory of Scott. She'd given him all she had, and he hadn't wanted her. Tears dripped into the mound of dirt she pushed back into the hole.

She straightened and stepped sideways, sinking to her knees to dig a new hole. She dropped in the seeds and scooped dirt. Patting the dirt reminded her of tucking a child into bed. A child she didn't have, but one she wanted with all her heart. Was this what Abigail felt? She loved the seeds and wanted them to grow into strong plants, to tassel and create life-sustaining corn. Her mother wanted that for her. But like Scott rejected Nora, she'd been pushing Abigail away.

Nora rose from the ground, feeling love for the seeds, for her mother, for a child she hoped to nurture someday. For her old dog who might be alone and frightened on the mountain. The Earth gave life to the corn, which nourished the people here in Hopiland. It was this way all over the world. Abigail gave life to Nora and loved her, tried to make life good for her, teaching her and protecting her in her own imperfect way. And if she were lucky, someday Nora would be able to do the same with a child of her own.

Words wouldn't form but rhythm and sound grew naturally, boiling up her throat and erupting from her mouth in a song. She danced, tears falling from her face, her voice loud and deep with love for the corn, for the Earth that would nurture it, for her mother, and even for Scott.

Seeds planted, Nora dropped to the ground, her back against a weathered fence post. Her eyes drooped and her mind floated.

When she opened her eyes a man stood in front of her. Two slits served as eyes in a face flat and smooth. A cylindrical peg looked like a mouth. His bare chest showed zigzags of blue, like lightning. He wore a woven white cloth around his middle like a kilt and carried a hatchet in one hand and feathers in his other. Why she didn't scream at this apparition, she couldn't say. It should have scared the bejeesus out of her. But she wasn't scared. The kachina—and that's what it had to be—didn't frighten her, despite his bizarre appearance.

He didn't speak but pointed to the mounds she'd planted. Small puddles pocked the field where she'd put her seeds. The kachina told her plainly, though he used no words and she didn't know how she knew what he meant, that he'd brought the rain.

"…brought rain."

Nora blinked at the words that seemed to be as real as the desert under her. She turned to the sound. The voice belonged to the kachina man, but he wasn't standing there.

She rubbed her eyes and stood, focusing on a lean figure silhouetted on the ridge. Cole trotted toward her. "Nora. What are you doing?"

Thank the kachina or luck or whatever power brought him here. She stood up, her legs weak and waited for him. "How's my mother? How's Charlie?"

"She was sleeping when I left and the hospital staff wouldn't let me see her. They wouldn't tell me her condition because I'm not family." He stopped in front of her, slightly invading her private space.

A tremor of despair began at the base of Nora's head and tears flooded her eyes.

Cole opened his arms and took the last small step forward. Without hesitation Nora leaned into him and poured her anguish, fear, regret, and sorrow into his beating heart. His arms closed around her, temporarily shielding her from any harm. He felt warm and smelled of sun and pine and safety.

When the worst of her storm passed, she pushed against him. "Okay. I'm done with that. Now let's get to Flagstaff."

He shook his head. "I just came out to see you. I'll go back and check on Abigail and Charlie, but you've got to stay here."

"I need to protect Abigail."

"This is the safest place for you. I'll take care of your mother."

Nora grabbed his arm. "It's Barrett. She thinks she's going to marry him and she can't. He's a killer. He killed Big Elk."

Cole stared at her. "Big Elk? When?"

"Yesterday." Nora started to tremble and tears spilled from her eyes. "My God, he had a man slit Big Elk's throat. Big Elk was working for Barrett."

Cole grabbed her by the shoulders. "I've got to go. Please, just stay out here for a while longer."

She shook her head. "I have to go with you."

A flash of anger lit his eyes. "You're going to get yourself or someone else killed."

"I've already caused murder. If I would have stopped snow making, Scott would still be alive."

"If you had stopped it, you'd be dead now too."

"What do you mean?"

He stood up, all business. "Never mind. Just stay here, Nora." He strode up the ridge. "I'll get this taken care of and be back for you. I promise."

Frozen, she watched him disappear down the other side. When an engine started she raced up the hill, desperate not to be alone. She sprinted up the next hill and stopped short.

The whole time she'd planted corn and let her imagination carry her away, Benny's pickup was sitting a short trot away.

She ran to the rusted hulk of a pickup and jumped behind the wheel, pulling the door closed with both hands. It wasn't very smart of Benny to leave the keys in the ignition, but then, he probably wasn't used to taking hostages.

THIRTY-SEVEN

NORA SPENT THE NEXT two hours with her right foot pushed to the floor, trying to make Benny's old pickup move faster. Unfortunately, it drove like he talked.

Nora fidgeted. Barrett could be with Abigail this very moment. Maybe he didn't have a reason to harm her, but maybe he did. He had to be tied to the explosion that put her in the hospital in the first place, right?

Then there was the dicey situation that if Gary found her before she got to Abigail, Nora would spend too much time trying to convince him of Barrett's guilt, leaving Abigail on her own, unaware of the evil monster she planned to marry.

The rusty truck finally puttered into the hospital lot and parked at the far edge. Nora jumped from the pickup, slamming the door. She struggled not to race to the front door. Her nerves strained like rubber bands stretched throughout her body, twisting tighter and tighter.

A vehicle moving way too fast caught her attention. In the next row Heather whipped her RAV4 into a parking space and jumped out. She'd changed from yesterday's clothes and had, from the look of her wet hair hanging down her back, had the luxury of a shower. She slapped toward the entrance in her flip-flops.

"What are you doing here?" Nora called to her. Despite everything, she envied Heather's shower and clean clothes.

Heather whipped around, obviously surprised. "I thought Cole wanted you to stay on the rez."

Cole could issue orders, but it didn't mean Nora had to obey. "I need to see Abigail and Charlie."

Heather hurried toward the hospital entrance. "He called me and asked me to be here with Abigail because he had to check something out."

Nora outpaced Heather. "Why didn't you wait for me this morning?"

Heather's face looked gray and cold as granite. "I came back early because I've got to talk to Poppy."

"Stay away from him!"

"Benny won't tell me who I am. He said I have to ask Poppy."

Nora grabbed the girl's arm and made Heather face her. "You saw what he's capable of, Heather. Don't go near him."

"Whatever he is, he's my father, even if I am adopted. He would never hurt me."

Nora opened the door of the hospital and let Heather enter in front of her. The cold of the air conditioning smacked her skin after the heat of the parking lot and the old truck. She hesitated, not wanting to ask the pink-coated volunteer for Abigail's room number.

Heather strode passed the front desk. "She's on the third floor."

Heather had more confidence than a normal sixteen-year-old. Nora wouldn't have thought to call hospitals and remember to get room numbers and generally take charge. At that age, passing out flyers about environmental issues or volunteering to plant trees ranked as her biggest accomplishment. And though blowing up the lift was definitely not a good thing, it did demonstrate Heather's ability to act.

Nora leaned over and spoke in a near whisper. "Try to look casual and not draw attention. Keep an eye out for the cops; I can't be seen here until I can get to Abigail."

They bypassed the elevator and opted for the stairs, hoping to avoid as much human contact as possible. At the third floor, Nora poked her head out the door and surveyed the hallway. Nothing but shiny linoleum, cream-colored walls, and bright lights. She slipped out with Heather behind her. The room numbers led them down the hall and to a nurses' station situated in front of the elevators. According to Heather's earlier phone call, Abigail's room sat on the corridor on the other side of the nurses' station.

Nora took a breath, straightened her shoulders and glanced at Heather. She had no choice but to march confidently by the nurses and hope they didn't take note of her shabby appearance and the smattering of scabs from the flying glass yesterday.

Heather met her eye and gave a nod.

Nora stepped out to round the corner. A splash of dark blue stopped her. She turned and shoved Heather back around the corner.

"Hi, Laurie." Gary's voice greeted someone who replied with her own hello.

Nora didn't know she recognized Gary's voice, but now he represented a major menace in her life and Nora was gaining survival skills. He must be here to interrogate Abigail. And he was still convinced that Nora had killed Scott and Maureen. Maybe he'd set a trap for Nora so he could snap the cuffs on her and drag her to a dungeon.

Nora leaned against the wall and strained to hear, but her beating heart made it difficult.

Heather tossed her hair and stepped around the corner.

Nora wanted to pull her back, but Heather moved so unexpectedly she lost her chance.

"Hi," Heather said as if she hadn't witnessed a murder yesterday or blown up a ski lift. Whatever the female version of ballsy was called, that was Heather. "I'm looking for Abigail Stoddard. She's on this floor, right?"

The nurse, or whoever Laurie was, answered. "She's in room 321. But you'll have to come back another time. She needs to rest now."

"How is she?"

Gary interrupted, "Heather McCreary, isn't it?"

Nora imagined Heather turning a royal countenance upon him and barely acknowledging his question.

"Your father said you were on vacation in Mexico." Suspicion sprinkled his voice.

"I came back when I heard about Abigail." She never missed a beat.

"Do you have time for a few questions?"

Now Nora knew Heather's plan: she would distract Gary so Nora could sneak by. The girl was cunning and, sweet in her own way.

Heather sounded annoyed, exactly as Gary would expect. "I don't have time now. I've got to be somewhere."

"You came to visit Ms. Stoddard. I think you've got a few minutes."

"Fine." Heather sighed with supreme teenage superiority. "But only a couple of minutes."

"We can use the lobby downstairs," he said. His black police shoes squeaked and Nora figured he'd moved to the elevator and pushed the button.

"Great. Let's do it in front of the whole world so everyone thinks I'm a criminal."

Easy, Heather, don't get him too riled up, thought Nora.

A ding, soft rattle, a little shuffling, a swoosh, and Nora assumed they were on their way down to the lobby. She poked her head around the corner in time to see the woman who must be Laurie scoot down the corridor on the other side of the elevator.

Nora stepped out and strolled past the station. She didn't see anyone behind the counter. Good thing nurses were busy people.

She read the room numbers as she hurried down the hall. She smelled like fire and fear and had to look like a homeless person. If Abigail felt anything close to her normal self, Nora had better brace herself for an epic lecture.

Laurie's friendly but firm voice floated out of the doorway to Abigail's room. Damn. Nora glanced in the door of the room next to Abigail's. The patient inside lay flat on her back with her eyes closed. With any luck, she—or he, it was hard to tell with all the white hair and sagging skin—was asleep. Nora slipped inside the room and into the bathroom next to the door.

"I'm going to ask you to come back another time," Laurie said. "Ms. Stoddard has had visitors all morning and she really needs to rest."

"Oh posh." Steel bands loosened around Nora's lungs. Abigail sounded like her regular self. "I'm not the least bit tired. Having visitors makes me feel better."

"That may be, but I'm going to have to insist." Laurie obviously didn't know who she dealt with.

"If you're going to be that way, at least give me a couple of minutes to finish our conversation." Now Nora detected fatigue in her mother's voice. To allow someone to tell her what to do really clinched it: Abigail was hurt. Nora fought not to run to her mother's bedside.

"Just a couple of minutes," Laurie said from the doorway. "I'm checking my watch and I'll be back down if you don't come out."

Abigail's visitor could be one of the women from her service club, but Nora hoped for Charlie. If so, it would mean he was okay. More than anything, she wanted her people safe and healthy and away from Barrett.

Laurie's shoes squeaked with infinite efficiency as she hurried down the corridor.

"Are you the nurse?" A crotchety voice called from the bed.

The voice jettisoned Nora into the air and sent her nerves jangling. She'd guessed incorrectly. The patient was a man.

Nora tried to be calm. "No. Just the wrong room."

His voice carried much louder than necessary. He probably didn't hear well himself and compensated by shouting at everyone else. "What did you say? I asked if you are the nurse."

She couldn't shout back. What if Abigail's visitor wasn't Charlie? What if Laurie came back and caught her? What if Heather broke under Gary's interrogation and told him Nora was on the third floor? What if a meteor struck Earth and they went the way of the dinosaur?

Sheesh. She always accused Abigail of exaggerating life to follow a movie script; it must be an inherited trait.

Still, Nora hurried to the old man's bed and spoke quietly. "I'm sorry I disturbed you. I'm in the wrong room."

His hand shot out from under the blanket, his grip surprisingly strong on her wrist. Nora's heart kicked in at the nightmare prospect of this frail-looking man actually being a demon. Or maybe a kachina, out to stop her from creating more chaos.

"The nurse hasn't been here for two days. No one gives me food. I haven't had a drink of water. She's trying to kill me so she can have my money."

His lunch tray sat on the windowsill, the gravy not even coagulated yet. An insulated pitcher with condensation from fresh ice water sat on his bedside table. He wasn't an evil sprite or Big Elk's faithful. He was an old, sick, and confused man.

Would life ever be normal again?

Nora reached over to grasp the pitcher, her other arm still in the old man's clutches. A bendy straw stuck from the top. "Let me help you," she said, grateful when he released her.

She put the straw in his mouth and he drew in the water, his rheumy eyes focused on her. The drink quenched his hostility and his eyes filled with the trust of a small child. He finished drinking. "You're the best nurse I've ever had."

She set the pitcher down and patted his hand.

His voice changed. "You are here to do good."

Moisture vanished from Nora's mouth and reappeared as cold sweat on her forehead. The old man's eyes closed and his mouth opened a bit, letting out soft snores as he immediately fell asleep.

The voice hadn't been that of the patient lying in front of her.

He'd spoken with the hesitant and abrupt cadence of the little kachina man.

Nora Abbott, you are certifiably nuts. Probably paranoid and delusional too. She tried to take inventory of what was real. Scott lay dead. Heather, and probably Alex, had destroyed the lift. Barrett had murdered Big Elk. Someone blew up her house with Abigail in it. Charlie risked his life to save Abigail.

Her mother rested next door. Nora had to touch her and know she was alive. She rushed toward the door … And stopped dead when she heard the low rumbled of a man's voice. It wasn't Charlie in Abigail's room.

"You should get some rest now. I'll be back later." Barrett sounded sincere and tender, all the wonderful things a man should be to the woman he intended to marry.

THIRTY-EIGHT

Barrett softly stroked the back of Abigail's hand. It might be the only spot on her that wasn't bruised or cut. He would prefer to take the pillow she rested her bandaged head on and smash it down on her face, grinding it until the life left her body.

"That Laurie is so bossy." Abigail pouted in a way he once thought attractive. "I want to spend more time with my fiancé."

He dodged stitches on her forehead and brushed his lips on her skin. "You've been through too much. First the gas leak and explosion itself, then to find out Nora is responsible." If Abigail hadn't turned at the last minute and ruined his aim with the tire iron, she wouldn't be lying here worrying at all. She'd be stretched out on a slab in the morgue.

Abigail's eyes sparked with indignation. "Nora is not behind this, despite what Gary says. He's determined to throw her in the clink. I'm glad she's on the lam, hiding from the Heat." Since Abigail's brush with the law she'd taken on a whole new language.

Why had he found her so appealing? She looked like an old woman and sounded like a harpy. The stitches and dried blood along the eight-inch gash on her forehead made her look like Frankenstein's monster. "I know it's hard to consider, but if the police are convinced Nora's at fault, they probably have strong evidence."

Barrett hadn't planned on killing Abigail. He'd left her at the police station in the care of his trusty attorney and rushed back to torch the apartment. But she'd shown up unexpectedly. After he decided killing her was the most expedient solution to the problem, it struck him as justice for rejection. She'd said yes to his proposal, but only for his protection.

Goddamn Charlie for his meddling. He'd somehow rescued her and now Barrett had another loose end.

A lioness protecting her cub would be no more ferocious than Abigail, even injured as she was. "It's Big Elk and his gang of thugs, maybe that big Indian friend of Heather's."

Barrett tried to soothe her. "You're probably right. At the very least, poor Nora has lost everything. Not even a memento of her husband is left."

Abigail sniffed in indignation. "Not that she needs to be reminded of his low character. The awful irony is that the only thing to make it through is that stupid box of Scott's."

This couldn't be. "I'm afraid nothing's left of the apartment."

"It wasn't in the apartment. I didn't want Nora to have to face it again, so I had Heather load it into her car to take to the dump."

Scott's fucking logs were still around?! Fiery claws ripped at Barrett's gut. Heather had the logs. Nora was with Heather. He had to find them. Now. "I can protect Nora until we get this all straightened out. Where is she?"

"I don't know. What if Big Elk has her?" The final word squeezed into a sob. He'd thought she was so dignified and classy. Her sniveling made him want to slap her face.

He had to convince Abigail of his grave concern for Nora's safety. "Big Elk isn't a threat. But I really need to find Nora if I'm going to help her."

"The last I knew, she and Heather were coming back from the Hopi reservation. Heather was really excited because she found out something about her family."

Her family. What the hell was this now? *He* was her family. Some big-mouthed Indian was filling her head with bullshit. He couldn't allow this. "What about her family?"

Fatigue crept into Abigail's voice. "She found out her name and is going to ask Charlie. Charlie knows a lot about Hopi people." Again her words tailed off into tears. "But now he's here because of me."

"Or because of Nora, if the police are right."

Abigail's indignation burst out. "They are most certainly not right. I won't have you casting aspersions."

Charlie's brain was probably so pickled he couldn't remember his last name, but what if it wasn't? He might know about Heather. Barrett couldn't risk Heather finding out. In for a penny, in for a pound: Charlie had to go.

"I'm sorry. Don't worry about Nora. I'll find her and protect her."

The last spurt of anger must have drained Abigail. She sounded exhausted. "Thank you, dear."

Barrett pulled her hand to his lips. "You said Charlie is in the hospital too?"

"He'll help her if he can. He's very fond of Heather." Abigail closed her eyes, already drifting off.

Barrett strode toward the door and spoke quietly to himself: "It's time Charlie minds his own business and leaves my family alone."

THIRTY-NINE

NORA HEARD BARRETT'S COWBOY boots clack under his bulk, then his voice as he exchanged friendly remarks with Laurie at the nurse's station.

This was bad. The same gaping slit across Big Elk's throat awaited Charlie unless Nora could warn him.

Nora checked the hall then snuck into Abigail's room. Her mother lay like a corpse, pale and lifeless, her eyes closed. One eye puffed in a bed of purple and pink, a stapled gash with blackened blood lined the eyebrow. If Nora had just given up the idea of making Kachina Ski a money machine, if she'd sold it or closed it and walked away, none of this would have happened. Scott would still have left her, but he and Maureen would be alive. Abigail would be flirting and probably planning her next wedding to some tycoon she met on a cruise. Nora was certain she had caused this disaster with her greed and pride. The guilt was almost unbearable.

She tiptoed to the bed.

Abigail opened one eye, the other swollen shut. "Oh, Nora." Tears spilled down the side of her face. "You shouldn't be here."

Nora took her mother's hand and leaned close. "I'm so sorry."

Abigail blinked, the struggle to be strong obvious. "Gary was here. He wants you for questioning. He thinks you killed Scott and blew up the lift and apartment for insurance. I know it wasn't you."

"Shh."

"He thinks you were in the apartment when I got there and snuck up behind me, hit me with something hard, then turned on the gas so the place would explode. Only you were on the phone with me. But I can't tell him that because he'll find out where you are."

"I'm sorry, Mother."

The fear that rode shotgun with Nora colored Abigail's words. "You've got to find Barrett. He'll protect you."

Abigail was so worried already; Nora couldn't bear to scare her more by telling her about Barrett. "Don't worry, Mom. I'll figure it out." Nora smoothed the hair on Abigail's forehead, avoiding the raw spots. "How are you?"

"Look at my face. This will leave a scar. This is where I hit the table when I fell. At least the mark on the back of my head will never be seen. But I'll heal. The real concern is for you."

No. The immediate threat was for Charlie. Barrett wanted something hidden from Heather, and he wouldn't hesitate to silence Charlie to do it.

Abigail patted Nora's hand. "I'm glad to see you, but you have to go before Big Elk or Gary find you here."

"I love you, Mom."

Tears returned to Abigail's eyes. "Well, I know that."

"No, I really mean it. You're a wonderful woman."

Tears left trails through Abigail's makeup. Of course nearly dying would be no excuse not to put on her face. Nora wondered where her mother had gotten the spare cosmetics. "That's nice of you to say, but we both know it's not true."

Nora pulled a tissue from the box by the bed and dabbed Abigail's eyes.

Abigail sniffed. "I'm not strong and smart like you. I so admire you."

"You admire me?"

"I wish I were more like you. You aren't afraid to be on your own. Look at me. I'm terrified of being penniless and alone." She sobbed.

Nora's bruised heart ached at the sight of Abigail's tears. "You're not alone."

"I wouldn't be marrying Barrett if I were more like you. I know he's the kind of man I appreciate. But this time," she sobbed, "this time I wish I had more courage to do what my heart wants."

Why wouldn't Abigail want to marry the man she thought Barrett was? "What does your heart want?"

"Charlie." Abigail dissolved into heaving sobs.

Blow someone up and the strangest things seeped from the cracks. Abigail and Charlie? That might be even crazier than a century-dead man showing up on Nora's doorstep.

"If you want Charlie, why not be with him?"

Abigail sniffed and wiped her eyes. "What security does he offer me? A decrepit cabin in a rundown mountain village. No shopping, no vacations, no retirement."

"Do you love him?"

Abigail looked at Nora in surprise. "No one has ever made me laugh the way Charlie does. He makes me happy just walking in the woods or sitting on the porch in the sunlight. I've never had that much fun at Macy's, even during a sale."

Nora smiled and shook her head. It would be great to stay with Abigail and continue the most genuine conversation they'd ever had, but it wasn't to be. If Nora didn't save Charlie, Abigail's dreams of enjoying the mountain with him would never come true. She'd already given Barrett too much of a head start as it was.

"I've got to go," Nora said.

"Yes. Go. Be careful. Be safe."

Keeping one eye out for the industrious Laurie, Nora strode as quickly and silently as possible, straining into every room, desperate to see that grizzled head she loved so much.

Up one corridor. Nothing but strangers in each room. Nora felt sad for every patient in every room and all their loved ones. They were living out their own stories of misery, woe, and hope. Hospitals are like normal life amplified. In here a headache doesn't mean two aspirins and a nap—it means a life-threatening tumor. A bruise becomes cancer. Affection is passion, anxiety is terror. Watching, waiting, praying. Life on the precipice. She hated hospitals.

At the far end of the hall a service elevator sat at the intersection of the two corridors. Nora hurried up the other side, checking each room. Charlie wasn't on this floor. Barrett could find and kill Charlie in slow torture by the time she checked each floor manually. Time for bold action.

Laurie and another staffer discussed a teacher at Laurie's daughter's school. Apparently, the teacher was the Antichrist.

Nora inhaled, straightened her shoulders, smoothed her clothes as much as possible and ambled to the station as if she felt no pressure. She smiled in what she hoped appeared a natural way, wondering if it looked like the desperate woman she was, fearing for her life and that of everyone she loved. "I'm lost, I guess. I'm looking for Charlie Podanski. I thought he was on this floor but I must have the wrong room number."

Laurie looked at her with the deep eyes of a Native American. She didn't return Nora's smile. Maybe she recognized Nora. Maybe she just didn't see the need to smile.

The other woman, a petite blonde, grinned, her teeth white in her tanned face. "Sure. Let me look it up."

The younger woman punched a few keys on the computer. "Here's the problem, you've got the wrong floor. He's in 408."

Laurie hadn't said anything. She studied Nora as if she were a new disease.

"Thanks," Nora said and tried to walk away when she wanted to run.

"You can take the elevator," the young woman said.

"It's only one floor. I'll walk." And hopefully avoid Gary when Laurie called him, which she would certainly do.

Nora rounded the corner and lunged for the stairway door. She bounded up the steps, taking off for room 408.

Charlie's room was on the same side of the floor as the stairs and Nora didn't encounter any staff as she dashed down the corridor. She glanced behind her to make sure Gary and Laurie didn't trail her before she ran into his room.

Charlie lay on his back, eyes closed. A white bandage-wrapped around his forehead. White cotton swathed his left hand and looked like a puff of snow lying on his chest. He should be out creating environmental mischief on his trails, not wrapped in disinfected sheets under artificial lights. Nora hurried to the bed.

"Charlie?"

He opened his eyes and focused them with effort. "An angel of the first degree."

Nora put a hand under his shoulders. "Are you hurt? Can you sit up?"

He grunted. "For you, darlin', anything."

He didn't weigh much but felt like a hundred-and-fifty-pound sack of sand. "I've got to get you out of here."

He gave her a blank smile. "You're breaking me out. I knew you were a good one."

Nora succeeded in sitting him on the side of the bed, but his speech and movements blurred around the edges. "Come on, Charlie. This is important. Barrett is coming after you."

He turned an amused face to her. "He better watch out. I'm coming after him."

"Are your feet or legs hurt? Can you stand?"

"Oh, sure. I can stand. I can take you dancing. I used to dance. Did you know that? I was dashing and the sweet girls lined up."

"That's nice, Charlie." He was so drugged up his arms and legs had less body than the hospital sheets. He'd never make it out.

Nora ran into the hall. There had to be wheelchairs somewhere. Two doors down a loud female voice, the tone perfect to get the attention of a deaf two-year-old, hollered. "Hello, Mrs. Robinson. I need to take you down for some tests. Let's just get your vitals."

The figure on the bed didn't respond. Nora wouldn't have responded, either, unless it was to tell the woman to speak like an adult. A wheelchair sat by the door waiting for Mrs. Robinson to have her pulse and temp taken.

"I'm Debbie, Mrs. Robinson. Your chart says your name is Deborah, so we're both Debbies. Debbie Robinson."

Amid the annoying and senseless chatter, Nora stole the wheelchair. Guilt nagged at her for not stealing Mrs. Robinson out from darling Debbie's clutches too, but there was only so much saving she could do in a day.

She rushed back to Charlie's room, half expecting Gary to be standing there with his gun drawn.

Charlie sat on the bed humming, arms out, swaying as if on the dance floor. "Do you suppose Abigail would like to dance with me?"

"Into the chair." Nora hefted him from the bed and plopped him into the chair not as gently as she'd have liked.

He grunted and tried to grab the chair rails but his mittened hand bounced off and landed in his lap, where he let it stay.

She inhaled. "Here we go. Act natural."

"Darlin', I'm the master at deceiving The Man."

She whisked him out the door and flew past Mrs. Robinson's room, where Debbie hadn't noticed the missing chair yet. No wonder hospital costs were so high with idiots like Debbie at large.

Chances were Laurie was no idiot. She probably put in a call to Gary before Nora had even hit the stairwell. Why hadn't he shown up yet with his handcuffs and billy club?

Nora stopped short of the corner where the nurses' station faced the elevator. She couldn't wheel Charlie in front of the nurses and get on the elevator. Even good ol' Debbie would have a better handle on her patients than to let strangers take them away. Any second, Debbie would burst from Mrs. Robinson's room and send the SWAT team after the missing wheelchair.

The elevator door whooshed open and Nora shrank to the wall.

Feet stepped out of the elevator onto the linoleum of the hall. Nora calculated the distance back to room 408. Maybe she could make it back to Charlie's room. And then what? Wait for Barrett or Gary to finish them off?

Footsteps approached the corridor. She lunged across the hall to the nearest room. She could shove Charlie into the bathroom and hide like she did next to her mother's room.

She didn't move fast enough. The footsteps sounded behind her.

If those feet carried Gary, the jig was up. She braced to swing the chair back, maybe charge into him and throw him off balance.

That was a stupid idea. She gave Charlie's chair a massive shove and dove into a room, not quite clearing the doorway.

A hand landed on her shoulder. She gasped. Heather's voice sounded irritated. "What are you doing?"

Charlie gave her a lopsided grin. "My beautiful Indian maiden. You make the world a better place just by being alive."

Heather raised an eyebrow and looked at Nora. "What kind of drugs is he on?"

Nora shook her head. "Can you distract the nurse so I can get him down the elevator?"

"That's a stupid plan."

"What do you suggest? We've got to get out of here before Gary finds us."

"No lie. But he took off for your mother's room and it won't be long before he figures out you're up here. When he does, he'll be on the elevator, or he'll have someone watching the lobby." Heather took hold of the handles of Charlie's chair, shoving Nora out of the way.

Charlie tilted his head back to look at Nora. "How is Abigail, that vision of grace?"

Nora patted his shoulder, trying to dam the panic flooding her brain. Think. There had to be another way to get Charlie out of here. Debbie was a blink away from storming out of Mrs. Robinson's room. They had to get moving.

Light bulb. Nora hurried back the way she came. "There's a service elevator this way."

Heather spun the chair around and sailed down the corridor past Mrs. Robinson's room, where Debbie shouted her sing-song nonsense.

Charlie's head listed to the right. "Like a chopper over the Mekong. Wind in my face."

No way would they get away with this. Gary or Debbie or Laurie or some other authority would find them, send Charlie back to his bed where Barrett would kill him like shooting a fish in a barrel. Nora would spend the rest of her life in jail for killing Scott and Maureen.

The hallway ended with a narrow corridor leading to the other side of the floor. The service elevator doors faced the corridor. Heather punched the buttons.

"Where are we goin'?" Charlie asked. He hummed a Doors tune circa 1968.

The numbers above the elevator marked the floors while her heart threatened to pound through her skin. Two, three . . . She held her breath, waiting for the doors to open on death.

The light stayed on four and the clank and settle of the gears and cables signaled the arrival of doom. The doors slid open.

But the elevator wasn't empty. Nora's heart stopped.

The young Native American man in blue scrubs looked up and gave them a distracted smile. He carried a plastic tray full of vials and other lab paraphernalia. "How're ya doin'?"

Heather shoved the chair into the elevator. "Good."

Nora stood paralyzed while the young man stepped out. He didn't give them a passing glance as he hurried away.

"Let's go, Lara Croft," Heather said.

Nora stepped into the car and the doors shut. They descended to the ground floor and out the back hallway to a courtyard with flowers, grass, and benches. All lovely, normal, no police chase, nothing but Charlie humming tunes from his psychedelic phase—his earlier one, that is.

Nora still couldn't breathe and her heart might quit again any time. But they strolled at a normal pace along the paved path, passing other patients enjoying the summer sunshine. Although Nora could only follow dumbly along, Heather even smiled and nodded at people.

A sidewalk veered off the garden path between two buildings, leading to the front of the hospital and the parking lot. Without altering their pace, Heather directed the chair into the deep shadows between the buildings. She reached into the pocket of her jeans and pulled out the car keys.

"Bring the car up and we'll load him in. Easy as pie."

Nora snatched the keys and scrambled for the car. Running through chocolate pudding would be easier. Her nerves were shot and she knew she was thinking like a crazy person. With every step she was sure Gary was closing in. When he discovered Charlie had disappeared he would call for backup. Police would circle them like sharks.

Eventually she reached Heather's car. It seemed like two moon cycles but it probably took thirty seconds. She fumbled to unlock the door and shook so badly it took three tries to slide the key into the ignition. She fired the engine and made herself take a deep breath to get control. Peeling out of the parking space might draw attention. She started to count. If she pronounced each number slowly, maybe her movements would slow to the beat and help her calm down. Thirteen, fourteen, back up, brake, sixteen, seventeen, put it in gear. Twenty-two, twenty-three, drive slowly down the row, turn. Thirty-five, thirty-six, pull up to the slit between buildings, put it in park.

Heather appeared with Charlie. His chin rested on his chest and his mittened hand dangled from the side of the chair. Passed out or fallen asleep. He was alive though. Right? He didn't move.

Heat rose from the pavement. Nora opened the back passenger door and she and Heather lifted and shoved Charlie into the backseat.

Nora grabbed a jacket and other clothes in the backseat to make a pillow and settled his head, arranging his legs.

"Let's go." Heather said then shouted, "Now. Now!"

Nora jerked her head up. Heather bounded around the front of the car and into the driver's seat.

Over the rumble of the idling engine, Nora heard what she'd been expecting all along:

"Stop!"

She still crouched over Charlie, his feet hanging out the open door.

Gary ran from the front of the hospital, reaching for the gun strapped to his side.

FORTY

HEATHER RAMMED THE RAV4 into gear and stomped on the gas, sending Nora tumbling across the seat. She bounced off Charlie and got wedged between the floor and seat. Her head slammed against the frame as the door closed, catching her hair in the jam. The door hit Charlie's feet and bounced open again.

Nora pulled herself up in time to see Gary raise his gun. She hoped he aimed for the tires or, better yet, shot like bad guys in movies and missed them entirely.

Heather raced from the parking lot, squealing a right onto the street, throwing Nora to the floor and sending the door swinging again, which took out another clump of Nora's hair and gave Charlie a new set of bruises.

Nora struggled to right herself and pull Charlie's feet inside. The vehicle swayed around corners and bumped through rough intersections, tossing Nora from side to side. With difficulty she managed to catch the door on one of its swings inward and *snick* it shut. She checked Charlie.

With his eyes closed he hummed tunelessly. He was conscious again, so they hadn't killed him, but enough pain medication flowed through him that the car door didn't seem to hurt him. For now he floated in a happy place.

Which was much more than could be said for Nora. She climbed to the front seat and looked out the window. They sped down a forest road, packed smooth but unpaved.

Heather stared down the road. "One thousand two hundred eighty-two what?"

Nora didn't have the patience for a game. "What are you talking about?"

"What are you counting?"

She didn't realize she was still counting. "Moments until I lose my grip on sanity."

"You could have stopped at five."

A giggle welled from somewhere in Nora's gut. It rose to a full boil of belly laughs.

Heather swung from the packed dirt road onto a trail and they slammed into rocks in the road, bouncing high enough to make Nora's head bang the roof.

Nora only laughed harder. Tears cascaded down her face.

Heather ventured a glance at her, then quickly back at the road. She swerved, throwing Nora against the door with a crash.

Nora's sides hurt. She was hysterical, and some part of her knew it. Soon she'd come completely unhinged.

Heather braked hard, made a nearly-ninety-degree turn, drove into a thicket of pines, and killed the engine. "Knock it off," she growled at Nora.

Nora sobered. There was nothing funny about this. What was the matter with her, anyway? She looked back at Charlie.

He knelt on the floor of the backseat. His voice sounded like he spoke around a mouth of cotton balls. "You girls know how to stage a jailbreak."

"You're a freak," Heather said to Nora, with as much irritation as a teenager can pack into a few words. And Heather was particularly skilled in that area.

Maybe they weren't exactly safe, but Barrett wouldn't find them here. They needed a plan. Nora took a breath but instead of words, she let out a laugh and started again.

Heather rolled her eyes. Then she smiled and chuckled despite herself. Soon her laughter joined Nora's in a tango of hysterics.

After a time, they settled down, wiped the tears from their eyes, and grew quiet.

"Charlie?" Nora asked.

"Don't suppose you grabbed some meds on your way out the back door?" he piped in.

She shook her head.

"Ah, well," he said.

Heather turned to the backseat. "You said you know a lot about people on the Hopi rez."

Charlie sounded fuzzy. "I spent a fair amount of time out there when I was young. Good people."

"Benny said I was from a powerful clan."

Charlie's words slurred even more than usual. "Are you Hopi? You look Hopi."

Frustration edged Heather's words. "Benny knows me."

Charlie's eyes drooped closed. "To know you is to love you."

Heather reached over the seat and took Charlie's hand. "Do I look like anyone you know?"

Charlie struggled to open his eyes. "You're a vision. A beauty."

"That's not what I mean. He called me Sikyatsi."

Charlie's head dropped back and he mumbled something that might have been a name, but it strangled in a deep snore.

Heather twisted in the driver's seat and glared out the windshield.

Nora wanted to comfort Heather, but she wasn't sure how.

Heather looked back at Nora. "Are you going to tell me why we kidnapped Charlie and what we're running from?"

Nora opened her door and stepped into the forest. She had to think.

Heather got out and walked around to her. "I saw Poppy coming out of the elevator while Officer Buttface interviewed me. Was he visiting Abigail?"

Nora nodded.

"Did he see you?"

Nora shook her head and finally spoke. "He was nice to Abigail but he wanted to know where I was. When he found out you were going to ask Charlie about your family, he got really upset."

Heather raised her eyebrows, adding insult to the sarcasm of her tone. "Oh good, she does something more than nod her head and laugh."

"Can you stop with all the smart-alecky attitude?"

Heather plopped down on a rock. "Sorry. I'm scared, okay? I don't know what to do about Poppy and I'm probably in trouble with the law too."

"You? Scared?" Nora sat down next to her. "You can blow up my lift, run in and out of the rez, go all *Starsky and Hutch* through town, and now you tell me you're scared?"

Heather put her chin in her hand. "I do what I have to do."

Nora stared into the silent forest, the Ponderosa pine thick and dark.

What was that? A flash of blue? Her heart lunged, followed by a flare of anger. No. This was crazy and she wouldn't look, wouldn't let her imagination and more hysteria make her believe the kachina man followed her.

"We've got to figure out what to do." Nora's voice sounded harsher than she expected.

"About what? Charlie in the backseat of my car? Poppy wanting God only knows what from you?" She licked her dry lips. "Poppy... Poppy ordering that man to kill Big Elk? Ordering Gary to arrest you?"

Nora rubbed her forehead.

"You know, when you do that, you look just like your mother," Heather said.

"Wouldn't it be nice if someone said something today that wasn't disturbing on some level?" Nora glared at Heather.

"And that's her look too."

"Gaa! Stop it." Nora couldn't help her outburst.

Heather laughed. "Really. You're almost as good at that you-low-life-scum look as Abigail."

"I'm an amateur compared to her."

Heather nodded. "She is good. She's got that Queen Abigail attitude, you know. But you're like the Lady Di of the family. You're classy and royal and seem sort of above everyone else. But you've got that soft vulnerable thing going on too."

Nora narrowed her eyes in irritation. "You're full of shit."

Heather burst out laughing. "Not Lady Di at all."

A small grin tugged at Nora's mouth before she remembered what a terrible mess they were in.

"We had to get Charlie out of there because your father threatened to hurt him."

The teasing smile vanished. "Not Charlie! Why would he do that?"

"Whatever Charlie might know about your family is something Barrett doesn't want you to find out."

"And he's going to hurt Charlie to keep him from telling me?"

"I think so."

Heather looked at her skeptically. "Where did you come up with this?"

Nora told her about the conversation she'd overheard.

Charlie mumbled from the backseat, his eyes still closed. "A cold wet can of liquid painkiller might keep me alive."

Nora opened a side door and put a hand on Charlie's forehead. He didn't feel feverish. One good thing. "I'm sorry, Charlie. It's almost dark. Maybe we can do something soon."

Heather leaned through the open back door and gently kissed Charlie's cheek. "I'll protect you from Poppy."

After Heather's calculating and calm attack of the situation, this tenderness surprised Nora. Just when Heather seemed like nothing but a Barrett clone, she flashed a human side.

Charlie took hold of Heather's hand and patted it. "You gotta stop trying to clean up Barrett's messes. He's a big man and he makes big problems. You can't make up for him and you're going to kill yourself trying."

Heather's eyes shimmered with tears. "You're probably right." She cleared her throat. "He's not even my real father, so I don't know why I feel responsible for the evil he creates."

Nora stood close to Heather. "Whatever Barrett is up to, it's not your burden. It's hard enough living your own life without having to make amends for someone else."

Heather nodded. "I know you're right. But in Hopi, we believe in balance. I should be able to balance Poppy's bad with my good."

Nora put an arm around Heather's shoulders. "Are you telling me that because Abigail is my mother, I am responsible for all her actions? That's a chore I'm not willing to take on."

"The Hopi elders say that two or three righteous people are enough to fulfill the Creator's mission. Some say even one truly righteous person can save the world."

Charlie smiled at Heather, still only half lucid. "You are good, no denying that. Let your goodness shine and leave Barrett off your scales."

Heather looked at the ground. "It would be different if he were my real father, I guess. Are you sure you don't remember Sikyatsi?"

Charlie shook his head. "It sounds familiar but my memory isn't as good as it used to be." He looked stricken. "We should have brought Abigail with us. She's not safe when Barrett is on the loose."

A spear of apprehension shot into Nora. "This is insane."

Charlie said. "Let's get the goods on Barrett and we'll all live happily ever after."

"I'd settle for all of us living."

Charlie's head then fell back and he snored.

After several minutes of silence, Nora shrugged in frustration. "Cole thinks Scott's murder is at the crux of everything."

Heather considered. "Okay. Then I guess we need to do some research."

"What do you mean?"

Heather walked to the back of the RAV4. "Don't get mad at me."

"Did you blow something else up?"

Heather shot her a withering look. "I said I was sorry about that. I didn't know you very well then."

"I'm not forgiving you yet. When we're safe from Barrett and your environmental and ethnic brethren, you and I are going to have a talk."

At least Heather looked contrite. She opened the back of the vehicle and reached inside to pull out a box.

That stupid box. It contained grief, anger, pain, and rejection. Nora remembered when Maureen's roommate brought it to the lodge. Why hadn't she burned it?

Heather looked at her with a mixture of embarrassment and guilt.

"It's okay," Nora said.

Heather carried the box to a flat rock and bent over it. She rummaged beneath odd items and pulled out a sheaf of paper. "Why was Scott working for Poppy?"

"Barrett? Scott worked for Barrett?"

Heather waved the paper. "This is from Southwest Consultants."

The box held her dead husband's possessions from a life she didn't know existed.

"Southwest Consultants is Poppy's uranium company."

Nora hadn't known that. But then, why would she care? "Okay. But I don't know why you'd think Scott was *working* there."

"He's got a whole stack of papers from them."

FORTY-ONE

Nora stirred herself and took the sheet of paper from Heather. It bore Southwest Consultants' logo. A matrix covered most of the page with printed column and row headings and Scott's scribbled figures in the boxes. "I don't know what this is," Nora said.

She stomped to the box and peered onto it. Just what she wanted, to paw through the remnants of Scott's secret life with another woman. Her stomach flipped and landed with a dull ache.

The first few items looked innocent enough. Racing magazines and old bike gloves. Under that she extracted a framed snapshot of Scott and Maureen standing in front of his backpack tent with a river in the background. Nora tried not to remember lying in that same tent next to Scott on so many of their own camping trips. When had she stopped backpacking with him? Two years ago, three? Something at Kachina always needed attention and even if she found downtime, the thought of strapping on a forty-pound pack and traipsing into the woods exhausted her.

She'd been stupid to think Scott, the man who loved an audience, would be happy alone while she worked. The pain of her loss made her want to fall to the ground and curl into a tight ball.

She started to put the frame on top of the magazines, but she didn't drop the frame as she intended. Instead, she raised her arms over her head and brought the frame straight down on the edge of the rock, shattering the glass and breaking the frame into two separate pieces held together by the photo inside. She picked up the mess and ripped at the picture and, with a final violent flourish, threw it into the trees.

"Wow," Heather said. "I never heard anyone scream like that."

Nora turned around, suddenly aware that her throat hurt. "I screamed?" She swiped at tears.

Heather nodded. "Feel better?"

"Not really."

"Want me to go through that stuff?"

Nora shook her head. "It doesn't do any good to deny the truth. I need to face it and put it behind me."

Heather's mouth twitched.

"I know. It sounds like Abigail." Nora scowled at her.

Seeing his things so neatly in the box hurt nearly as much as noticing Maureen's arm around Scott's waist in the photo. Scott didn't organize or keep anything neat. This had to be Maureen's doing. She took care of him, nurtured him. Nora forced herself to think the last . . . loved him.

Nora pulled out the stack of charts wrapped in a rubber band. The pages showed dates for twice a month. She flipped to the end of the stack. Over three years. He told her the affair ended two years ago. It had never ended. Damn it. Damn him.

She sank to her knees and gasped for air.

Heather materialized at her side, stroking Nora's back. "I'm sorry."

Nora struggled through the haze of anguish. She had something to do; exactly what, she didn't know. She couldn't fall apart. The world slowly took shape around her.

Heather stood next to her, uttering soothing words.

After many minutes, Nora pulled herself to her feet and cleared her throat. "Abigail called that one right. I wasted seven years on Scott."

Focus, Nora. Take care of business. It's what you do. She picked up the pages again. "What could these be?"

Charlie croaked from the backseat. "Bring them here and let me look."

Nora jumped. Charlie was like some spook that raised himself from the dead to spout prophecy and then collapsed, only to rise again.

She hurried to him to see if he looked close to death. She realized she didn't even know exactly what injuries he suffered in the explosion, other than a burned hand. But his face showed a healthy bit of color and his eyes sparked with life.

Charlie pushed himself to sit with his back against the door. With his good hand he took the page Nora held. He stared at the paper for a full minute, maybe willing his eyes to focus. Finally he handed it back to Nora. "Those are well logs. Scott was a logger for Barrett. He was checking groundwater."

"How do you know?" Nora asked.

Charlie smiled with reminiscence. "Protested a coal mine a couple of decades ago. Right before I lit the fuse in the office, I saw some logs like that. The company wanted to prove the water content."

The situation mushroomed in her mind, overwhelming her. "Who *was* Scott?"

Nora spun from Charlie and paced the clearing, anything to drag out the gremlins gnawing at her sanity. "I knew our marriage wasn't as good as it used to be. I didn't know how to make it work but I tried. Everything I did backfired. I should have known he was having an affair. I probably did on some level. But how could I have not known he worked for Barrett for three years?"

Charlie studied the page. "Did Scott know anything about water?"

Nora couldn't stop pacing. "He had an undergrad degree in environmental science. He knew a little about a lot of things. And yeah, I think he took some hydrology classes."

"So Barrett hired him to track groundwater," Charlie said.

"Why would he want to do that? Why not hire him outright with McCreary Energy?" Heather asked.

"There's something in the groundwater that interests Barrett and he doesn't want anyone to know about it," Charlie said.

Heather considered this. "Wouldn't Scott have needed an office and a lab to do the testing?"

"Maureen. Maureen was a graduate teaching assistant at the university," Nora said.

They both looked at her.

"She worked for a biologist."

"You knew her?" Heather asked.

Nora tried not to think about it. "She had a project tracking a vole or something out here a few years ago. She and some field techs camped on the meadow on the other side of the mountain. Scott probably met her there. Or maybe she chose to come here because they were already together."

Gradually Nora forced her mind from the Wronged Woman track. She didn't have time to mourn for a husband or life she never really had.

Heather frowned. "So Poppy hired Scott on the side. Looks like Scott took samples every two weeks from," she counted on the page, "ten wells. He hired Scott on the sly to keep the findings secret."

"And Scott found something he couldn't keep quiet about," Nora said.

"This is it! Got a phone?" Charlie sounded suddenly alert.

Heather found her bag under the backseat and grabbed her phone. When she handed it to Charlie he waved his bandaged hand.

Nora snatched the phone. "What's the number?"

Charlie recited and Nora punched, having no clue who she dialed. She didn't wonder long. She recognized Cole's voice the moment he picked up.

He sounded frantic. "Where are you two? Never mind. Stay put. The cops are everywhere looking for you. Charlie is gone and they think you kidnapped him."

"I did."

Silence. Big inhale. "Okay. We'll figure this out."

"Charlie's here. He wants to talk to you." She held the phone to Charlie's ear.

"We got it. Proof that Scott worked for Barrett. Well logs, pay stubs." He paused while Cole responded.

"Not sure where they're located. Got to be maps at Barrett's office with the wells numbered." Again he waited.

"No. You gotta stay with Abigail. I've got Heather and Nora with me. Take care of my girl, man."

Charlie nodded at Nora. "Wants to talk to you."

Cole spoke quietly. "I don't know if you want to tell Heather, but they found Alex. Cops think he stole Big Elk's Escalade and rolled it outside of Winslow. He's dead."

Big Elk and Alex both dead, along with Scott and Maureen. Corpses were piling up on Barrett. Nora had to make sure there would be no more.

She pushed the words from her mouth. "You and Charlie are working together on this, aren't you?"

"We're going to stop Barrett. I promise."

Nora swallowed. "Just keep Abigail safe."

"I'm on my way," Cole said. "Be careful."

Careful. As in, don't let the bad guys kill me and the people I love?

"Nora," Cole paused. "It will be okay."

"Okay." It sounded more confident than she felt.

"I really care about you, Nora" he said, his voice low and urgent.

She hung up the phone and turned to Charlie.

He nodded with conviction. "We're going into enemy territory."

FORTY-TWO

HEATHER CLIMBED INTO THE driver's side. "This is a good plan. Poppy will be all relieved to see me. I'll get him to walk to the stables. He thinks we always bond over horses. And you and Charlie can read the logs and maps and find the wells."

Fear lodged in the pit of Nora's stomach. "This seems ludicrous to go right into Barrett's grasp."

"He'll be so happy I'm home it won't occur to him that I brought you with me."

It might work in a perfect world. But the last few weeks proved how imperfect her world could be.

Charlie lay down in the backseat and before they even hit the main forest road his snores echoed in the vehicle. His excitement was no match for his tired body and a moving vehicle. Nora watched the mirrors for headlights, stared down the road ahead, turned to the side, then back.

"You're making me nervous," Heather said.

"Maybe we should go to the cops. I'll turn myself in. They don't have any evidence on me because I didn't kill Scott or Maureen or blow anything up."

Heather rolled her eyes. "Sure. Let's do that. You can convince them you didn't kidnap Charlie. Then you can tell them that Poppy really killed all those people and blew up your house, and you have a theory it has something to do with groundwater. That will fix everything."

"Okay, fine. But this is stupid. What if we do figure out which wells he's monitoring. How will that tell us anything?"

Heather shook her head. "I don't know. But it's all we've got."

Normally, the drive would take them back to the highway, through town, out to Interstate 40, and ten miles on the other side of the peaks: a forty-minute commute. But going through the peaks on a curvy, steep dirt road took much longer. The night grew darker and more sinister. Heather didn't spare the tires, suspension, or comfort of the passengers as she sped down the rocky mountain pass. Nearly two hours of driving tied Nora so full of knots her blood pressure nearly popped the veins in her forehead.

Still, when they turned down the one-lane blacktop road leading to the McCreary headquarters, Nora found her right foot pressing phantom breaks, dreading entering the lion's den.

They rounded the last corner to the imposing ranch house.

Heather frowned. "He's not home. Where would he be?"

"Maybe he is home, he's just trying to fool you."

Heather pulled up in front and put the Toyota in park. "What's the point in that? If he were home, the lights would be on."

Charlie stirred in the backseat. "Got a powerful headache. Sure could use a cold one."

Heather pulled the keys from the ignition and dropped them in the console. "Let's get that taken care of at least."

Nora got out and grabbed the well logs. "It's after ten. You're sure he's not in bed?"

"Poppy hardly ever sleeps."

Nora and Heather helped Charlie out of the backseat and up the porch steps. Heather opened the door and turned on the hall light.

"If he wasn't here, he'd have locked the doors," Nora whispered, already pulling back.

Heather led them through the front door, past an entryway and great room with enormous windows looking across the valley to the peaks. A three-quarter moon rose, brushing the tip of Kachina Peak. "Poppy doesn't lock doors. In his world, no one would dare cross him. Maybe he's right; we've never been robbed."

Heather left Charlie supported on Nora. She walked to a wet bar at the edge of the room and opened a small refrigerator. She pulled out three cans of beer and, lodging two between her forearm and belly, she popped the third open. She held it out to Charlie.

"Jewels in your crown, darling." He took it and tipped it back, chugging it down.

She opened another, handed it to him, and took his empty. "Feel better?"

"Immeasurably."

"Barrett really believes he's above it all?" Nora asked.

Heather stopped at a closed door and punched a code into the lock. "Yes."

"He doesn't lock the door to his house but he locks his office?" Nora asked.

Heather grinned. "That's to keep me away from his guns." She opened the door. "People hardly ever say no to him, and when they do, he's got ways to deal with them."

"Like Big Elk and Alex."

Heather froze. "Alex?"

Ugh, what an idiot. Nora put an arm around Heather. "I'm sorry. I shouldn't have told you like that. Cole said they found him dead in Big Elk's vehicle."

Heather stood motionless for three seconds, then took one deep breath. "Poppy needs to be stopped."

Nora shivered. "Thank God Cole is with Abigail."

Heather switched on the light, illuminating the office. She walked to the wall opposite the desk where a four-foot by three-foot framed map hung next to a full gun cabinet. "Okay, what are the well numbers?"

Charlie dropped into the leather desk chair and opened the third beer.

Nora spread a few logs on the desk and studied them. She listed off well numbers.

Heather turned around. "There are so many maps here. I don't know where to start or even what we're looking for."

"Do you have your phone?" Nora asked Heather.

Heather handed it over and Nora hit the last number. After two rings Cole picked up. "How's Abigail?" she asked.

She heard the smile in his voice. "Sleeping."

"Good. Is U the symbol for uranium?"

"Yes."

Nora leaned over and looked at the well logs. "Now that I can read the logs, I see that uranium levels are increasing in the last few months. We can't figure out where, though."

"What are the well numbers on the logs?"

She read off the list.

He paused. "Those are water wells on the Colorado Plateau."

Nora passed that along to Heather, who flipped charts. While Nora explained about finding Scott's logs and the increase in uranium counts, Heather located the wells on Barrett's maps.

"If uranium levels are increasing, it must mean McCreary Energy didn't do such a grand job of cleaning up their spills," Charlie said. He sipped instead of gulped his beer. A good sign. "But why would Barrett kill Scott because he discovered the contamination? Someone was bound to do a study and find out sooner or later."

"Unless he wanted to clean it up before anyone found out," Heather said.

Charlie shook his head. "You can't suck uranium from water in the middle of the night. It's a big operation and he'd have to get permits and jump through the EPA's hoops."

Cole listened, and then said, "The wells are in Hopiland."

"Scott knew it and was going to say something at the hearings," Nora said.

Heather nodded. "And Poppy must have found out about Maureen and figured she knew too."

Charlie rose from the desk. "Now he thinks you know, and maybe Abigail too."

"Barrett is getting desperate," Nora said. Cole didn't weigh in.

Charlie leaned back and picked up one of the log sheets. "My ancient eyes can't see this miniature log."

Heather leaned over the desk. "I think Poppy keeps a magnifying glass in the drawer."

Charlie opened the drawer and rummaged around under a few papers. He pulled out the glass, then stopped and stared. He took out an old snapshot of a woman, a little girl, and a man holding a baby.

He held the picture under the glass and stared at it. "Oh! How could I not know?"

Heather bent over the maps. "What?"

"I remember Sikyatsi."

Heather looked from the picture to Charlie.

He set the glass down but held the picture. "I don't know how I missed the resemblance. I'm getting old and forgetful, I guess. But you have her eyes."

"Whose eyes?" Heather demanded.

"Ester. The only woman besides our sainted Abigail that I ever loved."

Heather stared at him.

"Barrett's wife," he said.

"Poppy had a wife?"

"And what a woman she was. You are so much like her. How could I have not figured it out?"

Heather stared at him.

"You asked about Sikyatsi earlier, but I forgot." He pointed to the picture. "This is Soowi."

Heather leaned in to look.

Charlie's wistful voice croaked in the quiet. "She was your mother."

Heather's knees buckled and she caught herself on the edge of the desk. She grabbed the picture.

"You are Barrett's granddaughter." Charlie stood and walked to Heather. He held her face cradled in his one good and one bandaged hand. "I thought we'd lost you too."

Heather barely breathed the words. "My grandfather?"

Charlie stood back and let Heather process. She finally looked at him. "He had a wife. And kids?"

"A boy and a girl."

"Where are they?"

"Ah, angel," Charlie said, his voice thick with sympathy.

Barrett as a young family man. Nora had a hard time with the concept. "You'd better tell us the whole story," Nora said.

Charlie rubbed his hand along his grizzled jaw. "I thought Mac was a true believer. It was him who helped me with that logger's office. I took the heat so he could stay with Ester and the babies. He settled onto the rez and lived the good life."

Heather stared at him with dry eyes. "He lived on the rez? Which one?"

"Ester was Hopi through and through. She wanted good things for her people—your people. She worked hard to keep the old ways and fought to stop the rapers and extractors from tearing out the heart and lungs of the Mother."

Nora cringed at Charlie using the same vernacular as Big Elk.

"Barrett was a little less peaceful. More like me. But we needed to make people aware. It wasn't like now, with Al Gore making movies and everyone wanting to be green. Back then, it was all greed and exploitation."

Heather's voice sounded like a mouse. "What made Poppy leave the rez?"

"Choices, man. Bad choices." Charlie shook his head. "Blood is thicker and all that. Barrett McCreary the Second, your great-grand-father, had a heart attack. Bam. Dead. And just like that, Mac turned coat and became The Man. He left the rez and Ester and those babies. And he made a fortune gouging the vitals of the Mother, throwing away everything we'd worked for."

When Charlie stopped and Heather couldn't form words, Nora stepped in. "What happened to his family?"

Charlie stared at the beer while seconds ticked. Finally, he looked in Heather's eyes. "He broke her. Ester took the baby and went to the land for solace. Or maybe she just couldn't do anything else. She lived on the desert for months, eating in the old Hopi way, drinking from springs and seeps."

The story wasn't over, but Charlie stopped as if going on would be too hard.

Finally he inhaled and started again. "She and Mac had been working against the mining companies, trying to force them to clean up. She knew about the uranium leaks and contamination. But she drank from the springs anyway. And she nursed that baby boy."

Nora's stomach twisted.

"When she came back, there really wasn't anything we could do except watch them die. The baby went first. Even if Ester hadn't been so sick, that loss would have killed her. I was with her at the last." His breathing sounded heavy and labored. "She suffered." He drew in a shaky breath. "So much."

Heather didn't move.

Charlie sank to the desk chair. "And Mac wasn't there to see. He was making money."

"My grandmother and uncle died. What happened to the little girl? My mother. Did Poppy raise her?"

"The tribe hid her. They wouldn't let Barrett near her. But it was a hard life for the little darling. I kept in contact with her for a long time. But she ... " Tears filled his eyes and he swallowed. "Lost soul. The drink got her."

Heather stopped breathing.

"Alcoholism?" Nora asked.

He nodded. "Found her in Gallup in an old wash."

"My mother."

"If the tribe hid Heather and her mother from Barrett, how did he end up adopting her?"

Charlie stared at the desktop. His voice didn't rise above a whisper. "I heard Soowi sold the baby." Aside from a deathly pallor, Heather showed no signs she'd heard Charlie. "Wouldn't be hard for

318

someone with Mac's resources to have bogus adoption papers drawn up."

Nora hugged Heather, but the girl didn't soften. "He's a monster. We have to stop him."

The only way to help Heather was to finish this business. Nora studied the map and dialed Cole. When he picked up she said, "If the uranium is building in the aquifer, does that mean it will get in the Hopi water wells?"

His phone went dead.

"Cole?" Nora slapped the phone closed and redialed. It immediately shifted to voicemail. Something was wrong.

She turned to Heather and Charlie. "I've got to get to the hospital. Now."

FORTY-THREE

"WHAT DO YOU MEAN Charlie Podanski isn't here?" Barrett worried his heart would explode as his father's had.

The middle-aged woman with bags under her eyes lowered her voice even more. "Please keep it down. It's late."

Later than this old bat knew. Barrett wanted Charlie out of the way. "How could he be released? He was in a bad accident."

She eyed him like a confidante. "He wasn't really released. There was some hubbub here today with the police and everything. Two women kidnapped him."

"What?"

She warmed to her gossip. "Well, one was a girl. That woman from the ski place had this girl with her, and they just took him. They say the girl is a McCreary. No one seems to know why they did it." She obviously didn't know who Barrett was, the idiot.

Goddamn it. Abigail would know what's going on. He headed for the elevators.

The woman behind the front desk stopped him. "Wait. Visiting hours are long over. You can't go up there."

He lowered his eyes. "Please understand. I want to say good night to my wife. I would have been here earlier, but I had to keep the grandbabies until our daughter got done with her shift at the restaurant."

"I thought you came to see Charlie Podanski."

You meddling hag. "Oh, no. He's an old friend. I wanted to check on him while I was here. I came to see my wife on the third floor."

She would cave; she had that look. After a moment she said, "Okay. But please make it quick. I could get in a lot of trouble."

Nora had Heather, Charlie, and Scott's logs. Barrett only had Abigail.

But that was enough.

As Barrett approached Abigail's room, he heard Cole's voice murmuring. Barrett snuck closer and peered into the room. Abigail appeared to be sleeping.

Cole stood looking out the window, phone to his ear. "Those wells are in Hopiland."

And Barrett knew exactly what wells Cole referred to. He could guess who listened on the other end of the line, and he even had a pretty good idea where they were.

Everything he'd worked for was unraveling. Cole held sway over the congressional committee. Now he knew the secret of the wells. The Hopi would never give their permission to mine once they found out he hadn't cleaned up the uranium as he said. It was lost. Over.

Barrett stood in the hallway feeling his heart expand with the panic. He labored for breath. Fucking Cole had ruined everything.

What if Cole disappeared? Barrett had already gotten away with Scott, Maureen, Big Elk, Alex. One more. Then he'd be home free.

Once Cole was out of the way, Abigail would be Barrett's leverage, his ticket to everything he'd ever dreamed of for Heather.

Barrett slipped into a room across the hall with a sleeping patient. He cast about for something. Anything. A cell phone lay on the bedside table, the charging cord stretched to the outlet. Barrett snatched it, pulled the cord free, and spun around.

Cole still stared out the window, his back to the door.

Maybe he couldn't be quite as silent as his paid killer, but Barrett moved quietly enough. Cole was so shocked when the cord flew over his head and around his neck that it took him too long to react.

Barrett threw Cole face first on the ground and planted his knee in Cole's back. With all his bulk, Barrett pulled the cord and twisted it to cut off Cole's air.

Cole kicked and struggled but he was no match for Barrett's weight. It sounded like a riot to Barrett but it was certainly less conspicuous than a gunshot.

He hated what he was doing. Feeling the life seep from a body hurt his spirit, stole a bit of his own soul.

Goddamn these people for making him do this.

It seemed like hours, yet Barrett knew it couldn't have been more than minutes or even seconds. Cole quit moving but Barrett wasn't sure he was dead.

"Barrett?" Abigail leaned up on an elbow and stared at him.

He didn't move.

Her eyes widened. "Oh my God! Help!"

Dead or not, Barrett couldn't wait. He abandoned Cole and launched himself on Abigail.

FORTY-FOUR

"WE HAVE TO GO to the hospital. Something is wrong."

Charlie and Heather stared at Nora as if they couldn't understand what she said. A sudden telephone ring ripped through the room. Nora yelped and Heather lurched toward the sound. It rang again and Nora located it on the corner of the desk.

Heather grabbed it and punched it on. She listened for a second. "Where are you?" Hatred snapped in her dark eyes and she looked at the stand, punched the speaker, and set the phone back in the cradle.

"Can you hear me now?" Barrett's low voice snaked from the phone.

Heather dripped malice. "What do you want?"

"I'm glad you finally made it home. Is everyone safe? How is ol' Charlie holding up?"

Charlie raised his eyebrows. "Fine, Mac. Thanks for asking."

"Good to hear it. You have the cops concerned. They're trying to figure out how you're involved in all this."

"Look, Barrett," Nora said. "We know Scott was working for you and you killed him and Maureen to hide the increase in uranium in the groundwater."

He laughed. "Very good."

"We're going to the cops."

"I don't think you want to do that."

"You mean *you* don't want me to do that. Too bad."

"Here's what you're going to do. You and Charlie load up that box of Scott's things, including the well logs, and meet me up on the Peak. I'll be at the springs."

He paused. "Heather?"

Rage clouded her voice. "What?"

"You stay home."

She didn't answer.

"Give me another chance, Heather. When this is over, we'll take a world tour."

"Fuck you."

Silence sat for a moment. "Nora," Barrett said. "You have your instructions."

"Sure. Shall we bring wine or just the cops?"

"I think you'll want to do exactly as I say."

"Or what?"

"Or your mother might have an accident."

"Mother?"

Charlie jumped to his feet. He leaned toward the phone.

"You don't think you're the only one who can sneak past a few nurses, do you?"

Bile burned in Nora's gut. "What did you do to her?"

Barrett sounded as if he enjoyed the conversation. "Well, you know how she is about the great outdoors. But she's holding up fine.

Except she might trip and fall out here in the dark. Some of these cliffs can be treacherous—but I don't have to tell *you* that."

"Please don't hurt her." Nora could barely breathe.

"Bring the papers. If you don't, I'm sure the cops won't have a problem believing you are a very sick woman—a bad seed."

"Let me hear her. I need to know she's okay."

A shuffling sound came through the phone, then Abigail's voice, strong and angry. "Nora. He strangled Cole. Don't come out here. We do not negotiate with terrorists. Do you h—"

Barrett's voice came back. "Bring the box to the spring, Nora. And bring Charlie. It's been a long time since we've partied together, man."

He hung up.

Nora immediately reconnected.

Charlie's hand shot out and grabbed the phone. "What are you doing?"

"I'm calling the cops."

"You can't do that."

"I don't care if they throw me in jail for the rest of my life. We have to save my mother."

"One hint of cops and Abigail is a goner. We have to do this by ourselves."

Tears pushed at Nora's eyes. "He's going to kill us, isn't he? All of us."

Charlie's face sharpened. "I imagine he'll try."

"Oh God, what about Cole?" Another person dead because of her.

Charlie straightened his shoulders, setting himself for battle. "Cole's a tough one, honey."

She could only save one person at a time. Right now, it had to be Abigail. Nora started for the door. She stopped and looked around. "Where's Heather?"

"Didn't hear her leave."

Heather had more courage and ingenuity than either of them. They would be better off with her there, but that wouldn't be safe. "We've got to go without her."

Charlie reached back into the desk drawer and brought out a pistol. "We might need this, then."

FORTY-FIVE

HEATHER'S CAR WAS GONE when they got outside, and Nora lost precious time running to the barn to find a pickup. Lucky for them, Barrett's belief in his invincibility extended to his vehicles because the keys dangled from the ignition. Nora skirted town on the interstate and turned off on a dark road heading to Kachina Ski. At this time of night, there wasn't much traffic and thankfully they didn't run into any cops.

The chill of the mountain air swept across her face when she stepped from the pickup into Kachina's lot. She slid the box across the seat and threw the gun on top.

Charlie snatched the gun with his undamaged hand. "Better let me hold on to this. You've never used one before."

Her heart raced and she didn't want to waste time talking. "You have?"

He looked grim. "'Nam, remember?"

"Well, I'm not afraid to use it on Barrett if I need to."

Charlie shook his head. "She's important to me too."

They couldn't stay here and argue. She picked up the box and took off up the mountain to the spring.

Several feet from the clearing, she stopped and tried to still the panic pounding in her chest along with her heart. A dull light issued from a battery-powered lantern set on the rock.

Barrett's voice drifted to her. "Come on out, Nora. We're waiting."

Nora stepped forward. The moon cast just enough light onto the forest to reveal Barrett in the clearing.

"I'm sure you'll understand that I had to muzzle your mother. Her tongue can get sharp." He moved toward a boulder on which Abigail perched with her hands tied behind her back. Barrett bent over and pulled duct tape from around Abigail's mouth. He worked with one hand because his other held a gun.

Abigail gasped at the sting of the tape ripped from her mouth. "Nora, get away from here. He's insane."

Nora walked into the clearing and set the box down. "Here it is. Now let her go."

Barrett eyed the box, his gun dangling at his side. "You weren't stupid enough to make copies?"

The pristine spring at the base of the rocks looked like a virgin waiting for sacrifice. "This is it. All the evidence of increased uranium heading to the Hopi wells. If you keep quiet about this, you can go ahead and kill off the whole tribe and save Heather from ever living on the rez."

Abigail stirred on her rock. "Get out of here, Nora!"

Barrett ignored her. He addressed Nora. "You've got it wrong. I'm going to save the Hopi. There's no need to reveal the uranium because I'm going to make it all go away. I'm here to protect them."

"You can't clean it up if you don't admit it's there."

Barrett smiled, his teeth white in the night. "That's where you come in. Or more precisely, where snow making comes in."

Abigail stood, tottered, and dropped onto the boulder again. "You are a lunatic and I demand you release us this instant."

Barrett looked into the forest behind Nora. "Where's Charlie?"

The sound of a twig snapping to Nora's left was the only indication of movement. Charlie stepped into the clearing. "Right here, Mac."

Barrett didn't seem startled by Charlie's sudden appearance.

Abigail let out a sigh of irritation. "You couldn't go to the cops, just this once? I suppose it's your Communist leanings that keep you from doing the smart thing."

Charlie turned toward Abigail and smiled at her. "Your spirit is as full of fire as always."

"Okay, Casanova," Barrett said. "As with everything else, you don't know when to quit. You couldn't abandon the hippie, tree-hugging life when it became clear the old methods weren't working."

"Not like you, Mac. For some of us, the battle to save the Earth has real meaning. It isn't just something to pass the time while we wait to inherit our fortunes."

Barrett shook his head. "You poor, deluded fool. What has all your protests, petitions, demonstrations on the tops of flagpoles and wires strung across the trails accomplished?"

"It brought awareness, man. Changing the world I touch."

"The world I touch covers the globe. *Man.*" Barrett's voice carried contempt. "With my money and influence I've built clinics and cleaned up the rez."

Charlie interrupted, nodding. "Yep. Built clinics for people and took away their faith in their medicine men. Cleaned up the mess that wouldn't have been there but for your greed. A real hero. But what about the messes you didn't clean up? What about the uranium-tainted water on its way to Hopiland?"

Barrett toyed with the gun in his hand. "You read the logs, then?"

"What's uranium in the groundwater on Hopi lands have to do with snow making?" Charlie asked.

Nora took a step in Abigail's direction. Barrett didn't look at her.

"See, Charlie, you're always thinking in local terms. Saving this trail or that Spotted Owl. You've got to look at the big picture."

Nora knew Charlie's gun nestled in his waistband in the middle of his back. Why didn't he do something with it?

"What big picture is that, Mac?"

Nora moved one step at a time toward Abigail. Charlie's eyes, so often unfocused, were like lasers trained on Barrett.

"You think I only know about making money. That I'm only concerned with how to get what I can from the Earth and leave it in any shape as long as I turn a profit. But you're wrong."

"Is that so, Mac? What else do you care about?"

Charlie distracted Barrett with conversation and Nora didn't waste the opportunity. She was only a few steps away from Abigail.

Barrett held the gun toward Charlie. "You've seen my Heather. She's beautiful and smart and will inherit what all three generations of McCreary's have built. Everything I do, I do for her."

Charlie put his hands on his hips, the bandaged hand as well as the good one, inching closer to the gun tucked beneath his waistband. "I see. But Heather won't be happy with you when she finds out about the uranium killing off her people."

Barrett waved his hand. "The Hopi aren't her people. McCrearys are her people. Even so, I'm not going to let the uranium hit the well."

"What are you going to do with it? Suck it out?" Charlie's hand slid toward his back and the gun.

"Something like that. Even Scott had to agree I have a clever plan."

Mention of Scott made Nora's stomach flip. On the verge of shouting at Barrett and calling him murderer, she swallowed her rage. Another step and she'd be at Abigail's side.

"Tell me about this clever plan," Charlie said.

Barrett beamed. "Diversion. If I pump water from the aquifer here, under this peak, the water that would have hit Hopi wells will flow this way."

"What happens when that uranium-contaminated water gets to this well?" Charlie asked, his voice sounding dry.

Nora inched to Abigail's side and reached for the knots at her wrists with slight movements.

Barrett shrugged. "It's a mountain. Uranium is a natural element. People aren't going to be drinking the snow."

Charlie didn't say anything for a moment. "You're going to pump uranium on the sacred peak, and you think the kachinas will stand for it?"

Barrett let out a disgusted breath. "Kachinas. You don't still believe in those old myths, do you?"

"You used to believe, Mac. What happened?"

"I grew up. My family, supposedly protected by the kachinas, died a horrible death, and no one told me until years later. They kept my daughter from me, told me she died with Ester and Manangya, and they slowly killed her too."

"They didn't kill her," Charlie said.

"What do you call raising her in such poverty and despair she turned to the bottle? If they'd have let me have her, she would be alive."

Charlie's fingers closed on the gun behind his back. "What makes you think you'd have done any better? Your record with relationships isn't that great. Seems you thought if you left the rez, Ester would follow you."

Barrett winced. "She was a hypocrite."

"I might call her stubborn, smart, bull-headed, beautiful, and devoted to her people, but I never thought of her as a hypocrite."

Barrett's mouth twisted in bitterness. "What do you call it when she talked about her family and duty and sacrifice for her people. But when it came to me doing for my people, she wouldn't listen."

Barrett had more skill with knots than Heather, and Nora still struggled to loosen the ties on Abigail's hands.

Charlie took a tiny step forward. "She saw your abandonment for what it was: a chance for you to get back to the easy life."

Barrett bellowed like a bear in pain. "What do you know how she saw anything? She knew how much I loved her, cherished her and our children. She was punishing me for not living life her way."

Charlie shook his head. "Some punishment. She's dead. Your son is buried beside her. And you're amassing a fortune, living in a mansion, and allowing enough uranium to seep into Hopi wells to wipe out the whole tribe."

"Ester wouldn't listen when I told her about all the good we could do on the rez with McCreary money. If she hadn't run away she'd have seen the food deliveries that started immediately, the visiting doctors, the clinic, the school."

With the slightest movement, Charlie pulled the gun from his waistband. "She didn't want white doctors and water lines and electricity. She wanted the freedom to preserve the old ways. She believed in the Hopi way of life and their responsibility to the world."

Barrett waved the hand that held his gun, pretty much completely distracted by what was clearly an emotional argument for him. Words burst like bullets from his mouth. "Her bullshit religion and the kachinas and nature and balance. That's what killed her! She took my son, went out to the desert to pray, and it killed them."

332

"The uranium contamination in the wells killed her," Charlie said simply.

The rope fell away from Abigail's hands.

"If she'd have moved to town with me, her water would have been filtered and clean. She'd be alive. My son would be alive!"

Charlie shook his head. "The blame doesn't rest with a woman who was living as her ancestors lived."

"But I have Heather. She'll make up for her grandmother's stupid choices."

"Sorry, Mac. I don't think Heather's going to want anything to do with you from now on."

Barrett shook his head. "She's a teenager. She's going through her rebellion, but she'll come around. She'll claim her heritage."

"I think she's more inclined to Ester's side of the family."

"She'll never know about that weak bloodline."

"She already knows who she is. And she knows about the uranium in the wells."

A twig snapped in the forest opposite the clearing from Nora. Barrett turned his head.

The conversation ended.

Charlie pulled his gun.

Nora wrapped an arm around Abigail and threw them both to the ground, landing on top of Abigail to protect her.

A gunshot erupted in the night air.

FORTY-SIX

Silence fell on the clearing. It seemed the whole world paused. Who would have thought blurry, alcohol-sodden Charlie could be so razor sharp? He'd distracted Barrett and rattled him enough to get the upper hand. He was their hero.

Nora rolled off Abigail, anxious to see Barrett incapacitated and get Abigail back to the hospital.

Barrett stood by the rock, the gun pointed outward.

No! Charlie lay on his back. He let out a moan.

Abigail sat up and before Nora could grab her, jumped to her feet. "Charlie!" She ran across the clearing, flinging herself at Charlie's side, sobbing real tears.

No words of adoration from Charlie, just a weak grunt. A dark stain spread from a spot under Charlie's left shoulder.

"Oh, Charlie. Nora! He's bleeding!"

Barrett stared at the scene. "They usually do when they get shot."

Abigail sat on her knees and placed her hand onto the wound. "Get me something to dress this. I need to keep pressure on it."

Barrett sounded almost light-hearted. "Don't lose your head over it, Abigail. None of you are going to make it out of here alive."

Barrett swung the gun toward Nora. "They think you're crazy. They'll find you out here, your mother and Charlie murdered and a bullet through your brain, a tragic murder-suicide."

In a surprisingly sprite move for the big man, Barrett jumped toward Nora.

She froze like a fainting goat then darted to one side, out of his way.

Barrett swung an arm out and it brushed against her side as she twisted away.

Panting, he stopped and pointed his gun toward Abigail. "I can take care of your mother first."

"No!" Nora charged him, intending to knock the gun away.

Barrett wrapped an iron arm around her, pulling her close enough to smell his sour sweat. He put the gun to her head. "Got to make sure the angle is right for suicide."

Failure! She'd tried so hard but Barrett had outsmarted, out-planned, out-everything. She was no match. Why hadn't she gone to the cops? She couldn't save herself, Abigail, or Charlie. She'd done nothing for Scott. Cole probably lay somewhere in a pool of blood. She'd doomed the mountain to wither beneath the uranium snow.

Nora fought. She twisted her torso, kicked at the tree trunks that were Barrett's legs. If she moved at all, it was only centimeters, not enough to dislodge the cold muzzle from her temple.

Wait. Something moved in the forest.

It couldn't be the cops. Maybe the Hopi or Big Elk's people waited out there, chortling over Nora's demise.

There it was again.

Leaves rustled in the forest and a branch snapped. A flash of blue shone in the lantern's half-light. Suddenly a hulking figure burst into the clearing. Abbey trotted behind, tail wagging in welcome.

Barrett jerked his head toward the intruder and crushed Nora even closer to his side.

After a second of confusion, Nora finally identified the oddly shaped figure. He wore a kachina mask and full regalia of feathers and costume. He carried a hatchet adorned with ribbons and feathers. Usually frightening in its foreign aspects, the mask looked terrifying in the dark forest. In the sketchy moonlight, she saw the turquoise of the mask, its plug mouth and slits for eyes, long pheasant tail feathers rising behind.

The kachina rushed across the clearing toward Barrett and Nora with his raised hatchet. Abbey barked and raced with the kachina.

Though the kachina was much shorter than Nora originally thought, he swung his hatchet and hit Barrett in the throat with the dull edge.

Barrett grunted, his grip loosening on Nora.

She pulled away and Abbey lunged in.

Barrett jerked Nora close again and smacked Abbey on the head with his gun. Abbey yelped.

"Bastard." She squirmed to get free, but his arm tightened around her.

The kachina darted in again, striking at Barrett's gun arm, ripping the shirt on Barrett's biceps.

Barrett swung Nora as he turned and tried to get a bead on the dancing kachina in the shadowy clearing. Nora's feet slid along the ground and she lost her balance. Barrett's arm pinned her to his side and kept her from falling.

The kachina retreated across the clearing to Abigail and Charlie. He didn't slow his zigzagged dance but the masked face turned toward them, as if checking on them.

Barrett raised his arm and sighted in on the kachina.

Abbey snarled and bared his teeth.

Nora regained her feet and braced on the ground. She watched Barrett's finger and sprang against him when she saw it start to flex.

His shot hammered her ears, but the bullet whizzed into the forest.

Then something hit Barrett in the chest and fell to the ground. A rock.

One hand still pushing on Charlie's chest, Abigail reached for another rock. She pulled her arm back and let it fly. Maybe years of golf lessons had finally paid off in perfect aim.

Barrett ducked his head but the rock thudded into his temple.

The kachina circled back, hatchet raised.

"You bitch. I wanted to marry you. Give you everything." Barrett aimed his gun at Abigail.

Nora pitched and writhed and kicked, screaming in Barrett's ear.

With incredible force, he flung Nora toward the rock where Abigail had perched earlier. The back of her head cracked on the rough granite and she flopped to the ground. Her knee struck another rock and her leg went numb.

Abigail launched another rock. Stubborn, stupid Abigail. Nora struggled to get to her feet but her leg wouldn't move. "Run, Mother!"

Barrett took a step toward Abigail, the gun rising. He couldn't miss. At that range, he'd rip a hole into Abigail that would tear her in two.

Nora dragged herself, fighting to stop Barrett.

Suddenly, the kachina flew from the forest straight at Barrett.

Barrett didn't alter his aim at Abigail. A third shot exploded from his gun.

A woman screamed.

FORTY-SEVEN

ABIGAIL SCREAMED. AND SCREAMED again. The shrill sound ate into Barrett's brain like an ice pick.

Barrett had shot her. She should be lying on top of Charlie, her blood gushing onto the forest floor. Why wasn't she dead?

Abigail focused on a point behind him.

What was happening? Had he shot Nora instead? He swung his head around. No. Nora scrambled on the ground next to the boulder. He'd let go of her to aim at Abigail.

But Abigail was still alive.

Then he remembered. The kachina had darted from the forest. The fucking kachina. He'd ruined Barrett's plan.

Abigail sobbed, her hand still pressing Charlie's wound.

The kachina had flung himself in front of the bullet intended for Abigail. Barrett must have shot him.

Barrett looked at the spring. A pile of feathers, leather, and bright blue cloth soaked in the water.

Nora rose to her feet and took a numb step toward the spring. She started to shake her head, tears coursing down her cheeks. "No. Oh God, no."

Barrett's skin turned to ice. He didn't want to but couldn't stop himself from taking a step toward the kachina.

His shot had blown the kachina backward to splash in the spring. The motionless figure lay on its back.

Nora's knees buckled and she fell to the ground. A primal scream erupted from her core like the death throes of the Mother.

Please. No. No. Barrett pleaded with the spirits of the mountain. He couldn't look. He didn't want to know. But his feet carried him the few steps to the spring.

The kachina mask floated from the face. Glassy eyes stared from under an inch of water. Heather lay in the spring, blood washing away from the bullet hole in her heart.

EPILOGUE

SNOW FELL IN FAT white splats on top of Nora's Jeep. She hefted Abigail's tapestry suitcase into the back and slammed the tailgate closed. Abbey sat in the passenger seat staring out the windshield. He may not know where they were going, but he'd go with Nora anywhere.

Abigail stood behind her, arms folded as if the cold mountain air could penetrate her white down jacket. "I don't know why you don't get rid of this clunker and get a car more suitable to an executive."

Abigail could be blown up and shot at and still she kept her edge. What a woman. "No one will pay attention to what I drive, especially since I intend to ride my bike everywhere."

Abigail sniffed. "Always the fanatic."

"It's Boulder, Mother. I'll fit right in."

Abigail wouldn't concede. "I thought your tree-hugging days were over. You should drive a sporty, sexy car. You know what they say, 'Dress for the job you want, not the one you have.'"

Nora bent over and kissed Abigail's cheek. "I don't want that kind of job."

Charlie stepped close behind Abigail and put his arms around her, drawing her into him. "That's the spirit, darlin'. You keep a foot in the mountains and don't let the city corrupt you."

The tie-dyed rusted heap of Benny's pickup rumbled into the parking lot. They watched while he climbed out and walked to them, eying the suitcases in the back of the Jeep. "Heard you were heading north."

Nora grinned. "I suppose Nakwaiyamtewa told you."

He shrugged, a hint of smile around his eyes. "Did I tell you he is my grandfather?"

Made perfect sense. Nora took hold of his hand. "I'm glad you came to say goodbye. I want to thank you again before I left. Or apologize or ... I don't know."

"You've said that before."

Charlie kissed the top of Abigail's head. "Are you warm enough?"

Abigail stepped out of his embrace. "Don't be ridiculous. It's only October. If I can't handle the weather now, how do you suppose I'll survive January?"

Good question. How would Abigail fare in Charlie's little cabin on the edge of the forest with the nearest fashion mall 120 miles away in Phoenix, no luncheons to hostess or Junior League meetings to preside over?

Charlie shook his head. "Fire and vinegar. That's my Abbie."

Abigail fought the smile that crept to her face. She gave in and patted Charlie's cheek. "That's Queen Abbie, to you."

"As always, my dear."

Benny pulled a small cloth pouch from his jeans pocket and gave it to Nora. "I have something I want you to do." He placed the pouch in her hand. "When you get to Colorado, plant these corn seeds. Sing to them. If you do this one small thing, it will help me."

"How will that help you?"

He nearly grinned, big emotion for him. "It will help the whole world, but I like to think of you doing this to help balance me."

"Don't you grow enough corn for your own balance?"

He nodded. "But I have been given responsibility to spend a large pot of money the gray-haired followers of Big Elk gave to Hopi. It's guilt for the harm Big Elk did. We'll use it to clean up the uranium in the water."

Nora squeezed the seeds and already felt protective of them. She hugged Benny and then watched as he drove away.

She turned to gaze at the mountain visible from the road in front of Charlie's cabin. Snow accumulated in the pine boughs, the ground already blanketed in white.

Charlie followed her gaze. "One good thing came of all this. The mountain can be herself again."

Tears threatened. Scott's ashes lay on the ground of that mountain. Heather's blood soaked into the soil. "But at what cost?"

Charlie put an arm around her shoulders. "You sure you don't want that money, darlin'?"

Nora shook her head, throat too tight for words. While Barrett sat in jail without bond, speaking to no one, without the heart or life to even assist his attorneys with a viable defense, he'd sent Nora a complicated plan for her approval.

If she sold her interests in Kachina Ski to an environmental trust at an inflated price, the trust would secure protection for the mountain to remain undeveloped. It would be available to the tribes who held it sacred and would be forever named the Heather McCreary Wilderness Area. McCreary Energy set it up to fund the trust in perpetuity.

Nora agreed immediately, hoping Heather would have been pleased. She signed the money over to Abigail.

Of course Abigail protested. But Nora reasoned that since Abigail's husband gave Kachina Ski to Nora, the proceeds after her debt should go back to Abigail. This way her mother retained her pride and Nora could cut all ties with the mountain that had taken so much from her.

"Cole called to ask about you this morning," Abigail said. The woman was nothing if not relentless.

"That's nice." *Keep it short, Nora. Get in the car. Drive away before the litany begins.*

Too late. "I wish you'd give him a chance to explain."

Nora clenched her jaw. "He kept secrets from me. He wasn't honest, and I don't need another person like that in my life."

Charlie shook his head. "I lied to you too, sugar."

"And I'm not done being mad at you either." She kissed him on the top of the head anyway. "But you're in my life, and I already love you. Honestly, aside from you and Abigail, I want to forget everything about Kachina Peak. That includes Cole."

Abigail acted like a pushy salesperson. "You're being stubborn, Nora. He started out trying to nail Barrett for bribing Congress."

Nora turned her back and stepped toward the driver's door. "You've said all this before. I need to get on the road."

Abigail grabbed her hand. "But he was only trying to protect you. When he suspected Barrett was involved in Scott's murder, well, he ... "

Nora wrenched open the Jeep door. "Not listening, Abigail."

Her mother sniffed. "So now it's not 'Mother' anymore."

Nora kissed Charlie's cheek. "Take care of her," she said.

Charlie reached into his pocket and pulled out a beer. He started to pull the tab and glanced at Abigail. Her slight frown made him redeposit the can in his pocket unopened. "I believe we'll be taking care of each other."

Nora hugged her mother. "I love you." She climbed into the Jeep, set the wipers in motion, and pulled away.

Giving in to the urge, she let her eyes wander to the rearview mirror, certain of what she'd see.

It was no surprise to her that the kachina man stood in the trees watching her leave.

© Kelly Weaver Photography

ABOUT THE AUTHOR

Shannon Baker (Flagstaff, AZ) can often be found backpacking, skiing, kayaking, cycling, or just playing lizard in the desert. From the Colorado Rockies to the Nebraska Sandhills, the peaks of Flagstaff and the deserts of Tucson, Western landscapes play an important role in her books. Visit her online at Shannon-Baker.com.

ACKNOWLEDGMENTS

So many people conspired with me to get this book into your hands, and to them, I give my deepest gratitude. Without the undying support and brilliance of Sisters of the Quill—Janet Fogg, Julie Kaewart, and Karen Lin—I wouldn't have survived life, let alone been able to write a book. The Alphas—Margaret Bailey, Karen Duvall, Janet Lane, Alan Larson, Lawdon, Heidi Kuhn, and Joy Meredith—never fail to set me on the right track. I especially thank Jameson Cole, who was relentless in teaching me the basics. Rocky Mountain Fiction Writers (the best group EVER) has showered me with writerly blessings for close to two decades. An enormous hug of gratitude goes to Terri Bischoff at Midnight Ink, who plucked this guppy out of the sea, and to Nicole Nugent, who helped teach it to swim. Thanks also to cover artist Robert Rodriguez.

Because the Hopi revere humility and privacy, I won't splash her name across this page, but I am so very thankful to my Hopi friend, without whom this book would stumble and thrash against that gentle culture much more than it does. Thank you to Abe Springer, who showed great tolerance to a writer who knows next to nothing about groundwater. If I've failed to convey the proper respect for the science and the culture, it isn't because they weren't great teachers.

Thank you to the Hopi people of Second Mesa who welcomed a really white woman into their village and shared a small piece of their ancient culture. A big hug of appreciation to the Grand Canyon Trust, who not only paid me, but showed me a perspective uncommon for a Nebraska native. The passionate and dedicated staff opened my eyes to more than the perfect soyrizzo burrito.

As always, thanks to my brilliant and talented daughters, who will always be a great source of pride and inspiration. Mostly, thank you to Dave. He endured the thrill of victory and the agony of defeat—not to mention the depths of despair, the rays of hope, and the downright crazies—with equal faith and humor. Sorry about the helicopter.